Ana María
AND
The Fox

Ana María
and
The Fox

A LUNA SISTERS NOVEL

Liana De la Rosa

BERKLEY ROMANCE
NEW YORK

BERKLEY ROMANCE
Published by Berkley
An imprint of Penguin Random House LLC
penguinrandomhouse.com

Library of Congress Cataloging-in-Publication Data

Names: De la Rosa, Liana, author.
Title: Ana María and the fox / Liana De la Rosa.
Description: First edition. | New York : Berkley Romance, 2023. |
Series: The Luna sisters ; 1
Identifiers: LCCN 2022037542 (print) | LCCN 2022037543 (ebook) | ISBN
9780593440889 (trade paperback) | ISBN 9780593440896 (ebook)
Subjects: LCGFT: Romance fiction. | Novels.
Classification: LCC PS3604.E12266 A84 2023 (print) | LCC PS3604.E12266
(ebook) | DDC 813/.6—dc23/eng/20220920
LC record available at https://lccn.loc.gov/2022037542
LC ebook record available at https://lccn.loc.gov/2022037543

First Edition: April 2023

Printed in the United States of America
1st Printing

Book design by Tiffany Estreicher

For the eldest daughters,
who work so hard and do so much.
I see you. I am you.

Ana María
and
The Fox

1

London: July, 1863

The wind was relentless. It ripped at her once-neat coiffure, whipping strands of black hair against her face, the sting bringing tears to her eyes. It was the most frigid of welcomes.

Ana María wrapped her cloak tighter about her shoulders, burying her chin and cheeks in the warmth of the high collar. She glanced first one way and then the other, her eyes straining to see something—*someone*—who clearly wasn't there. Where was he?

"Qué feo," Gabriela—Gabby—muttered, her blue-tinged lips curling as she surveyed the neighborhood surrounding the docks. "Isn't England supposed to be green? I didn't expect London to be quite so . . . so gray."

Neither had she. Ana María sighed as she took in the coal-choked fog that clung to the docks like the arms of an illicit lover, doing its best to mask the filth and grime of the city. Yet the somber reality of their new home was apparent. The narrow buildings lining the wharf were worn and dilapidated, their brick facades stained gray by generations of coal dust. From her vantage point, she could make out piles of debris and refuse that littered the cobblestoned street, her stomach turning when she spied rats darting among the rubbish, fighting for scraps. Ana María ducked her head at the near constant stream of seagulls swooping down from above, their squawking grating her nerves like an out-of-tune pianoforte.

Discreetly shielding her nose with her hand, she inhaled the crisp leather scent of her gloves, thankful it smothered the acrid stench that wafted about her, a foul blend of the sea and human misery.

"Surely we'll encounter more green the farther we venture into the city," she murmured, ignoring her youngest sister's sniff of disbelief.

Of the three Luna sisters, Gabby was taking their exile the hardest, her lavish complaints annoying even Ana María's stalwart disposition. And Our Lady of Guadalupe knew there were no more difficult people than her sisters.

"Where do you think Tío Arturo is?"

Ana María struggled to keep the frown off her lips. "I don't know."

"Rather rude of him, isn't it?" Gabby peered around Ana María, her pretty features darkening. "It's not like our ship was delayed by a storm and we were pushed off course. The ship docked on the stated date, at the stated time printed on our tickets. He should be here."

He absolutely should have been, and Ana María sympathized with her sister's frustration. Two months at sea—first in a small skiff that delivered them from Veracruz in the black of night, then in a packet ship that stopped at Santo Domingo, followed by the very freighter they had just disembarked— had tested all of their resilience. Having been raised in wealth and relative ease, the sisters had struggled to share one small cabin, their sleep often interrupted by cries of alarm when the ship lurched and wobbled on the waves. Packed away were their extravagant day dresses and ball gowns, replaced by unassuming gray and brown calico and wool skirts. While unattractive, the simple dresses had kept them warm the farther the ship sailed north into the Atlantic.

But more so than trading in their affluence for anonymity, it was the forced proximity that had proved the most trying for the sisters. For they were not close. Constantly competing for scraps of affection and attention from their father had made them more antagonists than bosom friends, and the long journey had done little to soften the edges of their animosity for one another.

That their uncle was late to collect them after such an arduous journey was a sour conclusion instead of a promising beginning.

Biting back a sigh, Ana María laid a hand on Gabby's arm. "He should be here, but he's not. So I'm going to speak with the captain about hiring a carriage or hansom to deliver us to him instead."

"That's a good idea." Gabby tilted her head. "Would you like me to go with you?"

"No," she blurted, pressing her lips together as her sister narrowed her eyes. "I would rather you stay with Isabel. You know how taxing the voyage was on her."

They turned in tandem to where their sister sat among the stacks of their luggage, a book spread open in her lap. Her normally rich golden skin was drawn, and dark circles made her brown eyes appear sunken and hollow. The lurch and roll of the sea had caused Isabel to spend days on end huddled in their sparse cabin, sick and miserable, and they'd been shaken to see their poised sister so listless.

"Even at her sickest, she wanted to read a book." Snorting, Gabby shook her head. "I'll never understand it."

"They're her escape."

As the studious, bluestocking sister, Isabel had shown herself to be happy only when surrounded by the written word. She had insisted on bringing a satchel full of books with her on the voyage, something that had initially annoyed Ana María, for their quarters were tight. Yet Isabel's collection had come to entertain them those long days at sea.

And though she would never admit it, Ana María had long resented the refuge books granted Isabel. As the eldest, Ana María had been held to completely different edicts than either of her sisters.

Ana María blinked such thoughts away. She had committed herself to leaving her old grudges—and unrelenting bitterness—on Mexico's shores. This was her chance to truly know her sisters and improve their relationships despite the ways their father had worked to undermine them.

"I suppose I'll go wait with Isabel, then." Gabby sighed. "Reading one of her books is better than pacing the dock."

Ana María watched as her temperamental sister plopped down on a trunk next to Isabel. Pivoting, she glanced up the road again, willing her uncle's conveyance to rumble into view. She was not surprised when it did not happen.

Nibbling on the inside of her cheek, Ana María darted her gaze about as she pondered what to do next. There were a few hansom cabs parked along the docks not far away, but she hesitated. She had a hastily scribbled address for their tío Arturo in her reticule, information she had stumbled upon quite by accident when she had been rifling through the post one sunny morning. Ana María had recorded the direction, determined she and her sisters would not be dependent upon their father to convey them to safety.

It would appear she had been wise to do so.

Lifting her chin, Ana María looked to and fro in search of the captain. The older gentleman had been polite to them throughout the voyage, often asking after their health and offering them a cordial greeting. Ana María hoped a bit of that courtesy would make him willing to assist her now.

A gust of wind whipped off the sea then, and she fought back a shiver. A deep wave of homesickness engulfed her, and she blinked back tears. Ana María missed the warm sun on her skin, the taste of a tortilla fresh off the comal, the soft melodies her tía Susana coaxed from her guitarra on balmy summer nights. She ached for the feel of her mother's fingers threading through her hair, her nails scouring her scalp and soothing her anxieties.

Biting her lip, Ana María could admit now, with time and distance away from Mexico, that she even missed Fernando, her fiancé . . . or at least the aloof, efficient way he'd always seen to her welfare. Fernando would have secured a carriage for them by now, unwilling to let her and her sisters experience any discomfort.

But he was not here, and she had to secure their safety and comfort on her own.

Ana María paused to watch a group of sailors unloading cargo from the belly of the ship and carry it down the gangplank to be loaded onto wagons waiting nearby, the horses stomping their hooves in impatience. Perhaps the captain was among them—

And that was when she heard it. Shouts. Voices raised in anger. Gabby's incensed shriek. Her stomach sank like a steel anchor.

Gathering up her skirts, Ana María ran back the way she'd come, panic nearly choking her. The thudding of her boots on the wooden planks could not drown out the thundering of her racing heart.

They had escaped imminent danger when they'd fled Mexico City in the dead of night, with only the moonlight to illuminate their path, their gowns and corsets weighted with family treasures their maids had carefully stitched into the linings. But that fear could not compare to the terror coursing through her veins at the thought of Isabel and Gabby being injured by some unknown assailant, and so very far from home.

Gasping for breath in her too-tight corset, she finally saw them. Her sisters staring down a group of two—no, *three*—men. The fiends were attempting to flank them, but they didn't know their would-be victims. Isabel and Gabby were brandishing their hatpins like they were teputzopilli, their faces twisted in outrage. As she drew closer, Ana María could make out some of what Gabby said.

"I will stab you if you take one more step, pendejo," she growled, the words vibrating around her clenched teeth.

The man on her right, his grime-coated hand curled into a fist, inched closer. "You're a feisty kitten, aren't you, love?" His chuckle was a grating sound. "But do you know what we do to kittens who get in the way?"

Not waiting for a response, the man in the middle lurched forward and swiped his hand to knock Isabel's pin away. But her sister was fast, and Isabel jabbed the fiend in the fleshy part of his forearm, dashing back with large eyes as the man howled in pain. The other man darted at Isabel, his hand raised as if to strike her.

"No!" The shout burst from Ana María as she sprinted toward them, reaching to pluck her own hatpin free as she did.

The cutthroats spun about, their expressions morphing from amusement to concern in the span of a moment. That was when

Ana María noted the rapid footfalls pounding on the walk behind her. She whipped her head about over her shoulder, her mouth gaping when two burly men, who looked like they had just left a pugilist ring, barreled past her, their stern attentions fixed on the villains attacking her sisters. Before Ana María had even processed what was happening, one cutthroat was in the water, struggling to swim back to shore, while the other two had scampered away like the vermin they were.

"Are you hurt?" Ana María demanded when she reached Isabel, inspecting her hands for injuries.

"I'm fine," Isabel murmured, squeezing her fingers before stepping away.

Ana María blinked, a bit startled by her sister's composure. Mindful Isabel would not take kindly to her hovering, she pivoted to Gabby, who was in conversation with one of their rescuers. Only now that the adrenaline of the moment had begun to fade did Ana María realize the men wore the crisply tailored livery of footmen.

She approached, offering them a smile of gratitude. "I can't thank you both enough for your assistance." Ana María swept her gaze to include the other man, who hovered behind.

"It was nothing, miss." The man dipped his head. "I was just telling Miss Gabriela that we will get your trunks loaded up in the carriage and you don't have to worry about those wretches returning."

A frown puckered her brow. "What carriage?"

"Right there, miss." He jerked with his chin at a spot behind her. "Your uncle, Mr. Valdés, awaits you."

Ana María whirled about, her gaze landing on a sleek black carriage sitting at the end of the dock.

"Do you think it's really him?" Gabby whispered, moving closer to her side.

She didn't have a reason to doubt the footman's word, as he had saved them from whatever fate those thieves had planned for them. Yet cautiousness made her hesitate.

"Let's walk over together and determine whether it's truly him," Isabel suggested from her opposite side.

Ana María pressed her lips together when she saw how Isabel gripped her hatpin tighter. "Yes, let's."

Silent and somber, the sisters walked side by side in the direction of the carriage, their steps a metronome that harmonized with her heartbeat. When they were almost upon the conveyance, the door swung open and a figure appeared in the doorway. He was thin but fit, his black hair peppered liberally with gray. Grooves in his tawny complexion bracketed his mouth, and liberal lines branched from the corners of his eyes. And those eyes . . . they were their mother's. A striated greenish brown that Ana María had always thought the loveliest eye color imaginable.

"Tío Arturo?" she whispered.

His weathered face crinkled into a dashing smile. Ana María liked him immediately.

"Mis sobrinas hermosas! I apologize for my tardiness but am very happy to finally meet you."

Without hesitation, their uncle grasped first Gabby, and then Isabel, by the hands, kissing their cheeks while they exchanged introductions.

"And you must be Ana María," he murmured as he turned to her, his warm hands enfolding hers. "Your sister Gabriela is the spitting image of your mother as a girl, but *you* have her spirit. Puedo ver a mi hermana en tus ojos."

Ana María thought she may have smiled, but she couldn't be sure. All the air had been siphoned from her lungs, leaving a yawning emptiness inside of her. She adored her mother, but was she truly like her? Always acquiescing? Always striving to make others happy at the expense of her own happiness? Always enduring heartbr—

"Let us leave this foul place," Tío Arturo said, sweeping his hand toward the door of the conveyance.

The footmen had stored their belongings, and there was no reason to stay. Climbing into the carriage, Ana María settled next to Isabel and pondered their new life in London—*her* new life. It was poised to begin and she was happy for it.

Truly she was. And yet the past still cleaved to her, and her happiness was like the fog that floated above the waves; eventually it would burn away and reveal the turbulent, murky depths beneath.

Sometime later, Ana María sat nestled between her sisters on a sofa in a home that she quickly realized was not her tío Arturo's. An older woman greeted them upon their arrival, politely offering them tea with a big smile and a critical gaze. She was lovely, with graying curls and cornflower-blue eyes framed by long, dark lashes. The exquisite cut of her gown, the delicate Spanish lace that lined her bodice, and the tasteful elegance of her home were a testament to her wealth. The tilted angle of her jaw spoke of good breeding.

Who was she, and why had their uncle brought them here instead of to his own home?

As if understanding their confusion, Tío Arturo placed his teacup down on the walnut-wood table at his elbow and gestured to the woman, where she sat in an upholstered Morris chair next to him. "I'm sure you have many questions, but first allow me to introduce the Viscountess Yardley. Her ladyship's late husband was a friend of mine, and she has agreed to be your guardian during your time in London."

An uncomfortable silence rang loudly in the room. Surprisingly, it was Isabel to break it. "Our guardian? Will we . . . not be staying with you?"

"You will not." Tío Arturo drummed his fingers on the arm-rest as he considered them. "Out of an abundance of caution, we've decided to not reveal your identities as my nieces. We hope to conceal your close connection to the Juárez government."

Ana María frowned and looked to her sisters, who appeared just as baffled.

"In addition," Tío Arturo said, "we thought it would be more proper for you to be chaperoned by a well-respected member of society who could vouch for your wealth and consequence, and Lady Yardley is all that is respectable."

"So . . . who will the public believe us to be?" Gabby asked, her brow pulled low.

"You three will be wealthy Mexican ladies seeking refuge from the French occupation. There will be no reason for any-one to investigate your background . . . unless you plan to marry an English gentleman, I suppose."

Ana María exchanged a glance with her sisters, but Gabby's loud snort adequately summed up their collective feelings about that.

Their uncle flourished a hand. "Your parents appealed to me, as Mexican ambassador, for assistance, and in turn I asked Lady Yardley to sponsor you. Because she is gracious and kind, she agreed."

The viscountess nodded in agreement.

Tío Arturo continued, "Since I will not always be available to accompany you to social events, her ladyship will guide you through your stay in London and will ensure your time here is used wisely."

Ana María quirked her head. "'Used wisely'? What do you mean?"

Her uncle and the viscountess exchanged a look, but before she could ponder it, Tío Arturo spoke again.

"Did your father explain what he expected of you during your time here?"

"He expected us to eschew public gatherings. He said not to interfere with your work." Darting her gaze first at one sister and then the other, Ana María finally said, "And he reminded us that our every action, no matter how inconsequential, reflected on the Luna name."

Repeating her father's command brought her back to that moment of goodbye two months prior, when advancing Conservative and French troops forced Ana María from her mother and the only place she'd ever called home.

"Your tío Arturo will have a carriage waiting for you all when you arrive in London. See that you don't give him any problems."

"Of course, Papá," she'd whispered, dropping her gaze. In the stillness of the empty streets outside of Mexico City, her voice seemed to carry.

Her father gripped her arm. "I don't have to remind you of the very important load you carry."

The weight of that load had made it hard to breathe.

"Although your tío is an important man, especially now as he tries to convince England to side with Mexico in this war with the French, I expect you and your sisters to live quietly. No balls or social events. No drawing attention to yourselves. This is not a grand holiday." His dark eyes narrowed. "Do you understand?"

She'd swallowed. "I do, Papá."

"And do not think that because you're off on the other side of the Atlantic that you need not honor your engagement to Señor Ramírez."

Ana María had the good sense to gasp, truly scandalized her father thought her capable of being unfaithful to the commitment

she had made to Fernando. Or . . . rather one her father had made
for her.

"Good." He'd taken a step back, smoothing his large palms over
his simple black coat. Even in his nondescript attire, her father still
managed to intimidate. "Have a safe voyage, then, daughter."

Ana María pressed her lips into a firm line as he turned to
speak with Isabel and then Gabby. Even the dim lighting could
not hide their strained expressions, although Isabel was much
more adept at hiding her contempt. She could imagine his threats
to them were the same as the ones he'd uttered to her. After twenty-
four years as the eldest daughter of Señor Elías Luna Cuate, Ana
María knew better than to expect love and affection to fall from
his lips, even in farewell.

That she still craved such declarations had made her bite the
inside of her cheek until she tasted copper on her tongue.

Abruptly, Ana María was exhausted. They'd barely arrived
in London, and yet the stress of their escape, of their uncertain
future in England yawning before them, felt crushing.

Knitting her hands together in her lap, Ana María sucked a
greedy breath into her lungs. She had long learned not to voice
her discomfort. She dared not speak a word of her heartache at
leaving her home or her mother, for no one cared. It didn't matter that their father had secured their escape from the country,
not out of love or concern for their safety, but to protect his
daughters in their capacity as broodmares he could marry off to
secure political alliances.

"His letter to me said as much." Tío Arturo rose to his feet
and prowled around his chair, gripping the seat back as he
studied them. "However, having you three here will make my
work easier, I believe."

"How so?" Gabby voiced for them all.

"What I mean is that I now have three lovely, wealthy, *intelligent* heiresses to serve as goodwill ambassadors for Mexico."

Ana María's thoughts froze even as sweat trickled down her spine. "You want us to . . . to be goodwill ambassadors? How would we do that when we're supposed to be discreet?"

"Very simply put, you won't be."

The sisters gasped in unison.

For the first time since her greeting, it was Lady Yardley who interjected, her voice soothing. "What your uncle means is that you will accompany me to social events throughout the season. Balls, operas, boat races, garden parties, and all number of activities. Using what I am sure is your natural wit and charisma, Mr. Valdés hopes you will bolster the image of the Mexican people and show the British public that the French occupation is hurting citizens, like the three of you."

"And we'll do that by attending the opera?" Isabel asked, with a hard tone.

"Yes." Tío Arturo pounded his fist against his palm. "You will dress in your finest gowns, and you will laugh and charm every lady and gentleman you meet so the next time they read about how Napoleon the Third has claimed authority over the supposed Second Mexican Empire, the British public will remember the lovely Mexican heiresses they've come to know because they've cruelly been pushed from their home by the French."

"Public perception is everything," Lady Yardley added with a decisive nod.

"B-but," Ana María breathed, her heart racing with panic, "our father will not approve."

"He will not . . . but then he's not here, now is he?"

Had anyone ever suggested anything so blasphemous? It was almost as if Tío Arturo had claimed the Last Supper had not happened or that Juan Diego lied about la Virgen de Guadalupe visiting him. For Ana María to willfully disobey her father was the most foreign concept she could imagine. Just the idea of going against his strictly stated orders made her stomach flip.

After a lifetime of deference, the idea she could live free of the puppet strings she had come to recognize as her own was a freedom she could not fathom . . . but was desperate—so very desperate—to taste.

Their parents had fled to El Paso del Norte with the rest of Presidente Juárez's cabinet, and the sisters had been warned that correspondence would be limited out of a need for secrecy and security. So would their parents be privy to all the details of the girls' lives here, especially if Tío Arturo did not disclose them? And the longer the war continued, the lengthier their exile in England stretched before them into the unknown future. The fortune they had carried—the one they had already surrendered into their uncle's safekeeping—would ensure their lives would be comfortable ones. But if they could assist their uncle in his diplomatic efforts now, perhaps their time on English soil would be a finite thing.

Tío Arturo wasn't asking for their help for ambitious reasons; he truly believed they could help Mexico, even in this small way. And perhaps by helping her countrymen, Ana María could learn a bit about herself while she did it.

Sliding her gaze to first Isabel and then Gabby, she glimpsed in their eyes the same longing, the same hope that was sparking like a newly lit candle in her chest. This proposal their uncle was presenting might be their only chance to experience life on their own terms.

Setting her teacup on the table in front of her, Ana María lifted her chin as she met Tío Arturo's gaze. "When is our first outing?"

2

Gideon stepped out onto the cobblestone street just as the lamplighter was walking by, intent on igniting the lights up and down the street. Donning his top hat, he tucked his satchel under his arm and made his way to his rooms at Archer House.

Every step felt heavy. He was supposed to have left his office at Westminster more than an hour earlier, but had been inconveniently detained by a committee member inquiring about a bit of language Gideon had added to the proposal they were considering. Now he was running late for his evening engagement.

Not that said engagement was particularly interesting, but Gideon had long since learned that politics was more about networking and forging alliances than it was about the actual governing that politicians were elected to do. It had been a frustrating realization during his first year in Parliament, but Gideon was nothing if not driven, and quickly adapted to this environment where appearances were everything.

And appearing at Lord and Lady Montrose's ball was imperative. The marquess and marchioness hosted a ball every summer while Parliament was in session, and all matters of business were conducted over food, dancing, and card playing. This ball was only the second Gideon had been invited to, his first two years in Parliament seeing him snubbed an invitation. But through hard work and a tenacious drive, he had risen through the ranks of party leadership to chair his own committee, and he was not about to cede the small measure of power he'd earned by missing out on the biggest social event of the season thus far.

He arrived at Archer House several minutes later, hustling up the staircase to his set of rooms with only a brief wave to his proprietress. His pulse settled—somewhat—when he spied his evening clothes neatly pressed and draped across his bed. He'd left a note asking Mrs. Jones, his housekeeper, to see to the task. And while he had employed the older woman for the last year and had never had a complaint about her work, Gideon could not help but brace for disappointment, for life had taught him such an emotion was always waiting to be experienced.

Sinking into a chair at the narrow table that doubled as his desk, he pulled out a stack of papers from his satchel and tucked into the beef stew Mrs. Jones left for him. It was still a bit warm, not that Gideon cared much, his thoughts focused on the document in his hand. It was the latest report from the Royal Navy's West Africa Squadron, listing their newest slave ship seizures. When he reached the end, he poured all his frustrations into crumpling the paper into a tight ball and hurling it across the room into the rubbish bin.

Pinching the bridge of his nose, Gideon inhaled deeply until his chest heaved with the effort, expelling his breath along with his feelings of helplessness and impatience. With an effort born of years of suppressing his bitterness, he considered the Montrose ball and who would likely be in attendance. He cataloged in his mind whom he needed to speak with and with whom he could possibly enjoy a snifter of brandy without recriminations.

Not a half hour later, Gideon sat in a hackney as it rumbled over the divots and holes in the street on the way to Mayfair. Archer House was closer to Westminster than South Audley Street, but he'd become well versed in navigating both worlds. His ambition required such proficiency.

After he paid his fare, Gideon allowed himself a moment to simply study the stately Montrose House, ablaze with gaslight. Through the towering Palladian window, he caught glimpses of footmen weaving through the richly dressed guests, their trays piled with beverages and hors d'oeuvres. The sight made his stomach twist. Just two generations ago, his family were the ones in service—*servitude*—and now here he stood, in his fine black tailcoat, his shoes polished until they reflected his image. But unlike his ancestors, when he climbed those front steps, he would be welcomed as a guest.

Resisting the urge to fiddle with his cravat, Gideon paced down the walk, tipping his head back to stare at the sky. The stars were obscured by a cloying haze, but just knowing they were there was calming. His grandmother had looked up at the same sky when she had stolen aboard a freighter departing Charleston for London. If she could endure that awful voyage, he could certainly endure a grand ton ball.

"What are you doing skulking around out here, Fox?"

Dropping his head, Gideon took in Sebastian Brooks, the Duke of Whitfield. The man was just a year or two older than Gideon's eight and twenty years, and they had fallen into an easy friendship for all that they were different. Whitfield, the urbane, witty, arrogant duke who commanded attention wherever he went and couldn't bother to vote his seat; and Gideon, an upstart who strived for power and wanted still more to create change for others. But Gideon appreciated the other man's bluntness, and the advice he'd provided as Gideon ventured into high society had proven invaluable.

Skulk, indeed.

"I was simply enjoying a bit of fresh air before I plunged into the fray," he drawled, shaking the man's offered hand.

Whitfield snorted. "It does get deuced hot during these things."

"That's putting it mildly."

The duke fixed his shrewd blue eyes on him for a moment, and Gideon arched a brow. Whitfield's inspections had unnerved him when they'd first become friendly, but he'd since become used to them. Usually the duke would keep whatever observations he'd gathered about Gideon to himself, but on the rare occasions he deigned to share his thoughts, Gideon was often struck by Whitfield's insight.

"There's something else there, though, isn't there? Do they still make you feel like an outsider?"

A lump lodged in his throat, and it felt like an eternity for Gideon to work it free. Had his unease in these social situations been so apparent? And if Whitfield noticed, did others as well?

Was he treated as an outsider because *he* believed himself to be one?

Now was not the time for such introspection. Brushing past him, Gideon prowled up the steps, tossing out, "Don't be ridiculous," over his shoulder.

After they had surrendered their hats and coats to the butler, Whitfield was almost immediately pulled away into a discussion. Gideon was not surprised. Everyone wanted the attention of the young duke, and he knew they would find a way back into each other's company at some point during the night.

Gideon paused just outside the entrance to the ballroom. Despite his response to Whitfield, he *was* treated like an outsider. Oh, he knew he was respected to a degree and had begun to receive invitations to attend all manner of social events. But those things couldn't erase the stares. The whispers about his tawny-colored skin and dark eyes. About his imposing height. His childhood in Whitechapel. He may be a member of Parliament, but to many, he was still a grasping outsider.

But while Gideon may have had a humble start in life, his role models had been fierce. Determined. His grandmother's memory would never let him forget it.

"Are you ready to face the firing squad?" Whitfield murmured as he came to stand at his side.

"As ready as I ever am for these blasted things," he said, biting back a sigh.

It was a crush. Of course it was. Lord and Lady Montrose were well-liked, influential members of society, and invitations to their events were coveted. Gideon tried to remember that when stiff smiles were directed at him, the owners' gazes curious. Some critical.

A nine-piece orchestra serenaded the guests, the notes bouncing off the high coffered ceilings. Women in gowns of every color twirled about the parquet dance floor in their partners' arms, observed by guests seated at tables and lined up along the perimeter, and up and down the sweeping staircase. Gideon pressed his lips together to smother his amusement when he spied several women trying to maneuver their large crinoline-lined skirts through the packed crowd. He knew little of women's fashion, but such silhouettes seemed like a cumbersome trend to him.

"Your grace, Fox, it was good of you to come."

Gideon pivoted, a polite smile sliding onto his face when his gaze landed on his host, Lord Montrose. The marquess's return smile was cordial.

"I was told this was the place to be, so I am happy to have been invited."

The men made idle chatter about the festivities, before Whitfield was waylaid by a marchioness who asked to introduce him to her granddaughter. Her *unmarried* granddaughter. Gideon bit the inside of his cheek to contain his amusement at his friend's resigned expression as the older woman led him away.

Montrose took a sip of his champagne, his eyes dancing over the guests who milled about. "Did you read the latest report from the Royal Navy squadron?"

He slid his gaze to look at the marquess askance. How had he not known Montrose received squadron reports? He'd specifically set his secretary to the task of discovering who else in Parliament had shown an interest in the squadron's operations, and the marquess's name was never mentioned.

His palms were abruptly clammy. "I did. I confess to being frustrated so many ships were spotted."

"I, too. I had imagined that with the war in the States, the slave traders would have slowed their horrific activities, but I understand there's still much demand in Brazil and Cuba."

"Sadly, there is. Plus, I can imagine the Confederacy is always in need of soldiers."

Gideon enunciated the word *Confederacy* with so much disdain, he almost winced.

Lord Montrose appeared nonplussed, merely cocking his head. "I understand you're working on a proposal to pressure these foreign governments to cease their support of this inhumane practice."

"I am." Gideon licked his suddenly dry lips, his pulse thundering in his ears. "If I accomplish anything during my time as an MP, let it be the absolute abolishment of the slave trade across the world."

"And that would be a legacy worth leaving." The marquess swiped a champagne flute from a passing footman and handed it to Gideon. Clicking their glasses together he said, "Let us deliver such a condemnation together."

Elation . . . *hope* . . . robbed him of breath. It was more than he would have thought possible. To have an influential, well-connected member of Lords as an ally in this mission was an answer to his prayers. With Montrose adding his support to the cause, suddenly the idea of delivering a death blow to the transatlantic slave trade seemed possible.

Gideon dipped his head, smothering the first real smile he'd felt in . . . *forever.* "I would be honored to work on such a worthy cause with you, my lord."

He and Lord Montrose discussed the issue for several more minutes, and after agreeing to let their secretaries decide upon a meeting time, the marquess excused himself to see to his guests. Gideon did his best to hide his good mood, but it was hard not to gloat at the prospect of securing such a powerful ally.

"Christ, did Montrose offer you one of his daughters to take as a wife?"

Rolling his eyes, Gideon didn't bother to look at Whitfield, who had reappeared out of the crowd next to him. "You're uttering all manner of ridiculous things this night."

The duke chuffed. "I insist you give me my due, sirrah. I'm certain that at least eighty percent of the words that fall from my lips on any given day are ridiculous. I don't save my antics for you alone."

"I certainly hope you didn't subject the Marchioness of Everard's granddaughter to said antics."

"Rest assured that I was all that is charming and ducal." Whitfield took a sip of his drink, the amber liquid hinting at something stronger than Gideon's own champagne. "Because I confess that I do enjoy subjecting you to that eighty percent."

"Why am I so lucky?"

Whitfield shrugged. "I'd wager it's because you're one of the only people I've met who doesn't find my antics amusing."

Gideon had sensed that about his friend. Whitfield enjoyed being challenged, relished a lively debate, and yet so few people dared contradict a duke.

"You have a very dispassionate personality," Whitfield continued, swishing the liquid about his glass as he surveyed the room, ignoring the people who tried to snag his attention, mostly marriage-minded mamas as best as Gideon could gather. "And I am determined to crack it. I live for the day you laugh so hard you shoot water from your nose."

"Well, you will die a disappointed man," Gideon said, a smile in his words if not on his face.

"Oh, most assuredly."

Frowning, Gideon swung his head to his friend, but before he could question his words, Whitfield whistled under his breath.

"That must be one of them."

Gideon shook his head. "One of whom?"

Whitfield jerked his head to a spot across the room. "The heiresses."

"The . . . what?"

The duke snorted. "The sisters from Mexico. Apparently, the Mexican ambassador is sponsoring them. Word is they fled the conflict with France with their fortune."

He was aware of the French occupation of Mexico but hadn't given it more than a passing thought. Not when he was concerned with his own directives within Parliament and the Civil War in the States.

Curious, Gideon turned to consider one of the women Whitfield had identified. She was young, not long out of the schoolroom, he imagined. With her rich mahogany hair and enticing hazel eyes she was undoubtedly pretty, a fact emphasized by the group of fawning young men who surrounded her. He watched her, waiting for her to smile, but she never did.

"She's quite the lovely bird," Whitfield murmured, his deep tone containing a note of interest.

Gideon shot him a glare. "That's no way to speak of a lady."

"Touché," the duke agreed, his gaze steady on the young woman in the green gown. "But then I'm certain she's well aware of her loveliness."

To argue the assertion would have been foolish. The lady in question did indeed appear aware of her charms, the slight curl of her pink lips as she listened to the swains about her a contradiction to the hard glint in her eyes. Gideon felt certain that this was not the first, and would not be the last, time she'd entertained a court of admirers.

"I believe I will request an introduction, if only to learn her name." Whitfield winked at him before he slipped into the crowd, his broad body making its way to the heiress holding court across the room.

Stifling a sigh of resignation, Gideon skirted the edge of the group, watching with amusement as Whitfield sidled to the young woman's side, dipping his head to whisper in her ear. It was apparent he hadn't bothered to ask for an introduction and seen to the task himself, a faux pas only a duke could be forgiven of.

Leaning on a column, Gideon sipped idly on his champagne

for a time, taking in the festivities around him yet ignoring most of it. His gaze skipped over many MPs and lords he should speak to, if only to be courteous, but for the moment Gideon was content to just observe. Socializing would come again, soon enough.

All pretenses of aloofness dissipated when an effervescent laugh had him turning his head, seeking out the source before he knew what he was about.

Gideon's skittering gaze landed on her with the force of a cannon blast. She was flanked by guests, like a sun in the center of the universe.

She was dressed in magenta, the fabric embroidered with exotic flowers in gold thread, blossoms he suspected flourished in her homeland. The brilliant color set off her luminous tan skin and accentuated her every enticing curve. Brindled brown eyes twinkled in amusement as she listened to the chattering man next to her, her body turned toward him as if she were genuinely interested in what he had to say. But Gideon knew the man who stood next to her, Stephen Avery, a fellow MP, was an empty-headed fool. Given how the lady smiled at him, perhaps she was just as foolish.

The thought disappointed him to a confusing degree.

"Miss Luna, your gown is so *unique*. I've never seen a color quite like it before."

A break in the music brought the feminine voice to him, and even Gideon could dissect the mocking implication of the woman's words. Stepping to the side, his gaze fell on the speaker. Lady Emily Hargrove flicked her fan about, her guinea-colored hair framing her pretty face, even as her mouth twisted into a serpentine grin.

Gideon walked several paces to his right until he could see Miss Luna's face unobstructed. A warmth traveled over his skin as he took her in. She was obviously one of the Mexican sisters Whitfield spoke of, and for a reason he couldn't pinpoint, Gideon found her more arresting than her prettier sister. Maybe it was her easy smile? There were no hard edges to it. He took a sip of his now tepid champagne, bracing himself for her response.

"Thank you, Lady Emily." She grasped her voluminous skirts with both hands, and showcased the craftsmanship for her admirers. "Mexico is a colorful, vibrant place, and this color reminded me of home."

Her lips were tight for a moment, perhaps a bit wistful, but they tipped up again in an instant.

Miss Luna tilted her head to the side as she considered the marquess's daughter. "I know not everyone is partial to bold colors, and not everyone looks good in them, for they can be overpowering, but I fancy this magenta fit the happiness I felt being here."

Several of her gentlemen admirers quickly offered compliments, and Gideon rolled his eyes.

"My French modiste has assured me that delicate colors, like this green"—Lady Emily ran a hand down the beaded bodice of her gown—"are all the rage in Paris. And everyone knows Paris is the leader in fashion."

"Parisians are very stylish." Miss Luna's expression was open and amiable. "The dressmaker who created this lovely gown lived in Paris for many years. Her late husband was a diplomat, and when he died, he left her a sizable portion, which she used to open her own dress shop in Mexico City."

"She went into service?" Lady Emily sputtered, pressing a hand to her chest.

Miss Luna's brows knit together. "I've never considered what Señora García did a service, but I suppose you could say it was."

"What did you consider it, then?" Avery asked.

"Artistry." Running her black-lace gloves along the intricate stitching that graced the front panel of her gown, Miss Luna smiled. "Some artists coax beautiful notes from piano keys and violin strings, while others combine oils and canvas and produce vivid scenes that rob us of breath. Señora García takes fabric and thread, and creates masterpieces that are worn for the whole world to see."

Gideon's breath hitched in his throat. What an intriguing way to think of fashion, as art and beauty. He wasn't sure he agreed, remembering how ungainly the wide crinoline skirts appeared to be.

Still, he moved a step closer to the group as if an invisible string reeled him in.

"So she has Paris to thank for her creativity and style." Lady Emily's laugh was sharp.

"Or perhaps living in Paris, surrounded by the fashion and art, was her muse." Miss Luna fixed her gaze on the glass of lemonade in her hand. "I've always thought an artist could be inspired by all manner of things, but the desire to create was inherent."

She looked up, an unreadable expression on her face. "Do you suppose anything outside of Europe is incapable of beauty and culture and art? That only British history, European history, is worth knowing? As if the greatness of the British Empire, the Spanish Empire . . . the Roman Empire . . . weren't built on the backs of those they stole from. Those they pillaged from, all while they claimed to be civilizing the native people."

A scowl darkened Lady Emily's face. "I'm sure everyone would agree that the British Empire's influence has brought stability and civility to the world."

"If you define *everyone* as the British and those who directly benefit from their exploits, and *stability* as wealth and power, well, then I think you might be correct."

A small snort slipped from his nose before Gideon could dam it, and he thought it may have escaped notice until Miss Luna's brown eyes collided with his, pinning him in place. Even across the distance, and people who stood between them, her scrutiny felt important, and he stood a bit taller. It was an alarming thought that he craved this woman's approval, and a voice in the back of Gideon's mind wondered why he cared.

Her expression changed not one whit, but he glimpsed a glint of interest in her gaze.

Lady Emily exited the group with her cluster of friends, leaving Miss Luna to hold court over her cast of sycophants, and Gideon debated whether he wanted to join their ranks. Watching her toss back her head to laugh at a comment, her white teeth flashing against the backdrop of her tan skin, made the muscles in his shoulders tense. Then she dipped her head to allow Avery to whisper in her ear, and it was like a douse of cold water to the face.

Gideon's political future stretched before him, and he had no intention of distracting himself from his goals and ambition for a laughing pair of brown eyes. If he were to court the attentions of a woman, she would have the impeccable connections needed to benefit his career, not be a young heiress who would be returning overseas to a future on foreign shores.

With that uncomfortable truth in mind, Gideon offered Miss Luna a brief nod and disappeared back into the crowd, in search of a strong drink.

3

"Did she really have to bring the dog along?"

Isabel uttered the words softly, in Spanish, and Ana María bumped her shoulder in commiseration. Lady Yardley's Maltese was naturally exuberant, but as the landau navigated the afternoon crowds in the park, the animal's incessant barks and yelps had quickly become tiring.

"Oh, she's not so bad," Gabby answered, again in Spanish, as she reached out a hand and stroked Dove's soft white fur. The dog submitted to her sister's affection for a moment before turning to bark at a passing carriage.

Ana María managed to stifle a laugh when Isabel grumbled under her breath.

When Lady Yardley had suggested they take her landau for a ride around Hyde Park, they'd eagerly agreed to the proposition. The day had dawned with a cloudless sky, the warm sunshine heralding a pleasant outing.

Yet Ana María was well aware the viscountess had suggested such an activity because she wanted to capitalize on their debut the night before at the Montrose ball, a showing she had called perfection.

And their night had been a smashing success. They had socialized in Mexico, but always under their father's watchful eye, and the fear of error had made the events more stressful than enjoyable. The same was not the case with the Montrose ball.

Lady Yardley had been impressed with their wardrobes, and had happily riffled through their gowns, personally selecting their attire. Ana María had drawn courage from wearing her own dress, for although she was determined to start anew in London, the familiar reminder of home fortified her resolve.

The majority of the people they met had been friendly and welcoming, although a few, Lady Emily and her ilk, had been less so. But Ana María was no stranger to the haughty, judgmental attitudes levied at her and her sisters. She was the daughter of Elías Luna Cuate after all, a man who had shrewdly worked his way from a poor village in Michoacán to a sweeping villa in the capital, with a peninsular for a wife and the ear of the presidente. Whispers, innuendos, and vile gossip had surrounded the Luna sisters like a toxic cloud since their first public appearance as schoolgirls, and such an early exposure had hardened Ana María's spirit against frivolous attacks.

What it hadn't prepared her for was the sting that lanced her when the most captivating man she'd ever set eyes upon had simply acknowledged her with a nod before disappearing back into the crowd. Ana María had seen him approach, his expression placid but his obsidian eyes fervent as they considered her and her new group of friends. His dress attire had been austere, with no embellishments aside from a crisp white cravat tie, but she supposed such things would have been overshadowed by the harsh beauty of his face.

He had appeared interested in their conversation but never joined it, content to watch from the fringe as she maneuvered around Lady Emily's cutting jabs and fended off the overtures from swains more concerned with her dowry than any thought in her head. Ana María had thought this mystery man might be different . . . but then he'd left with barely a nod.

His disinterest had stung.

And why she should care about this man's lack of attentiveness, Ana María knew not. She was in a new city, at complete liberty to reshape her persona . . . a persona that had garnered curiosity from engaging people and attractive men the night before. Yet the thought of that gentleman's black eyes nagged her. She had never been found wanting, working hard to ensure she met—no, *surpassed*—all expectations her father set her to. And she could not manage to hold this man's regard for longer than one conversation.

A new worry emerged in the back of her mind, taking the inconvenient shape of her absent fiancé. Theirs was a political union brokered by her father, but Ana María respected Fernando, and her flirtatious behavior at the ball had not been respectful of the promise she'd made him. Although Tío Arturo had made no mention of her fiancé, Ana María couldn't imagine he would agree with her behavior the night before.

Despite this, thoughts of the dark-eyed gentleman continued to play through her mind, and guilt soured her stomach. And that feeling sparked her anger, for hadn't she longed to leave behind the old constraints that had bound her? And guilt had long been a tool her father had used against her.

Dove's incessant yapping pulled her from her disappointed memories to the noisy present. A present that included Isabel's glower of discontent and Gabby's lighthearted laughs while she greeted new acquaintances as they rumbled past.

Hyde Park was bustling with the elite and powerful this time of day, the walking paths burgeoning with the fashionable, and the riding paths a slow queue of carriages. Not that Lady Yardley seemed annoyed with the congestion, her merry waves and flirtatious smiles to riders who stopped to greet them making her intent apparent.

So when she spoke, her gaze trained on the path before the landau, it took Ana María a moment to understand her words.

"Remember to refrain from speaking Spanish." Lady Yardley tipped her fan at a gentleman who rode by at a trot. "No one likes to be left out of the conversation."

Knotting her fingers together in her lap, Ana María's chest tightened at the scold. Of course they should not be excluding Lady Yardley from their conversation, and embarrassment made her cringe.

"And yet no one seems to mind when French is spoken. I heard plenty of people speak French last night," Gabby pointed out, her black brows rising.

"And German, too," Isabel added.

"I'm surprised you heard much of anything considering you spent the majority of the ball locked away in the library." The viscountess leveled her sister with a gimlet stare.

She bit back an inner groan. Ana María had, of course, noted Isabel's absence in the ballroom last night, but would never have dreamt of embarrassing her with this knowledge. Isabel was shy and avoided social gatherings, and had often found ways to escape them, much to their father's frustration.

Lady Yardley obviously had no sisterly compunction to hold her tongue.

Scarlet infused Isabel's cheeks, and she looked away without a response.

"And German is spoken because the prince consort is German," Lady Yardley continued, flicking her fingers.

"Well *I'm* Mexican and will speak Spanish when I feel like it," Gabby pushed, turning in her seat next to the viscountess to face her directly.

"Gabby, her ladyship has a point." Ana María leaned forward to press a hand to her youngest sister's arm. "She's the only one in this carriage who doesn't speak Spanish, and it's rude of us to speak it when she cannot understand us."

Her sister pressed her lips together for a pregnant moment, holding Ana María's stare. There was so much anger festering in her sister's hazel eyes. So much bitterness. And although playing peacekeeper exhausted her, Ana María refused to allow Gabby to treat her as the enemy.

Heaving a sigh, Gabby looked to Lady Yardley. "Please accept my apologies. That was rude of us."

The viscountess dipped her head, cuddling Dove close to her chest.

"*But*," Gabby continued, "while we've agreed to dance to this merry tune of Tío Arturo's, I refuse to contort myself into an English rose simply to curry favor."

Ana María scowled. "No one's asking us to be anything other than what we are."

"Are you certain of that?" Isabel murmured from her side, her mouth a firm slash.

As Ana María debated what to say to appease her sisters, the viscountess suddenly yelped in alarm.

"No! Dove, come back!"

Ana María gasped as the white dog leapt from the landau, unconcerned with the traffic congesting Rotten Row and the carriage wheels and horse hooves that could maim her. Dove darted around every obstacle, each step punctuated by her high-pitched yips, and by the time Lady Yardley's driver had managed to steer the landau to the side and out of the way of other conveyances, the dog was nowhere to be seen.

"Oh no," Lady Yardley wailed, her hand pressed to her mouth and her eyes quickly filling with tears. "I'll never find her now."

Ana María immediately grasped Isabel's hand. "I saw the direction she disappeared in, and between the two of us, we'll find Dove, your ladyship."

Without giving her sister a chance to object, Ana María hauled her down the carriage steps.

"What about me?" Gabby demanded, gripping the edge of the landau and looking down at them.

"Tend to Lady Yardley." She gestured with her chin to where the viscountess cried into her handkerchief.

"Teach her some Spanish," Isabel called, taking off in the direction Dove was last seen and not hearing their sister's annoyed growl.

Ana María trailed after Isabel, weaving through the crowd, offering quick hellos and friendly waves when she encountered a person she met the night before. When her sister abruptly halted to survey the landscape, she heaved a breath.

"Of course Dove jumped from the carriage. The little beast was no doubt beside herself with all the smells and noise," Isabel grumbled, her dark eyes darting about. "It was cruel for Lady Yardley to bring her."

"Come now, you know her ladyship was not trying to be cruel." Ana María winced as she wiggled her toes. Her slippers were more suited for drawing room visits than mad dashes after wayward dogs. "Dove loves attention and has certainly received more of it on this drive than any of us."

Isabel snorted, flashing her a look of disbelief.

Her brows stitched together. "What's that supposed to mean?"

"It means that the landau has been stopped no less than ten times since we departed because admirers have wanted to greet you. Or Gabby. Shower you both with praise."

Her middle sister pivoted away, but not before Ana María glimpsed the harsh tilt to her chin. Was Isabel jealous? Her reserved sister, who was the living embodiment of the Luna family's Purépecha roots, had long been subjected to lingering glances and whispered sneers. And her beauty was always compared to Gabby's, and to a lesser extent Ana María's own.

But perhaps her ambivalence for social situations was a mask for her sister's desire to be seen as more than the quiet, bookish Luna girl. It was hard to stand out when one's sister shined so very bright.

"Isabel, that just means we're doing what Tío Arturo has tasked us to do. I'm sure if you stopped hiding away in the library and actually met new people, you'd be pleasantly surprised by how affable they are," she said calmly.

Isabel's glare could have cracked the thickest ice. "But I'm also doing what I've been tasked with."

Ana María jerked her chin back. "What do you—?"

"There's the tiny fiend," Isabel exclaimed, and Ana María looked over in time to see a flash of white disappear between the trees that lined the path. Grasping her skirts, Isabel gave chase.

Sighing, Ana María set off after them. She really should have worn better shoes.

Doing her best to catch up, Ana María smiled politely at a gentleman who tipped his hat as he walked toward her. She vaguely recognized him from the Montrose ball. Mr. Edwards? Edmond? She couldn't recall.

When his steps paused, she realized he intended to converse with her, and annoyance set her teeth on edge. Offering him a quick wave, she skipped away, quickly following her sister's trail through the trees and around the bend . . .

Only to miss the sudden dip in the earth.

Without even a moment to stop her forward motion or attempt to regain her balance, Ana María fell into a bed of primrose and phlox, crushing the delicate blooms under the weight of her body. The crinoline of her skirts protected her from injury but couldn't prevent how the air was knocked from her lungs, leaving her stunned.

Gasping for breath, Ana María rolled over and stared up at the cerulean sky, wondering how her day had turned so unpleasant.

"Are you injured, miss?"

A familiar face loomed over her. With his onyx eyes and striking face, this man had inconveniently plagued her thoughts since the night before. Her mouth gaped when she realized he cradled Dove against his broad chest.

"Dios mío, Ana, are you all right?"

Isabel appeared at her side, grasping her upper arm and helping her sit up. Ana María winced, the boning of her stays cutting into her sides. She did her best to avoid looking at the gentleman who lingered nearby, but he must have noticed her pained expression, for he suddenly crouched down on her other side.

"Why don't we try to help you stand? I'm sure lying under this crushed cage is not very comfortable."

Ana María nodded her consent, inhaling sharply as she stood upright, her head swimming for a moment. Isabel immediately adjusted the fall of her sister's skirts, brushing decapitated flowers from the folds and reaching up to tuck errant curls back into place. The gentleman continued to hold Ana María's arm, his warm palm turning her thoughts to sludge.

"Are you well?" he asked softly.

Gritting her teeth, she finally dragged her gaze up to meet his, her face unbearably hot. "I'm well, thank you. The only thing injured is my pride."

His full lips twitched for only a moment, but amusement shone in his eyes.

Directing her attention to Dove, who sat in the man's arms with her tongue lolled to the side, Ana María scowled. "All this tomfoolery just so you could chase after who knows what."

"Look at how pleased the little beast is," Isabel huffed, rolling her eyes as she scratched Dove's head.

A distant part of her mind noted the dog was indeed emitting an air of smugness, but Ana María found it a colossal task to look at anything but the man who held Dove close, his large hands gently stroking the dog's white coat. He glanced down at her and held her gaze, just as he had done the night before. A pulse of awareness reverberated under her skin.

Ripping her eyes away, Ana María schooled her features, struggling to disguise how his presence discomfited her. If she'd thought him handsome under the dim glow of gas lamps, it was nothing compared to how the sun kissed his bronze skin and made it glow. His dark beauty was hypnotizing, and her tongue felt glued to the roof of her mouth.

Isabel did not appear as affected by his presence, for she offered him a genial nod and said, "Dove here has led us on a merry chase through the park, and we appreciate your assistance in capturing her and helping my sister, Mr. . . . ?"

"Fox, Gideon Fox," he murmured, his deep voice like crushed velvet.

Ana María gasped. "Gideon Fox, the member of Parliament? The one who wrote that editorial in the London *Times* in support of the Union army?"

Mr. Fox's brows rose, and he opened his mouth before snapping it closed again. "Yes. It was the right thing to do. Britain should be publicly stating its support for President Lincoln, who will be remembered fondly by history, no matter what his countrymen say about him now." He coughed into his hand. "I'm surprised you took note of that."

"Why should you be? My sisters and I are doing our best to read the newspapers and learn about how the British view the world and their place in it. Also, having an understanding of how politics works here and who the political players are seems important." She cocked her head. "Many people we know are hoping President Lincoln and the Union are successful, especially as they fight to grant freedom to enslaved Africans. And seeing as how African people were also stolen and trafficked to Mexico by the Spanish, many members of Mexican society have African antecedents, so we share an affinity."

His expression turned thoughtful. "Thank you for the reminder that the British were not the only ones who benefited from colonialism."

Ana María pressed her lips together to smother her smile.

"I know we're breaking protocol by not being properly introduced, but seeing as how you've come to our aid, perhaps we can be forgiven the oversight," she began.

"I won't tell if you don't," he said, the corner of his mouth quirking.

Her eyes widened. Was he flirting with her? Ana María found it hard to believe the stoic man she glimpsed at the Montrose ball would showcase a playful side. It teased a grin onto her lips.

"Well, since we have immunity, allow me to introduce to you my sister, Miss Isabel Luna Valdés."

Her sister bobbed an impeccable curtsy, flashing a rare, brief smile at Mr. Fox, who bowed to her in turn.

Pressing a hand to her chest, she said, "And I am—"

"Miss Ana María Luna. Yes, I know. All of London knows who the Luna sisters are by now."

It does? Sliding her gaze to Isabel, her sister looked back at her with a frown, as if she was just as flummoxed.

Seeming to sense their surprise, Mr. Fox chuckled. "While British society has welcomed several dollar princesses from America, we have yet to be graced by any from Mexico."

"What an unfortunate label," Isabel said.

"Well, we are happy to end your unlucky streak," she hastened to add, hoping to deflect from her sister's words.

But if the way Mr. Fox mashed his lips together and made a show of bouncing Dove in his arms was any indication, he'd not missed her statement.

After a pause, he handed the dog to Isabel, who scowled while she tucked Dove into the crook of her arm. Mr. Fox leaned on his cane. "Now tell me, ladies, between you, me, and Dove here, what is your opinion of London?"

For the next several minutes, the sisters shared observations gleaned from their brief time in the country. Based on how his eyes crinkled at the corners when they explained several interactions with well-known members of society, Mr. Fox was amused by their opinions of the Montrose ball.

He effortlessly transitioned the conversation to the conflict that sent them fleeing from Mexico, and Ana María abruptly walked a tightrope, not wanting to provide too many details about their father and his important role in the government, and yet wanting to share a bit of her uncertainty and fear with a sympathetic ear. And Mr. Fox was sympathetic, but never in a way that felt false or cloying. His questions were thoughtful. His replies sincere. The light in his eyes comforting.

But Ana María quickly learned his graciousness was a cloak for his tenacity.

"Why did your parents not accompany you when you fled Mexico?" His brow dropped low, darkening his mien. "To send three unmarried daughters, with no protection, across the Atlantic, was nothing short of dangerous."

Shame, defensiveness, *anger* fused in her gut, and Ana María fought to keep those emotions off her face. Isabel, it appeared, was battling to do the same.

She fiddled with her gloves to give herself a task to channel her frustration. "I assure you that our parents would not have sent us if the prospect of remaining in Mexico were not more dangerous than the journey."

And Ana María *knew* this . . . yet she couldn't soothe the bitterness that festered like an open wound deep in her soul.

"But what could be more important than ensuring one's own children were safe?"

"You assume, Mr. Fox," Isabel interjected, "that we are more important than their other interests."

A fire surged up her throat, bringing tears to her eyes. Turning away, Ana María feigned an interest in the violets and primroses that had cushioned her when she fell. Nothing Isabel said was untrue, but the bald way she had revealed their father's commodification of their safety made her want to dash away and hide.

Although she couldn't see Mr. Fox, she could sense how he shifted his weight on his feet.

He cleared his throat. "The gentleman in me wants to argue your words, as if I could possibly know your circumstances." Ana María finally turned to look at him. "So allow me to say that I'm glad you escaped a grave situation, and are here now, chasing mischievous canines through Hyde Park and brightening my monotonous day."

His words melted the protections around her resolve, and Ana María chuckled. "You forgot the part of the narrative when I gracelessly fell and crushed the flowers. That was definitely the part that stood out in my mind."

"Fall? I don't recall being witness to a fall." Mr. Fox tapped a finger against his jaw.

The tips of his ears turned pink when she reached out and grasped his arm, her delight at his playfulness making her forget herself. Ana María touched him for only a moment, and yet it was enough to make gooseflesh erupt across her skin.

Jerking back, she whispered, "I apologize."

Mr. Fox shook his head, but before he could respond, Isabel huffed loudly.

"We've been found."

Looking over her shoulder, Ana María saw Lady Yardley and Gabby walking down the path toward them, the older woman waving a handkerchief at seeing Dove safely in Isabel's arms.

"If you would excuse me, Mr. Fox," Isabel said, lifting Dove as if to showcase her as a prime specimen of empty-headed idiocy, "I should deliver this miscreant to her anxious owner without further delay."

They watched from a distance as the viscountess was reunited with her beloved dog, her relieved laughter carrying on the breeze.

"I overheard part of your conversation with Lady Emily Hargrove last night."

A fluttering sensation filled Ana María's chest. "Oh. I fear I may have upset her."

"I thought you were quite gracious, especially since she was not particularly gracious to you." Mr. Fox cocked his head to the side as he studied her. "Had you hoped to win her good opinion?"

Ana María dropped her gaze to study her dirt-smeared gloves. "We're new here, and I would hate to alienate those who might well be my friend."

Also, a person of Lady Emily's stature would make for an influential ally, and one Tío Arturo would approve of.

"But perhaps you and Lady Emily are cut from a different cloth, and she showed you as much at the ball?"

"Perhaps," she conceded with a wry smile. "I simply sought to make a good impression."

"And who said you didn't?" Mr. Fox moved a half step closer. "*I* was impressed."

Her breath faltered as she met his piercing dark eyes. "Th-thank you."

"Will you be attending the Ralston ball tonight?"

Swallowing, she nodded. "I believe we are."

He digested this information for a moment. "Will you save your supper waltz for me?"

"I'd be honored to," she murmured, her voice hoarse.

"I look forward to it." His smile was brief but devastating, and she rocked back on her feet at the sight of it. "Until tonight, Miss Luna."

With her heart thundering in her ears, she watched as Mr. Fox greeted Lady Yardley and her sisters, patted Dove one last time on her head, and ambled away as if he hadn't just sent her composure careening into the ether.

Ana María could only aspire to reclaim her poise.

24

"You told me you weren't going to be here."

Gideon glanced at his friend askance. "Whitfield."

The duke crossed his arms over his chest, a glass of wine dangling from his long fingers. "What made you change your mind? I know it wasn't the crowd." He gestured to the guests conversing and laughing around them, a hint of a scowl on his lips. "It's the same boring lot we saw yesterday."

"I don't know; I'd wager there are some among this sea of faces worth speaking with."

"Not likely." Whitfield turned to face him fully, his pupils contracting as he studied him. "Last night it looked like you were waiting to have a tooth pulled, but now, well, now you seem almost . . . dare I say, eager?"

Ignoring the way his heart rate spiked, Gideon scoffed. "Being absurd again, I see."

Not rising to the bait, Whitfield unwrapped his pointer finger from around his glass, tipping it at Gideon. "When I saw you at the coffeehouse this morning, you specifically said you would not be attending tonight. What happened in the ten or so hours from then until now?"

A husky laugh met his ears at a break in the music, and Gideon turned toward the sound. Taking several steps to the right, he craned his head for a better look, heaving a sigh when he did not find *her* in the throng.

"Ah, you met someone. That's it, isn't it?"

Swiping a glass from a passing footman, Gideon took a healthy gulp in lieu of answering.

Whitfield's chuckle was as dry as the red wine on Gideon's tongue. "Who is she?"

"You're assuming a good deal."

"And you're deflecting a good deal."

Gideon snorted, pivoting to scan the other side of the ballroom. His gaze skipped over the crowd without landing on his quarry, and his stomach sank a tad.

"Are you looking for Montrose?" Whitfield continued. Like the headstrong mule he was, he refused to give up his line of questioning. "He's not here, but then you knew that. Anderson mentioned it this morning."

"Did he?" Taking a sip, he leveled a look at the duke. "Not much Anderson says is worth remembering."

Whitfield rocked back on his feet, his blue eyes blinking rapidly. "Did you just make a joke? I feel laughter bubbling up my throat, but surely I'm mistaken."

"You are. It's probably indigestion."

"Christ, man, you cannot do this to me." The duke wiped a hand across his mouth. "If you have developed a sense of humor, whatever do I have to live for? Needling you to smile was my purpose in this wretched life."

"Perhaps you can dedicate yourself to the betterment of our great country." Gideon bumped his shoulder into Whitfield's. "Vote your seat. Throw your title and good name behind the proposal I hope to craft with Montrose's support."

"Good name?" The duke scoffed into his drink. "Of course I'll support your proposal . . . just as long as you don't expect me to flatter any of those idiots in Lords."

"I know better than that. I can't have you undoing all my negotiating with your droll tongue."

Whitfield raised his glass to salute him.

Gideon cocked his head. "For all you've made of my presence here tonight, why are *you* here? You've made it abundantly clear you hate these things."

"How unfortunate. I don't hate them at all." The duke sniffed. "I *loathe* them. But beggars can't be choosers, or whatever that silly idiom is."

"Beggars? What do you mean?" Gideon frowned.

"Oh, don't mind me. I am in a mood," Whitfield replied with a wave of his hand.

"You're always in a mood."

"So I am." Taking a sip of wine, the duke sighed. "Egad, Lady Everard has spied me. It's time for a hasty retirement to the cardroom. Are you coming with?"

Shaking his head, Gideon said, "I'm sure I'll make my way there eventually, but not quite yet."

Whitfield winged up a brow before he sauntered away.

Sweeping his gaze across the crowd, Gideon pondered where Miss Luna might be. He guessed there might be two more sets before the supper waltz, so there was no reason for him to rush to locate her . . . but then she *was* the primary reason he was here.

A small smile tugged at his lips as he remembered how she had tumbled over the hedgerows and landed in a graceless heap on the ground. Gideon had initially been worried she had injured herself, but her pink-tinged cheeks and self-deprecating words made it clear the only thing maimed had been her self-possession.

And from that ungraceful introduction had sprung a truly diverting conversation. In just a handful of minutes, Miss Ana María Luna had proven herself to be clever, witty, and effortlessly charming. Although Gideon had told himself he did not have time to indulge his attraction to the foreign heiress, in that moment in the park, with the sun shining down on her black hair and turning wisps copper, it had been impossible to ignore her appeal. Like a meteor drawn into her orbit, Gideon had been riveted.

Clearing his throat, he looped his hands behind his back and strolled about the room, dipping his head in greeting to those he passed and stopping a time or two to exchange pleasantries with acquaintances. As Whitfield had said, it was the same scene as the night before, with many of the same faces. The social season was a monotonous loop, and Gideon had no notion of why such events drew a crowd when it was damn near impossible to distinguish one from the next.

Except for this ball. Gideon had a very clear idea of why he was in attendance, and for once he would not allow himself to be concerned with politics or current affairs as he normally would. When his thoughts turned to examining his uncharacteristic behavior, Gideon pushed them ruthlessly away. There was a time and place for self-reflection, and it was not while maneuvering through a ton crowd.

His cravat tie was suddenly strangling, and Gideon resisted the urge to yank it loose and toss it away. Instead he dropped his glass on the tray of a passing footman and prowled in the direction of the ballroom. He was here to dance with Miss Luna, and dance he would.

And then he heard it. Gideon had doubted he would be able to hear her laughter above the din, but it floated to him through the noise, and Gideon's seeking gaze finally found *her*.

She wore a stunning shade of green. It was the color of lush verdant valleys, the bodice trimmed with delicate blond lace, which contrasted gloriously with her warm, tawny skin. Cream-colored roses were nestled in her ebony tresses, a crown on her beauty.

He'd grown used to the colors of the season, yet on Miss Luna, those shades were brighter and more vivid. She was so . . . so . . . *alive*, and Gideon could not look away.

Then she placed her hand on the arm of the gentleman next to her, tipped her head back, and laughed gaily.

There was something in her laughter that felt *off*. He took a step closer, his gaze darting over her in examination, trying to determine what it was that seemed diff—

And then Gideon saw it. In the flush of her cheeks. In the sway in her stance. In the manner in which she clutched the gentleman's arm as if trying to maintain her balance. She was foxed.

His shoulders drooped under the weight of his disappointment. He'd thought Miss Luna was a singular young woman, but he'd obviously been mistaken. Gideon's toes curled as he watched heads turn in her direction. Cringed as he noticed eyebrows rise and lips press into grim lines. Miss Luna continued to laugh and converse, her voice a shade too loud, completely unaware of how the other guests sniffed their noses as if they had smelled something foul. A quick glance made it apparent she was not the only person in her group who had imbibed too much, but the scornful gazes were directed at *her*, for transgressions were always magnified when committed by a woman.

Yet Miss Luna seemed immune to the stares. The whispers.

But Gideon noticed. From the fledgling beginnings of his career, he'd quickly learned to pay attention to the opinions of those who made society go around. And their distaste made his skin turn cold.

By instinct, he stepped back, his subconscious whispering for him to have a care. To maintain a distance.

Such warnings felt like vinegar on his tongue.

Movement behind the group of young people snagged his gaze, and he watched with his brow creased as a gentleman approached, two glasses of punch in his hands. The gentleman next to Miss Luna, Lord Simon Ripley, stepped back to intercept him, a leonine grin on his pale face. Snatching a tumbler from the man, the lordling slipped a flask from his pocket and poured the unknown contents into both glasses. The men lifted the crystal aloft, toasting each other, before Lord Simon stepped back into the circle of friends and handed one to Miss Luna.

"Gracias, Lord Simon," she exclaimed with a laugh, before taking a large drink.

It suddenly occurred to him that perhaps Miss Luna was unaware of how her new friends were taking advantage of her . . .

Gideon considered her closely. Her smile was blinding as she spoke with the gentlemen around her. He identified several as known rakes and libertines, and his hackles rose. Where was Lady Yardley to keep such fortune hunters away from her? How had she not considered the possibility that villains might exploit her naivety? He was surprised *and* frustrated the viscountess was so lax in her duties to her young charges. How could Miss Luna, as a foreign guest, know who was friend and who was foe?

"They've made quite a splash, have they not?"

Looking askance, he spied a murder of dowagers perched several feet away, their sharp gazes trained on the group he had just been studying. Gideon took a small, inconspicuous step toward them.

"I've found them to be quite charming," a blond-haired woman murmured. Gideon recognized her as Lady Langley. Or was it Lampley? Gad, he could hardly keep these guinea-haired toffs straight. "Polite. Well spoken—"

"And also fast, unscrupulous, and unfit to socialize with innocent young ladies," a snide voice interjected.

Gideon swallowed down an uncomfortable knot.

"That's rather harsh. Perhaps things are done differently in Mexico," an older woman pointed out.

"Do you suppose they allow their young, unmarried women to imbibe at social events?" The question was uttered with undisguised disdain, and Gideon turned to identify the speaker. It was Lady Montrose. Apparently she had attended although her husband had not. "Even so, they're not in Mexico anymore."

The desire to defend Miss Luna made him teeter on his feet, but he couldn't afford to charge out on his white steed, his banner waving in the wind, without courting criticism himself. Thus, ignoring how his ribs seemed to constrict around his lungs, Gideon directed his gaze elsewhere.

Yet he still kept one eye on Miss Luna. On the glassy sheen in her eyes. On the pink tint that rose from her décolletage and up her neck. On the way Lord Simon Ripley stood a tad too closely by her side. When Lord Simon leaned down to whisper in her ear, Gideon gnashed his teeth together.

Tearing his gaze away, he wandered a few steps to create some distance in which to corral his wayward emotions. Gideon could not understand why they were in such tumult. He'd engaged in only one conversation with Miss Luna, had yet to dance with her, and still he could not deny that he had an intense desire to protect her from rogues who would disgrace her. To shield her from the stinging tongues of the ton.

From his periphery, Gideon noted how the dowagers continued to whisper behind their fans, lips curled in disapproval. Surely Lady Yardley had been made aware of Miss Luna's behavior. Would she not come and rescue her young charge?

Yet she continued to chat with Lord Simon, the very scoundrel responsible for her current state.

The notes of a Viennese waltz strummed through the air, and Gideon pivoted about, his teeth clenched. He could either leave now and pretend he hadn't engaged Miss Luna for this set, or whisk her away onto the dance floor and explain the danger she was in.

Gideon focused on his quandary. It appeared that Lord Simon was trying to coax Miss Luna to waltz with him, but she shook her head with a friendly smile. The man did not release her hand, though, despite her obvious denial, and Gideon mentally ordered himself to relax as his stiff limbs weaved through the crowd toward her.

"Come now, Miss Luna, I thought we were friends."

A glower darkened her mien, but in a flash was gone. "Of course we're friends, my lord. But as I have told you, my waltz is spoken for."

Miss Luna looked in his direction then, a manufactured smile frozen on her lips but relief shimmering in her eyes.

"But where is your partner now, Miss Luna, darling?" Undeterred, Lord Simon moved a step closer to her, his hand suddenly a manacle about her wrist. "Come now, dance with me—"

"Miss Luna, buenas noches. Cómo está?" Gideon asked in halting Spanish, his gaze locked with hers and uncaring for Lord Simon's presence.

A grin lit her face. "Señor Fox, I was unaware you knew Spanish."

"I doubt I can claim to know it when I use it in such a horrific way," he said, unable to keep a matching smile from his lips.

"Not horrific at all." She sank into a curtsy, which wobbled as she rose. "No one has tried to converse with us in our home language, and mi corazón hurts to hear it."

Gideon resisted the urge to shift on his feet. "I don't mean to cause you pain."

Miss Luna's expression softened. "Pero, you didn't. Rather you've brought me joy." When the man next to her snorted, her face fell. "Have you met Lord Simon Ripley?"

He had met the man on one occasion or another, but they ran in very different circles. Still, Gideon inclined his head. "My lord, how do you do?"

"Fox." The lordling murmured his name as Gideon suspected he summoned his butler. Or his valet. "How clever of you to learn a spot of Spanish."

"I don't know if it was clever so much as kind," Miss Luna interjected.

"Did I tell you I know some Spanish?" Lord Simon said, angling his chin toward her.

Her brows knotted together. "You did not, my lord."

Lord Simon nodded, the liquid in his tumbler sloshing over the rim and onto his hands. "I spent a summer in Cádiz, in the south of Spain. Have you ever been?"

Gideon shook his head while Miss Luna said, "I have not had the pleasure."

"Truly?" Lord Simon scowled. "I thought surely you would have visited."

Miss Luna blinked in apparent confusion. "My mother and

grandparents emigrated from Spain, but I have never had the opportunity to visit."

Lord Simon tugged on his ear and looked at her as if she had spoken Spanish to him. It suddenly occurred to Gideon where the lordling's confusion came from.

"You are aware that Miss Luna is not from Spain, yes?" he ventured.

"You're not?" he said, jerking his chin back.

She hiccuped a laugh. "I'm from Mexico, my lord."

"But that's the same thing, isn't it?"

Gideon had no notion of what to say as he watched the light in Miss Luna's eyes snuff out like a candle. How could this fool believe Mexico was the same as Spain? And then it occurred to him. Lord Simon could believe it, for when had he—or anyone of his set—ever considered anything or anyone outside of Britain? Or Europe, for that matter?

Looking at Lord Simon's perplexed expression now, Gideon could wager a guess.

"Mexico was called New Spain—by the *Spanish*—for a long time." Miss Luna's tone was polite but crisp, even as her words slurred a bit. "But Mexicans won their independence more than forty years ago, and we have been an autonomous country ever since."

The fact that she felt compelled to be so polite in the face of such horrid ignorance—or willful disregard—made Gideon curl his hands into fists so tight the material of his gloves popped at the seams.

"Fascinating," Lord Simon murmured, a jaunty smile twisting his lips.

"World affairs are indeed interesting." Gideon took a step back. "You should try reading the other sections of the newspaper, my lord. There are many *fascinating* international topics outside of the gossip pages."

Without another word, Gideon swept Miss Luna onto the dance floor. His well of patience had abruptly run dry.

It took him several moments to realize that his partner was struggling to keep up with the pace he set for their waltz, her eyes large and her hand holding tightly to his shoulder as she attempted to regain her balance. Holding back a sigh, Gideon slowed, tucking Miss Luna a bit closer to his chest. For support, of course.

Her head barely reached his chin, but with his hand on her waist and her palm pressed against his, Gideon was overwhelmed by a sense of rightness.

Which would absolutely not do.

Their initial turn about the dance floor was done in silence, and Gideon wondered if she was as attuned to his every movement and breath as he was to hers.

"Thank you for arriving when you did, Señor Fox," she said as they stepped around another couple. "I was almost afraid I would have to accept Lord Simon's offer to dance."

He glanced down at her with a frown. "You didn't want to dance with him? You seemed to be enjoying his company when I approached."

She scoffed. "Did I?"

"You were drinking his brandy, so I'd say yes."

Her mouth froze in a perfect O. Relief filled his chest at the sight.

"I take it you didn't know Lord Simon was slipping brandy into your punch." Gideon didn't bother to hide the bite in his voice.

"I did not." Miss Luna swallowed, a sickly cast sweeping over her complexion.

He raised a brow. "Did you not notice the sharp taste? Or how it made your head swim?"

"I did, but I suppose"—she pressed her lips together—"I just assumed that was how it was supposed to taste. I've never imbibed before."

"You haven't?"

"No." She wrinkled her nose. "My father would never allow us to partake of spirits. He said it was unladylike."

Gideon's mind flitted back to the dowagers' cutting remarks, and his lungs constricted.

He narrowed his eyes on her face. "Surely your friends have told you what signs to look for. Told you what sort of gentlemen to avoid."

Her laugh was sharp, like the harsh toll of a bell. "You assume I've had friends, Señor Fox."

His pulse pounded in his temple. "Truly?"

Miss Luna turned her head, presenting him with her profile, but a bit of her pinched expression was still visible. "My father dictated whom I could speak to and where I could go. My friends were not really my friends but those he paid to serve as companions."

Any irritation Gideon felt for her and her behavior bled away, leaving a yawning ache in his chest.

"Have I made a fool of myself?" Her velvet brown eyes were wide as they met his.

A lie danced on his tongue. Gideon's hand flexed at her waist as he deliberated what he could say to dispel the worry from her gaze. But in the end, he respected her too much to withhold the truth.

"I've overheard talk."

Dropping her gaze to his chest, she deflated with a long exhale.

"Of course there's been talk. A woman's reputation is a tenuous thing. She could live her entire life virtuously, be held up as an example to follow, and one wrong step will see her tumble from grace." She raised her head to scan the crowd. "And of course a foreign woman, one whose accent declares to every ear that she is an outsider, will be afforded less leniency."

Unable to think of an adequate reply, Gideon held his silence.

"I suppose the same censure being directed at me has spared Lord Simon or the others in the group."

It was not a question.

Gideon's nod was terse. "Lord Simon is the Duke of Westerley's second son. Titled young men are the darlings of the ton."

"Of course they are. Men of his cloth derive their worth from their familial connections, which buffers them from rebuke, even while they expose young women to scorn." Her snort was soft but discernible. "Men of his caliber exist in Mexico, too."

"They do?"

"Sí." Her lips twisted in distaste. "While Mexico has no noble titles to convey, a hierarchy exists in society. There are the peninsulares, or those born in Spain. My mother and her family are peninsulares."

"I did not know that." Gideon quirked his brow. "What part of Spain is she from?"

"Zaragoza. Her family emigrated to Mexico when she was a young girl." Miss Luna stared unseeing over his shoulder. "She doesn't remember much about it, but my grandparents speak of it frequently."

"So because they were from Spain, they occupy a higher caste?"

"That and because they are related to some of the richest,

most influential families in Spain. Even now, my mother's surname carries great weight."

Gideon should have known, for Miss Luna carried herself
like a queen.

"And what of your father?" he asked, holding her a bit tighter
as he led her through a turn.

Her expression shuttered. Gideon could think of no other
way to describe how Miss Luna's face went blank. "My father
comes from more humble roots."

Gideon battled with a frown. Did Miss Luna not wish to
discuss her father because his antecedents didn't match her
mother's glorified ones? She did not strike him as an elitist, but
then what were the reasons for her reticence?

"Where does *humble* fall on the Mexican hierarchy, then?"

A small, sad smile curved her lips. "My father's people *are*
Mexico. Like the maguey or águila or even the great mountain
Popocatépetl. Long before the Spanish burned and pillaged
their villages, and imposed Catholicism upon them, the Purépecha have lived and prospered in Mexico, and yet they are
treated with derision."

Her words washed over him. So much of what Gideon had
learned about Miss Luna's family explained what he saw in her.
Her fierce pride. Her resiliency. Her poise and grace.

A poise and grace that had now been tarnished. He allowed
his gaze to roam about them, his stomach turning when he met
Lady Montrose's disapproving eyes.

"What have they said?"

Gideon blinked and glanced down at her. "Do you truly
want to know?"

She stared up at him for a pregnant moment and then
nodded.

He chewed the inside of his cheek for a pause. "That you're fast."

"Truly?" When he nodded, she smirked. "I've never been called fast before."

"I offer my congratulations." Gideon chuckled when she smacked his back, but sobered quickly. "Some have been a bit more gracious and opined that perhaps you are unaware of our norms."

"I'm sure that's true to an extent, but what norms would they be referring to?"

Her tone was inquisitive, but the set of her jaw was sharp enough to cut granite.

After a quick mental battle over how to express the sentiments shared, Gideon blurted, "I believe they think you too expressive."

"Too expressive?" Miss Luna closed her eyes and sighed. "As in I smile too much?"

"And perhaps laugh too loudly."

She stared at him, her mouth a firm line. Her eyes had lost some of their luster. "I can't say I'm surprised such behavior would earn their ire."

Miss Luna remained silent during several circuits around the floor, her expression devoid of emotion. She kept her gaze trained on a point over his shoulder, so Gideon could not catch a glimpse of her thoughts. Yet her distress bothered him, and Gideon stroked his thumb over the backs of her knuckles.

Finally, he ventured, "Surely Lady Yardley has instructed you on the sort of behavior expected of young ladies during the season?"

Her eyes found his, and Gideon was unprepared for the firestorm brewing in them.

"Instruct us? Do you suppose my sisters and I do not know

proper manners? That because we were not educated in England we could not possibly know how to behave in a social setting?"

"Of course not." Still, Gideon couldn't stop himself from whispering in her ear. "But seeing as how you were drinking liquor in a ballroom with a group of known scoundrels, I do not think it wrong of me to inquire."

"That is unfair," she hissed.

"Perhaps it is, and for that I apologize." He glimpsed the imposing figure of Lady Montrose from the corner of his eye. "Yet surely you realize the unsteady ground you now tread."

"I understand that I made a mistake tonight. I am sorry for it." Miss Luna sucked her cheeks in for a moment. "Nevertheless, I won't apologize for showcasing emotions other than quiet cheerfulness and docility."

"Nor should you have to." Gideon shook his head. "The sticklers are just unused to your expressiveness."

Miss Luna rolled her eyes. "Isn't it silly, though? That young women are to showcase only the most benign of emotions? If they are amused or delighted by something or someone, their smiles cannot be too broad? If they find something humorous, they best not laugh too loudly?" She curled her lip. "Ay, it would be unwise to show too many teeth."

Before Gideon could think of a response, she barreled on.

"That is the sort of condemnation I grew up with. But the criticism came not from those outside my home, but from those within." Her dark eyes dropped to his cravat tie. "I thought that here in London I may be able to breathe. Just a little. That my sisters and I wouldn't have to measure every step we took or word we uttered. How foolish I was to think such a thing."

"I didn't mean to distress—"

"And yes, Lady Yardley did provide instruction on what

to expect and what would send people's tongues wagging," Miss Luna interrupted, her tone firm. "You would also be pleased to know that she informed us of who the libertines and fortune hunters were so we may have a care. But when one engages me in conversation, I cannot give them the cut direct, so what do these busybodies suggest I do? What do *you* suggest I do, Señor Fox?"

This was not going at all as he had expected. Gideon had thought to warn Miss Luna, assuming she had simply been unaware of her missteps. Instead, he had sparked a fire in her she'd obviously battled—and lost—before.

His hand flexed at her waist, his fingers holding her tight. "As I am not a young lady—"

"Indeed you are not." Her gaze raked over his face. "I suspect that no one would think twice if you were to laugh in public."

"I would never laugh in public"—he feigned a haughty look—"for it would blemish my reputation."

Miss Luna's lips twitched.

"I'm sorry you find yourself in this unfair situation." Gideon filled his lungs. "Perhaps it would be best if you kept close to Lady Yardley's side at events such as this. She would provide a stately influence, and the rogues would give you a wide berth."

"So you recommend I . . . cling to the viscountess's apron strings?" she articulated, her head tilted to the side.

"That is not how I would phrase it, but . . . essentially yes."

She huffed a breath. "I thank you for your suggestion, but I will not be doing that."

Gideon pulled his chin back. "Why not?"

"Because, Señor Fox, I have already spent my entire life trying to please an audience of one. His opinions, of me and others, have been *my* opinions, whether they were fair or not. I agreed to marry the man he chose for me with no argument. But he is not here now." Miss Luna pressed her lips together, her mien fierce. "And I do not need a nursemaid."

Agreed to marry the man he chose? A loud ringing filled his ears. "You're engaged?"

Her dark eyes became saucers, but Miss Luna quickly recovered her composure. "I am. My fiancé, Señor Ramírez, stayed behind to work for the rightful president."

Lead filled his gut, for there was no other way to describe how his stomach crashed to his feet. Doing his best to ignore the disappointment coiling around his chest, Gideon managed, "Well, I'm quite certain your future husband might have a different opinion about your need for a nursemaid."

A flush swept over her features, but her jaw was firm. "And my *future* husband is welcome to share his opinion when he's locked his chain about my finger and his surname around my neck."

Gideon blinked down at her, every muscle in his form stiffening at her harsh tone. Whatever had her fiancé done to cause her to react—

"Despite what you or the other men in my life may think, I am not an idiot. I am perfectly capable of spotting a cad, and even engaging in a conversation with him, without somehow falling prey to his charms."

"And what of tonight?" Gideon pushed, despite himself.

Miss Luna straightened her spine. "I learned a lesson tonight."

"And at what cost?" Gideon swept her into a series of turns to the far end of the dance floor, where fewer guests and dancers lingered. Anger simmered on the surface of his skin, pulling it taut, and he wasn't sure if it stemmed from her stubbornness or the fact that she could never be his . . . "You must know that moving about in society is a game. There are rules, and those who do not play by them will lose. You've *lost* tonight."

"Perhaps I have." Her voice was a jagged whisper. "But like any good game of whist, play continues as long as there are tricks to be played, and I'm not ready to retire."

The last strains of the waltz echoed about them, and they slowly came to a stop. Gideon released her, but Miss Luna did not move away from him, and he remained rooted to the spot. Her gaze held his, challenging, resolute . . . but a hint of sadness lurked there as well.

Gideon didn't know what to say. Even if she had run afoul of the matrons this evening or if her reputation managed to remain intact, Ana María Luna was still engaged to be married to another man. Her good name was not his concern.

Gideon allowed his eyes to wander over her features, casting this moment to his memory to hopefully recall with fondness and not the frustration currently twisting his insides.

Taking a step back, he offered her a polite bow. "Thank you for dancing with me, Señorita Luna."

"It was my pleasure, Señor Fox," she murmured, sinking into a curtsy.

When she rose, Miss Luna flashed a bland smile—notably devoid of her white teeth, *damn it*—pivoted, and disappeared into the crowd.

5

Ana María did not remember the carriage ride back to Lady Yardley's home. She did not remember much about the remainder of time she had spent at the Ralston ball. Oh, she knew she had continued to smile and laugh, but everything had rung hollow to her ears. Her smiles had felt artificial, and she wondered if anyone had noticed.

Or cared.

She stood in her chamber now, staring at her reflection in the gilded mirror above her dressing table, while she waited for the maid she shared with her sisters to attend her. Her gown was impeccable, the rich green color bringing out the gold in her skin. Her black curls were still artfully styled, the cream roses tucked among the strands in their first shade of bloom. Her father would be pleased with her appearance.

Abruptly, Ana María wrenched a rose blossom from her hair and threw it down, crushing it under her heeled shoe. With a locked jaw, she ripped the other flowers from her hair before she plucked the hairpins free, allowing them to fall to the floor with satisfying pings. Her hair fell down about her shoulders, draping across her face like a curtain and hiding her reflection.

Nevertheless, Ana María clenched her eyes shut as her chest rose and fell with her rapid pants. Despite being an ocean apart, she had not been able to outrun her father. His judgment followed her still. In the disapproving stares of the dowagers who reigned over the ballroom; in the pinched expressions of young ladies she'd desperately like to befriend. And while their condemnation stung, it was not surprising. Ana María knew some would view her and her sisters as threats. Some would find a reason to dislike them and relish in any opportunity to ostracize them, whether it was because they were foreigners or wealthy or attractive or any other excuse the human mind conjured to justify such behavior.

What she had not expected was to find a note of rebuke lurking in the obsidian eyes of Mr. Fox.

Shuddering a breath, she sank onto her bed, uncaring for her crinoline underskirt and voluminous layers bundled about her. She covered her face with her hands and willed herself not to cry.

Ana María had been anticipating her waltz with Mr. Fox all evening. Since they had talked in the park, she had replayed their interaction, smiling over the memory of his witty words and kind smiles. And if her palms tingled and her heart raced at the idea of being in his arms as they danced around the ballroom, well, she allowed herself the indulgence of that private pleasure.

She had dressed with care that evening, selecting one of her best gowns and styling her hair in a fashion she knew flattered her features. When she and her sisters arrived, her dance card had filled quickly, but she steadfastly reserved her waltz, penciling in Mr. Fox's name when several gentlemen asked for it. And though she had spoken with a variety of people, some more diverting than others, Ana María had nervously awaited

Mr. Fox's arrival. She supposed now that it was those very nerves that had blinded her to the acrid taste of her beverages. She'd simply been relieved that as the minutes ticked by, her anxieties gradually abated until Ana María wasn't in a position to question why.

And then he was there, greeting her in halted Spanish, and her heart felt too big for her chest. That he had taken it upon himself to learn a greeting in her language had made her want to grab his face and plant a kiss on his lips. Of course she did no such thing, although it was a tempting thought, for he was incredibly handsome. His attire was elegant but simple, almost severe in its crisp lines and lack of adornment . . . but then his face was so striking that embellishments were not needed.

Although she'd struggled with her poise at the beginning of their waltz, he'd taken her into his arms, and it felt as if she were floating . . . but the illusion popped as easily as a raindrop in a storm.

So caught up was she in the replay of the night, Ana María did not hear the door open.

"Are you unwell, Ana?"

She jerked her head up, and her wide eyes fell on Gabby framed in her doorway, their maid, Consuelo, standing nervously behind her.

Hastily smoothing her hair back and twisting it over her shoulder, Ana María turned her lips up into a semblance of a smile. Or so she hoped. "I'm simply tired, thank you."

Gabby nodded, but her brow remained furrowed as she considered her. It remained as such while Consuelo helped Ana María undress and plaited her hair for sleep. Ana María stayed seated at her vanity table after she wished Consuelo a good night, her eyes following the young maid in the mirror as she departed, before she dropped them to her knotted hands.

A tense silence filled the room, and just when Ana María was going to ask Gabby why she was still here, her sister spoke.

"What happened?"

Their eyes met in the mirror. "I don't know what you mean," Ana María hedged.

Gabby's snort was sharp. "Of course you do. You were smiling all evening . . . until you weren't."

"Like I said, I just grew tired." She severed their eye contact, fidgeting with the hairbrush. "We've not had much time to rest since we've arrived."

"Well, there's one truth in your lies. Tío Arturo and Lady Yardley have had us doing tricks as if we're Dove."

Just as Ana María opened her mouth to respond, her door swung open again. This time Isabel stood on the threshold, and she said not a word as she slid the door closed and crossed the room to perch on the edge of Ana María's bed next to Gabby.

"Has she told you what happened?"

Ana María huffed in annoyance while Gabby shook her head. "She claimed she was merely tired."

Isabel rolled her eyes. "Not likely."

"Whatever is that supposed to mean?" Ana María demanded, spinning about on the bench to face them directly.

"It means that we know how you behave when you're tired. Not only have we known you our entire lives, but we were just sequestered on a ship with you for two months." Isabel flourished a palm. "This is more than exhaustion."

Damn them for their perceptiveness. She worried her cuticle so she could look away and collect her thoughts.

"Ana, I know we've never been particularly close—" Isabel began.

"Father made sure of that," Gabby added.

"But we're in this together." Isabel's throat bobbed for a moment, and then it was her turn to look away. "Only you two know what we left behind and why. Only you two know the secret we carry and the treasure we guard."

Ana María pressed her lips into a thin line to keep her chin from trembling.

Isabel looked up then, her black eyes shining with unshed tears. "If we can't trust each other, who can we trust?"

Who indeed? Ana María had learned a painful lesson just that night about the merits of trusting new friends.

Sighing, she clasped her hands together to keep from worrying her cuticles further. "Apparently I've been the source of gossip."

Her sisters frowned in unison, but it was Gabby who spoke. "You're not unused to gossip. What is it about this time that has you so upset?"

"The person who told me about it."

She held her breath before she said more.

"Was it . . . Señor Fox?" Isabel asked tentatively.

Ana María nodded.

"Señor Fox?" Gabby looked back and forth between them. "The gentleman who rescued Dove in the park?"

"He secured her waltz." Returning her gaze to Ana María, Isabel asked, "Did it . . . not go well? He could barely keep his eyes off you when we encountered him in the park."

Heat rushed over her face. "Yes, well, I'm certain he feels differently now."

"Why do you say that?" Isabel pressed.

Ana María shook her head, unwilling to share her shameful secret.

"Tell us, Ana," Gabby said, her tone just short of a command. "I'm certain it will make you feel better."

"I'm sure it won't," she muttered.

She looked up to see her sisters exchanging a perplexed look.

Pressing her fingers to her temple, Ana María released a small moan. "Do you remember the people I was conversing with?"

Isabel shook her head, while Gabby's lip curled. "Their smiles didn't reach their eyes."

Regret dropped like an anvil in her stomach. "I wish I had noticed that."

"Why?"

Looking first at one sister and then the other, Ana María hid her face behind her hand. "Because then I would have known better than to drink the punch Lord Simon offered me."

"Why, Ana?" Gabby's voice was sharp and commanding. "Tell us."

So with a pout, Ana María did. She told them how the first glass of punch Lord Simon offered had tasted terrible but she drank it to not be rude, and then the subsequent glasses had lost their bitter edge. How as the evening wore on, she felt simultaneously lightheaded and carefree, until—

"You've never had alcohol?" Gabby's expression turned impish. "Not even a gulp of tequila to celebrate el Día de la Independencia?"

"Of course not," she sputtered. "Have you?"

Isabel snorted while Gabby threw her hands wide. "Sí. Many times."

Ana María's gaze darted between her sisters, who stared back with exasperation.

"Siempre tan perfecta," Isabel murmured, but there was no ire in her words.

"Not anymore it seems. And the worst part is that the only reason I even knew what had happened was that Señor Fox told me." She moaned, dropping her head to her chest.

"He strikes me as an honorable man, Ana. Surely he told you out of concern rather than mockery," Isabel said gently.

Mr. Fox's charcoal eyes had intently inspected her when he'd first arrived for their waltz, and she'd been touched by his regard. Now she knew it stemmed from something darker . . .

"I believe he was, it's just . . ." Ana María nibbled on her lip. "When he warned me that my behavior had generated talk, I was disappointed."

"Why were you disappointed?"

"Because I felt judged." She pursed her mouth. "It reminded me of how Father would scold me for the smallest infraction."

"Oh," Isabel whispered, while Gabby scowled.

"But Father is *not* here." Gabby slapped her hands on her thighs. "We have been tasked by Tío Arturo to socialize and befriend members of society. And while what happened tonight was regrettable, it does not mean you need to take up Father's switch simply because he's not here to wield it himself."

Gabby's declaration landed like a blow, and Ana María gasped. Was that what she was doing? Punishing herself for infractions she knew would have displeased their father?

"Was that the only thing Señor Fox warned you about?" Isabel asked.

She huffed. "Sadly, no. Apparently the British do not like it if you smile too brightly or laugh too loudly."

"Truly?" Isabel wrinkled her nose.

Ana María splayed her hands. "According to what he overheard."

"How ridiculous," Gabby growled. "Smiling and laughing are somehow sins? Or are they only when a woman does them?"

"Considering how Lord Simon and his friends were just as, if not more, inebriated than I was but no one was condemning them, I'd say society's judgment is not as readily concerned with men's behavior," Ana María grumbled.

"I swear that people thrive on being critical of women." Gabby crossed her arms over her chest, her expression mulish. "If it was not Father's reproach, it's now these nonsensical edicts."

"Perhaps Señor Fox thought to warn me because I imagine he knows a bit about being an outsider," Ana María offered.

The sisters exchanged a knowing look.

"Which was kind of him," Isabel said.

And she had lashed out at his kindness. Remorse festered in her chest. Surely her waltz with Mr. Fox was the last time she would ever spend in his arms.

"I had thought things would be different here. That *I* would be different here." Her shoulders sank. "And yet I'm still the same Ana, always wanting to please others."

"Don't be so hard on yourself." Gabby patted the back of her hand. "And you are different . . . you were borracha at the ball, and I am immensely proud of you."

A bark of laughter burst from Ana María's lips before she knew what she was doing. Gabby grinned openly, while Isabel's trembling lips were smashed into a firm line. Something about the manner in which her sister was trying so hard not to smile quadrupled her own amusement, and Ana María leaned forward and pressed her face to her thighs as amusement shook her frame.

She could feel the tension leave her shoulders, her jaw . . . her mind as she chuckled along with her sisters. When was the last time she had shared in a bit of humor with Isabel and Gabby? The fact that she could not remember made her infinitely sad.

Whatever had happened before was no more. They were here now, together, and once again Ana María was reminded that no one could stop them from being friends.

Sitting up, she wiped tears from the corners of her eyes, pleased to see that Isabel and Gabby both had flushed cheeks, their breaths rapid as they, too, gathered their bearings.

"I know you esteem Señor Fox, Ana," Isabel began, her tone abruptly sober, "but perhaps it's a good thing that matters unfolded the way they did with him. It's not as if you could have a future with him. Señor Ramírez is waiting for you back in Mexico after all."

If Isabel had doused her in the face with a bucket of cold water, she could not have dampened her spirits faster. *Fernando.* Her fiancé had been far from her thoughts—a remnant, almost, of a past life—until her conversation with Mr. Fox. And now Isabel's inconvenient reminder rudely reiterated how even an ocean could not separate her from his specter.

"I told Señor Fox about Fernando, so as you can see, it worked out as it was supposed to," she confessed around her dry throat. "I have a fiancé waiting for me. And even if I didn't," she continued, her tone growing firm, fierce, "why would I ever want to be with a man who would so easily concern himself with the opinions of others?"

Pleased with her rationale, Ana María nodded her head and pointedly ignored the dubious look Isabel and Gabby exchanged.

She barely knew Mr. Fox. Had shared only two conversations and one waltz with him. No matter that she found him intriguing and enigmatic and painfully handsome, Ana María refused to tilt at windmills for men who were of the same mold as her father.

And she would keep laughing, because, Dios mío, she had earned that right, and she would not allow anyone to tell her to stop.

6

Covent Garden still managed to enchant him . . . when he was not distracted from the performance by chattering attendees.

Gideon tapped his foot in a rapid beat as Lady Wenthrop described her daughter's extensive fasting routine in great detail. Lady Grace, the topic of conversation, sat on the other side of her mother, her expression frozen in what Gideon could only imagine was horror.

"And then she drinks tea six times a day, with a dinner of milk and eggs." The countess dipped her head as if to share a great secret, and Gideon darted his gaze to Lady Grace, whose complexion had turned a sickly shade of green. "I have hopes that with this new diet, she will finally secure a husband this season."

Well, now all of Lady Wenthrop's machinations made sense. Apparently there was no worse fate for a young debutante than to have multiple seasons with no marriage offer. As if a gentlewoman's only purpose in life were to marry and bring forth the next generation of lords and ladies. And the countess was determined to see her daughter settled, even if she had to ply her with disgusting concoctions in some misguided belief that Lady

Grace would finally land her lord if she, what? Lost weight? As if anyone could tell much of her figure when it was encased in a crinoline cage.

Sneaking a quick glance at Lady Grace's stoic face, Gideon felt for the girl.

"I had no idea such"—he cleared his throat—"*regimens* would be considered useful."

Lady Grace's facade cracked for just a moment as her expression clearly said, *That's because you're a man*, before she turned her head to look at the stage.

Well. Gideon didn't know what to think about that, and all at once Miss Luna came to mind. He suspected she would have a great deal to say about Lady Wenthrop's recitation. Mentally shaking away thoughts of the young woman, Gideon directed his attention back to the countess.

". . . Mrs. Sanders, my dear sister, told me that Empress Elisabeth is known to go on fasting diets or liquid diets, and sometimes only eats eggs and milk. And everyone knows the empress has the tiniest waist in Europe."

This was news to Gideon. Still, he nodded knowingly.

The countess patted her daughter's arm. "So if it's good for the empress of Austria, surely it's good for my Grace."

"Surely," Gideon murmured. "She appears to be the embodiment of good health."

Lady Grace did not turn her head in his direction, and he fancied she had mentally escaped to a faraway place where her mother did not tell young men that she was being coerced into consuming disgusting diets in the hopes of snaring a husband.

What an odd, vexing situation.

Rather than voice such a thought, Gideon nodded politely as the countess continued to prattle on about various topics, most revolving around her poor daughter, and Gideon did his best to appear interested. He was sure he'd not succeeded when he spied Lady Grace glancing in his direction with an amused tilt to her lips.

Eventually, a visiting guest snared Lady Wenthrop in conversation, and Gideon stifled his sigh of relief. When Lord Montrose had invited him to enjoy a performance of *Satanella* in his private box, he had readily agreed. In the fortnight since he'd learned of the marquess's interest in putting an end to the slave trade to South America, Gideon had not had a chance to speak with Montrose again in person. They had exchanged messages through their respective secretaries, but the last two meetings they had agreed upon had both been canceled by the marquess at the last moment because of sudden conflicts.

Frustration, and an impending sense that sand was slipping through some invisible hourglass, had kept Gideon on a knife-edge. With each new West Africa Squadron report that made its way across his desk, his feeling of helplessness grew. And Gideon despised feeling helpless. He'd worked too damn hard to reach a point where the possibility of cutting off such a horrific practice, a practice that had once ensnared his grandmother, was within his grasp. And like bait on a line, it was continuously jerked from his grip.

That was until the invitation to join Lord and Lady Montrose at the opera had arrived. Gideon had once again donned his dress attire, paid a hackney to deliver him to Covent Garden, and had entered the Montroses' private box intent on discussing their shared initiative with the marquess . . . only to find himself seated next to the loquacious Lady Wenthrop instead.

Gideon glanced over his shoulder, his gaze falling on Lord Montrose conversing with guests who'd visited the box at the start of intermission. A dull pain throbbed in his jaw, and it took him a moment to realize he was clenching it so tight his teeth ground together. Which would not do.

Turning forward, he flipped his opera glasses to scan the audience. The auditorium was filled to the rafters, the burnt scent from the gas lamps melding with the haze of perfumes and the acrid tang of sweat from the mass of human bodies packed together to watch the production. Gideon had never been a fan of crowds, but something about Covent Garden always filled him with awe. Perhaps it was the soaring ceilings that amplified the music notes; the rows of opulent boxes lining the perimeter of the auditorium; or the orchestra, whose members seemed just as invested in the performance as the actors and singers onstage. He'd not attended his first opera until he was already a member of Parliament, and instead of conversing and negotiating with his peers as he had expected, he'd been completely charmed by the entire experience.

Which was the only consolation he would accept if he were not able to converse with Lord Montrose.

The conductor tapped his stand, and the air was suddenly peppered with an assortment of musical notes as orchestra members began to tune their instruments, signaling the end of intermission. Hopefully his chance to chat with the marquess would arrive with the next intermission.

The second act began in a breathless swell, and Gideon was soon lost in the show, his gaze fixed on the action on the stage. Loud whispers from Lady Wenthrop on his left disrupted his attention, and he bit his tongue until the taste of iron filled his mouth. While he waited for his temper to settle, Gideon surveyed the crowd. The gas lamp glow made it convenient to people watch, which was a large reason why performances at Covent Garden were so popular. Everyone wanted to be seen, and guests dressed in their finest attire to make the best impression.

His gaze skipped over familiar faces he knew from commit-tees or from the boxing ring, where he exercised several days a week. Whitfield didn't appear to be in attendance . . . unless the duke had already disappeared into a dark corridor with his paramour of choice. A smile stretched his lips when he spied the familiar blond head of his friend Captain Sirius Dawson. He wasn't aware the captain was even in town, and Gideon made a mental note to look for Dawson next time he visited their club.

His wandering gaze came to an abrupt halt, as if the spin-ning arrow on a compass had found true north. Miss Luna was seated between her two sisters in a box across the auditorium, all six of their eyes staring transfixed at the stage. It appeared that Lady Yardley was seated behind them, but Gideon refused to call attention to himself by raising his glasses to confirm. For he did not need them to see that the box was filled with young men, all of whom seemed a bit bored, if the number of chins propped in hands or nodding heads were any indication.

Gideon's eyes returned to Miss Luna once again. He had not spoken with her since the night they danced at the Ralston ball, but he had replayed their conversation multiple times. The truth she revealed about her father and the control he exerted over her life. How she continued to feel judged and condemned for the most innocuous of behaviors even with her father an ocean away. Gideon could understand her frustration; however, it had been obvious—to him, at least—that someone needed to stress the precarious situation she had inadvertently placed her-self in.

He regretted that it had been him.

Gideon regretted even more that a man waited for her back in Mexico.

And while Miss Luna hadn't behaved inappropriately as far

as he knew, Gideon had watched as she laughed and smiled through several events since their ill-fated waltz, his chest feeling just a bit tight anytime he did. Although she always seemed to be surrounded by a crowd of admirers, Gideon felt her gaze on him, and he wondered if she replayed their last conversation as much as he did. Did she, too, feel that sting of wistfulness anytime their eyes met?

Her name had appeared in the gossip pages a handful of times, with speculation that this rake or that libertine was paying her court, but Gideon did not put much stock in those rumors. Miss Luna was engaged to be married, and regardless of her friendliness, Gideon knew she was too honorable to engage a man's affections when there could be no future between them.

Despite that, it felt as if a million knife cuts lanced his skin whenever Gideon spied her in conversation with someone else. Whenever his mind wondered about the man she was to marry . . .

The Luna sisters had garnered a good deal of admiration, as well as jealousy and envy, during their short time in England, and Gideon reminded himself—continuously—that he should be relieved not to have such fervent, insidious attention shone his way.

But he still liked to admire Miss Luna when he had the chance. Like in this moment, when she remained perfectly still, as if one errant move would disrupt the intricate and lovely world that had been created onstage. Even across the auditorium Gideon took note of her eager eyes. The soft pink color that stained the crests of her cheeks. How her red lips gaped when something amazed her. When a young man—was that Lord Nicholas?—leaned forward from his seat behind her to whisper in her ear, Miss Luna didn't even flinch at his nearness. Didn't appear to acknowledge his words or presence in any way. Her whole being was completely immersed in the wedding between the disguised demon handmaiden Satanella and Count Rupert, and Gideon was glad for it.

So when she looked up suddenly and her eyes found his, Gideon bit back a gasp. They stared at each other for the span of two of his staggered heartbeats before she dipped her head, all politeness, and returned her gaze to the stage.

Gideon felt as if he had been hit upside his head. There was nothing earth-shattering about exchanging a glance with a beautiful woman, yet his thoughts were in a scramble. Her dark eyes had been guarded, but perhaps a bit curious, and that smidge of interest he saw in her gaze glowed in his belly for reasons he absolutely refused to identify.

For truly, what was the point? Nothing had changed between them, and Gideon did not want them to.

No, things were better left as they were. In time, his interest in her would fade to polite regard, and seeing her in public would no longer be a reason to brighten his day.

Gideon prayed as much, at least.

"He's looked over here no fewer than five times," Gabby whispered to her in Spanish, the glee in her voice evident even though Ana María did not turn to see her expression.

"I don't know whom you speak of," she said, locking her eyes on the stage. The female singer was truly extraordinary.

"Of course you do." Gabby bumped their shoulders together. "I suspect you noticed him as soon as he entered the box across the way."

"Across the way, you say?" Ana María allowed herself a reprieve to look to the other side the theater, knowing perfectly well who sat there. Despite the noise around them, and the gentlemen vying for her attention, she'd instinctively known Mr. Fox had arrived.

And just like a magnet, her gaze was continually dragged back to him throughout the show, and she prayed desperately to la Virgen that her perceptive sisters didn't notice.

"You're a terrible actress," Gabby grumbled. "I must say, I'm surprised Señor Fox is here."

Ana María found she was as well, but chose not to voice it. "Why are you surprised?"

Gabby raised a shoulder. "He's just so serious. At the Richardsons' soiree, I don't think I saw him smile once." Her brows drew together. "Although he was with the Duke of Whitfield, so that might be the reason."

"Perhaps you didn't give him a reason to smile at you."

"That's nonsense. I give everyone a reason to smile . . . even when I wish that they would go to el infierno."

"Traviesa," Ana María huffed before returning her gaze to the stage.

Dipping her head closer, Gabby whispered, "You truly don't find Señor Fox dour? When Isa danced with him at the Hamilton ball, she said he barely smiled."

"But she also said he was friendly and asked interesting questions."

"Sí, well, I guess I don't see his appeal," Gabby said, pinching her arm.

Ana María stealthily leaned away from her youngest sister. "How can you not? He's witty. Observant. Incredibly intelligent." She slid her eyes to where Fox sat quietly watching the performance, his somber dress attire cloaking him in darkness. "He's very compelling."

Her sister's sudden silence caused her to turn to her, and

Gabby stared back with an arched brow. "*And* handsome. I *can* admit that Señor Fox is very attractive."

"Sí . . . that—that, too." Ana María fidgeted with her fan, hoping Gabby didn't take note of how her ears burned. "He was probably looking over here to see who our guests are and whether it would be beneficial for him to speak with them or not."

"I rather doubt he'd have an interest in estos tontos. They're all empty-headed and not at all the sort of men a serious politician like him would spend time conversing with."

"But at least they're nice to look at," Ana María volleyed back, stifling a laugh when her youngest sister snorted.

Isabel leaned forward in her seat and speared them with a reproachful look. "Cállense, por favor," she hissed. After a tense pause, she leaned close. "Or at least tell me what's amused you so I can laugh, too."

Pressing her trembling lips together for a moment, Ana María finally whispered, "Gabby is unimpressed with our guests."

"I didn't realize we were allowed to have an opinion on the company." Isabel made a soft noise in the back of her throat.

"They're not all bad," Ana María murmured.

Isabel curled her lip. "If you say so."

Ana María held her silence and was relieved when her sisters said nothing more. In the lull, she couldn't stop herself from sliding her gaze to the box across the way. As she covertly studied Mr. Fox, an usher increased the brightness of the gas lamps in their box, for the second intermission had begun.

"May I fetch you a glass of punch, Miss Luna?"

Blinking up at Mr. Avery, Ana María hesitated. But his expression was open, containing only earnest interest. "How kind of you to offer, sir," she murmured, rising to her feet.

While she waited for the gentleman to return, she risked a

glance across the way. Mr. Fox appeared to be in deep conversation with Lord Montrose, both of their expressions serious and intense. It seemed he no longer had a reason to glance at her.

A bittersweet twinge pinched under her ribs. It seemed cruelly appropriate that the first man who'd sparked her interest, the first man she would have chosen for herself rather than being presented to him as some sort of enticement for the sake of her father's career, had found fault with her. Fernando's indifference never stung; Mr. Fox's was razor-sharp.

Thankfully, she did not have time to consider this sad fact because Mr. Avery returned with her beverage, along with his eager stories about his work in Parliament. Ana María was left with little room or reason to speak aside from polite exclamations at the appropriate moments in his narrative.

". . . and then at the cricket match, Fredrickson mentioned that a deal could be made if I was willing—"

"Cricket?" Ana María stood straighter. Cricket sounded like a sport she would enjoy watching. "I've never had an opportunity to attend a cricket match. It was played in Mexico, but not widely."

A scowl marred Mr. Avery's expression. "But surely a cricket match would be too unruly for a lady of your gentle breeding."

Ana María just barely kept from rolling her eyes. "I assure you that my temperament is much more stalwart than that."

"Still," Avery began, his censorious look melding to one of placation, "it's merely a group of men reveling in their baser instincts. A lady such as yourself would not find any enjoyment in such an aggressive sport."

"Aggressive? I confess I've never heard cricket described as aggressive." She took a moment to take a sip of punch, containing her wince at the oversweet taste. "I'm interested in all manner of topics, contentious and otherwise. I assure you that a woman can be both gently bred and also of an inquisitive, hardy temperament."

The man's mouth slid open to deliver what Ana María assumed would be a biased rebuttal, but it was cut off by a dry laugh.

"Come now, Avery. Surely you've learned never to underestimate the prowess of a determined woman."

Ana María stiffened as a buzzing sounded in her ears. She *knew* that gravelly voice. In an effort to allow herself time to compose her nerves, she raised her glass to her lips . . . and sputtered as a rush of the sticky-sweet liquid rushed down her throat. Wet coughs rattled past her lips, and her eyes watered as she gasped for breath.

As she struggled to collect herself, a handkerchief was thrust into her free hand. It was a simple cotton square in a deep navy blue, but it was soft against her skin, and as she placed it to her mouth, Ana María noted its citrus and mint scent. A blend that had imprinted on her memory since she'd enjoyed her solo dance with him.

"Are you quite well, Señorita Luna? I did not mean to surprise you."

"Yes, that was not well done of you, Fox," Avery scolded.

"No, apparently not," Mr. Fox murmured, his eyes not leaving her face. "I do apologize."

She patted her mouth with his handkerchief. "You have nothing to apologize for, I assure you."

Mr. Fox arched one black brow, and she could have sworn a smile teased along his lips, but then she knew the man rarely smiled.

"I couldn't help but overhear your conversation as I walked up." He said the words to Avery, but his gaze was heavy on her.

"And I can't think of anything that might occur during a cricket match that would offend your delicate sensibilities, Señorita Luna."

Avery blustered, throwing his arms out. "Surely watching sweaty, crass men engage in their baser tendencies for sport is unworthy of her attention."

Ana María darted her gaze to Mr. Fox, who stared back at her, his expression almost taunting, as if to say, *Yes, surely such behavior is beneath you.*

Amusement collided with circumspection in her chest, and it took her a moment to suppress the laughter fizzling in her throat. "You give me more credit than I deserve, Señor Avery."

"What do you mean?" the other man said, his eyes large with offense.

"What I mean," she began, mirth curling her lips, "is that Mexicans, like their Spanish ancestors, have a fascination with crass sports. Bullfighting, for example."

"Bullfighting?" Mr. Avery whispered.

Ana María nodded. "Of course. If we are to speak of aggressive, barbaric sports, one cannot exclude bullfighting."

Mr. Avery's befuddled expression had her battling with laughter once again.

Instead, she swallowed her mirth and said, "Great matches take place in Mexico City and other places throughout the country. I attended my first match when I was barely ten years old. I cried so loudly my father ordered our nursemaid to take me home."

While Avery opened and closed his mouth, Fox met her gaze head-on. "I can't claim to have attended a bullfight, but I've heard they can be . . . brutal."

"Brutal indeed." She raised her glass to her lips for a sweet, fortifying sip. "And infinitely sad."

"Why sad?" Avery asked, suddenly regaining use of his tongue.

Before Ana María could answer, Mr. Fox interjected. "Because when is a story about man against beast ever not sad?"

She took an eager step toward him. "Which is why I always cheer for the beast . . . or the woman or the creature that finds itself on the opposing side of such an encounter."

Fox cocked his head, his warm gaze holding hers. Ana María longed to ask him what he was thinking, so curious about the thoughts he kept carefully hidden behind his unflappable veneer.

But such things would be futile. Blinking, severing the connection, she refocused her attention on Mr. Avery.

The man shifted back and forth on his feet, his brows pulled low. "Lud, Miss Luna, you sound like one of those suffragists who like to stir up trouble."

She pressed a hand to her chest. "Do I really? How interesting."

"They're not interesting." Avery yanked on his dinner jacket, a scowl darkening his countenance. "They are termagants."

Doing her best to ignore Mr. Fox and what his reaction was to Avery's assertion, Ana María crinkled her brow. "I would not know, but quite frankly, your assessment has made me curious."

Avery looked down his nose at her. "You know what Shakespeare said about curiosity, don't you, Miss Luna?"

Ana María opened her mouth to say she was familiar with the quote from *Much Ado About Nothing* that he referred to, but Fox's rich tenor interrupted.

"Shakespeare also said that curiosity is a sign of intelligence and a lively mind, did he not? 'I will keep where there is wit stirring, and leave the faction of fools.'"

Her palms grew clammy as her mouth went dry, and Ana

María could only stare at him. Never would she have thought a man quoting an obscure line from *Troilus and Cressida* would be so attractive. But Fox snagged her gaze then, and she would not have been able to look away if she tried.

That confusing warmth . . . the one she experienced anytime she was in Mr. Fox's presence, rushed through her blood once again. And she was abruptly annoyed, for how could he say such flattering things to her in one moment and then scold her in the next?

Her annoyance, her frustration at her own foolishness, at the embarrassment she felt knowing Mr. Fox had been witness to it, sparked her temper. The temper she had long ago corralled behind a thick wall of decorum.

"So you are not only an ambitious politician, but also a literature scholar." Ana María held herself so stiffly she practically vibrated. "Tell me, Señor Fox, is there anything you can't do?"

"Oh, my shortcomings are numerous." He took an infinitesimal step closer, and she doubted she would have noticed if she weren't so spellbound by his every move. "I fancy my intentions are always honorable, but then intentions are of no concern when harm is done."

Was he apologizing . . . or was that what she wanted to believe? The men in her life had never respected or valued her enough to apologize for their transgressions, so Ana María rather doubted she could trust her own perception.

"You're an upstanding fellow, Fox. Or so I've always believed." Avery's forehead crinkled. "I doubt Miss Luna would find much to shame you for, if she were to look."

A curtain dropped down over Fox's eyes, and the color in his cheeks deepened. "You are kind to say so, Avery, but I assure you that Miss Luna would not have to look hard to find a reason to criticize me."

It was an olive branch. And even if it wasn't, Ana María respected Mr. Fox enough to extend him a bit of grace in return. "My mother would say there is never an excuse to shame a gentleman."

"Even when the man is deserving of contempt?"

His gaze darted up to meet hers. Whether he was talking about himself or generally, Ana María did not know . . . but then perhaps that was the point.

Swallowing, she nodded. "My mother believed it was not a woman's place."

A frown clouded his expression. "Then who is to hold him accountable?"

Lifting her shoulder, she smirked. "God."

Mr. Fox tilted his head. "And have you taken that lesson to heart?"

"It remains to be seen."

His eyes widened and then humor shined in his gaze. In fact, his lips stretched around his teeth in what could only be described as a grin. Ana María felt her own mouth tremble in response.

She had made him smile. She had made this bastion of male pride and power smile, and while Ana María knew better than to assign any sort of assumptions to his uncharacteristic grin, it brightened his whole face, morphing his dark beauty into something approachable. Something precious.

And as soon as the thought came to her mind, she banished it, for that way lay trouble.

Mr. Fox moved closer, his dark, dark eyes holding hers, but before either of them could say anything else, a new person intruded into their conversation.

"Señor Fox, Señor Avery, how good of you to visit."

Jerking her head about, her gaze landed on her tío Arturo.

Mr. Fox recovered from his surprise before she did. "Señor Valdés, when I learned you were in attendance, I had to come pay my respects." He extended a white-gloved hand in greeting. "It has been too long since we've spoken."

"It has indeed, sir." Tío Arturo swirled the dark liquid in his tumbler as he considered him, as if taking his measure. "I hope Señorita Luna has told you of our people's fight under France's egregious occupation."

She had not seen her uncle since the day after the Ralston ball. He had visited to inquire after her health, and then politely but firmly reminded her how much he was depending upon her and her sisters to serve as respectable symbols of the Mexican people. Tío Arturo had not been cruel or even scolding, but Ana María had been so embarrassed, she claimed a megrim afterward and retired to her chamber for the rest of the day.

Thankfully, Mr. Fox spoke before she did.

"She's touched on it." Fox met her eyes for a passing moment before turning to her uncle once again. "Any situation that would drive three gently bred young women from their home is cause for concern."

"Bueno." Tío Arturo gestured with his arm to the other side of the box. "Let's get both you and Avery a beverage, and I'll tell you more about what the rightful government of Mexico has been dealing with and why we need Parliament to publicly denounce the unlawful occupation of the country."

Clapping a hand on Mr. Fox's shoulder, Tío Arturo led the gentlemen to the opposite end of the opera box, where an attendant was serving refreshments. Cocktails that were available for others, but for which Lady Yardley warned were strictly off-limits to her and her sisters. They were allowed to partake in private, but the viscountess did not wish to invite trouble if they were seen imbibing in public. The older woman's explanation had made Ana María cringe.

Mr. Fox glanced back over his shoulder as he walked away, his dark eyes unreadable.

But what Ana María could read was the pounding of her heart, which beat out a warning that the more she spoke with the indomitable Mr. Fox, the more trouble she would bring down upon herself.

And where there was trouble, there was bound to be heart-ache.

7

"Sir Baldwin has sent a letter regarding your thoughts on Bill 155."

Gideon pulled his gaze from the sunlit-dappled path ahead of him to pin it on his secretary, Mr. Stansberry, who walked in step beside him. "Oh, I can imagine my thoughts on the Casual Poor Bill irritated him to no end."

Stansberry avoided Gideon's gaze. "It would seem so."

Jerking to a halt, Gideon turned, cocking a brow at the man. "What did he say?"

"He . . . he . . ." The secretary worked his throat. "He said—"

Gideon held up a hand. "I know Sir Baldwin is an arse. Thus, I will not be surprised by any word you utter. Now tell me."

"Right." Stansberry jerked his head about and raised his shoulders as if he were preparing to enter a pugilist ring. "Sir Baldwin's letter stated that though you managed to raise yourself up out of poverty, not everyone is as ambitious. He, and I quote, 'refuses to watch as vagrants and undesirables suck at the teat of the city of London and contribute nothing of value in return.'"

Biting off the last syllable, the secretary dropped his head to study his shoes. Shoes that were always shined to perfection. Gideon covertly glanced down, not at all surprised to see his distorted reflection staring back at him.

Even in the shiny leather of Stansberry's shoes, he looked displeased.

Because he *fucking* was.

"Send it to the paper."

Stansberry jerked his head up. "Sir?"

Spinning about, Gideon prowled down the path. "Send the letter to Miss Assan. She'll know what to do with it."

After a moment's pause, Stansberry hustled after him. "You want me to send it to Miss Assan? But she'll plaster it all over the front of the *Times*."

"Precisely. That's what I want."

Miss Effia Assan was the finest investigative journalist in the realm, for all that her detractors liked to comment that she was a woman. But upon their first meeting, Gideon had recognized a kindred spirit; a Black woman making her way in a world determined to squelch her ambitions and remind her of her place every chance it got. He had no doubt that Miss Assan would give MP Chambers, and his deplorable letter, the treatment it deserved.

"If you insist, sir," his secretary murmured, taking a small notepad and pencil out of his coat pocket and scribbling a note.

"Was there anything of import I should know before this meeting with Lord Montrose?" he asked, tipping his hat at a trio of ladies as they passed.

Stansberry pressed his lips together, which immediately set Gideon's teeth on edge. "Just this, sir."

And without another word, the man shoved a folded bit of newspaper into his hands.

Unfolding the paper, Gideon glanced down and read . . . a frown slowly contorting his face.

The showing of Satanella *on Thursday evening proved to be a crush, with a sellout crowd featuring society elite rubbing elbows while the riffraff enjoyed the opera from the gallery below. A quick perusal of the grand boxes lining the auditorium hinted at the illustrious lords, ladies, and dignitaries who were in attendance. But it was the comings and goings of the Mexican ambassador's private box that enraptured the crowd, for the enigmatic Luna sisters were his guests. Since their arrival in London more than a fortnight ago, the young ladies' actions have been cause for talk and speculation. So of course when the elder Miss Luna was spied in conversation with Parliament's most ambitious and most dour politician, Mr. Gideon Fox, word spread like vellum soaked in alcohol. But it combusted when the gentleman in question smiled . . . showcasing all his teeth! This author didn't think Mr. Fox capable of such a human emotion, but is happy to have been proven wrong. The allure and charm of the Luna sisters, most especially Miss Ana María Luna, must be legendary indeed.*

He swallowed his tongue. All movement seemed impossible, as if his body had been encased in ice.

Gideon must have made some sort of sound, for Stansberry stumbled to a stop and turned to him, his blue eyes wide. "Are you quite well, sir?"

"Yes," he choked out, his voice unnaturally loud in his ears. "I'm fine."

Stansberry studied him for a long moment before he nodded. "Is there anything you'd like for me to do about the article?"

"Nothing at all." Gideon smoothed down his lapels, relieved his hands weren't shaking. "It's just a gossip column after all."

But it was gossip about *him*. About him and Miss Luna. And they had mentioned him smiling. With teeth. The very sin Miss Luna had been accused of. Chagrin made his toes curl in his boots.

"It is indeed a gossip column, but . . ." Stansberry pressed his lips together so tightly they showed white. When Gideon arched his brow, the man deflated like an aeronautical balloon with a leak. "I think it's good you've found yourself in the gossip pages."

"And why is that?"

Stansberry raised a shoulder. "It shows you're human."

Gideon jerked his chin back. "I beg your pardon. Do I not comport myself as a human? Were you in doubt of my humanity?"

"Of course not, sir," the secretary mumbled, dropping his head.

"Did you perhaps think me a newly discovered breed of bird? Or perhaps like my surname, you believed me a rare breed of fox," Gideon pushed, his tone crisp.

Although his secretary did not raise his head, the corner of his mouth tipped up. "It never occurred to me, but perhaps you're right."

"I am always right." When Stansberry nodded mutely, Gideon chuckled. He smacked the man on the arm with the rolled-up newspaper. "Now explain what you meant by this *human* comment of yours."

Rocking back on his feet, Stansberry opened his mouth but

quickly snapped it shut when two ladies strolled past, a foot-man walking behind them with three small dogs tethered on leashes. Gideon and his secretary dipped their heads in greet-ing, and when the women had disappeared around the bend in the path, Gideon cocked his head at the man.

"Right." Stansberry fidgeted with his cuff link to avoid his gaze. "Your whole life is your career in Commons. I plan your schedule, so I know the events that occupy your time. I know that even if you attend the opera"—he gestured to the news-paper in Gideon's hand with his chin—"or a ball or Venetian breakfast, your presence is for political reasons."

"That's not a bad thing," Gideon could not help but assert.

"No, not at all," Stansberry quickly agreed. He licked his lips. "It's just . . . well, I've heard it said that these Mexican heir-esses are lovely, and I think it quite nice that you have been conversing with a pretty lady simply for the enjoyment of her conversation."

Gideon scoffed. "And how do you know I enjoyed my con-versation with her?"

"Because you smiled." Stansberry smiled himself. "I've never seen you smile, and I've worked for you for almost two years."

"Surely I've smiled once during that time." Gideon swiped his hand through the air. "I'm not as dour as that."

"Not dour at all, sir. Just focused. Driven."

Yes, Gideon liked to believe he was those things, and he cer-tainly had to be to accomplish everything he wanted in Com-mons. Heaven knew that he had to work twice as hard for an ounce of the success he'd earned, because for some of his col-leagues, he would always be an overreaching Black man from the East End.

And Gideon feared any success he had found could be

snatched away if he were to misstep. So while he enjoyed his evening chatting with Miss Luna—and she deserved all his smiles—Gideon could not afford to give her any more.

Pivoting about, Gideon continued his walk down the path, determined to outpace the uncomfortable feeling that crept along his spine. The sun was out, the temperature was mild, he didn't have a meeting until later in the afternoon, and for the first time in a week, he had several free hours to simply enjoy a walk in the park.

And now that walk had been intruded upon by all manner of inconvenient thoughts of Miss Luna and his now very public connection to her. Gideon curled his hands into fists as his mind raced with what such a connection could mean for him and his goals.

Stansberry's rapid steps crunched over the gravel as he hastened to catch up with Gideon. "I sense you're not pleased with this development," he panted.

"How very astute of you."

"That's why you keep me on the payroll, sir."

Despite himself, Gideon snorted. "Either a foolish or brilliant decision."

"Definitely brilliant." Stansberry finally fell into step with him, their footsteps thudding a rhythm on the walk. "Is there another reason you are displeased that the papers have linked you to the eldest Miss Luna?"

"My God, you are a dog with a bone," Gideon huffed, shooting his secretary a scowl.

"My dear mother used to say I was stubborn because I was the youngest." There was a fond smile in Stansberry's voice. "She said I needed to be dogged to get answers . . . or the attention I believed was my due."

"She must be very proud of you now."

"I believe she would be." When Gideon turned to him, Stansberry's jaw was held so tautly it could have crushed rock. "She died five years ago, when I was at university."

An inconvenient ache pulsed in his chest, and despite his desire to avoid personal conversations, Gideon heard himself say, "I lost my parents when I was twelve. We were all felled by a fever, but I was the only one who survived."

He usually kept thoughts of his parents at bay. While his ambitions were consumed with honoring his freedom-seeking grandmother, Gideon tried not to let the memories of his mother and father haunt him. They had very few tangible things to offer him as a boy, but they were rich in love, and they showered him with affection and praise. His father, Ronan Fox, had fled his ancestral home in the Highlands during the Clearances, finding himself in Manchester working in a colliery when he met Gideon's mother, Emmy, a young secretary who worked for the foreman. It had been love at first sight, according to his father at least . . . but then even now, sixteen years since their death, Gideon could remember the soft look that filled his mother's eyes whenever she had looked at his father.

"I'm sorry to hear that, sir," Stansberry murmured.

"Yes, well." Gideon fixed his gaze on an indeterminate point farther down the lane. "Everyone has a story of loss."

"Indeed. And Miss Luna has lost much recently." When Gideon turned to him with a frown, his secretary shrugged. "She's lost her home, her parents, her whole life in Mexico, really, with no guarantee she'll get it back."

"That is . . ." Working his jaw, Gideon considered what to say, steadfastly ignoring the heavy weight in his gut. "That's quite gracious of you, Stansberry."

A dusky pink crisscrossed his cheeks. "It's not hard to extend grace when it seems as if she is still getting her footing. But

I wager you're still not pleased to be connected to her in such a way."

"Of course I'm not pleased." Gideon tapped the paper against his palm. "It serves no purpose to be linked to a woman whose future lies somewhere else"—and *with* someone else— "and who cannot help bolster my career in Commons."

"Of course," his secretary murmured.

"Plus," Gideon continued, as if listing Miss Luna's "faults" would somehow convince him of them, "I've heard some members of the ton consider her a bit fast."

"I cannot imagine why."

With his brows hiding in his hairline, Gideon stared at the man. "Can you not?"

"Truly." Stansberry frowned. "From what I have gathered in the gossip sheets, she hasn't done anything untoward. Her behavior doesn't hint at scandal, but rather a bit of merrymaking."

Gideon threw his hands into the air. "But that's just it. Young women are not allowed to engage in merrymaking, no matter how innocent the fun. Society searches for any excuse to judge them, and friendly smiles or lighthearted laughs are reasons to extract the claws."

"It's rather unfair, don't you think, that women are criticized for the very thing men do all the time."

Rotating his head, he considered his secretary with a sad smile. "This is why I continue to pay you."

Stansberry arched a brow. "Because I annoy you?"

Snorting, Gideon shook his head. "Because your capacity for kindness and empathy reminds me of my own. Especially because every moment I spend within the walls of Westminster tenaciously tries to steal those things from me."

A deep rumbling noise sounded behind them, interrupting any response Stansberry may have planned. As Gideon glanced over his shoulder, his gaze fell upon a curricle racing and bumping along the path, coming right toward them. Without a word, both men moved off to the side, shielding their eyes from the sun as they looked up at the conveyance as it barreled past them, the sharp sounds of laughter the only thing left in the curricle's wake.

His stomach sank when the laughter reached his ears, for he knew its owner.

"Was that . . ." Stansberry paused, staring after the departing carriage, his mien darkened in confusion. "Miss Luna?"

Following the conveyance in the distance, Gideon could make out Miss Luna's dark head as it tipped back to laugh. Grasping the gossip sheet still clinched in his hand, he whacked it against Stansberry's arm.

"Now do you think it unkind of me to be wary of associating with her?"

He didn't allow his secretary a chance to respond. With a stifled sigh, Gideon followed the direction the carriage disappeared into, an unhappy coincidence.

"You're in the paper again, Ana."

Dropping her pen onto the escritoire with a ping, Ana María looked to Gabby with a sigh. "I'm sure I don't want to know what it says this time."

"To be fair, the column discusses who was at the opera last night." Isabel flipped a page in the book she was reading. The worn cover told her it was from the collection she had them lug across the Atlantic. "It mentions that you were seen conversing with Señor Fox and—"

"He was smiling!" Gabby's voice pitched high with glee. "The writer said"—she paused and held up the paper to read—"*This author didn't think Mr. Fox capable of such a human emo-*

tion but is happy to have been proven wrong. The allure and charm of the Luna sisters, most especially Miss Ana María Luna, must be legendary indeed. Allure. Charm. My, we mustn't let these compliments go to our heads."

"It's too late for you," Isabel murmured dryly, not looking up from her book.

Gabby rolled her eyes but kept her attention on Ana María. "Whatever were you and Señor Fox talking about that made the dour man smile?"

"As I told you already, he's not dour," Ana María declared before she promptly clamped her mouth closed.

"I am merely quoting the article this time." Gabby narrowed her eyes. "Now don't evade the question."

Turning back to the unfinished letter she was writing her mother, Ana María considered her swooping handwriting. She had managed only a few mundane lines, in which she described the cool, damp weather, Lady Yardley's Mayfair townhome, and the Catholic parish where they attended Mass. The urge to describe the people she had met, the sights she had seen, the visceral manner in which her body ached for the warm, familiar surroundings of their villa in Mexico City had her pen vibrating in her hand. But she could not write the words. Not when she knew her father would read them and know they had not obeyed his edict.

For Ana María knew that if her father learned she and her sisters were gallivanting about London, tasked with charming the very men who could choose to keep England out of Mexico, he would find a way to leave his hiding spot in El Paso del Norte and travel across the sea to collect them.

And that thought, the idea of having her puppet strings reattached in some macabre display of authority, had her opening her mouth and saying, "He quoted Shakespeare and we discussed bullfighting."

Gabby's brows drew together. "Why would you discuss that?"

Ana María tapped her pen against her hand. "Señor Avery seemed to believe cricket would be too much for my feminine sensibilities, so I told him of Mexico's fascination with bullfighting."

"And Shakespeare?" Isabel asked.

"A well-timed rejoinder."

Staring down unseeing at the half-written letter, she replayed in her thoughts the fleeting smile that had brightened Mr. Fox's face. For the span of several seconds, he had been transformed. Like a curtain being lifted, his true self took center stage to take a bow, and that glimpse made her want to know more. Made her infinitely curious for why he hid himself away behind a mask.

But do you not do the same thing? her mind whispered to her. *Do you not hide your true passions under a veil of docile, feminine obedience?*

"I have to say, Ana, that I'm surprised you even chatted with Señor Fox after the Ralston ball." Isabel closed her book with a snap and settled it in her lap. Her intense dark eyes settled on her eldest sister, and the hairs on the back of Ana María's neck rose. "I would think after the conversation you had with him, you'd want to avoid him."

A scowl twisted her lips. "He greeted me. Do you wish for me to have ignored him? Given him the cut direct?"

"Of course not. But you could have excused yourself from the conversation."

"That would have been rude. The box was not overly large, and all the other guests would have been mindful of my snub."

Ana María lifted a shoulder. "Señor Fox does not deserve such reproof."

Isabel slowly shook her head back and forth. "Perhaps not. But then by engaging each other, you brought reproof down on yourselves anyway."

Ana María tossed her pen on the desktop and launched herself to her feet, rucking up the bulk of her skirts as she took a step toward her sister. "And why does that bother you? It's not your name being bandied about in the gossip rags."

"It bothers me because I never would have expected you to court impropriety." Isabel held her book so tightly in her hand, her knuckles showed white. "I never thought you the kind of woman to trifle with other men while in an agreement with another."

The room fell silent, the only sound the steady tick of the grandfather clock that stood sentinel in the corner. Even its morose beats were damning to Ana María's ears.

"How am I trifling with anyone, Isa?" She narrowed her eyes. "That is an unfair claim to make."

"You like Señor Fox. It's so obvious that you do, and I worry you are allowing it to cloud your judgment."

"Cloud my judgment?" She threw her arms wide. "How so? Have I not told him of my engagement?"

"And yet the two of you still continue to circle each other," Isabel hissed, her black eyes firing.

Ana María pressed her lips together and looked away.

"Dios mío, Isa, get off your high horse," Gabby grumbled into the silence. "For all his solemnity, Señor Fox has been very amiable. He's paid me more regard than Señor Ramírez ever did. Plus, he's infinitely more handsome. His cheekbones make me want to cry, and those lips . . ." She pressed her palm to her chest, and reclined as if she were swooning. "Do you think

Señor Fox's lips are as soft as they look? Like two feather-down pillows. I bet he'd whisper dirty words in your ear before he'd nibble across your jaw to claim—"

"Gabby!" Ana María and Isabel exclaimed in unison.

"¿Qué?" Gabby snorted. "Las dos son tan puritanas."

"I'm not prudish," Ana María and Isabel cried, again in unison, each glaring at the other for their continued agreement.

"The fact remains that Ana is here and Señor Ramírez is in Mexico." Gabby waved a hand in the air. "It's not like she would even be engaged to him if it weren't for Father."

This time neither sister said a word, for it was true. Fernando was not the man Ana María would have chosen for herself. But then she'd long known it was foolish to set her cap at any man, because her father would have the final say in whom she took as her husband. When he had announced that he had brokered a deal for her to marry Fernando—as if she were livestock he'd sold at auction—Ana María had almost been relieved to not have to wonder when she'd be married off. The not knowing, the stress of waiting, had been unbearable.

"And why shouldn't Ana flirt with any man she chooses?" A sour expression twisted Gabby's face. "It's not like Señor Ramírez has stopped gallivanting all over the city with Señora Romero."

Her muscles locked into place as warring emotions washed over her. Disappointment, shame, and embarrassment coiled in a ball in her chest, and Ana María dropped her gaze to the floor. She thought of the letter to her mother, and wondered if she was brave enough to ask for instructions on how to hold her head high when one's husband flaunted his affairs in front of all of society.

"Señora Romero is not Ana María's concern," Isabel began, holding the book in front of her like a shield. "Men will be men."

Sucking in a breath, Ana María clenched her eyes closed. The words were their mother's, lessons she had dropped through their childhood and adolescence like bitter seeds . . . and the seedlings that sprouted had poisoned so much more than the sisters had realized.

"It shouldn't be that way," Gabby declared, tossing the newspaper on the ornate coffee table, her hazel eyes flashing. "Ana shouldn't have to excuse such disrespect because Mother always did."

"What can she do, then?" Isabel leaned forward, her normally calm, dulcet voice sharp. "She has to marry him, but I doubt he will end his affair with Señora Romero simply because of his new wife."

"But he should." Ana María paced to the fireplace and back again. "Fernando should want my respect—he should respect *me*—enough to end a relationship that intrudes upon our own."

"Of course he should," Gabby echoed, clapping her hands together.

"And just because Mother espoused certain ideas doesn't make them right." Ana María twisted her fingers together. "She's so unhappy. Surely you noticed how miserable she was."

Gabby nodded . . . and after a moment, so did Isabel.

"Well, I refuse to resign myself to such misery. I refuse." She stomped her foot. "I will respect Fernando, and I expect him to respect me in return."

"And if he doesn't?" Isabel quirked a brow. "How will you possibly hold him accountable?"

Accountable. The word brought to mind Mr. Fox and the way his deep, dark eyes always considered her so keenly. As if every word that fell from her lips were interesting and smart and worthy of his undivided attention.

It was a heady feeling, and Ana María would never again settle for anything less.

"Maybe it's not my responsibility to hold him accountable. I'm to be his wife, not his mother." She bit the inside of her cheek for a moment before she squared her shoulders. "And who's to say that this engagement will move forward anyway."

"Indeed. This conflict could last for years, and Fernando could marry Señora Romero instead." Gabby's brows rose while her tone dropped. "You know she went with him to El Paso del Norte."

Ana María did know, and the fact that the older woman could stay behind when Ana María could not had grated less as the weeks passed.

A rustling sound drew her attention, and she turned to see Isabel approaching, her face expressionless. Without a word, she reached out to grip Ana María's hand, squeezing it for a moment.

"Despite how it may seem, my allegiance is to you." Her throat bobbed. "I have great respect for Señor Ramírez, for he was one of the few men in Father's circle who made me feel seen."

"That's because the men Father interacts with are fools. Great statesmen, but fools."

Isabel's smile trembled. "But regardless, I want you to be happy. And I've long known you could never be happy if you were not valued, and is there any greater sign of value than respect? And I respect you, Ana. More so now than ever before."

Tears clogged her throat, and Ana María blinked rapidly as her sister's form went blurry before her. Isabel was always so hard to read. Always an enigma, she'd given up trying to understand. So her words now were like the warmest embrace.

"And I you." She looked down to where their hands were

still linked together. "I appreciate that you consider situations from a different perspective, and I've come to value your opinion . . . even when it stings."

"Hopefully it doesn't sting too much," Isabel murmured.

"Only a little."

The sisters smiled at each other for a heartbeat, until the door to the drawing room swung open, Lady Yardley framed within.

"Are you ready for visiting hours? Your gentlemen callers are lined up down the walk, I'm told."

Looking first to Gabby and then to Isabel, Ana María shared a secret commiserating smile with her sisters.

One they had not shared in many long years.

Gripping Isabel's hand, Ana María urged her middle sister to sit next to her on the settee, Gabby nestling on her opposite side. "Open the gates, Lady Yardley. We're ready."

8

Before she knew it, Ana María had settled into a routine of sorts. It consisted of waking a few hours after dawn and joining her sisters and Lady Yardley at the breakfast table, where she did her best to eat the bland eggs and oatmeal that were staples of the viscountess's morning meal. The bacon and occasional rashers of sausage that made an appearance were always cause for silent celebration, but she still longed for fresh, zesty salsa to liven her eggs or vanilla bean for her porridge. After their meal had ended, she retreated to the drawing room, where she and her sisters read the morning papers and hypothesized about what was happening in Mexico based on the scarce reporting that appeared in the British newspapers. It was a damning sign that unless British resources were directly affected by international events, the reporting on such events would be wanting. It had irritated the ladies to no end, until they learned their tío Arturo received frequent dispatches from his connections within the Liberal government. There had been no word of their parents specifically, but Tío Arturo seemed to think that meant they were safe and hale.

Despite her simmering resentment, Ana María hoped and prayed they were well.

After reading the newspapers, the sisters set out with Lady Yardley to brave the ton at the slew of events she had accepted invitations to on their behalf. And even if their schedules were free, visitors called every day. Gabby wagered it was because most guests hoped to report on their activities or the topics they discussed, even the style and cut of their attire. Ana María knew her sister was right, for their names appeared in the gossip pages with regularity, even if they had done nothing of note. She longed to give the busybodies of the ton something to talk about, but Ana María knew any mistake on their part could hinder Tío Arturo's quest to earn British support. The urge to rebel, to revel in her newfound freedom, was not as strong as her desire to win international support for her countrymen.

Ana María had glimpsed Señor Fox across a crowded ballroom or while passing each other on the walking path in Hyde Park, but he'd never stopped to converse with her. Had not sought her out as a dance partner. Of course he greeted her politely and murmured nonsensical and benign compliments, but his niceties ended there.

No longer did he smile at her in that manner that made his dark eyes twinkle and her knees turn weak.

"You're staring."

Jerking her head about, she met Isabel's amused gaze. Although she knew it was fruitless to deny it, she couldn't help but mount some sort of defense.

"I was simply studying Lady Carole's ornate wallpaper. I've not seen walls decorated with"—she squinted, a frown tugging on her lips—"is it chickens?"

"Poultry-inspired wallpaper. I never would have imagined such a thing existed." Isabel snorted. "How very . . . unique."

"And a bit bizarre," Ana María whispered, leaning close to study the pattern.

"I suppose if you have a great affinity for birds, it makes sense."

"Or eggs."

A bubble of laughter burst from Isabel, and she clamped a hand over her mouth, her shoulders shaking with suppressed giggles and tears pooling in her eyes. Ana María could not recall the last time she'd seen Isabel—her serious, bookish sister—so overcome with mirth she could not contain it. Which was a shame because Isabel had the most infectious laugh, and her toothsome smiles seemed to be illuminated from within.

Ana María grinned outright, the etiquette hawks be damned. Sliding a handkerchief into her sister's hand, she patted Isabel on her back. "It's the eggs and you know it."

Blotting under her eyes, Isabel said, "What I know is that the only reason you spotted the poultry wallpaper is that Señor Fox is seated against the wall."

"Is he really? I was unaware."

As far as lies went, it was rather pitiful, but Ana María had no intention of admitting that her sister was right. Since Mr. Fox had entered Lady Carole's drawing room for the woman's annual poetry reading, Ana María had been unable to think of much else. Her gaze was drawn to him, over and over again, as if she were a moon snared in his orbit. It did not help matters that he'd yet to look in her direction. Not even once. Did he know she was in attendance, or was he ignoring her intentionally? Would he greet her politely—distantly—and then act as if she didn't exist?

Since their names had been attached together in the paper, he seemed to go out of his way to avoid her. Every time his gaze met hers and quickly glanced away, every time his shoulders tensed when he heard her voice, and the way he politely excused himself whenever they found themselves in the same vicinity made her teeth clench and her nails dig into her palms. Was she really such a pariah, so undeserving of even a few moments of his time? Never in her life had she been rejected so thoroughly.

And despite his indifference, Ana María couldn't stop thinking about him. About his sarcastic rejoinders. His intelligent mind. The intense way he considered her when she spoke.

The thought that he might snub her in such a small, intimate gathering made her heart feel as if it were lurching out of rhythm in her throat.

"You're an awful liar, Ana. Has anyone ever told you that?" Isabel asked dryly.

Smoothing her gloved hands over the skirts of her day dress, Ana María chuckled. It was a harsh, brittle sound. "And yet I've been playing a role my entire life, Isa. If I'm good at anything, it's pretending to be something I'm not."

After the silence between them had stretched for several minutes, Ana María finally angled her body to look at her sister fully. "You have no admonishments for me? No timely reminders of my engagement to Fernando? Surely you have some opinion as to why *he* keeps avoiding me."

Ana María did not dare utter his name aloud, even though they spoke in Spanish. The thought of her tongue shaping the syllables tasted like bitter melon in her mouth.

"He avoids you because he is a politician who must act in a manner that benefits him politically, and he does not benefit from an association with you." Isabel lifted her glass of lemonade to her lips, and then lowered it again. "I know you know this, but it bears repeating."

Grasping Ana María by the hand, Isabel whispered, "This is

not our home. We can't afford to put down roots here. Not when we'll have to rip them up again when we depart back to Mexico."

Dipping her chin to her chest, Ana María clamped her eyes closed.

"He knows you're engaged, Ana, so why indulge your emotions in a manner that will never see the light of day?" Isabel ran her thumb over her knuckles. "You're charmed by him because he doesn't treat you as some exotic doll he can attach his fantasies to."

"He's also handsome. Don't forget that detail."

Isabel patted her hand. "He is. I was foolish to make such an oversight."

A laugh slipped past Ana María's lips. "Now you're being ridiculous."

"Am I? Or are you?"

She paused, her amusement frozen on her face. She *was* being ridiculous. Once again, her desire to be accepted, to meet expectations, to be the perfect eldest daughter of Elías Luna Cuate had overruled her thoughts. Dictated her self-worth. Inhaling until her lungs felt full to bursting, Ana María exhaled on a slow breath.

"Thank you." Her fingers twisted in the lace overlay of her skirts. "We've been taught since birth to seek the approval of men, and it's a hard lesson to relinquish."

"Especially when the man in question is such an enigma."

"So you do understand his appeal," Ana María joked, bumping her shoulder into her sister's.

"I'm not blind." Isabel huffed sharply. "I may find men bothersome overall, but I am not ignorant of their charms."

"I suspect you've found many things bothersome since we've arrived."

"Haven't you?" her sister volleyed, a knowing smile ghosting across her lips.

A flash of jade-colored silk materialized on Ana María's opposite side, and she turned to spy Gabby sliding onto the narrow chair next to her.

"The poetry reading is about to start," her youngest sister stated. "How many people do you think will be reading original pieces? Dios mío, this will be either vastly amusing or the most vexing of tortures."

Ana María's eyes darted to meet Isabel's gaze.

"A bothersome thing," her sister mouthed.

And it was Ana María's turn to stifle her amusement.

"You are an oak, Fox."

Gideon directed his gaze from where Lady Emily Hargrove scribbled on a sheet of paper at the front of the room to his friend who sat beside him. "What are you getting on about?"

Whitfield scoffed, the grating sound conveying annoyance. "Either you are determined to play ignorant or you are the world's most clueless man." The duke considered him with shrewd blue eyes. "My wager is on being clueless."

"Fancy coming from you, when you seem determined to perfect the clueless lord routine."

"I beg your pardon." The duke lifted his chin and looked down his Roman nose at Gideon. He was certain the look had intimidated more than one man in Whitfield's lifetime, but Gideon knew his friend was all bark and no bite. "But I am no mere *lord*. Show my illustrious title some respect, sirrah."

"Forgive my oversight, *Your Grace*," he said with an exaggerated wave of his hand.

Taking a lazy sip of his lemonade, Whitfield winced. "I'd

sooner forgive you, and your rudeness, than Lady Carole for serving this foul beverage."

Gideon chuckled. "I assure you that I'm not the first person accused of being clueless over your nonsensical ramblings."

"Ramblings? And here I thought I was pontificating in a manner that befitted my ducal station." Whitfield pressed a fist to his chest in a very dramatic fashion. But then most things the duke did were dramatic.

"You feel too deeply about things to ever be truly ducal." Gideon snagged punch from a passing footman, carefully avoiding the lemonade. "Now do I want to know why you have compared me to a deciduous tree?"

"Now you're just trying to impress me by using big words." Whitfield set his glass on a nearby table and crossed his arms over his chest. "You have studiously kept your gaze from traveling to the other side of the room."

"Have I? I hadn't noticed."

"Interesting. So you didn't know that two-thirds of the Luna sisters are sitting like lovely roses in the sun in front of Lady Carole's front window?"

Gideon dropped his gaze from Whitfield's and stared instead at the liquid in his glass. "Are they really?"

"Indeed." The duke drummed his fingers on his forearm. "Miss Isabel is wearing blue, which I must say looks striking against her dark skin."

"Miss Isabel is quite striking all on her own," Gideon murmured.

"And Miss Luna could probably wear any color, although I do prefer this primrose color she's wearing now."

"She's not wearing primrose."

Gideon realized his mistake when Whitfield's lip curved up. *Damn it.*

"What color is she wearing then, Fox?" The duke's voice was low so only Gideon could hear him. "Seeing as how you seemed ignorant of her attendance, I'm curious how you're knowledgeable of her attire."

Disregarding how his muscles were rigid, Gideon turned until his back faced the side of the room Miss Luna sat on. "Must you always be such an arse?" he asked through his clenched teeth.

"Yes." Whitfield's expression was exasperated. "My late father gave me the impression that such behavior was necessary for a duke."

And just like that, irritation seeped from his blood. Whitfield had a talent for dropping nuggets from his childhood into random conversations and completely disarming Gideon. He suspected his friend did it on purpose, but he was kind enough to ignore it.

"Why don't you go talk to her?" The duke raised a brow. "It's obvious to anyone who knows you that you want to."

"You're the only one who knows me, Whitfield."

"Oh, that's right." His friend tugged on his lapels. "You really should make new friends."

Gideon rolled his eyes by way of answer.

Whitfield propped his shoulder against the wall. "So why don't you go speak with her?"

"Because I have no interest in providing the gossip rags with another reason to speculate about us," Gideon growled.

"Aah, yes. I remember now. But only because it was reported you smiled at Miss Luna when you've only ever frowned at me."

"Frowns are all you deserve, Whitfield."

The duke chuckled until the sound abruptly died as his eyes narrowed at a spot beyond Gideon's shoulder. "You're not the only one who thinks so."

Gideon glanced over his shoulder, his gaze immediately snagging on the subject of their conversation. On the object of his thoughts, despite how he had tried to purge her from his mind. Her day dress was a simple shade of blushing rose. It lacked embellishments, yet it stretched across her body in a manner that seemed indecent, even as it failed to provide even a peek at forbidden skin. After Gideon stared at her arresting face for a long moment, his gaze shifted to her side, and his eyes widened.

"Are you referring to Miss Gabriela?" he asked, swinging his head about to look at the duke.

Whitfield raised a shoulder in a manner that may have been dismissive if not for the hard look in his blue eyes. "It doesn't matter. I have never had an interest in winning the approval of shrews."

Gideon's lip twitched. "I never would have pegged Miss Gabriela as a shrew. She has always been polite and engaging in her conversations with me."

"Yes, well,"—the duke spread his palms—"she has only ever been critical and caustic when we've conversed."

"It sounds as if she treats you as you treat others."

"That is"—Whitfield's brows dropped low—"rather disconcerting of you to point out."

Before Gideon could respond, Lady Carole clapped her hands together at the front of the room, silencing the audience. After consulting a piece of parchment in her hand, their hostess announced the name of a young lady who would be starting the exposition with a piece by John Donne.

Whitfield groaned softly as he took a seat next to Gideon. "This is going to be torturous."

Gideon bit back a snort, but knew not to argue the point.

As predicted, the next hour passed at an excruciatingly slow pace, and for almost every one of those minutes Gideon endeavored to keep his expression passive, or at least mildly diverted. But it proved difficult as yet another young man stood to recite some bit of nonsense from Byron. *Christ, why was everyone so enamored of the man?* And it wasn't just Byron who was a favorite among the gathered crowd, for the audience had been subjected to multiple renditions of works by Wordsworth, Keats, and others. It was almost a reprieve when an original poem was shared, no matter how the abundance of similes or metaphors employed made him cringe. Soon Whitfield began whispering his prediction for what the speaker might read, be it original or from an esteemed poet, and Gideon was amused by how accurate his friend proved to be.

But his amusement died when Lady Carole looked down at her sheet and called, "Miss Isabel Luna."

Gideon whipped his head about, not at all surprised to see the middle Luna sister staring back at Lady Carole with large eyes, her face frightfully pale. As he watched, she turned to Ana María with a panicked look.

"She didn't request to read a piece," Gideon murmured, anger prickling across his skin.

Whitfield's nostrils flared. "It would appear not."

Darting his gaze about the gathered crowd, it landed on a group of young ladies sitting near the front of the room, their shared demeanor one of exuberance. They appeared to relish Isabel Luna's embarrassment, and Gideon rose to his feet without thought, taking a step toward where Ana María sat with her sisters—

"It seems there was a mistake, my lady."

Blinking, Gideon paused when Gabriela Luna stood, a bright smile on her pretty face.

She raised a white-gloved hand. "It was I who wished to recite a poem, not my sister."

Ana María and Isabel flinched in unison, but neither contradicted her.

"My apologies, Miss Luna," Lady Carole said, a smile spreading over her face when Gabriela joined her at the front of the room. "But you are here now, and what poem will you be reciting for us today?"

Lifting her pert chin, Gabriela declared, " 'In a Storm' by José María Heredia."

A low murmur spread across the gathered crowd at the announcement of the selection, but the youngest Miss Luna appeared unaffected as she cleared her throat and pressed her folded hands to her chest.

It was no secret that Gabriela was of a fiery disposition, but seeing her orate—no, *perform*—a poem, solely in Spanish, was like watching a thunderstorm in all its ferocity. Most of the audience appeared enraptured, if a bit confused, as they could not understand what she was saying. Gideon snuck a glance at Whitfield, who was staring at Gabriela intently. An improvement from the sardonic look he showcased throughout the earlier readings.

While Gabby performed, Gideon found himself traversing the space that separated him from her sisters, coming to a stop behind her empty chair, his fingers curling around the seat back. He did not look down at Ana María, but being in her presence, noting the subtle whiffs of her jasmine scent, eased some of the ire pounding in his head.

When she was finished, Gabby flourished a curtsy like a dancer, teeth flashing brightly as she beamed at the applauding audience. Gideon took a step back as she regained her seat, acknowledging her impish smile with a tilt of his head.

His eyes traveled to the group of young ladies he had spied earlier, disgust over their mean-spirited antics souring his stomach.

"What a . . ." Lady Carole paused, her brow pinched as she opened and closed her mouth. Gideon imagined she was searching for the right words. "An *emotional* ending to tonight's exhibition. Thank you, Miss Luna."

As the crowd clapped, Gideon heard himself cough politely. "Lady Carole, were there no other poets or poetry lovers who signed up to read?"

The older lady shook her head. "Miss Luna's performance was our finale. Why do you ask, Mr. Fox?"

Ignoring the eyes fixed on him, Gideon clasped his hands behind his back and said, "Because I could have sworn I saw Lady Emily put down her name, and I was looking forward to hearing what poem she recited."

The room went still, Gideon's unspoken assertion echoing through the space. Lady Emily Hargrove *had* signed up to perform, but she had not written her own name. The implication was clear, and as several heads turned in her direction, the lady in question turned red to the roots of her hair.

"Is that correct, Lady Emily?" Lady Carole's brows disappeared into her hairline as she looked to the young woman and her friends. "You are more than welcome to do a reading, if you'd like."

Lady Emily shook her head frantically, her blond curls slapping against her cheeks. "Thank you, my lady, but that's quite all right."

She slid her gaze to Gideon for a moment, her expression darkening, but he affected a look of surprise and, he hoped at least, of disappointment. If Lady Emily experienced one-tenth of the humiliation she attempted to bring down upon Isabel Luna, Gideon felt justice had been served.

After being thanked by their hostess, and encouraged to partake of the arrangement of refreshments prepared by the kitchen staff, the audience members rose from their seats with one last applause. Almost immediately, all three Luna sisters pivoted about in a whirl of colorful fabrics and greeted him with broad grins.

"Señor Fox, that was very . . ." Ana María paused, her throat bobbing as she looked up at him with her doe eyes. "Thank you," she finished simply.

Hearing her voice after weeks of depriving himself was like taking in a full gulp of air; his lungs rejoiced at being filled, and his blood sang. Gideon knew there was nothing particularly special about her voice . . . aside from its effect on him. How her melodic timbre curled about him, making him equal parts appeased *and* impossibly hard.

Gideon shifted on his feet to relieve the pressure his cock was placing on his placket.

"I didn't do anything. Miss Gabriela was the one who spoiled their plans." Turning to her, he shook his head. "You were brilliant."

"Please call me Gabby," the youngest Luna sister said, grinning at him. "I'm relieved I remembered the poem." She paused, a wicked light sparking in her gaze. "Although no one would have been the wiser if I had just spoken nonsense."

"Isa and I would have known," Ana María interjected, "and then our laughter would have ruined your passionate spectacle."

"If I were to laugh at anything, it would have been at Lady Emily's face when you asked when she would perform." A gentle smile curled Isabel's lips. "Thank you, señor."

He opened his mouth to respond with some demure comment, but Ana María placed her hand on his arm, and his heart abruptly seemed to beat in the spot where they touched.

"You were firm but polite. No one can fault your manners, especially in light of Lady Emily's lack of them."

"Gideon Fox is all that is honorable and true." Whitfield's voice sounded from behind them, drawing their heads about.

"Your Grace," Ana María murmured, bobbing a curtsy, "as I am sure you guessed, we were discussing Mr. Fox's chivalrous display."

"It was quite well done, Fox," the duke murmured before his arctic blue gaze turned to Gabby. "As for you, Miss Gabriela, I found your recitation quite inspired. But then you've always struck me as a young woman with a strong theatrical streak."

Gabby glared. "What is that supposed to mean?"

Stifling a sigh, Gideon watched as his friend and the youngest Luna sister squabbled, various inanities flying back and forth between the pair. Eventually, Isabel rolled her eyes and declared she was going to find Lady Yardley, leaving him standing with Ana María, who watched her youngest sister gesture about with her arms as she scowled at Whitfield.

"I confess I'm surprised to see you here today, Señor Fox." Her gaze darted up to meet his. "You don't strike me as a lover of poetry."

Steadfastly ignoring the way she rolled the *r* in *lover*—even though his body did not—Gideon said, "Just because I no longer spend my free time penning sonnets about a field of wildflowers or the tempting nature of the bow in a woman's upper lip . . ." He paused when Ana María tucked her own lip between her teeth. Swallowing down the swell of inconvenient thoughts, he continued. "Doesn't mean I enjoy poetry any less than the next person."

Her slippered feet moved closer. "*No longer?*"

Gideon winced, which made her laugh. "Well, it's possible I've written a few poems. Back at university. Like any other young man, I found it quite useful for turning the heads of comely barmaids."

She smirked. "You must have thought yourself quite dashing."

Glancing down at his feet, he shrugged. "I was eager. A bit full of myself."

"So, like most young men, then."

"It would seem," he said, grinning down at her upturned face. When a telltale blush spread across her cheeks, his pleasure grew.

Exhaling, Ana María asked, "If you had been in the position where you had to recite a poem at a moment's notice, would you have chosen one of your own?"

He shook his head so fast she chuckled. "Definitely not. If I had to choose, I suppose I would select . . ." Gideon tapped his mouth. " 'Bury Me in a Free Land' by American poet Frances Harper."

Ana María's lush lips parted as she stared up at him. "I've never heard of it."

"It was first published in an abolitionist newspaper. A friend in Philadelphia that I correspond with sent me a copy."

"Would you share it with me?" she asked breathlessly.

His stomach rolled and his head swam, but she appeared so curious—fervid, even—that Gideon squared his shoulders and quietly recounted the verses to the deathbed poem. His tone dipped and rose with the lines, inspired by the avid way Ana

María watched him, her breath hanging on every word he uttered. Gideon was almost disappointed when the last line dissolved into the air, for being the sole focus of her attention was a powerful feeling.

She blinked rapidly for several seconds at his conclusion. "That was beautiful in its rawness. So emotional and unflinching." Ana María considered him. "You feel very strongly about abolition, don't you?"

Always to the heart of the matter. Ana María Luna seemed to know exactly what to say to leave him off balance.

Gideon raised a palm. "I do, and I don't understand why my peers don't as well."

Dropping her curious gaze, Gideon stared at the garish wallpaper without really seeing it. "My grandmother was eight and ten when she managed to steal aboard a London-bound steamer ship with the aid of abolitionists working in Savannah. She had spent her life toiling on a plantation there. When she finally arrived here, she was lucky enough to receive help from a Catholic women's group, and she soon found a position as a seamstress in a dress shop in Manchester. Only then did she learn she was pregnant."

"Who was your grandfather?" Ana María's voice was nothing more than a whisper, as if she didn't want to ask the question.

And Gideon didn't want to answer it.

He flexed his jaw for a moment. "My grandmother never said."

Ana María closed her eyes, and when she opened them, her brown depths were clear. "What was her name?"

"Sabine." He rubbed his thumb over his forefinger as memories of his grandmother washed over him. "She had a low, melodic voice, and when she smiled, her whole face lit up."

"She sounds lovely."

Gideon hummed. "She was. Despite everything she endured, she still believed the best in people. I try to remember that when those I work with in Parliament refuse to look past the end of their noses."

Her pretty face turned contemplative. "Those in power have grown desensitized. It's easy to prioritize concerns and plans of action when certain issues do not affect you directly." Ana María's mouth quirked. "Or there is a profit to be made."

"Ah, money. The world's great evil."

"Isn't that why armies invade and far-off countries exert dominance over others? To claim their resources, be that gold, silver, land, or human flesh?" A deep sigh seemed to drain her. "It's why I speak Spanish and why you fight for those who have been stolen away from their homelands."

"And it's why you're here now."

Ana María clasped a hand to her mouth, her eyes wide and glassy. "Oh God, it is."

Never had Gideon been overwhelmed with the desire to comfort someone else. His hands twitched to grasp Ana María by the shoulders and pull her into his chest, enfolding her within his arms. Gideon yearned to bury his face in her hair and inhale her lulling scent into his lungs. He rather doubted words would be possible with her so close, but Gideon would make it clear with his hands—his lips—that she was safe.

Instead, Gideon moved toward her, his gaze intent on hers. "I know your exile has been forced upon you, and your reception here in London has been tenuous at times, but I think you very brave, Miss Luna."

Gideon gestured with a tilt of his chin to the crowd of guests chatting around them. "These people? These pillars of polite London society? They would be helpless as newborn babes if they were forced from their homes in the middle of the night. They balk at cold baths and cold cups of tea, as if such things were a necessity instead of a sign of their privilege. Strip away all that bestows their elevated status, and their refinement and gentility would melt away like snow on a rainy morning."

Ana María's breath hitched when he dipped his head, his mouth now a hair's breadth from the delicate shell of her ear. "But you and your sisters, Miss Luna? I imagine you were frightened, but not cowed. Now here you are, an ocean away from your home, charming and beguiling everyone you meet."

She angled her chin to meet his eyes, a playful smile on her lips. "Not everyone, señor."

Without thought, Gideon grasped her hand, his thumb skating over her knuckles. Ana María gasped, but returned his tight grip.

"I assure you, no matter what they may say, no one is immune to your charms."

And Gideon squeezed her hand in his, for once uncaring of who saw.

9

"You want to attend *what*?" Ana María cried.

Isabel shifted on her feet, her gaze fixed on the plush Aubusson carpet. "Surely you know I've read his work."

Glancing down at the pamphlet Isabel had shoved into her hand, Ana María read:

Announcing an in-depth discussion of natural history with renowned British biologist Charles Darwin on his groundbreaking work, On the Origin of Species.

The pamphlet went on to list the date, time, and location of the event, which was occurring that afternoon.

She jerked her chin back. "You have?"

Isabel stared at her before covering her face with her hand. "Of course I have. Padre Ignacio used to give me new books or science journals on all manner of subjects."

"Padre Ignacio?" Ana María frowned.

"The priest who gave us our first Holy Communion?" Isabel snorted. "The very same."

"But why would he give you a copy of *On the Origin of Species?*"

"Because he has read *everything.* Father Ignacio knows English, French, and German, and he says his Portuguese is passable, so he has more texts at his disposal than the common reader. He once told me that the teachings in the Bible were to nurture his heart, while it was his responsibility to find books to nurture his mind."

"I—" Ana María stumbled to a stop, her thoughts sluggish. "I'm impressed. I didn't realize there was quite so much depth to the man. A bit of a rebel, isn't he?"

"The disciples were rebels, too." Isabel's dark eyes turned shiny. "He's whom I miss most. Not Mother, and certainly not Father. But Padre Ignacio always made me feel smart. And understood. He saw something in me that others didn't when—"

Ana María waited for her sister to continue, but instead Isabel shook her head and looked away. Glancing down at the pamphlet in her hand, Ana María finally released a long breath. "I'll accompany you."

A small sound escaped her sister, and if Ana María guessed, she'd say it was a gasp.

"You will?"

She nodded. "I want to understand why you find this so interesting. And also"—she waggled her eyebrows—"you know Father and Mother would never permit us to attend, so we can be rebels together."

As devout Catholics—or, in her father's case, a Sunday Mass Catholic—their parents would be mortally offended by the hypothetical research of Mr. Darwin.

But Ana María could admit, if only to herself, that the snippets of information she'd gleaned from the newspapers were fascinating. And while she never would have entertained learning more on such scandalous—or *devilish*, as her mother would say—ideas, the taboo nature of it made it all the more appealing.

Isabel's onyx eyes sparkled. "I like the sound of that."

"Very well," Ana María said. "How do you intend to get there? Surely Lady Yardley would object to our using the carriage if she knew where we were going."

"Has she objected to anything we've done since our arrival?" Isabel drawled, tilting her head to the side.

No, she hadn't. Aside from instructing them on British etiquette, the viscountess had been content to let them explore. She managed their social calendar, and accepted invitations for them to events she deemed worthy of their presence, but Lady Yardley had not balked when the sisters went on afternoon walks sans chaperone or made shopping trips to Bond Street. Gabby had even attended several ladies' club meetings with only Consuelo as her companion.

Ana María appreciated the freedom Lady Yardley afforded them, but she often wondered why the viscountess had agreed to host them in the first place. Gabby suspected Lady Yardley fancied Tío Arturo, and the more Ana María watched the two older people interact, the more she agreed that there was more to their relationship than either would admit.

Several hours later, Ana María allowed a footman to help her step from the viscountess's landau. With one hand clutching her reticule, she used the other to shield her eyes from the afternoon sun slitting its way through the surrounding buildings. Walking to the lecture hall at the Victoria and Albert Museum, Ana María gaped in awe at the large frieze featuring the queen staring down at them in the inner courtyard, surveying all who entered.

"It's quite the crowd," Isabel whispered from her side. Her

gaze was not on the impressive architecture, but on the people who had queued up to enter the facility.

Most appeared to be students, along with what were presumably faculty members. Yet Ana María spied several people she recognized from various ballrooms and drawing rooms, including an earl and a marquess. An interesting development to be sure.

"They're staring at us." Isabel pulled out her fan and waved it casually in front of her mouth, all the better to shield her words. Or perhaps to hide her face.

Ana María considered her sister. She'd noticed that Isabel could be uncomfortable and tense in a crowd, and seeing the amount of people in attendance, Ana María was worried her sister might be regretting her wish to attend the lecture.

Isabel's voice cut through her concerns. "I sincerely hope they don't think to approach us with the intent to explain Mr. Darwin's work to us."

"But, Isa, surely we need a gentleman to translate science for us." Ana María swept her hand toward the lecture hall entrance. "I mean, I may even need assistance determining where to enter, let alone make sense of Mr. Darwin's specified analysis."

"Do not worry, hermana." Isabel grabbed her wildly gesturing arm and tucked it around her own. With a placating smile that made Ana María snicker, she patted her hand. "I'm here to help explain difficult things to you. As the ugly sister, I have had more opportunities to learn, for I was never expected to perform for Father's many allies."

Spinning about on her heel, Ana María dug her fingers into Isabel's arm. "That is a lie, Isa. Whoever made you believe you were anything but beautiful was the worst kind of liar."

"Father told me, Ana." Isabel's expression turned to marble. "Maybe not in those words, but his opinion of me was clear every time he allowed me to disappear to the library during a ball, or when guests came to visit and he only ever called you and Gabby to greet them." She glanced down to where Ana María held her tight. "I've never been an asset to him."

"Isa, it's because you look like—"

"But I *will* be an asset to others."

With her brows drawn together, Ana María cocked her head. "What do you—?"

Her question was halted when her sister gasped softly.

"My fear is about to come true, for a gentleman approaches," Isabel murmured, already adopting a look of polite interest.

Ana María struggled to do the same. Her chest was painfully tight, and a knot of tears festered at the base of her throat. Their father's treatment of Isabel was so unfair, but almost more so because Ana María had not once thought to counteract his actions. She'd never questioned or challenged their father's conduct toward her. Instead, Ana María had been resentful of Isabel, for she had not been held to the same standard as she was; her sister had seemed able to do whatever she pleased, while Ana María jumped through hoops like a circus animal. In reality, Isabel had been made to feel inferior simply because she looked like their father.

Further realizations were halted when a gentleman came to a stop before them. Ana María studied his face, a vague memory of having been introduced to him during one of her promenades through the park coming to mind. He was a former enlisted officer, a hero in the Crimean War, from what she could recall. What she knew for certain was that he had been friendly and courteous.

"Ladies, it is a pleasure *and* a bit of a surprise to see you here today," the blond-haired man said as he bowed his greeting to them.

His name came to her in a flash. "Capitán Dawson," she murmured, sinking into a curtsy. "We are merely two young ladies of a curious nature hoping to learn about a curious subject."

He was handsome, Ana María noted as she observed Captain Dawson furrow his brow as he considered his response. She appreciated a man who thought before he spoke.

"In my somewhat limited experience, gentlewomen are often not permitted to read texts such as Mr. Darwin's." He slid his blue-eyed gaze to Isabel, who met his look with an arched one of her own. "As if science and numbers were capable of corrupting a woman."

"It seems as if some in society believe a woman can be corrupted by a gusty breeze. A springtime shower." Isabel narrowed her eyes minutely. "The attentions of a handsome gentleman."

Ana María did her best to hide her surprise by coughing into her hand, but Captain Dawson remained focused on her sister, his expression changing from cordial regard to teasing flirtation in one blink of his striking eyes. "Are you worried my handsome face will corrupt you, Miss Isabel?"

Taking a step forward, her sister chuckled. "You presume much, Capitán Dawson. I don't believe I ever said you were handsome."

The man opened his mouth for a long moment before snapping it closed with a clack of teeth. "Indeed you did not. Do forgive me, ladies. It seems that I've been presumptuous, and for that I apologize."

Offering them a crisp bow, Captain Dawson pivoted and disappeared back into the crowd.

"Really, Isa," Ana María murmured, nudging her sister with her hip, "did you have to embarrass the man?"

"I wasn't trying to embarrass him." Isabel furiously fanned herself, pointedly looking away. "I just wanted to remind him not to assume."

"And I believe you succeeded." Concern swept over her, and Ana María lowered her voice. "The gentleman should not have presumed, but have"—she cleared her throat—"you and el Capitán met before?"

"A time or two." Isabel shrugged, still not meeting her gaze. "Why do you ask?"

Ana María carefully kept her expression neutral. "No reason. He seems like a pleasant gentleman."

Isabel scoffed. "I would not call Captain Dawson a gentleman."

"Then what would you call him?" Ana María asked, blinking.

"Rake. Scoundrel." Her sister's lip curled. "Mujeriego."

A damning judgment from Isabel . . . and now Ana María wondered what the man had done to warrant such an assessment.

"Faith, Isa, those are strong words."

"But they're the right words." Isabel angled her face until her hat shielded everything but the stubborn set of her chin. "I first met the capitán in a less-than-ideal situation, and I quickly learned he is not a man I have any interest in knowing or interacting with again."

Ana María blinked. "What do you mean by *less than ideal*?"

"Dios mío, Ana, not now," Isabel growled.

Pressing her lips together, Ana María paused a moment. "Very well, let us hope you have no reason to interact with him in the future."

Isabel made the sign of the cross, her countenance devoutly pious. "So let it be done."

"I thought it was *His will* be done."

"Yes, well, the book of Mark says we should also ask for what we want, so I am making it clear what exactly it is that I desire."

Ana María choked on a laugh before she winged an arm out at her sister. "Shall we? Before there are no seats left for two young women of a curious mind."

The dual entrance doors had been propped open, causing the queue of eager attendees to surge forward, their excited voices rising and falling like ocean waves. In the crowd, Ana María spotted Captain Dawson's brown bowler hat moving among the swarm of people as they made their way to the entrance, and she slid her gaze to Isabel. Unsurprisingly she found her sister's dark gaze following his path, and it took all of Ana María's self-control not to ask again how her sister knew the man.

It must have been something distasteful for her serious, stoic sister to have developed such a dislike of him, and still Ana María was simply happy to see her sister moved by something other than her books.

A short time later, the pair found themselves seated in the back of the auditorium, chattering university students flanking them on all sides. Several of the young men had attempted to start conversations with them, eager and hopeful. But as neither Ana María nor Isabel were in the mood for forced niceties, they pretended not to know English. Isabel offered a pointed commentary in Spanish about a certain gentleman's bad breath with sweet smiles and a friendly tone, and not for the first time, Ana María was struck anew by her sister's witty, sharp banter. Isabel had always given the impression she was more comfortable with fictional interactions than real ones, perhaps concerned with being too awkward or shy. But Ana María found Isabel wasn't awkward in the least, but droll and intuitive, catching subtle details that escaped Ana María's notice.

Once again, she was reminded of how little she knew of her sisters, and her heart ached a tad.

She was ripped from her reflections when an older gentleman stepped to the lectern, and the roar of voices in the room immediately tapered off. After welcoming the crowd, the man launched into a long and effusive introduction of Mr. Darwin, touching on various aspects of his career and work, and Ana María found herself intrigued, for it seemed there was more to the man's studies than she had known.

And truly, how would she have known? Her father closely monitored what she had read, and the only reason Ana María had any frame of reference in regard to Mr. Darwin was that she had overheard snippets of conversations at various gatherings, all spoken with ridicule and scorn, and in some cases true offense. If the people she had overheard were to be believed, Mr. Darwin claimed men were no better than beasts, and rather than being created in God's image, they were no more special than the birds of the air or creatures of the earth. It had made her lip curl when she'd first heard her father rail about it at the dinner table, but in the span of several months, Ana María had learned that much of what she thought she knew had been simply a means to keep her obedient.

It was that epiphany that spawned her need to prove she was more than just a docile doll to be manipulated as her handler saw fit. So Ana María clapped politely as Mr. Darwin took his place at the lectern and greeted the attendees.

Within just minutes of Mr. Darwin's talk, she was mesmerized. As Darwin utilized various charts and grand sketches of animals she had no notion even existed, she found herself balancing on the very edge of her seat as the biologist spoke of his observations in the Galápagos Islands, and the hypotheses he extrapolated from them. Some of his verbiage was unknown to her, but the pitch of his voice made it readily apparent that he was fascinated by the natural world and intent on learning its secrets.

Ana María was awed to learn nature contained more nuances than she had ever realized or been given the time to consider. She'd been taught to think in terms of black and white, right or wrong, all while her father routinely acted in shades of gray. But listening to Mr. Darwin hypothesize how mockingbirds in the Galápagos had changed and adapted to environmental conditions made her realize how, in essence, she had done the same. She, Isabel, and Gabby had arrived in England with very rigid orders on their shoulders, but in their new environment, they were changing. Adapting.

Evolving, perhaps.

Now she listened, a bit spellbound, as she considered the metamorphic change she'd experienced since she arrived on English shores. Oh, she was no scientist, but she had enough sense to know her circumstances were not comparable, yet it made sense to her own mind. She had been raised with particular standards and rules set for her by outside forces, and Ana María had lived for them. Strived for them. However, now the conditions had changed, and the rules that had defined her were no more. She was changing, and she fancied she liked who she was becoming.

"I'm going to walk to the stage to study Mr. Darwin's sketches more closely."

Startled, Ana María blinked until her eyes focused on Isabel. "Por supuesto."

A frown flattened her sister's mouth. "Are you all right?"

She nodded. "Quite well. Mr. Darwin simply gave me much to think about."

"A mí también." Isabel jerked her thumb over her shoulder. "There's quite a crowd up there, so I don't know how well I'll manage to look at the displays, but I intend to try. I'll return in a few minutes." She paused, chewing her lip. "Will you be well?"

A warmth spread in her chest to hear of her sister's concern for her, even if it was not warranted. "Isa, rest assured that I will be fine. Now go and get a good look at that sketch of the tortoise so you can tell me about it. I'm quite curious if it resembles the image I envision in my mind."

Isabel's cheeks went pink as she chuckled. "I have a mental image, too. I'll let you know if we were correct."

Ana María watched as her sister walked to the front of the lecture hall and effortlessly navigated through the bodies of other curious guests, until she lost track of her in the crowd.

Gripping the lecture program in her gloved hands, she pondered all she'd learned from Mr. Darwin's talk. But instead of focusing on her own mental and emotional evolution, she considered what she thought of the man's conjecture and how it contradicted the teachings she had learned in Mass every week. Was it possible to be a good Catholic and embrace Mr. Darwin's evolutionary view at the same time?

"I have never seen quite that look on your face before."

And for the second time in a handful of minutes, Ana María's heart lurched in surprise.

"Mr. Fox," she managed, pressing her hand to her chest. When she had caught her breath, she stared at the man in question. "I was not aware you were in attendance."

He dipped his dark head, but not before Ana María spied how the corners of his plush lips twitched.

Plush lips? Whatever was she on about? She was certain Mr. Darwin had made no mention of plush lips in his speech.

"I must admit to being a bit surprised to learn you were in attendance. I would not have thought such a discussion would be of interest to you."

"Do you know you are the second man to tell us that tonight?" She arched her brow. "Count yourself blessed that it was I you divulged such a thing to and not Isabel, who has already flayed a gentleman for expressing the same opinion."

"Yes, Captain Dawson told me about finding himself on the cutting edge of Señorita Isabel's sharp tongue," he murmured, his dark eyes sparking.

Ana María snorted. "Yet you risked similar treatment by revealing such a thing to me?"

Mr. Fox lifted his shoulders, shrugging as much as his severe black coat would allow. "You strike me as a woman who values honesty, and I was honestly surprised to learn you were here."

"Well, Señor Fox, I contain a multitude." She spread her arms as la Virgen de Guadalupe did in every rendering Ana María had ever seen. "And I confess that I enjoy learning new things and have tried, as of late, to be more open to differing opinions and beliefs."

"An admirable thing." He stared down at her for a long moment, his dark gaze hypnotic as she stared back at him. Blinking, Mr. Fox seemed to snap from his thoughts. He gestured to the seat one over from her own. "May I?"

"Please do."

Swiping his coattails out behind him with a wave of his hands, he sank on the nearby chair, the movement wafting his citrus-and-mint scent her way and filling her nostrils. It was crisp. Comforting in a way that made her want to snuggle into his side and bury her face in his chest so she could saturate her lungs, her blood, with *him*.

"So why the intense, thoughtful look, Señorita Luna?" Mr. Fox angled his broad shoulders until he was facing her, his arm draped over the back of the chair between them. "You seem quite perplexed."

Chewing on the inside of her cheek, Ana María opted for honesty, for he was not wrong when he claimed she valued it. "I find myself waging an internal battle between the truths I have been taught from catechism and what my logical mind is able to grasp from the observations Mr. Darwin has noted."

Mr. Fox made a sound in the back of his throat that Ana María thought might signify agreement. "When I first read *On the Origin of Species* and realized that it was possible my existence was a result not of divine creation but rather because creatures had evolved slowly over generations, I was flabbergasted."

"That is the perfect way to describe how I am feeling at this moment." She folded the program in her hands, smoothing her finger over it until there was a crisp crease. "The thing is, I don't doubt that this is exactly how things evolved for other animals b—"

"But not for humans," Mr. Fox interjected, with an understanding nod.

"Exactly." She added another fold to the program. "Scripture says we were created in God's image, but how can that be possible if we're just evolved apes?"

"Well, if you must know, I'm certain several members of Parliament have not evolved much past our supposed ape ancestors."

Laughter surged up her throat before she could contain it. Although he did not join in her amusement, the light danced in Mr. Fox's dark eyes as he watched her.

Eventually Ana María quieted, and her conflicting thoughts pinged around in her brain once again.

"I can tell by your expression that there's more on your mind."

Her chuckle was dry. "I've always been so good at keeping my thoughts from my face."

Mr. Fox's own manner turned thoughtful. "Well, I will take

it as a compliment that you feel comfortable enough to not shield your inner thoughts from me."

"I don't know about that . . ." she said, laughing in truth when he scowled at her. After a moment, Ana María glanced down at the paper in her hand. "I suppose I'm trying to reconcile a lifetime of teachings. A notion of who I thought I was and what I believed, with this . . . new information. These new *experiences*."

She wasn't just speaking of Mr. Darwin's lecture, and she suspected Fox knew it.

He twirled a ring on his finger, one she had never noticed before, his jaw working as he seemed to formulate his response.

"I think it"—he cleared his throat—"commendable that you are not the sort of person to dismiss ideas or suggestions or theories out of hand because they contradict your own beliefs. Many people are like that, and I believe they are the worse for it. I myself am quick to form an opinion, and it is always an uncomfortable thing when I realize that what I believed"—Fox looked up and captured her gaze—"was wrong."

It was her turn to clear her throat and look away. Perhaps it was an apology for how he had been avoiding her, and maybe it wasn't. Regardless, his words were a balm.

"Now," Mr. Fox continued, "how does that apply to this situation? Where emerging scientific discoveries are challenging religious teachings? Honestly, I don't know."

He shrugged his shoulders. "My priest is of an inquisitive mind. He believes God has given us the curiosity to explore the natural world and the intelligence to make sense of what we find. I'm sure if he were here at this talk, Father Duncan would be pushing aside all those fancy gentlemen and eager students up at the front of the room for a better look at Mr. Darwin's sketches."

"That's what Isabel did." Ana María canted her body toward

him. "Are you Catholic, Señor Fox? Is your Father Duncan a parish priest?"

Fox blinked before he nodded his head. "I believe we are still called *papists* here in England."

Her wits dissipated, and it took Ana María a moment to say, "We've met so few Catholics since we arrived that I'm genuinely surprised to learn you follow Rome's teachings."

"Yes, well, ole Henry the Eighth, and most of the monarchs succeeding him, did their best to erase Catholicism from England, and they have prevailed to a great extent." He spun the ring on his finger again. "But seeing as how my father was a Catholic Scotsman and my grandmother worked on the plantation of a French immigrant family, Catholicism was something both of my parents agreed upon."

Fox focused on a spot in the middle distance, and Ana María knew he was miles—possibly *years*—away. "When my parents died, it was Father Duncan who arranged for me to have a home in the nearby orphanage where he taught, and it was he who ensured I was fed and clothed. Without his patronage, I never would have afforded university or even have had the ambition to attend it."

"It sounds as if he was another father to you, in a way," she whispered.

His normally stern features softened. "Indeed. I'm blessed to still see him every Sunday for Mass."

Her heart leapt. "Where does he hold Mass? Would it be possible for us to attend?"

Frowning, Fox turned to look at her. "It's in Whitechapel. I highly doubt Lady Yardley would approve of you and your sisters venturing there."

Ana María scoffed. "Señor Fox, we literally fled a war. I assure you that any sight we witness will not shock us."

His expression did not change, but Fox nodded. "Very well. I'm willing to escort you and your sisters from Yardley House to Father Duncan's parish this Sunday."

"I would like that very much." A grin pulled her cheeks taut. "And then I can meet this man who encourages you not to be afraid of the world around us, but instead to explore it."

Rubbing a hand along his jaw, Fox turned thoughtful again. "It stems from fear, doesn't it? This need for some people to avoid the pursuit of knowledge, to suppress their curiosity, and to ridicule, shame, and threaten those who do. I find it incredibly frustrating—"

"Howbeit not surprising." Ana María wrinkled her nose. "It would seem to me that some are content to relegate things they do not understand to the realm of magic or witchcraft or otherworldly monsters, instead of approaching new things with a curious mind."

"Are you a science convert, then?" Mr. Fox arched a dark brow. "As Catholics, we have centuries of church history and superstition to guide us through such discoveries. Are you comfortable ignoring that precedence?"

His tone told her he was teasing; nevertheless, she felt his question warranted a serious answer.

"I . . . wouldn't say I'm comfortable ignoring precedence, as you call it." Ana María stared down at the folded program as she ordered her thoughts. "Instead, I want to think that my beliefs are strong enough to withstand counterarguments. And if they aren't able to stand up to scrutiny, then I should examine why not, and make adjustments accordingly."

"How very scientific of you," Mr. Fox said with a chuckle.

"This is my attempt at being logical. For the first time in my life, I'm in a position to explore and learn and grow in ways that aren't dictated to me by others. And part of doing that, in my mind at least, is reconsidering my own personal truths." Ana María opened the folds of the program, revealing the fan she had inadvertently created. "Do I know if Mr. Darwin's assertions are correct? I do not, but he has crafted a convincing argument supported by scientific findings. Just the same, for all that I strive to be logical, it must be said that we humans are still enslaved to our own emotions."

"Mankind is an emotional being." He paused, his mouth quirking. "Do you suppose it is our emotions, and not our intelligence, that separates us from the rest of God's creation?"

"Interesting question." She considered him with keen eyes. "But how very sad it is to think that animals, like Lady Yardley's little Dove, are not capable of feeling emotion. She seems quite devoted to the viscountess, and it would be depressing to think such behavior was not done out of some form of love."

"But if animals have emotions, is it possible to reconcile how we treat them?" he pushed.

"Of course." Ana María's chuckle was dry. "A war is being fought right this minute because one group of men think it their God-given right to own another group of men. If we are willing to treat our fellow humans so horribly, what chance do the creatures of the earth have?"

"Excellent point."

Pulling a handkerchief from his coat, Mr. Fox coughed into it, before neatly folding it and putting it away. She noticed it was a simple square of cotton, with no embellishments or initials stitched into the material. Her fingers suddenly twitched with the desire to do just that for him. To stitch a *G* and an *F* into the cloth, as a sign that someone valued him enough to gift him something pretty. Ana María suspected Mr. Fox had been on his own so long that he'd grown used to the utilitarian, and such details were beneath his notice.

Ana María ached to give him a reason to notice beautiful things again.

With a start, she realized she had been staring at his hands—his large hands, which did odd things to the pit of her stomach. Lifting her gaze, she tensed to find him considering her with intense, smoldering eyes.

By instinct, she rubbed her knuckles against her cheek, thinking she must have something on her face. Or worse. "What is it? Did I say something silly? So much about this topic leaves me out to sea."

Rather than breaking his stare, Mr. Fox continued to regard her, his mouth curving up. "I was simply marveling over your expressions."

"My expressions?" she repeated dumbly.

He nodded, propping his chin on his fist, his gaze unwavering on her face. "You're like a prism, displaying your thoughts and emotions in an array of colorful expressions. I'm sure I could watch you all day."

Her heart slammed against her ribs so forcefully that Ana María was certain Mr. Fox would see how her frame vibrated from the impact. Hypnotized by his gaze, she searched her memory for a time someone—anyone—had ever looked at her as he did now. As if she were fascinating. Intelligent. *Beautiful.*

"Do you know what I have been working toward in Parliament?" he asked all of a sudden, catching her off guard.

Ana María pressed her lips together as she reordered her thoughts. "I believe the Duke of Whitfield mentioned you were hoping to expand the Lyons-Seward Treaty," she murmured.

"In a simplified manner, yes." Propping one leg over the other, Fox relaxed into his seat, his head falling back slightly to look at the ceiling. "I've been working on a matter that is twofold: a proclamation that England will no longer do business with any country that offers port to any ship engaged in the slave trade. The treaty you mentioned outlaws the practice at ports in Britain and the United States, but I want it to include countries in South America. Like Brazil, where slavers' ships still find welcome."

She stared at him unblinking.

"And two, I hope to form an alliance of merchant shippers who not only vow not to engage in the practice, but record information on ships they see on the open seas that do, and report that data to the Crown." He waved a hand. "For compensation, of course."

Her breath stuttered out of her. "How have others responded to your proposal? Do you have support?"

"I do. Lord Montrose has agreed to be my partner on the legislation in Lords." Fox rubbed his chin. "But I would love to add more, so I've been requesting meetings with as many different MPs as possible to win their support."

"And have they agreed to meet with you?" she couldn't help but ask.

His sigh fluttered against his lips. "Most have, but not all."

Her eyes fixed on his face, studying every movement of his features. "Why not?"

"Because sometimes a man of humble origins, with more tenacity than connections, is not afforded the same consideration as his peers." Fox rotated his head to look at her. "Sometimes finding even a smidge of success requires he must forgo his own wants and desires. This is something I've desired, a great wrong I've sought to correct, since I first learned my grandmother's story as a boy."

She bit down so fiercely on her tongue, she tasted copper. Ana María tried to drop her gaze, fought to sever their eye contact, yet it felt as if his dark eyes pinned her in place. So this was the why. Why he had been so circumspect with her. His quest to secure support for his initiative would be thwarted by any public association with her, the Mexican woman whose name found its way into the gossip rags simply because she stepped outside her door. Ana María thought back to the article that had appeared in the paper. The one that had linked them together. The speculation about their relationship must have made his job that much more difficult.

Shame coursed like magma through her veins. Ana María had always done what was expected of her. Had always met every expectation and behaved as the daughter of the formidable Elías Luna Cuate knew she must. But now that she and her sisters were away from their father's influence, whether on them or others, their simple presence in London had separated her from the first man she ever thought she might desire to have for herself.

It was the bitterest of tonics. Ana María could not change who she was—surprisingly did not want to—and she refused to allow society's criticism, or the possibilities of what could have blossomed between her and Mr. Fox, if her hand were free, to change that. She and her sisters deserved the chance to shape their own futures, and while it was a blow to admit it, Mr. Fox would not be a part of hers.

Refolding the program in her lap, Ana María offered him a genuine smile, infused with as much warmth as she could manage. "I admire you, Señor Fox, and I'm certain your parents, and your grandmother, would admire who you've become. I know you'll garner the support you seek, and I hope it, in turn, brings you the greatest satisfaction."

10

"I see you have brought guests with you. How surprising."

Gideon snorted. "Oh yes, I'm sure *surprise* is what you're feeling."

Father Duncan pressed a hand to his mouth, his act of offense surprisingly convincing for a man of the cloth. But Gideon knew better.

"You've never brought friends to Sunday Mass before—"

"Almost all of my friends are Anglican, Father—"

"And then when you do, you bring a trio of pretty young women." The priest clucked his tongue. "Of course I'm surprised."

Gideon slowly lifted his brow. "And?"

Staring at him unblinking for a long moment, Father Duncan finally sighed. "Oh, very well. I am also a bit proud of you."

"Proud of me?" Gideon bumped his shoulder into the old man's. "You are too kind."

"And you are too snide for your own good." Father Duncan folded his hands together behind his waist, his eyes trained on where Ana María and her sisters stood on the narrow walkway leading into the church, speaking with several members of the congregation. It was not every Sunday they received guests, and certainly not guests of the Luna sisters' stature.

Not that the ladies had dressed or behaved ostentatiously. On the contrary, they had sat near the back of the nave wearing simple dresses devoid of embellishment and in nondescript colors. Despite this, the cut and quality of their attire, the tilt of their chins, and the healthy glow of their cheeks bespoke their wealth. They proclaimed their quality.

Ana María looked over at them then, a soft smile on her lips as she spoke with a young female parishioner balancing a baby on her hip and with a toddler clinging to her leg. She held his gaze for a passing moment before turning back to continue her conversation with the young mother, yet it took Gideon's heart longer to return to its normal pace.

What was it about seeing Ana María in this situation that made his chest ache? Was it how effortlessly she seemed to fit into the flock? Was it the gentle manner in which she interacted with the parishioners, many of whom society would curl their lips at in disdain? But Gideon had not once glimpsed disdain on Ana María's face . . . because he had found it very difficult to look away from her. For while he had always thought her lovely, in this setting, surrounded by people he had known for years and whom he considered friends—even *family*—sunshine bathing them in a warm glow, she was stunning.

This is where she belongs, his heart whispered to him, not in some Mayfair drawing room where she would be a doll in some pompous lord's collection. Not in a villa in Mexico City, the forgotten wife of some elevated politician. For here, among the modest people of the neighborhood, she shined, for she was herself.

Gideon tore his gaze away. It was not his place to tell Miss

Luna where she belonged, and it was certainly a flight of fancy to believe she might belong with *him*.

Just thinking such a thing felt forbidden and sent heat flooding his cheeks and racing to pool low in his belly.

"I assume these are the sisters from Mexico that the papers have spoken of."

He nodded. "The very same."

"Where have they been attending services?" Father Duncan asked, dipping his head in goodbye at a parishioner who walked past.

"St. Monica's."

The priest whistled through his teeth. "That's quite a trek from Mayfair."

"I suppose next you'll say it's a sign of their devotion," Gideon drolled.

"You know me well." Father Duncan's tone turned from diverted to contemplative. "Still, they seem quite comfortable here among the parishioners. Perhaps they will return." Gideon could feel the priest's gaze on him. "Would you mind if they returned?"

"Of course not," he blurted out a tad too quickly, imagining the knowing smile on Father Duncan's face but not looking to confirm its presence.

"Is that because you are—perhaps—interested in spending more time with the eldest Miss Luna?"

Gideon scowled at the man, before he peeked at the young woman in question. She was nodding her head while an older widow gestured about as she spoke. Ripping his gaze away to refocus on Father Duncan, the man was watching him with a triumphant smile.

He rolled his eyes. Gideon knew there was no use in prevaricating.

"Miss Luna has a future husband waiting for her in Mexico." He flexed his jaw. "And even if she didn't, I cannot allow myself to be distracted. Too much is on the line."

With a strong clasp on Gideon's shoulder, Father Duncan dropped his voice. "Have there been any developments?"

Gideon nodded.

"Come tell me about it," the priest said.

Father Duncan turned to walk back inside the dimly lit sanctuary, but Gideon paused on the threshold, his gaze seeking Ana María's once again. But the baby she had been admiring was now in her arms, and her pink lips were stretched into a broad smile. Gideon's throat felt impossibly tight as he looked on, his mind wandering down inconvenient paths—

"Gideon, are you coming?" Father Duncan called.

After pausing to collect his bearing, Gideon made his way to the priest, who invited him to sit on the hard wooden pew right before the altar, a spot where they had sat and discussed all manner of things during his childhood. He and Father Duncan had always spoken freely with each other, and already the thought of sharing some of his burden with his old friend lifted a weight from his shoulders he had not realized was there.

Angling his body on the pew so he could keep one eye on the sanctuary door, Gideon divulged all that had transpired since they had last spoken. He told him of the MPs and lords that he and Lord Montrose had identified as men who had supported the original treaty the year before, and who may be open to Gideon's new iteration.

"But we need additional support if we're to have any impact," he confessed.

Tucking a fist under his chin, Father Duncan furrowed his brow. "Whose support, if won, would ensure your proposal passed both houses?"

Gideon pinched the bridge of his nose. "Montrose and I have identified several men, each more unlikely than the next."

"And yet great things often occur when the odds are unfavorable."

Huffing a breath, Gideon shook his head, the saying reminding him of all the times the old priest had recited it to him.

"Yes but—"

"Excuse me, gentlemen?"

Glancing to the open vestibule door, Gideon found Ana María standing within the frame, bathed in bright sunlight. He blinked several times at the sight.

"Have I kept you and your sisters waiting?" Rising to his feet, he jerked on the fall of his coat as he stepped into the aisle.

"It does not feel much like waiting when surrounded by good company," she said with a warm laugh.

Coming to a stop before her, Gideon permitted his gaze free rein to study her large doe eyes and full bow-shaped mouth. "Still, you are supposed to be my guests, and I've slipped away and left you unaccompanied. My apologies."

"It is I who should be apologizing." Father Duncan slapped him on the back. "Much has happened since I saw Gideon last, and I was eager for an update. I apologize for my rudeness, Miss Luna."

"I assure you that apologies are unnecessary. My sisters and I have had a thoroughly diverting visit." Ana María grinned. "Padre, your congregation is filled with truly gracious people, and we have enjoyed ourselves immensely."

Father Duncan winged out an arm to her, and when she accepted it, he escorted her back into the gleaming sunshine. Gideon followed behind them, listening as Ana María asked the priest about the social programs the church hosted, sharing how her parish in Mexico City had health clinics for the parishioners once a month. Father Duncan exclaimed what a clever idea that was, and Gideon contained a smile as the two chatted animatedly about the details. Stepping from the building, he spied Isabel in conversation with an elderly couple while Gabby played with several children nearby.

"I'm ever so pleased you and your sisters took the sacraments with us this day." Father Duncan patted her arm. "I hope you return soon."

Ana María glanced over her shoulder then, her serious dark gaze meeting his. "I speak for my sisters when I say we would love to . . . if Señor Fox does not mind, of course."

"Of course not," he answered automatically.

Gideon knew he should mind, but it was getting harder and harder to remember why.

The return ride to Yardley House proved to be enjoyable. Not because Gabby, and to a lesser extent Isabel, chattered excitedly about the people they met and Father Duncan's sermon, but because Gideon rode next to Ana María on the narrow squab. Shoulder to shoulder. Thigh pressed against thigh. Gideon felt delirious with her jasmine scent floating about him, and it took every bit of his self-control to focus on her sisters.

"Señor Fox, please tell me that we are allowed to return," Gabby exclaimed.

Although it took a moment for his brain to relocate to his head, he managed a nod. "O-of course. Father Duncan already extended an invitation to your sister."

"He was most gracious, too," Ana María said, laughing when Gabby clapped her hands.

While her two sisters continued to discuss their morning at Father Duncan's parish, Ana María turned her chin toward him and whispered, "Thank you."

"For inviting you?" When she nodded, Gideon continued. "It was my pleasure. And I'm a bit relieved you and your sisters enjoyed yourselves."

"Relieved?" She tilted her head. "Why relieved?"

Gideon lifted a shoulder. "You ladies spend your days surrounded by fine things. With people who are cultured and sophisticated—"

"I believe you're giving the group as a whole too much credit," Ana María interjected with a wry smirk.

"Probably," he said around a chuckle. "Still, the parishioners who attend Father Duncan's parish are everyday, working-class people."

"The salt of the earth," she said.

He nodded, glancing down to hold her gaze. "Precisely. And I've found that those who occupy high society have no interest in fraternizing with those who are the backbone of our country. They turn their noses up at them as if their wealth and comfort and privilege aren't dependent upon the very same people they scorn."

Ana María wrinkled her nose. "And you believed I would scorn the parishioners?"

His shoulders sagged a bit. "Actually, I didn't. From what I have come to know of you these many weeks, I could not see you behaving in such a manner. But then receiving confirmation was a relief."

"Aah." She dropped her gaze to stare at her hands knotted in her lap. "It was a relief for me, too, if I'm honest."

Gideon angled his shoulders about to look at her fully. "In what way were *you* relieved?"

Her lashes were dark fans against the swells of her cheekbones. "It was a relief to see that you are just as austere and reserved with these people you've known for years as you are with me."

"You believe me austere?" he asked.

Ana María nodded, still not meeting his gaze. "I believe you can be. Not all the time, of course, but the more I come to know you, the more I think it just a part of your character."

"Interesting," Gideon murmured, angling his head to stare out the carriage window.

He sensed rather than saw her look up at him. "I hope I have not offended you."

"Of course not." Against his better judgment, Gideon patted her knotted hands, his skin feeling hot and flushed. "It is just unfathomable to me that I've managed to hide how much you affect me."

Unable to keep his gaze away, Gideon glanced down to discover her lush lips had parted into a perfect O. "What do you mean?" she asked breathlessly.

His palms were clammy and his throat was dry, but Gideon refused to look away. "Every second I'm with you, Miss Luna, is like—"

"Whoa," the driver called from outside the carriage, and their bodies swayed forward with the force of the stop. Isabel grasped the door handle without waiting for the footman to open it, but allowed the servant to assist her down the carriage steps. Gideon watched as Gabby followed her out, before he dared to look at Ana María once again. Color was high in her cheeks, and her pulse raced at the base of her throat. For a moment Gideon imagined what her skin would taste like if he pressed his lips there.

"Mr. Fox?" she whispered, not making any move to exit the carriage.

He had to tell her. Ana María Luna may have been promised to another man, but she had to know how she left him at sixes and sevens whenever she was near. Whenever he smelled her alluring scent. Met her soulful dark eyes from across a ballroom. How no day had passed that he hadn't thought of her. She could never be his, but Gideon had to tell her of how much he wished she could be.

Licking his lips, Gideon opened his mouth—

"Ana, are you coming?"

They turned in unison to see her sisters standing together on the walk, their brows stitched together as they stared back at them. Ana María exhaled raggedly next to him.

"Yes, my apologies," she called, moving to exit the carriage. On the top step, though, she paused and looked at him over her shoulder. "Good day, Señor Fox."

Gideon allowed the footman to close the carriage door, before he dropped his head on the seat back and pounded a fist against his mouth.

"I haven't been this happy about going to Mass in months. Maybe years," Gabby announced as they entered the sitting room situated among the family bedrooms on the second floor of Yardley House. Plucking her fascinator from her mahogany curls, she tossed it onto a nearby cushion, where Consuelo immediately snatched it up lest it get damaged. "The people were much more friendly and welcoming than any reception we've received since arriving on this godforsaken island."

"Gabby, really, watch your language," Ana María scolded distractedly as she watched Mr. Fox's carriage disappear down the street. *What had he been about to say—*

"But it's true. Don't you agree, Isa?"

"I do." Isabel sorted through a basket she had filled with various books from her collection before she selected a brown leather-covered book and sank into a deep armchair. "The experience was much less about being seen and more about the message and service itself. Quite a refreshing change of pace."

"And Father Duncan was quite good, was he not?" Gabby added.

"He was charming." Ana María smiled vaguely as a maid wheeled a tea cart into the room. "Very engaging and personable."

Gabby snorted. "High praise, indeed. It seems that most of the people we have met are incapable of even smiling."

"It's the fear of wrinkles." Isabel smirked from over the top of her book. "Can't smile too much, you know."

"What is this talk about wrinkles?" Lady Yardley inquired as she sailed into the room, Dove tucked under her arm. After she situated herself in her wingback chair and allowed a maid to slide a tufted ottoman under her feet, her blue-eyed gaze focused on each of them in turn. "Was there discussion of wrinkles at this papal church you attended?"

"There was, your ladyship. We were reminded that the sacrament of Communion erases lines and wrinkles, and makes gray hairs disappear." Gabby raised her brows. "Perhaps you should join us for Mass next Sunday."

The words were uttered with such easy droll, it took Ana María a moment to realize her sister was joking.

The viscountess's expression changed not one whit, for she was now quite acquainted with Gabby's sharp tongue.

"I asked about wrinkles because Mrs. Palmers, who owns that stylish perfumery on the Strand, sent around a note that she had received several new beauty products she thought might be of interest to me." She patted her cheek with a gloved hand. "She knows how keen I am to keep my complexion refreshed and the glow in my cheeks."

The sitting room door opened then, and Bauer, the viscountess's maid, strolled in carrying a parchment-wrapped parcel topped with an elegantly tied pink bow. Setting it on the table at the viscountess's elbow, she retreated to a chair in the corner of the room with Consuelo.

"Let's see what treasures Mrs. Palmers has sent," Lady Yardley squealed.

Placing Dove on the floor, she eagerly grasped the pink bow and untied it, before lifting the top of the box and setting it aside. With impatient motions, the viscountess tossed the packing paper included in the box behind her head and pulled out bottles, reading the labels aloud to the sisters.

"Cold cream, with a bit extra added for that coveted glow." The viscountess shimmied her shoulders. "A dewy complexion has never been amiss."

"If a dewy complexion is all the rage, than I am an original, for I positively glow every year during the rainy season in Mexico City." Gabby smirked as she scratched Dove behind her ear after the dog had settled into her lap.

"I'm certain a dewy glow is quite different from a . . . from a—"

"Perspiration glow?"

Gabby succeeded in coaxing an eye roll from Lady Yardley.

The viscountess continued to catalog the skin care products that Mrs. Palmer had included, exclaiming over several, and encouraging Ana María and Gabby to sample them. Ana María tried to muster the excitement Lady Yardley was obviously expecting, but her thoughts were in an uproar. *How do I affect Mr. Fox?* If the fire burning in his dark eyes was any indication, his words would have reduced her to ash. So why would she care about having a dewy complexion or pillowy lips when—

"And this one is for you, Isabel," Lady Yardley said, extending a white tube toward her.

Isabel slowly lowered her book, her brow furrowing. "For me? What is it?"

"It's whitening cream. I thought it might help you feel"—she gestured with the tube to Isabel's face—"more confident in the ballroom."

Ana María's mouth fell open as her jaw unhinged. She could not even gasp, for the room was suddenly devoid of air, and she carefully slid her wide eyes to her sister.

Blinking rapidly, Isabel set her book aside and rose to her feet. Her footfalls across the carpet were silent, but Ana María's heartbeat slowed to match every step. Taking the tube from Lady Yardley, she pivoted and walked back to her seat without a word. Isabel had dropped her chin, but the position could not hide the crimson staining her cheeks.

"Why do you think that would help Isabel with her confidence?"

Gabby asked the question with a blithe tone, but Ana María knew better. Her sister's eyes were hazel flints, and her nostrils flared with every breath she took.

Lady Yardley shrugged, not looking up from a small vial she was studying. "Well, she's quite dark, isn't she? I thought if we could lighten her skin a bit, she may feel more comfortable engaging with other young people and dancing with gentlemen at balls. Surely she would have more fun doing that than retreating to the library to spend the evening with a book."

"Escaping with a book sounds lovely to me, and I am not even a great reader," Gabby declared.

The viscountess snorted as she removed her gloves and dabbed cream on the back of her hand.

"Isabel doesn't need this." Gabby crossed the room and ripped the white tube from Isabel's hand. "Why would she want to be a pale version of herself when she was born to stand out? When her skin has been touched by the sun?"

Looking up, Lady Yardley stared with a frown at first Gabby and then Isabel. "There is no reason to be upset, Gabriela. I was simply trying to help. A light complexion has always been prized, so I thought such a cream might prove useful."

"I appreciate your concern, my lady," Ana María began stiffly, "but there's no need—"

"Not *everyone* prizes light skin," Gabby hissed, stomping her foot. "Isabel's features, including her dark skin, are gifts from our people. Of those who lived and breathed and loved for hundreds of years since before the world knew it as Mexico, and were never defeated by the Tenochca Empire." She flung a hand out at Isabel. "Her bronze skin was worn by warriors. By survivors. To bleach it away because of some grotesque beauty standard would be a cruel sin."

Ana María pressed a handkerchief to her mouth at Gabby's fiery defense of their sister, but Isabel just stared at her, a sad smile on her lips.

"Gracias, Gabby, pero no hay nada de qué preocuparte."

"Of course there is!" Gabby dropped down to her knee in front of Isabel's chair, quite a feat in her skirts. Grasping her hand, she said, "You're beautiful, Isa. I've always been so envious of you, with your lovely skin that looks stunning in every color. You don't look washed out and sickly when you wear yellow."

Isabel chortled.

"And your hair can hold a curl and is only prettier when it rains, while mine droops and makes me look like Dove after Bauer has given her a bath."

"You're being ridiculous," Isabel said, fond exasperation in her voice.

"But I'm not. What's ridiculous is that people think if you somehow look like everyone else, you'll be beautiful. But that's boring." She squeezed Isabel's hand. "And you're anything but boring, Isa."

At some point during Gabby's passionate speech, Lady Yardley returned to studying the contents of the box with a huff, unable to understand their rapid Spanish. But Ana María had begun to cry and only realized it when Dove jumped into her lap and began to lick her cheeks. Pushing the little dog away, she took a moment to clear her throat before she rose and crossed to her sisters. Pressing next to Isabel's side, she joined their hands together.

"Isa, I hope you know that Father's opinions are not ours." She stared down at their hands rather than meet her sister's gaze. "I believe he sees Abuela in you . . . and he's tried so hard to overcome that past. But however he views you, whatever he has planned for your future, doesn't have to be how you view yourself. His plans don't have to be yours. You know that, right?"

From the corner of her eye, she saw Isabel nod. "I know. Being here in London . . . with the two of you . . . has made it easier to think that's true."

"Same with me." Gabby plopped onto the settee on Isabel's other side. "In Mexico, I knew it was only a matter of time before Father sold me into marriage, like he did Ana."

Ana María flinched, and Isabel squeezed her fingers in response.

"And that still may be my future. We may return after the

French are defeated and Presidente Juárez is reinstated, and an ally of Father's is waiting to claim me . . . and my dowry." Her frustrated sigh drew Ana María's gaze. Instead of finding Gabby looking forlorn, her sister had her shoulders thrown back, her chin high, with a hard look in her hazel eyes. "But until that happens, I intend to take advantage of this freedom I have and get to know the Gabriela Luna I want to be, and not the one Father tells me I am."

"They wanted to put me in a convent."

Clutching a hand to her mouth to stifle a gasp, Ana María looked at Isabel with wide eyes. "What do you mean?"

Isabel lifted a shoulder. "I overheard them speaking on their balcony. I was walking around the garden because I had read there was to be meteor shower and I didn't want to miss it."

"What did they say?" Gabby demanded.

"Father was . . ." She shuddered a breath. "Complaining that I kept hiding during events. Just like her ladyship. He was angry I continued to show more interest in books than in any of the gentlemen who came to court his favor."

"Well, of course you'd be more interested in your books," Gabby scoffed. "I'd be more inclined to read your books than to be forced to hold a conversation with those tontos."

Ana María nudged Isabel's shoulder with her own. "And what did Mother say to this?"

Isabel was quiet for a pregnant moment, and when she finally spoke, Ana María had to lean close to hear her words. "She said that they should ask Padre Ignacio for recommendations for convents that might be a good fit for me."

Ana María clenched her eyes closed. That their mother had suggested Isabel take up the habit was a cruel twist.

"Perhaps she thought you would be happy as a nun," she offered quietly.

"Perhaps," Isabel whispered.

"But you don't want to be a nun, do you, Isa?" Gabby asked. Isabel shook her head.

"Well, then you won't be," Ana María declared. "And you don't have to use any of these nonsensical products to make you into something you're not." She shifted until she faced her sisters, meeting first Gabby's earnest gaze and then Isabel's guarded one. "If only for this time we are on English shores, we will be the truest forms of ourselves. No more living up to expectations we did not set for ourselves. No more treating each other like enemies when we were born to be friends."

Plopping her chin on Isabel's shoulder, Gabby nodded. "Friends."

Isabel blinked until her tears cleared her eyes. "Friends."

Ana María beamed at her sisters, although the sight of them grew a bit blurry behind her watery eyes.

"Considering you all were speaking in Spanish, I have no notion of what has just transpired, but it appears as if the three of you have come to some sort of pact."

Lady Yardley's drawl brought their heads about, and the older woman regarded them from her chair, Dove happily curled in her arms.

With a prim nod, Ana María said, "We wanted Isabel to know she didn't need to change anything about her appearance."

"She's quite perfect just the way she is," Gabby added, glaring at the viscountess.

"Put away your claws, Gabriela. I did not mean to cause offense." Lady Yardley looked to Isabel. "I apologize. I should have been more thoughtful."

Isabel nodded, but said nothing more.

The older woman's gaze skimmed over the three of them before she raised a teacup and saucer to her lips. "I fancy I'm starting to understand some of the Spanish words you use."

"Please don't," Gabby replied, "for then how will we be able to speak of—"

"Your ladyship," Ana María interrupted, casting her youngest sister a censorious look, "it's never a wasted skill to be proficient in another language."

"I would agree, but then who do I know that speaks Spanish aside from you and your uncle?" the viscountess grumbled.

"But think about how you can gossip about your friends right in front of their faces, and they would never know," Gabby countered.

Lady Yardley sucked in her breath. "I wouldn't dream of doing such a thing."

Ana María pressed her lips together rather than respond, and apparently her sisters were of the same mindset, for neither of them spoke. They'd quickly learned that the viscountess enjoyed knowing the latest gossip and was not above passing it along to others.

When the silence in the room had stretched for an uncomfortable moment, Lady Yardley finally chuckled. "Although, I do so much like the idea of being able to have a private conversation in the midst of a crowd."

"It is definitely a perk," Ana María agreed.

Exchanging an amused glance with her sisters, she was once again thankful for these simple moments when they could be diverted together.

11

"Ladies, the carriage will be at the front curb in exactly ten minutes, and if you are not ready by then, you will be left behind."

"That's quite cutthroat of you, your ladyship," Gabby said as she donned an emerald earring.

"Well, if you had begun dressing for tonight's festivities when I told you to earlier this evening, you would not be rushing now." Lady Yardley gestured to where Ana María lounged by the fire, sipping a glass of claret. "Your sister heeded my words and now she won't be flustered when she steps into the carriage."

"Not everyone can be perfect like Ana," Gabby grumbled, but any sting that may have been present in her words was blunted by the teasing look she tossed Ana María's way.

"I don't like to rush." Raising her glass, she waggled her brows. "It's a shame you don't have time to enjoy a glass with me."

"Oh, I intend to have a glass, or at the very least sneak a fla—"

A knock on the front door halted her words. The sisters turned to Lady Yardley, who had crossed to the windows that overlooked the street, pushing the drape aside to peer out.

"I believe it's your uncle."

"Tío Arturo?" Ana María set her half-empty wineglass aside, her legs abruptly shaking as she rose to her feet. "Why would he be here?"

"And at this time?" Isabel added.

The sound of footsteps in the hallway drew their attention, and at the sharp rap on the door, the viscountess bid the person to enter.

Evans, Lady Yardley's butler, stood on the threshold. "Mr. Valdés is here to see you, my lady."

Without waiting to be invited in, Tío Arturo stepped into the room. With a soft thank-you to Evans, he promptly closed the door behind the man.

Her stomach sank, for Ana María had never seen him in such an unsettled state. While his physical demeanor appeared unchanged, there was a hitch in his step, a manic fret to his motions, and a wildness in his hazel eyes that reflected his agitation. What could have possibly upset her normally jovial tío in such a way?

"Mr. Valdés," Lady Yardley breathed, setting her own wineglass down and advancing toward him to grasp his hand. It was apparent she, too, had recognized his distress. "Has something happened?"

Tío Arturo squeezed her hand before he swept his black coattails out behind him and sank like a stone into one of Lady Yardley's armchairs. In a macabre sort of way, it reminded Ana María of the afternoon they had first arrived in London . . . but instead of his gracious smiles, they were met with his anxiety and distress.

"I think it would be best"—he jerked on his coat—"if my nieces were removed from London for a spell."

"Why?" Ana María demanded, her tone neither soft nor deferential.

"Because"—Tío Arturo ran a hand along his chin—"we've received intelligence that French sympathizers have been targeting Mexican citizens or individuals with ties to Mexico to leverage them for bounty or favors from the French."

Ana María sucked in a breath, the sound not quite drowning out Gabby's exclamation or Lady Yardley's startled gasp.

"Are they in danger, Arturo?" the older woman managed.

"I don't believe so, but I don't want to take a chance." He clasped his hands together and tapped his closed fist against his mouth. "We were wise to keep the girls' connection to the Juárez government secret, but that certainly doesn't mean their true identity hasn't been discovered. Luna is not the most unique of names."

The room was silent, the air heavy and thick with tension before Isabel broke it.

"So let's think this through," she said, standing to pace across the room. "If it were discovered our father is a Mexican government official, how would they be able to use us against the cause for freedom?"

"They could hold you for ransom." Tío Arturo rubbed his temple. "And if these hypothetical abductors were smart enough, they could petition the Valdés family for your return."

"As if the Valdés family would pay our ransom," Gabby scoffed.

"I would make sure we did," Tío Arturo avowed, and her sister sagged a bit at his words.

"But that is assuming they discover the connection. What if they don't?" Lady Yardley pressed as she extended a glass of wine to him.

"I don't know." Tío Arturo raised the glass to the light, studying the dark liquid for a tense moment before he put the glass to his lips and took a long slug. Wiping his sleeve across his mouth, he said, "Do you know several influential British papers lauded Napoleon for capturing Mexico? One said he was to be praised for defeating"—he raised an arm to crook his fingers into quotation marks—"'one of the most degenerate and despised races of either hemisphere.'"

"Did they really print that, Tío?" Isabel asked on a whisper.

"They did, mija." He plopped his elbows on his spread knees and dropped his head. "The English only care about men named Napoleon when they believe he is a threat to them. To Europe. But for his offenses in Mexico, they've congratulated him. I've been proud to represent Mexico, to speak for the Juárez government here in London, but that article, and dozens of others like it, reminded me that the British see no pride in my role, for Mexico holds no value to them."

Fire burned in Ana María's throat and in the backs of her eyes, and she clenched them closed, desperate to contain the tears, the sobs, that threatened to overwhelm her. Inexplicably, Mr. Fox's fierce face appeared in her thoughts. Wasn't he fighting for something similar? Wasn't he demanding the British government—the people—recognize an injustice and fix it? Dios mío, how she wished he were in the room with them now to help them plan. To strategize. To hold her hand and tell her everything would be well.

"That's why I thought it imperative for you three to be the faces, the voices, of the Mexican people. I knew we needed to challenge the notion that Mexico was nothing but mestizos in need of a master, and what better way to do it than with three charming, intelligent, furiously proud mexicanas." Tío Arturo expelled a noisy breath. "And I fear I have made you targets for our enemies instead."

The walls of Yardley House suddenly felt too confining, as if they were inching closer and closer about her with every second that ticked off the clock on the mantel. Ana María reached for her own wineglass again, purposely ignoring how her hand shook and sloshed the acerbic liquid about. Although she took an ample mouthful, her tongue and mind registered no taste.

"I think a break from town would be just the thing." Lady Yardley stalked to the narrow box perched on the side table next to her preferred armchair. Bauer used it to sort and store the various invitations they received for the viscountess's convenience. Now, with a single-minded focus, the viscountess shuffled through its contents while Ana María willed her wine to numb her tumultuous emotions.

"Here it is," she exclaimed, brandishing a simple but elegant envelope in the air. Gliding across the room, she thrust it into Tío Arturo's hand. "Will this work?"

Unfolding the invitation, he skimmed over the lines before a weary sigh fell from his lips. "Lord Tyrell is a longtime member of Parliament with an estate in Devonshire, and he commands a great deal of respect from his peers."

"Is he of the type to agree with that hateful sentiment you shared?" Gabby asked, her expression mutinous.

"He is." Lady Yardley cast Tío Arturo a scowl when he opened his mouth to argue. "Earl Tyrell is a cold, calculating man, and I had intended to send our regrets to the invitation. But now—"

"But now we can't afford to wait for a kind host when we simply require a welcoming one," Ana María intoned.

She slid her gaze to Isabel and Gabby, who both stared back at her with wide eyes. They sought reassurances, and as their older sister, she ached to do just that. Instead, Ana María looked away. How could she possibly reassure them, pretend everything would be well, when so much about their present situation was precarious and unknown?

"Do you wish for me to send our acceptance, then?" Lady Yardley strummed the corner of the invitation against her gloved finger, the sound muffled yet still distinctive. Probably because the action served as a metronome for Ana María's own heartbeat.

"Yes." Tío Arturo scrubbed a hand down his face. "I want you all safe, and I will feel a measure of confidence if you are away from this blasted city."

Icy fingers crept up her back and along her scalp, and Ana María fought the urge to shudder. Their life in Mexico had been spent living under a display case, their every movement dictated and watched, if not by their father, then by the guards who had been hired to mind them. Ana María had always chafed at these high-handed ways . . . but now she almost wished to have that level of protection again. To be viewed as something treasured, instead of something to despise.

They had been living an idyllic dream since landing in London, but that bubble had now popped. Now their blitheness, their gaiety, was gone, and once again they had to worry about their own safety. Ana María hiccuped a sob at the thought.

"And what of tonight?" Gabby asked. "Are we not to attend the Maddox ball after all?"

Tío Arturo shook his head. "We do not want to alert anyone that we are aware of the threat. I want you to continue to behave as if nothing has occurred, so when you leave for Tyrell's house party, it is not seen as suspicious."

"So we're supposed to act like nothing is wrong even while French sympathizers could be working to abduct us?" Isabel threw her hands up.

"I'm a terrible actress, Tío," Gabby interjected.

Their uncle slashed his hand through the air, and the room fell silent. "I will escort you tonight, and anywhere else you must go before the Tyrell house party." He fiddled with his gold cuff link. "I have hired additional security, and they will shadow us as discreetly as possible."

Clearing her throat, Ana María ventured, "With all due respect, any desire I had to attend tonight's festivities has been smothered after this revelation."

Isabel and Gabby nodded in agreement.

Their support caused her to raise her chin as she slid her gaze back to their uncle. "I believe it would be best if we skipped tonight's ball, and instead discuss any contingency plans we may need to execute should one or all of us fall into enemy hands."

Tío Arturo stared at her for a taut moment, until he slowly nodded his head. "Very well. If that will make you all feel better, I agree, mijitas. I promised your mother I would keep you all safe, and I intend to do that."

"Gracias for telling us about the danger." Ana María rose and pressed a quick kiss to his cheek. "Our father would have kept the threat from us, so I appreciate your trust. Mis hermanas and I will return it by doing what we can to keep ourselves safe."

Gabby's loud grumble brought their heads about. She had peeled off her gloves and was staring at the decanters on the sideboard. "I'm not heartbroken to have missed the Maddox ball tonight, but I have enjoyed going to museums or salons or for walks in the park without requiring permission first. Are we to be locked away again?"

Ana María went still, darting her gaze to her uncle.

Tío Arturo's expression was soft as he gazed at Gabby, and then slowly took in Isabel, before he finally met her eyes. "Of course not, Gabriela. It is still important that you showcase that winning personality and beautiful face for Mexico, for until the French are driven from our shores, their threat will remain. We will just be cautious from here on out. ¿Sí?"

"Perfecto," Ana María answered, finally allowing her back to relax against her chair.

"I spoke with Anders this morning at the club, and he committed his support. So we have another yes vote."

Gideon dropped back his head and tapped a fist against his forehead, uncaring that Montrose's office door was open and anyone walking by in the Westminster halls could see his uncharacteristic display of emotion. But he was just so damn relieved. After months of working with the marquess to garner support for their measure, they were now within a handful of votes of moving the resolution forward.

The massive, invisible load that rested on his chest grew lighter with each vote they procured. If Ana María were here, she would make some droll comment about him looking almost happy. His mouth quivered around a smile thinking about her reaction—

"I take it you are pleased with the news."

He coughed into his fist. "Very pleased. I wasn't optimistic Anders would be open to the idea, but I am relieved to have been proven wrong."

"Old Anders is a lot of hot air until you pinpoint his pet interests." Montrose raised his teacup but paused, cocking his brow at Gideon. "And I know what those interests are."

"And for that I am thankful."

"Don't be too thankful," the marquess tsked under his breath. "for not even my stellar negotiation tactics could appease my lady wife's distaste for your friend."

Gideon frowned. "My friend?"

"The eldest Miss Luna," Lord Montrose said archly.

A litany of curse words assaulted his thoughts, but Gideon did his best to school his expression. "I find Miss Luna to be quite charming and clever, if a bit bold."

It felt like a diplomatic answer, and the marquess merely held his gaze for a tense moment, and returned his attention to the paperwork before him.

He had worked side by side with Lord Montrose over the weeks to bring this issue before Parliament, and Gideon had learned a great deal from the man along the way. Not just the maneuvers the marquess employed to accomplish his objectives, but about the *air* he carried about himself. As if he believed the world waited with bated breath for his opinion. As if every vote, every decision, every critical national issue would benefit if only Lord Montrose shared his thoughts on it.

A childhood spent in Whitechapel had not taught Gideon such self-possession. He had never believed society was eager for the ramblings of his mind. His position in Parliament was not because it was his *due*, but because he had worked and worked, some nights until he could barely keep his eyes open and his fingertips were worn raw from scrubbing at the floors and fixtures of the university library, where he earned extra money in between classes. There was no room for hubris in such places while completing such tasks.

But watching Montrose wield his knowledge of his contemporaries and capitalize on their weaknesses, Gideon was reminded that while he never felt entitled to success, he had enough pride in his work to expect it.

His grandmother made sure of that.

Fortifying his spine with his signature grit, Gideon reached for his teacup and added an extra sugar cube simply because he could.

"We're still short several votes." Montrose relaxed into his chair, linking his hands over his waist. "But I have some ideas on how we can win them."

The men chewed over the marquess's ideas for a time, when

Montrose pushed his seat back from his desk and rose to his feet. Crossing to the small table nestled under the narrow window on the other side of the room, he considered the liquor bottles on display, before peering at Gideon over his shoulder. "What will you have?"

"I'll have whatever you're having," he murmured.

A moment later a glass was dropped down with a thud on the desktop before him. Without taking a moment to consider its contents, Gideon grasped it and tipped back the glass, welcoming the warmth that calmed his mind.

The marquess propped one leg over the other and considered Gideon over his own glass. "I confess that I had an ulterior motive for offering you a drink when I did."

Tilting his head to the side, Gideon ignored how his pulse jumped at the man's words. "Am I to assume liquor is required for this revelation?"

Montrose grunted as he studied the alcohol in his glass. "It may make it more . . . palatable."

"What is it, then?" he asked, setting his glass down with a thud.

"The Tyrell house party."

Gideon's racing thoughts stumbled to a halt. "I beg your pardon."

"Earl Tyrell is hosting a two-week house party at his estate in Devonshire. He doesn't entertain very often, so the fact that he is holding such a gathering is *fortuitous*." The marquess uncurled one of his fingers from his glass to point it at Gideon. "I secured you an invitation to attend."

He jerked his chin back. "Why me? I don't even know the man."

Not that he had not heard of Earl Tyrell. The earl had been an active, loud, and influential voice in Lords since Gideon was a child. Although they'd never been introduced, he'd seen the man in the halls of Westminster, Tyrell always surrounded by a gaggle of assistants and sycophants. From the talk he'd heard, the earl was rumored to be a hard man who possessed a sharp intellect and a cruel wit. But he never lacked for support on his proposals, and securing his vote on a measure almost guaranteed its success.

Which was why gaining Tyrell's support would be crucial. Gideon expelled a loud huff.

"The house party conflicts with a wedding Lady Montrose and I are attending in Suffolk, so we cannot attend." The marquess speared Gideon with a sharp look. "And this is your proposal, Fox. I know I don't have to tell you how instrumental Tyrell's support would be."

"From what I heard, he was opposed to the Lyons-Seward Treaty." Gideon shook his head. "Why do you believe he would support this?"

Montrose tapped his pen against the desk, his gaze unfaltering. "I don't know that he will. Tyrell has always been a bit hard to pin down. But what I do know is that the more men we prevail upon, the greater our chances of success."

Raising his glass, Montrose took a deep swallow. A predatory look darkened his features. "And one day in the future, when the sins of slavery are not up for debate, I intend to use every no vote against the man who delivered it."

Although the thought of attending a house party for a fortnight caused the backs of his eyes to throb, Gideon couldn't deny the satisfaction that swept through his blood at Lord Montrose's declaration.

"And I will delight in helping you."

12

The terraced gardens at Tyrell Manor stretched out before him, the lush expanse of lawn bisected by topiaries, boxed hedges, and limestone steps leading to gravel walking paths that extended into the distant Devonshire countryside.

Gideon was a bit awed by the grandeur of Tyrell Manor. Not that he had expected anything less from the ancestral estate of the Tyrell earldom. Much like the man who wore the title, the landscape seemed to have been carved from the hillside, as if even the soil and bedrock could not withstand the unrelenting power of something so implacable.

Yet for all its perfect right angles, colorful flower beds, and expertly trimmed hedges, the landscape was sterile. Beautiful but not warm. His grandmother had once said that the plantation where she was born, the one where she toiled, was the most strikingly beautiful *but* accursed place on earth. Gideon had never understood what she meant. But something about the earl's home left his spine ridged and his teeth on edge.

He glanced up at the manor house, his gaze skimming over the sash windows and ornate balusters. He felt as if eyes were watching his every move, and he figured they probably were.

Anytime he visited grand English estates, it wasn't just the guests and servants who tracked him with covert stares. For he saw the dark shadows lurking in the brightly lit ballrooms. The veneer of gentility that failed to mask the tainted history imprinted on the foundation. The stares were in the bricks and stones and mortar that comprised the manor itself. The blood of their makers, whose flesh was bought and sold to support such idyllic country houses, called to him. To the burning flame inside his heart that his grandmother protected and carried, and passed on to him.

Gideon was still surprised Lord Tyrell had extended an invitation for him to attend the house party. He had almost expected the earl to turn up his nose at the idea of hosting at his ancestral home the son of a biracial woman and a papist Scot. He'd learned from a footman that the manor had been rebuilt in the late 1690s, when the original structure was destroyed by fire. Gideon was relieved he'd managed to hide the hitch in his breath with a well-timed cough.

Allowing his eyes to touch on the grassy steppes and perfectly manicured flower beds, Gideon released a long sigh. Regardless of what the earl or his lofty guests thought of him, he deserved to be here. Tyrell would not have extended an invitation to him if it weren't true.

Clasping his hands together behind his waist, Gideon pivoted about and returned to the pleasant warmth of the manor. Expelling a sigh to find the entry empty, he proceeded up the staircase and to his room, where he sank onto a brocaded chair at the small escritoire in the corner, pulling out the newest version of his talking points. Gideon had reviewed them extensively, having memorized them word for word, but he was determined to be prepared for any question Earl Tyrell had for him. Montrose had helped him fine-tune every point in anticipation of Tyrell's objections, and the marquess had assured him there would definitely be objections.

The small clock on the desk chimed, bringing his head up. Guests were expected downstairs soon, but he'd been dressed in his evening attire for an hour, resisting the urge to yank on his cuff links every one of the thirty-six hundred seconds in that hour.

Gideon dropped his gaze to his notes again. Montrose had wagered that Tyrell would balk at another parliamentary measure focused on slavery, so they had worked on ways Gideon could combat such claims.

If he were successful in winning Tyrell's support, his proposal, his dream of bringing about an end to the slave trade, would be realized. The thought that the grandson of a formerly enslaved woman could have the most powerful empire in the world not only condemn but also abolish the heinous slave trade around the globe formed a knot of bubbling emotions in the back of his throat.

Folding his notes, Gideon tucked them into an interior pocket of his coat. Crossing to the mirror hanging over his dressing table, he took a moment to straighten the fall of his tailcoat and smooth out the nonexistent wrinkles in his cravat necktie. A simple gold pin lay nestled in the white folds of the tie, and Gideon focused his unblinking gaze on it. He'd been employed as a solicitor's clerk for three years before he could afford it. The first time he'd pinned it into place, Gideon had felt like a giant, mighty and powerful. Unstoppable.

Through hard work and plenty of late nights, he was now in a position where he could purchase another pin. Or two. Perhaps with a jewel. But he didn't, for this simple gold pin was enough. *He* was enough. And soon enough, he would be wearing it when he secured Lord Tyrell's support to end the wretched practice that brought his mother's ancestors to America . . . and then chased them from it in desperation and despair.

Every hair was in place. No wrinkles in sight. Gideon looked every part the gentleman. Worthy to set foot in Lord Tyrell's storied home and dine at his table. Yet his nerves were raw, and thus his temper short. How he was to manage two weeks of this madness, Gideon knew not. But for his initiative, for Montrose, for his stubborn pride, he would persevere.

With one last check in the mirror, he squared his shoulders and lifted his chin, as his grandmother had taught him so many long years prior. Gideon left the sanctity of his chambers and proceeded to Earl Tyrell's drawing room.

Thirty minutes and a glass and a half of claret later, Gideon had exchanged a tepid greeting with his host, a few stilted conversations with other guests, before he'd retired to a spot near the fireplace. The burning grate offered more warmth than the other guests in attendance, and Gideon knew better than to expend too much energy convincing people he was worthy of their regard.

It was going to be a long fortnight.

A commotion at the door halted his wineglass's ascent to his lips. From what he could gather from the hushed talk sprinting through the room, surprise guests had arrived who sparked equal parts interest and disdain, and his fellow partygoers were unsure of how to respond. Gideon rolled his eyes. Thinking of his own lukewarm reception, he hoped these new guests were made to feel more welcome than he was.

Turning back to study the fire roaring in the grate, he figured he would greet the new arrivals once the commotion over their appearance had died down.

A tinkling laugh met his ears. A sound that had continued to bewitch him despite his fortitude and better judgment.

Tipping his glass back, Gideon swallowed the entirety of his wine in one bitter gulp.

With his veins pulsing alcoholic fortification to his extremities, he slowly pivoted, his gaze taking in various faces from the crowd by the door—as if they mattered. As if he could delay the inevitable.

But when he saw *her*, she was all he could see. Her sisters who stood by her side, the guests who flanked them as they issued their greetings, were all part of the void. Faceless, unimportant figures blotted out by the sheer brightness of Ana María's presence.

And when her gaze met his, her pink lips tilting up into a secret smile, his goddamned heart soared. For that shy smile was meant only for him.

Gideon watched from his perch by the fireplace as Ana María and her sisters advanced into the room, offering salutations and friendly warmth to every guest they met like bits of pollen on the wind. He hoped, rather fruitlessly he knew, that he was allergic to her particular brand of charm.

Perching his elbow on the fireplace mantel, he aimed for casual and confident, even while his blood roared in his ears. Ana María walked a circuit around the room, slowly moving in his direction and sending his pulse skittering with every step she took. Gideon may have thought of her incessantly since the carriage ride from the parish church, but he'd not spoken with her. In the weeks that passed, he'd been decidedly off-kilter, replaying those moments together in his mind, seeing the kaleidoscope of expressions that played across her face every time he closed his eyes. Feeling flummoxed when he caught whiffs of her jasmine scent as he went about his day.

When he should have been focused on his job, Gideon had been thinking of her.

Burnt-umber eyes shyly met his as she approached, and Gideon could not recall why such a thing should concern him.

"Señor Fox, I did not know you would be in attendance," Ana María said, bobbing a graceful curtsy. "I hope my presence here this next fortnight will not cause you undue stress."

His brain stuttered. "Whyever would you cause me stress?"

Although her bearing remained friendly, there was a sad turn to her lips. "Come now, I thought discussing religion and science together had made us bosom friends."

Gideon's mouth trembled around a laugh. "Do you suppose there's atonement on Dante's grand sketch of heaven and hell that takes into account the unique occurrence of a discussion about the marriage of religion and science that *doesn't* result in a holy war?"

Ana María tapped her lace-gloved finger to her lips and cast her eyes heavenward, as if awaiting divine inspiration. "I cannot vouch for Dante's opinion on the subject, but what I can say is that despite the diverting conversation we shared regarding Mr. Darwin's work, being seen with me in this setting might not be to your benefit."

And with that salvo, Ana María tilted her head at the crowd that milled about them.

Gideon couldn't bring himself to look away from her, although he longed to. Her claim was true, and though shame-fueled flames heated his cheeks, he held her gaze. For if she was brave enough to confront him about his fickle nature, well, then he could be man enough to look her in the eyes while she did it.

Filling his lungs with her sweet scent, Gideon ordered himself to say, "I think you are one of the most fascinating people I have ever met. You left behind everything you'd ever known to come here, and despite that upheaval and uncertainty, it hasn't made you hard, Miss Luna. You've embraced the change with a smile, and have tried to do right by you and your sisters." He dropped his gaze to his feet, vulnerability wrapping about him. "I respect you immensely . . . nonetheless the gossip that follows our interactions is a detriment to all that I'm trying to accomplish."

How he heard her swallow over the chatter in the room, Gideon did not know. "Do you know I have never appeared in the gossip rags before?"

Gideon jerked his gaze up, his brows high on his forehead. "Indeed?"

Ana María chuckled, although the sound was not merry. "I know it's hard to believe, but it's true. As my father's eldest daughter, much was expected of me, and I was mindful of that responsibility. My father is very ambitious. He worked hard to elevate himself from his poor childhood and has battled for every scrap of success he's won." She paused, her gaze tracing over his face. "In so many ways, you and he are similar."

Abruptly feeling cold, Gideon tensed.

"And because my father had to work so hard, I knew better than to step out of line. I had a role, and I knew what was expected of me." Her shoulders appeared to curl in on themselves. "My whole life has been spent living up to his expectations. For the betterment of his political career. He's not here now, Señor Fox, but still . . . I feel the need to conform. To behave."

Gideon took a step closer to her. "Why?"

The silence stretched like a too-tight piece of twine, and right before Gideon was certain it would snap, Miss Luna whispered, "Because if I want to bring about change, I need to play the game. I didn't understand my father's rigidity, the fierce hold he kept on all of us, until I saw how carefully you held yourself. How every step you take is methodically considered. I hold you in great esteem, Señor Fox, and I would not be able to forgive myself if our friendship were to distract from the very important work you are doing."

A suffocating heaviness twined itself around his neck. The incomparable Ana María Luna, the woman who had haunted his dreams and every one of his waking hours, esteemed him . . . and thus knew they could not be friends.

A rebuttal was acid in his mouth, his mind reeling from her confession, but she spoke before he could.

"I have no doubt you will change the world." Ana María's gaze was hypnotic. "Where my father is cold and ruthless in pursuit of his goals, you are empathetic and gracious. But while you may be different, your association with me could affect all that you work for just the same."

With her chin trembling, Ana María turned to stare at the flames in the grate, which jumped and sparked in crimson and gold bursts of light and heat. Standing this close to her felt hotter still.

"I have no desire to cause a stir or be the object of ridicule, but it took a venture across the Atlantic Ocean to help me realize that I refuse to bend to the opinions—the standards—of people who do not know me. Who do not know my past nor have any interest in my future." She shook her head, ebony curls sliding against her cheeks. "And even if my hand were not already spoken for, it's obvious, don't you think, that your future will be very different from mine?"

Gideon pressed his mouth together in a tight line.

"So let us be friendly acquaintances, señor." Her hopeful tone unclenched his teeth. "This house party will see us thrown together in multiple ways, but if we keep our distance, and make the platonic nature of our affiliation clear to the other guests, hopefully all of your good work will not be over-shadowed by the gossips."

As if you could ever be a simple acquaintance, his mind bellowed. And Gideon slashed that thought. Ana María was providing him with the answer to his dilemma—his *infatuation*—and rather than embracing it and being thankful, he was prevaricating.

Gideon's whole damn chest ached at the idea that Ana María recognized the very real consequences of their friendship. The burn of disappointment and anger churned in his gut and bubbled up in his throat. Had he become so caught up in his ambitions that he had lost track of what he had been fighting for? Did his grandmother give two damns if he forced England to publicly denounce the evils of the slave trade, or did she care that he had found a measure of happiness in this bleak, terrible world?

And being with Ana María—in any way he could, even as just her friend—had made his days brighter.

The sudden arrival of Isabel Luna halted his spiraling thoughts.

"Señor Fox, I'm surprised to find you among Lord Tyrell's guests," she said baldly.

Gideon crossed his arms. "I admit to being a tad surprised to have received an invitation. But then seeing as how we're both politicians committed to the betterment of Britain and her citizens, perhaps that's why."

Isabel rolled her eyes, an uncharacteristic expression from the normally reserved young woman. "From what I can tell, Lord Tyrell has no interest in bettering the plight of his fellow Englishmen. More so his own bank ledger."

"How do you know that, querida?" Ana María asked before he could.

"Oh, I've heard talk," Isabel mumbled, waving her hand as she looked pointedly away.

Suddenly feeling the urge to excuse his presence at Lord Tyrell's house party, Gideon met Isabel's stubborn gaze and then Ana María's curious one. "Our host has a notorious reputation as a miserly knave, withholding his opinion and vote for the highest bidder. The only reason I can count myself his guest is that I need him to throw his support behind my proposal. It's due for a committee vote this month."

"What is the possibility you can tack on support for the Juárez government to your proposal?"

"Isa, really." Ana María scowled at her sister. "I'm certain Señor Fox has enough to contend with without adding our cause to his docket."

"Your cause?" Something about the manner in which she said the words caught his attention.

She raised a narrow shoulder, not quite meeting his eyes. "If you must know, Señor Valdés has tasked us with our own objective."

Intrigue crept along his spine, and he moved closer to her. "What task did he set you to?"

Ana María glanced askance at her sister, who merely stared at her with an unreadable expression. Her shoulders relaxed. "Upon our arrival in London, Señor Valdés asked us to be visible and active within society to bolster the image of our countrymen."

Gideon's mouth sagged as the significance of her revelation settled on him. Of course Mr. Valdés had met Ana María and her sisters and immediately recognized how their charisma, their beauty, and their story could help generate sympathy and support for the Mexican people. A sudden thought occurred to him; was this why Ana María had been so willing to create distance between them? Because she had as much to lose if their names were paired in the gossip pages together?

"I see I have surprised you." Ana María clicked her tongue. "Especially after the speech I just gave."

He shifted on his feet, mindful Isabel was watching them with a notch between her brows. "Of course not. I'm not at all surprised you would do everything in your power to help those you left behind in Mexico."

Ana María's throat worked as she looked down at the ornate fan she twisted about in her hands. "It was something we wanted to do, not something we were told to do. The difference mattered."

Gideon could absolutely understand that. "Mr. Valdés was very wise to have chosen you as the face of the occupation in Mexico."

A pink tinge touched her cheeks. "We're trying to make it real. Mexico is on the other side of the Atlantic, a place most Englishmen will never visit. And with Europe invested in the war in the States, the French occupation of a sovereign country, their attempts to expand their empire, is of small concern."

"And that is unacceptable," Isabel interjected.

Linking her arm through her sister's, Ana María continued. "Señor Valdés hoped that members of Parliament, of society, would remember us, think upon us kindly, when he lobbied those same people to intercede in the conflict."

It was an ingenious plan, really. Three pretty Mexican heiresses find their way to London after they've been driven from their homes, and the ambassador sees a way to make their strife recognizable and understandable to the masses. But one thing nagged at him—

"Why did your parents send you to London?" He shook his head. "Would not a location closer to home have been better?"

"Well, we weren't going to go to the States—" Isabel started.

"Our parents are acquainted with Señor Valdés." Ana María waved a hand. "It made sense to them to entrust us to his care."

Except that did not make sense to Gideon. Their parents had sent three daughters across an ocean to an acquaintance?

The questions went unasked because a smiling face appeared on Ana María's other side.

"At least there is one person in attendance I am happy to see." Bobbing a curtsy, Gabby favored him with a simper. "I am quite glad to see you will be a guest along with us this fortnight, Señor Fox." She paused, darting her gaze about. "But do tell me, is His Grace with you?"

Gideon barely contained his snort. "Whitfield will not be in attendance. He is busy hunting with our friend Captain Dawson."

Isabel stiffened in the corner of his eye. "And does Captain Dawson live close by?"

"His estate is about a three-hour ride from here." Gideon's mouth quirked. "Is that too far or too close?"

"Much too close and not far enough."

"I concur, Isa dear," Gabby drawled.

The group's laughter was drowned out by the butler announcing that the guests could proceed into the dining room for dinner. He offered Ana María his arm, and she accepted with another of her shy smiles. Heat rushed through Gideon's veins at having her so close.

"You know that escorting me is going to send the gossip-mongers into a flutter," she whispered.

He did. "Why did you accept, then? I would have understood if you demurred."

"Because I didn't want to. I will be forced to interact with all manner of individuals during our fortnight here"—Ana María lifted a shoulder—"so I figured I should take advantage of the company I truly wish to keep when opportunities present themselves."

Gideon was mortified to feel heat sweep up his neck and spread across his cheeks. "I confess I was dreading this house party. If I did not need Lord Tyrell's support, I would have stayed in London, where the moments I had to spend with pompous, self-important lords were limited. But knowing you're here, even if we're *only* to be acquaintances"—he smirked when she rolled her eyes—"promises to make these next two weeks enjoyable. Somewhat."

"Somewhat?" Ana María smacked his arm with her fan. "It will definitely be enjoyable, but only if we're able to devise a means of communication that will not alert the prattlers. Hand gestures or some such thing. That way we can share our observations and exasperations without drawing undue attention."

"How very clever of you."

She chuckled. "Have I surprised you again?"

"No," Gideon said simply, looking down at her. He wasn't surprised at all.

Once they entered the room, he found they were seated on opposite ends of the table, the two dozen or so guests stretched between them. He wanted to mourn the distance that separated them, but it was for the best. He was in attendance on business, and despite their witty repartee, Gideon had never believed in mixing business with pleasure.

The long ordeal of dinner progressed in a mundane fashion, a fact Gideon was thankful for. The women who sat on either side of him were pleasant, but their names left his mind like water through a sieve. He managed to engage in some friendly discussions with several of Lord Tyrell's neighbors, although he had yet to speak with the man himself.

Raising his glass, he watched the older man chuckle at something Gabby said. Gideon had noticed that the sisters were assigned seats flanking the earl, and the earl seemed quite enchanted with his young guests. Not that Gideon could blame him. The full weight of Ana María's regard was a heady thing.

After dinner was finally concluded, the men excused themselves to Tyrell's study for liquor and cigars. Gideon adjusted his waistcoat as he followed the queue into a dimly lit room lined with bookshelves, an imposing fireplace adorning the far wall. As a footman poured various spirits from an array of crystal decanters, the earl extracted a leather-covered box from a locked drawer in his desk. Withdrawing a key from his pocket, he quickly unlocked it and raised the lid, revealing neatly packed cigars.

Holding one up to the light from the lamp on the corner of his desk, Tyrell ran it under his nose. "From Cuba. The best money can buy."

Gideon was never much a fan of cigars, finding the taste and the scent rather unpleasant, but he knew how to play the game. He hadn't come this far in his political career by skirting good decorum.

While Tyrell helped his other guests select their cigars, Gideon requested a tumbler of whisky. He swished it around his glass, watching as the dark liquid clung to the sides before melding back down into the whisky. It looked like a good vintage, and when he raised it to his lips and it hit his tongue, he hummed in the back of his throat. A superb quality.

"And what of you, Fox? Which would you like?"

The earl gestured with his hand to the assortment of cigars arranged before him. Holding up his glass, Gideon shook his head.

"I thank you, but this deserves to be savored on its own."

Tyrell arched a brow. "I hadn't realized you were a whisky connoisseur."

The earl's tone was just a shade shy of mocking, and Gideon suspected it would have been sharper had he not been Tyrell's guest for the next fortnight.

But Gideon knew condescension when it was directed at him, and he certainly knew how to handle it.

"Oh, I would never claim to be a connoisseur." He held up the tumbler to the light just as the earl had done with the cigar. "But my father taught me that a good Scots whisky should have a clean, crisp bite, and this most certainly does."

"Aah." The earl closed his box and set it on his desktop. Propping his hip against his desk, he took a long puff on his cigar, exhaling smoke rings as he considered Gideon. "So did your father come by his knowledge because he was a Scot or because he was a drunkard?"

Several men in the room hissed their displeasure while others chuckled. Gideon ignored them, keeping his gaze firmly on Lord Tyrell. The earl thought he could intimidate him. Other men had believed the same.

But Gideon was unmoved by Tyrell's attempts. As if he would ever be shamed by such pathetic volleys.

Taking a long, slow drink, he quirked his mouth. "He was a Scot, my lord. He used to say that he was saved from getting lost in the bottom of a bottle by his proclivity for expensive, quality whisky. Not exactly something that could be purchased on an assistant factory manager's salary."

"How surprising." Tyrell cocked his head to the side. "I had no notion you were part Scot. I've heard it said that you're the grandson of an enslaved woman." He looked at him with gimlet eyes. "Is that true?"

Gideon lifted his chin. "'Tis true. My grandmother escaped

on a packet ship departing Charleston and came to London many years ago."

"Interesting." The earl's gaze narrowed on Gideon as if he were an intriguing cipher. "So you, the descendant of a Scots father and a Black grandmother, have risen to hold a seat in Commons. However did you manage that?"

The room had gone silent. Gideon could feel the gazes of the other guests bouncing between him and the earl, the atmosphere in the room thick with apprehension. Tyrell's question dripped with scorn, but Gideon was resolved to maintain his unperturbed facade.

Pausing to take another sip of whisky, Gideon shrugged. "Through a lot of hard work and a healthy dose of luck."

"I thought it was the Irish who believed in luck," another gentleman chimed in, but Gideon did not seek out the speaker. He did not care.

"I've heard it said that luck is what you make of it, and I believe that is true to an extent. How useful is a stroke of good fortune if you do nothing to seize on it?" Gideon swirled the liquid in his glass. "I think it's easy to downplay hard work and a bit of luck when one has not had to rely on it. When one is born into privilege, it makes it difficult to comprehend any additional paths to success that do not mimic one's own."

Certain he was advancing onto fractured, unstable ground, Gideon took another sip of whisky.

Lord Tyrell puffed another ring of smoke and nodded his head. "It's true that it is hard for me to imagine such a meteoric rise considering the various hardships I'm sure you encountered. Because it's true that not everyone can boast that their antecedents are tied to the Conqueror. Can you even trace your antecedents, Fox? Surely not on your maternal side."

Gideon managed not to curl his lip, but just barely. Instead, he tipped his tumbler at the man in what he hoped was a jovial manner. "I cannot. Another evil of slavery. It stole away entire family trees. Entire communities lost their connections and identities. Who my grandmother knew herself to be is not who her enslavers told her to be. And that is something no one in this room will ever be able to understand."

"Indeed not. This is why the Lyons-Seward Treaty has not done enough in your eyes, correct?"

Dragging his gaze away from Lord Tyrell's arrogant face, Gideon turned to the speaker. It was Avery, whom Gideon had not spoken with since the opera so many weeks before when he had engaged him in conversation with Ana María. Gone was the usual carefree expression the man usually wore, replaced instead by earnest interest.

"It is. The Lyons-Seward Treaty has helped suppress the Atlantic slave trade in British and American ports, but what about the rest of the world? Although it's supposedly been outlawed, African people continue to be stolen from their homes and brought to countries like Brazil and Cuba. Can Britain claim to be a world leader, an expansive empire, if it allows such an evil practice to not just exist, but thrive?"

No one spoke, but Gideon felt the weight of everything that was not said in the air he breathed.

"My grandmother fled to this country because she thought she would find safe haven here. She was under the impression that the British were staunch abolitionists. Not just here in England, but around the globe." He inhaled, filling his chest, and his resolve. "I want the government to publicly admit that she was right by passing this measure. And I want the power of the empire to enforce it."

A few gentlemen murmured their agreement, and Avery nodded his head eagerly, an obvious ally Gideon had not intended to find. Perhaps Avery wasn't the only ally he would find among this lot.

Gideon slid his gaze back to his host, finding the man was still watching him, his expression unreadable . . . except for a certain harsh light in his blue eyes.

"Yes, well," he drawled, taking a long draw from his cigar, "I'm not entirely sure it's wise to issue a parliamentary declaration about slavery at this time. It doesn't seem wise to alienate the Confederacy."

"And why is that, my lord?" Gideon applauded how curious he sounded, while disdain made his teeth clench.

"Because the great war in the States still rages." The earl studied the wisps of smoke that rose from his cigar. "And truthfully, I'm uncertain if I even side with the Union. The Confederates seem to value gentility and aristocratic decorum. Plus, the majority of American cotton grows in the South, so it stands to reason we should not alienate our suppliers."

"Suppliers? Of course." Gideon swept a hand through the air. "For what does it matter if that crop is grown and harvested by enslaved people, as long as peers in England can cheaply clothe their footmen?"

Such a rejoinder was a douse of alcohol to flames, and the men's voices rose the more glasses of brandy and whisky that were consumed. They argued about whether Britain had an obligation to take a side in the American war, and if they did, whether the British should support the Union or the Confederacy. As for Gideon, he chimed in with a comment here or there, managed a chuckle when the moment called for it, and refrained from requesting another refill of whisky. After Lord Tyrell's chilly reception, the liquor lost a bit of its magic.

13

"What is on the agenda today? Watching the men try to hit an archery target? An afternoon of charades?" Isabel slipped onto the settee next to Ana María with a sigh. "More dancing so Lord Tyrell can run his gnarled, evil hands all over his female guests?"

Ana María stiffened, her eyes flying to her sister. "Has the earl been untoward with you?"

"No." Isabel's lip curled. "But I've overheard a few of the other women mention that he has been overly familiar."

"He's a boor," Gabby exclaimed as she sailed into the room. "If we didn't need to be here, I would demand we return to London." She waggled her brows as she plopped into an armchair across from them. "Preferably after I jabbed him in his a—"

"Gabriela, really," Lady Yardley hissed as she entered, a maid following close behind. After directing the maid to set the tea tray on the table in front of her, she turned a hard stare on Gabby. "I know you are capable of controlling yourself, so why must you court trouble?"

Her youngest sister scowled. "How am I causing trouble?

Only my sisters were in attendance, and this was a private conversation. Perhaps it is you who should apologize for interrupting a private moment."

"Gabby," Ana María scolded, heat creeping up her face at her sister's rude behavior. "That's no way to speak to her ladyship."

Rather than apologize, or even look chagrined, Gabby reached forward and plucked a biscuit from the tea tray. Taking a bite, she relaxed into her chair, unconcerned with the crumbs that now lay scattered about her skirts.

"I do not require an invitation to enter this room. It is a sitting room Lord Tyrell set aside for all of us to utilize." The viscountess swept over them with her narrowed eyes. "A courtesy not all guests have been granted."

Ana María figured as much. The room was not terribly large, but with a grand window that overlooked the manicured gardens stretching across the back of the estate, delicate cherrywood furniture, and tasteful art and draperies, it was an attractive space. So why had the earl offered it to them for their private use? It was not as if Lady Yardley was closely acquainted with the man.

Not for the first time, she wondered why he had invited them. Why provide them with such lavish guest quarters? Why seat her and Gabby on either side of himself at dinner? Ana María had no answers, but plenty of uncomfortable hypotheses . . . the majority of which involved the earl looking for a young bride with a hefty dowry.

Smoothing her hands down her skirts as she attempted to smooth the uncomfortable thoughts from her mind, Ana María asked, "So what are the plans for today, my lady?"

Lady Yardley cuddled Dove to her face, whispering nonsensical cariños to the dog, before she allowed her to settle in her lap. "Landaus will be available to take guests into the small village nearby to shop or visit the local posting inn for a meal. Lord Tyrell's housekeeper indicated the earl was taking some gentlemen into the home woods to scout the terrain in preparation for next week's fox hunt."

"Fox hunt?" Gabby visibly recoiled. "What a barbaric sport."

"No worse than bullfighting," Isabel retorted. "Not that I approve of either, of course."

"Yes, well, perhaps we should refrain from mentioning our own shortcomings when others can use them against us," Gabby said in Spanish, angling her head suggestively in Lady Yardley's direction.

The viscountess stroked her manicured hand over Dove's small head, her expression bored. "I will offer no excuse for the sport—"

"Is it even fair to call it a sport when the fox is not equally matched?"

"But I've long suspected that the aristocracy has continued to indulge in the barbarity of foxhunting as a means of exercising their will over nature." Lady Yardley snorted. "For in what ways do these men, ensconced in their elegant Mayfair homes and ancestral estates, ever exert their dominion upon those creatures less than themselves?"

"Ummm," Isabel began, frowning.

"Should I prepare a formal speech—" Gabby waved her hands about.

"Every day, your ladyship." Ana María flattened her mouth as Lady Yardley's eyes widened. "Those men believe everyone is beneath them. That God blessed them with wealth and pedigree, and in some cases a title, because they are special. When truly, they are anything but."

With her gaze darting among the trio, the viscountess finally sighed. "Since I was certain you would have no interest in the scouting mission nor the trip into the village, I indicated we would be hacking out with the stable master for a tour of the estate."

Ana María sucked in a breath, then turned to take in her sisters' equally puzzled expressions. "Thank you, your ladyship, but my sisters and I have not ridden in—"

"At least a decade."

"A long while," she amended, flashing a scowl at Gabby.

The viscountess studied them for a long moment, and then leaned forward in her chair . . . causing Dove to yelp in disgruntlement.

"I confess that I haven't ridden since—"

"Waterloo?"

"Gabriela, I swear it will be a miracle if you do not find me with my hands around your throat at some point or another," Lady Yardley growled.

"Your ladyship," Ana María gasped, before slowly allowing her lips to twist into a harlequin grin, "at least allow me to hold her down for you."

Rolling her eyes, Gabby snagged another biscuit from the tray and pointedly turned away from them to stare out the window.

"The stable master asked for everyone interested in touring the grounds to meet at the stables at one of the clock, where we'll select our mounts." Lady Yardley raised her brows. "Did you have Consuelo pack your new habits?"

"Of course. We assumed we'd have more use for them here than we have so far in London."

"But perhaps after getting reacquainted with the saddle, you'll want to hack out in the park on occasion." Lady Yardley offered Dove a portion of her biscuit. "There are several stables that will rent mounts by the hour or day."

"I suppose we'll judge our interest upon our return," Isabel added despondently.

"Oh, cheer up, you lot. I think you'll have fun," Lady Yardley exclaimed, hoisting her teacup in the air in a mock toast.

Sliding her gaze to both her sisters, Ana María found that neither seemed as excited or as confident as the viscountess did.

The rest of the morning passed in an easy manner, with the sisters keeping to their rooms to read or relax. So much of their time in England had been spent bustling from one social event to another, or entertaining guests and visitors, all while wearing bright, engaging smiles. That sort of never-ending performance took its toll. Ana María was incredibly grateful for the opportunity they had been granted to experience life away from their father's suffocating influence, but she didn't realize how much they needed a break until those few quiet hours.

At the appropriate time, the sisters helped each other don their new habits, ensuring the velveteen draped in just the right way, before they grabbed their crops and made their way to the stables. Ana María smiled politely at members of the staff they passed, ignoring how Gabriela used her crop as a sword, and swished it about in an imaginary battle that had even Isabel chortling in amusement.

When they arrived at the stables, they found a handful of other guests milling about. Ana María noticed that some matrons steered their daughters and young charges away from her and her sisters, but the majority were friendly and welcoming. Thus, Ana María dipped a deep curtsy to the Marchioness of Hampstead and her daughter, Lady Mallory, when they greeted her. The women had treated her graciously from their introduction, and she was happy that the long ride would allow them to become better acquainted.

Yet even while they chatted, Ana María held her breath when other riders joined the group, hoping one would be Mr. Fox. She knew it would be best for them not to interact any more than what was polite, but her stubborn heart yearned for a glimpse of him all the same.

The crowd around them grew silent as an older gentleman with a hitch to his step and a long crop in his hand approached. Stopping before them, he cleared his throat.

"Ladies and gentlemen, I am Mr. Davies, the stable master here at Tyrell Manor. I'm honored to have been tasked with giving you a tour of this storied estate." He swung his hand to the line of young grooms standing behind him. "If you would please follow me, my grooms and I will select a mount that will match your ease and comfort in the saddle."

Ana María swung her head to her sisters, whose expressions ranged from muted interest to resignation. Stepping forward, she beckoned Isabel and Gabby to walk with her, hopeful a bit of her enthusiasm wore off on them.

A half hour later, the party set off after Mr. Davies, Ana María being careful to direct her mount to walk with Lady Hampstead and Lady Mallory. Sharing a room with her sisters after the train ride from London had begun to wear on her, and she was happy for a break from Isabel and Gabby. Although she knew they had been on their best behavior since they had arrived at Tyrell Manor, Ana María relished the reprieve from worrying when one of them would do or say something that would draw attention.

The trio engaged in light conversation for a time, Lady Hampstead regaling them with tales of her time spent on the

Continent as the daughter of a military officer. Eventually, the marchioness directed the discussion to Ana María, asking about her home in Mexico and the tumult that sent her fleeing its shores. The women were thoughtful listeners, and for the first time in a long time, Ana María allowed herself to relax in company that was not her sisters'.

"It would seem that despite the frightening reason for your exile from Mexico, coming to England has permitted you a bit of freedom, wouldn't you say, Miss Luna?"

"I would." She ducked her head to hide her flushed cheeks. "Some might say it's granted us *too* much freedom."

"Only a young lady could be granted *too much* freedom," Lady Mallory grumbled. Her stare turned assessing. "But I'm curious, if you were granted the freedom to make choices for yourself, what would you do with your life?"

The inquiry filled Ana María's mind with soundless noise. What would she do? If the question had been posed to her while she was still in Mexico, she would have been scandalized by it. Of course she'd want to do whatever her father wanted of her. But now . . . now her long months in England had blown away the fog that had always obscured her gaze, the fog her father had always seemed to shine a light through to guide her way. Now she was unfettered and, at the very least, able to express her own wants and desires.

"I think . . ." She cleared her throat as her hands tightened on the reins. Her thoughts skipped over her conversations with Tío Arturo about swaying public opinion and the glimpses Mr. Fox had provided of the important work he did in Parliament. She even thought of Father Duncan and the good work his church was doing for its parishioners. "I think I should like to be involved in politics in some way. Developing and writing proposals for public projects that would make day-to-day life easier. Perhaps organizing education reforms. Health efforts."

"That's a very admirable and practical goal, Miss Luna." Lady Hampstead studied her from under the brim of her hat. "Do you suppose the conflict that sent you and your sisters from Mexico is responsible for this interest?"

Certainly years of watching her father maneuver and scheme to see his political goals come to fruition played a part.

Ana María nodded. "There were many influences, but the conflict has absolutely played a part. And the French occupation was not a sudden thing. The machinations that made it possible for Napoleon to find victory were set into motion years ago. But I have had many long days and nights since we fled Mexico to ponder the decisions made by past administrations, and President Juárez most recently, and whether a woman's viewpoint would have made a difference."

"How intriguing." The marchioness pursed her lips. "As a girl, I often had time to consider the various battles and skirmishes my father participated in, and more often than not, I came to the conclusion that things would have been very different had a woman, or *women*, been a part of the decision-making."

"And that's what I hope for. That one day young women are granted the opportunities that are afforded to young men," Lady Mallory said, pounding a closed fist onto her pommel.

"I hope that day comes sooner than later, for—"

A sudden commotion in the hedgerows bordering the path sent their horses into a sidestep, and they snorted and stomped the ground. When a pair of rabbits burst forth from the foliage and darted in front of them, Ana María's mount reared back, its hooves pawing at the air as its whinny echoed through the clearing. Thudding its hooves back to the earth, the mare dashed away in the opposite direction, carrying Ana María with it. She had a fleeting glance of Lady Hampstead's and Lady Mallory's terrified expressions before she disappeared into the bramble.

Ana María tried to pull back on the reins to stop the terrified mare, but the beast shook its mighty head, yanking the reins from her hands. Aghast, Ana María clung to the mare's neck, whispering a Hail Mary in between dry sobs, desperately hoping the horse would tire soon and not toss her off in the process.

But it continued its mad dash, carrying her over several hills and through multiple clearings, jumping over a brook, and splashing Ana María's habit with cold waters. Crouching low over the horse's neck, she murmured gentle, soothing words she was not certain the mare could hear over the sound of its thundering hooves.

And that clamor disguised the approach of another rider. Ana María was only aware a rider had run them down when a gloved hand appeared in her line of vision, reaching to grasp the dangling reins. With a firm "Whoa" and an unyielding hold, her mare began to slow, its breath puffing in thick clouds as its great chest heaved. Only when the horse had managed to slow to a clipped walk did Ana María feel safe enough to look up at her rescuer.

"Are you all right?" Mr. Fox maneuvered his mount close to her side, reaching out to clasp her shoulder.

His touch electrified her, and the air whooshed from her lungs. "Yes. I'm fine. Just a bit shaken, if I'm honest."

"I would be surprised if you weren't." His grip on her shoulder tightened. "You've always struck me as a composed woman, but even you must be shaken from time to time."

A laugh burst from her mouth, chasing some of the tension from her body. "I assure you that despite my quest for perfection, I am but a mortal."

Mr. Fox's dark eyes lingered on her lips before rising to lock with hers. "Let me lead you to that tree over there, and I'll help you dismount. I'm guessing you could use firm ground under your feet for a spell."

"Firm ground would be welcomed, thank you," she said, her voice hoarse.

Within minutes, Mr. Fox had managed to tether their respective horses to a low-hanging tree branch before turning his attention to where she sat in her sidesaddle. He hesitated for a moment, his gaze fixed on her booted foot, slowly traveling up the drape of her habit, to finally meet her eyes.

"Allow me to help you down."

His tone seemed to have dropped an octave, scraping across her nerve endings and making her shiver.

Mr. Fox paused in the act of raising his arms to her, his brows disappearing into his hairline. "Would you prefer I not assist you?"

"No, no, you're quite fine." Ana María giggled. "If I was left to my own devices, I am certain I'd find myself in a heap on the ground below."

"Well, we cannot allow that." He dragged the back of his hand along the draped material. "Mauveine is a lovely color on you, and it would be a shame to ruin this habit."

A gasp caught in her throat, but before Ana María could respond, Mr. Fox had his hands on her waist, his long fingers dipping into her flesh. Even through her corset and stays, his palms were hot to the touch, and she closed her eyes and allowed herself a moment to simply relish the feel of his hands on her.

She had only ever shared a dance or two with Fernando during the months of their engagement, his hold on her polite and impersonal. But nothing about Mr. Fox felt impersonal, and her heartbeat roared in her ears as he gently brought her down to the ground, his body sliding against hers in the descent, sparking wildfires across her flesh. When her feet hit the earth, Ana María looked up at him, her teeth catching her lip to find his pupils wide. His gaze locked on where she abused her lip, and when his head lowered ever so slightly, she inhaled, certain he was about to kiss her—

Mr. Fox dropped his hands from her waist and took a step back, wrenching his hand through his hair. Spinning on his heel, he prowled to his saddlebag and extracted a water flask. Unscrewing the top, he held it out to her wordlessly.

Desperately trying to hide her ragged breaths, Ana María accepted the offering with a polite nod.

The water was cool and refreshing, and she closed her eyes as it soothed her parched throat. Re-centering herself, she opened her eyes to Mr. Fox staring at her with a darkened expression.

"Care to tell me how you found yourself to be on a runaway horse?"

Toeing at the ground with her boot, Ana María lifted a shoulder. "She was spooked by a pair of rabbits. I tried to calm her, but I'm not the most accomplished horsewoman. I thank you for stopping us when you did." She frowned. "How did you come across us?"

Pulling on the fingers of his gloves, Mr. Fox slowly stripped the leather from his hands. Ana María tracked every inch of skin that was exposed. If he had the power to set her ablaze with his gloved hands, what would it feel like to have his bare skin touch her own . . . ?

"I rode out with Lord Tyrell and the other gentlemen to inspect the hunting grounds."

Ana María scrunched her nose. "I wasn't aware you intended to take part in the fox hunt."

"I don't. A loutish sport, if you ask me." He quirked his

mouth into a semblance of a smile. "And I will always root for my namesake."

She chuckled. "I'm delighted to hear it."

"I only accompanied the men, for the ride allotted me time to chat about my proposal with some of Lord Tyrell's guests."

"But not the earl himself?"

He shook his head. "As I expected, Lord Tyrell will be a harder nut to crack."

"Perhaps." Ana María thought of her host's shrewd, calculating manner. She found him rather unnerving, and she was tempted to tell Mr. Fox as much, but clamped her mouth closed instead. Her opinions on the man did not much matter when his support was necessary to secure Mr. Fox the votes he needed to see his proposal go before Commons.

The pounding of hooves sounded behind her, and Ana María turned to see one of Lord Tyrell's grooms approaching at a gallop. His expression lifted when he spied her standing with Mr. Fox.

"Miss Luna, how relieved I am to find you uninjured. Lady Hampstead alerted us to what had occurred," the young man exclaimed, ripping his hat from his head as he approached her.

"Yes, it was a frightening experience, but thankfully Señor Fox was able to stop my mount before anything disastrous occurred."

"I am happy to have been in the right place at the right time."

He uttered the words with such nonchalance, except Ana María remembered the panicked look in his eyes when he had reined in her horse. He'd been frightened. *For her.* That knowledge made her whole body feel light and airy.

"I'm happy you were there as well." She directed a full grin his way, pouring all her gratitude . . . and a bit more into it. "Thank you, señor."

He dipped his head politely, but his gaze was potent as he stared back at her.

The groom moved forward a step. "Would you like for me to escort you back to the manor, Miss Luna?"

Ana María unconsciously looked to Mr. Fox and she opened her mouth to respond—

"I will escort her," Mr. Fox murmured.

"You will?" she parroted, blinking.

He nodded. "If you approve, of course."

"Oh." She darted her gaze to the groom, who shrugged in response. She turned back to Mr. Fox, her cheeks burning hot when she said, "I would appreciate your escort."

The groom looked between the two of them for a moment and then nodded. "I'll let Mr. Davies know. Have a good day."

They watched the young man mount his horse and ride away, the silence stretching between them until only the sounds of birds chirping, squirrels scuttling about in the tree boughs above them, and the distant bleating of sheep were all that surrounded them. It was not until the groom disappeared beyond a bend in the path that Mr. Fox broke the silence.

"Did you wish to remount your horse, or would you prefer to walk?"

Thinking back to her recent scare, she snorted. "A walk would do me good."

"Me, too." He unwrapped the horses' reins from the post and led them to where she stood waiting. Gesturing with his hand to the path the groom disappeared down, Mr. Fox said, "After you."

They ambled for several minutes in silence, but Ana María was not bothered by it. The weather was mild, with a soft bite to the air, and she tipped her head back to soak up the sunshine whenever there was a break in the tree canopy along the path.

"Devonshire is quite rural, and is known for its coastal cliffs. I'm surprised the earl has not organized a trip to the seaside."

"I've had quite enough of the sea, gracias," she said succinctly.

His dry chuckle made her smile. "Well, in that case, you will have to content yourself with these inland hills and valleys."

Ana María stumbled to a halt. Planting her hands on her hips, she surveyed the landscape. Rolling hills extending to the horizon, with fields segmented by crops of different varieties. Clusters of birch, ash, and beech trees stood like islands in a sea of green. "Hills? I must confess that I have a very different idea of what constitutes a hill."

"Is that so?" Mr. Fox's brow tipped up. "I was not aware you were also a geographer, among your many talents."

"Well, you did not ask me, now did you?" Ana María angled her chin up. "And I was taught that a lady should never be boastful."

"What a ludicrous lesson," he declared with a scoff.

She couldn't hold back her laugh at his disgruntled expression. "And why do you say that?"

Mr. Fox looked at her askance. "Because when a young man excels at a certain subject or is learned in a particular area, no one expects him to not talk about such things. On the contrary, most men would prefer for us to believe them experts on topics they actually have no notion of."

"I'm sure you encounter such men all the time within Parliament."

It was now his turn to snicker. "And I am certain you encounter them every time you step outside your door."

"And sometimes even inside my home, during what you British refer to as visiting hours."

His face stretched into a grin right as he stepped into a patch of sun, and Ana María caught her breath, for never had she beheld a man quite so captivating.

"I'd like to return to the manner in which you turned your pretty nose up at these quite *imposing* hills." He widened his stance, and Ana María forced herself not to gawk at his form. "Am I to assume that your home in Mexico features hills grander than these?"

Mr. Fox swept his hand at the surrounding countryside, and Ana María noticed he'd yet to put back on his gloves. She stared, transfixed, at the sprinkling of dark hair that peeked out from under his shirtsleeve, and she perversely wondered if it was as soft as it—

"Miss Luna?"

Ana María flinched, darting her gaze up to meet his. Mr. Fox stared at her for a pregnant moment, and slowly arched his brow.

Her face went up in flames, and she was certain it now matched the vivid color of her habit.

Pacing a few steps away to give herself a moment to regain her composure, she aimed for breezy when she murmured, "My apologies. I was just distracted by—" Her thoughts tumbled about in her suddenly empty head. How had a bit of forearm scrambled her mind so thoroughly?

"Distracted by . . . ?" he encouraged, his lips stretching into a smirk. A smug smirk, damn it.

Her spine went ramrod straight. "I was *distracted* by my inspection of the landscape and comparing it to my home. But Mexico City is surrounded by mountains, so these hills do not quite measure up."

"Do *not* tell Lord Tyrell that." Amusement sparked in his eyes. "It sounds as if Mexico City is quite grand."

"I think so," she whispered.

A fierce wave of homesickness swamped her so suddenly, it left her gasping. Stumbling forward, Ana María propped her hand on the trunk of a nearby tree, regaining her balance as she sucked deep breaths into her lungs. She rested her head on the abrasive trunk, clenching her eyes shut, blocking out the rolling English hills, and bringing forth images of her home behind her eyelids. The vivid colors. The crisp scents. The sweltering sun on her skin.

Tilting her head back, she welcomed the sunbeams that caressed her cheeks . . . but they lacked the warmth she craved. Ana María feared she'd never be warm again.

"Describe for me what you're seeing in your mind." His voice sounded close behind her, and she shivered. "I want to know what it's like."

Planting both hands on the tree trunk, she squeezed her eyes tighter. "It's cool, but not cool enough to need a rebozo. The breeze carries the scent of tortillas cooking on el comal and maíz roasting on an open fire." Ana María licked her lips as if she could taste the sweet and spicy treat. "There is music playing in the distance. Una canción de amor. A love song."

"What else?" he asked, his voice stirring the strands of hair along her temple.

"I'm on the rooftop patio, and the city is stretched before me. The colorful buildings, the thatched roofs, the cobblestone streets filled with wagons and bustling crowds. And in the distance is the cathedral, and its bells are chiming, calling worshippers to afternoon Mass."

"What's beyond it? What lies beyond the city and its humming crowds?"

A tremulous smile pulled on her lips. "The mountains. The snow-capped Popocatépetl."

"What is Popo-cat-é-petl?" he asked, his careful pronunciation dancing across the back of her neck.

"It's a volcano. Popocatépetl is a name in náhuatl that means 'smoking mountain.'" Ana María swayed slightly until she felt the ghost of his chest against her back. "There is a Mexica myth that says the mountain was once a young warrior who ventured out of the city to visit the grave of his beloved. The gods took pity on the grieving man and turned him into a mountain, covering him with snow."

"So he could be with his loved one forever?"

Ana María shivered as his breath caressed her cheek. "I suppose."

"Have you noticed that many myths, no matter which culture they originate from, focus on love or loss or revenge?" Gideon rested his chin on the crown of her head. "Why are humans so consumed with the three?"

"Because they remind us we're alive."

The breeze whipped around them, enveloping her in his citrus-and-mint scent and lulling her senses. She was a puddle of want with him pressed against her, his nose and chin nuzzling at her hair. She had never been this close to a man before . . . and frankly, she couldn't imagine permitting anyone else such liberties. Not even Fernando.

For no one had ever made her feel the way Señor Fox—Gideon—did. From the moment their eyes had met, she'd felt as if she knew him. And he knew her. This dance they had performed to avoid each other had stung worse, for each of them knew it was prudent to stay away. Yet their connection still pulsed and pulled like an invisible force whenever they were together, whether across a crowded ballroom or separated by the length of a dining table.

But there was nothing separating them now.

Squaring her shoulders, she pivoted on her heel and brought her eyes up to meet his. Gideon's broad form engulfed her, overwhelmed her, and yet she felt safe. In the depths of her soul, Ana María knew he would never hurt her.

He stared down at her now, his bottomless onyx eyes trailing over her face as if her features were a map to some long-sought destination. And when his gaze landed on her mouth, her lips fell open as her tongue darted out to wet them.

"Señorita Luna"—her name was a growl—"I should very much like to kiss you."

Ana María took a step closer to him, daring to wrap her hands around the hem of his coat. "And I would very much like it if you did."

His mouth hitched up at the corner for a second before he mashed his lips together in a determined slash. With slow movements, he brought his hands—his deliciously bare hands— up to cradle her face, his thumbs sweeping across her cheek- bones in reverent strokes, before he slowly, ever so slowly, brought his mouth down to meet hers.

Until that moment, Ana María had never considered that a kiss could feel like an embrace. That the simple meeting of lips could channel a flood of emotions, each more comforting, more all-consuming, more *fervid*, than the next. For under Gideon's hands, she became lost in the onslaught of all the things they had tried so very hard to ignore. That they had each fought to suppress. For now, as his lips moved over hers, nipping and sa- voring, his tongue sweeping across her mouth as if she were his first taste of heaven, the dam broke, and Ana María intended to submerge herself in the waves.

"I've wanted to do this from the very first moment I saw you," he breathed, breaking free to press his cheek to hers. He wrapped his arm around her waist and hauled her closer still. When he nuzzled his nose along her jaw, gooseflesh swept over her body. "You've made it impossible to stay away."

Giving into the multitude of sensations assaulting her, Ana María lifted her arms to twine them around his neck. "I wasn't trying to tempt you. I know you have responsibilities and can't afford to indulge in dalliances."

Gideon scowled, his dark gaze holding hers. "You deserve more than dalliances. You deserve a man who will recognize how clever you are. How you think deeply about things, and approach new ideas or viewpoints with empathy. How despite a childhood spent in competition with your sisters, you refuse to view them as antagonists, and seek their happiness instead."

Stroking his knuckles down her cheek, he kissed her temple, inhaling deeply of her scent. "You are an amazing woman, Miss Luna, and you deserve the world. And that's the crux."

"It is?" she whispered.

He hummed. "Because I'm not free to give it to you."

It was Ana María's turn to pull back, frowning as she considered him. His cravat was askew, and his hair, always impeccably styled, was mussed. But it was his lips, pink from their assaults on her own, that made him look boyish. His eyes stared at her intently, and she glimpsed sadness lurking in their midnight depths. Although his confession was like a lash across her heart, Ana María knew he was right. Gideon had made it abundantly clear that his career was his priority, and knowing him the way she did now, she understood why. He wasn't working just to realize his own ambitions, but to atone for the past and to create a better future for so many people like him. And although she ached to have him for more than just this stolen moment, *her* future was in Mexico. With another man.

"I'm not asking for the world, Señor Fox." She adjusted the

fall of his cravat, and then settled her palm over where his heart thundered in his chest. "I'm simply asking for another kiss."

His eyes went wide, but he didn't hesitate to acquiesce, lowering his head to capture her lips with his own.

Ana María sighed into his touch, his lips and hands drowning out the fruitless warnings that sounded in the back of her mind. For there would be time to mourn what could not be, and it was not now. Now was for indulging in the impossible.

Gideon had just slipped his hand into her hair when a distant sound cut through her trance. Breaking their kiss, Ana María craned her neck to listen more closely.

"Someone's coming," he whispered, dropping his arm from around her waist and stepping away. Spinning about, he tended to their neglected mounts, taking turns to rub their snouts and croon soft words to them.

Ana María watched him with her arms wrapped tightly about herself, bitterness curling about her and stinging her eyes. She knew this interlude could not last. Although her heart lurched at the thought of never feeling his lips on hers again, never tasting his smooth skin, never hearing his gravelly voice say her name as if she were the most precious, beautiful thing in the world, Ana María blinked back her tears and raised her chin. For heartache had become her old friend.

As the clop of horses' hooves drew closer, Ana María quickly fixed her hair, ensuring all wayward strands were tucked back into place, before she smoothed her hands over the skirts of her habit. By the time the riders appeared around the bend, she fancied she appeared as unruffled as she willed her emotions to be.

"Ana, there you are," Gabby called, waving her arm in greeting. "When we heard what happened, we wanted to find you, but that gruff Mr. Davies insisted his groom would bring you to safety."

Her horse came to a stop, and Gabby leaned over her pommel to inspect her eldest sister. "But then the groom returned without you, stating you were uninjured and being escorted to the manor by Señor Fox. As if such an explanation would possibly appease us. Of course we had to see for ourselves."

"Thankfully, I am just fine, as you can see." She inclined her head in Gideon's direction but couldn't bring herself to look at him. "My guardian angel placed Mr. Fox exactly where he needed to be to ensure all was well."

"Thank you for rescuing our sister, sir," Gabby said, flashing her most winsome smile at the man.

Gideon held his silence, but bowed his head in response.

"Gabby insisted we come and escort you back ourselves." Isabel slid her gaze to where Mr. Fox continued to stand stoically with their mounts. Her eyes narrowed for just a moment, before she blinked and looked back to Ana María. "If that is all right with you, of course."

She was nodding her head before Isabel finished speaking. "I would like nothing better than to enjoy this pleasant afternoon weather with the two of you."

Isabel rolled her eyes, and Ana María suppressed a sigh. "Señor Fox, do you mind playing escort for all three Luna sisters instead of just one?"

"It would be my pleasure," he murmured, holding her gaze for a tense moment and then looking away.

Ana María believed him, and that made the inevitable separation to come that much more painful.

14

The first ball of the Tyrell house party was a grandiose affair.

The ballroom was ablaze with the glow of immense candelabras bedecked with hundreds of beeswax candles that filled the expansive space with a pleasant scent. Gas lamps were placed in strategic locations to add to the ambiance, and ornate double doors were propped open to the veranda, inviting guests to wander about the lamplit gardens. A nine-piece orchestra ensured music notes serenaded guests at all times, coaxing the many attendees to engage in various dances. Lord Tyrell's neighbors came from miles around to partake in the earl's hospitality, and the atmosphere was festive and jolly.

Ana María fiddled with the edge of her dance card as she studied the various names that had been scribbled on it. When they had arrived in the ballroom for the festivities earlier that night, she and her sisters had been promptly greeted by and introduced to every eligible gentleman in the room, and some who were not so eligible, and their dance cards had quickly been filled. As Ana María listened to this viscount discuss his fondness for Spanish rococo architecture, and an older MP from a London borough spent more time looking down her bodice than holding her gaze, she noticed the glances from the debutantes and their mothers. They were critical but without the disdain she had come to expect. A small victory, indeed.

For a passing moment, she permitted her gaze to seek *him* out. The one man she longed to dance with, the one she automatically searched for every time the notes of a waltz strummed through the air. But he had not asked to partner her. Had not spoken with her. Not once.

Oh, she'd felt his gaze on her several times throughout the night, and while they had exchanged a loaded glance a time or two, it appeared that their stolen moment in the home woods was all she could expect of Gideon's company. Ana María knew the ache would lessen with time, but it didn't make it any easier to bear, especially when she observed him leading other women out for a set. Each of her sisters had danced with him, as had Lady Mallory, and in stolen, covert glances, she watched him move about the dance floor, his broad body somehow both imposing and graceful. Ana María did not recall the majority of conversations she engaged in during her sets because her attention had been so ensnared by the one man in the room she could not have.

Now as she made her way to the ladies' retiring room, she delivered a mental admonishment to herself.

You knew *you and Señor Fox could not be. You must remember Fernando. It may be wartime, but an engagement should not be broken so lightly.*

Do you really want to make England your permanent home? For you know Señor Fox would never consent to live in Mexico, not when his work in Parliament is so dear to him. Are you willing to give up your home for his?

It was just a kiss, Ana.

Ana María rubbed at her brow as she walked, for the last

was hard to believe. Not when Gideon had held her so tenderly. Kissed her so desperately. Made her feel . . . so much.

Such thoughts were a waste of time, for Gideon was destined for great things here in England, and she was destined to return to Mexico and Fernando.

A knot lodged in the back of her throat, and Ana María tried in vain to swallow it.

A muffled sound reached her ears as she passed a half-opened door to her right, and her footsteps halted. Was that a cry? A whimper? Did someone need help?

Lifting her skirts, she tiptoed to the door, gingerly bracing her hands on the frame as she angled her head to peer around it. Her eyes widened as a sharp gasp fell from her lips.

Throwing the door open so hard it thudded off the wall, Ana María stalked into the room. "Get your hands off my sister, cabrón!"

Lord Tyrell whipped his head about, his open mouth snapping closed when his gaze fell upon her. After a beat it twisted into a sardonic grin. "Ah, Miss Luna. How good of you to join us."

Ana María glared at the man, her teeth grinding to dust, before lowering her eyes to where he still maintained his vise on Isabel's arm. Her sister's face was red and splotchy as if she had been crying, but she continued to try to shake off the earl's manacle-like hold as if she were a wildcat that had been caught in a snare.

"Unhand her at once, my lord," Ana María demanded again, careful to pitch her voice an octave higher.

"I don't believe I will. Not after I caught her sneaking around this room and rifling through my desk," he replied, giving Isabel a hard jerk for good measure.

"I was doing no such thing," Isabel hissed, scrabbling at the earl's hand on her arm. "I told you I lost my way to the women's retiring room."

"I doubt that." Lord Tyrell lowered his head to snare Isabel's gaze. "The butler has said he's seen you more than once snooping around. Has found you in rooms and wings of the house you do not belong." He suddenly caught her chin between two long fingers. "Why is that? What are you searching for?"

Ana María raced forward, angling her shoulder down as she'd seen Enrique Ugartechea do in a lucha libre match, and collided with the side of the earl's back, taking him by surprise and sending him sprawling onto a nearby chair. While Lord Tyrell collected himself, Ana María clasped Isabel by the hand and hauled her to the door.

"If you ever lay a hand on my sister again—on any woman at this party—I will stab you with my hairpin." Ana María pointed a finger at the man, rage making her entire body tremble. "I know exactly where to put it for maximum injury, and I would be more than happy to show you."

The earl took a step forward, running a hand through his hair, his face twisted in rage. "Listen, you little bitch—"

"Whatever is going on here?"

Jolting in surprise, Ana María glanced over her shoulder to see Lady Yardley and Lady Hampstead in the doorway, their expressions matching thunderstorms. Several heads were visible behind them, and from the cacophony, it seemed they had arrived with a crowd.

The viscountess immediately crossed to her and Isabel, her blue eyes wide with concern. "Are you all right? What happened?"

Before either Ana María or Isabel could answer, Lady Hampstead advanced into the center of the room, her unerring gaze locked on the earl. "What did you do, Tyrell?"

"What makes you think I have done anything—"

The marchioness held up her hand, cutting him off. "Because you are a notorious abuser of women. Oh yes, we women warn our daughters and charges about you and your presumptuous hands and crude words."

The earl smoothed down his lapels, and his expression turned positively terrifying. "And still you accepted my invitation to join me here at Tyrell Manor. How frightening could I be if you're willing to partake of my hospitality?"

"If the choice had been mine, we'd not be here now," Lady Hampstead declared, planting her hands on her hips.

"Come now, your ladyship, do not allow yourself to be swayed by lies. I am always respectful to women, especially those I have welcomed into my house as guests. And anyone who says differently is a liar, no doubt spreading such malicious rumors for their own gain or to draw attention away from their own sins."

"Sins indeed, Tyrell," a gentleman said from the doorway, a scowl on his lips. "My lady wife told me you had said inappropriate things to her, and I did not believe her, much to my shame. And now we find you in here, harassing two young women."

"Harassing? Hardly." The earl threw his arm out to point at Isabel, where she stood enclosed in Ana María's arms. "I found her rifling through my drawers. No doubt looking for state secrets she could pilfer for her savage countrymen."

Their twin gasps were drowned out by Lady Hampstead's raised voice. "That's quite the accusation to throw around, Tyrell, and no doubt unfounded."

"You shame yourself by making such baseless claims, your lordship." Lady Yardley considered him as if he were a foul thing stuck to the bottom of her shoe.

While the earl attempted to argue his case with Lady Hampstead and the other guests, the viscountess turned to them and dropped her voice. "Make haste to your room now. I will follow as soon as I can."

With a quick nod, Ana María clutched Isabel's hand and dragged her through the crowd gathered around the door until they could make a mad dash up the grand staircase. Once they reached their room, Ana María pressed her back against the door as she flipped the lock, her lungs heaving against the confines of her corset with every panting breath. Isabel collapsed onto the bed, her voluminous skirts swallowing her frame until only the tips of her slippered heels were visible.

A few minutes ticked by on the clock as the sisters struggled to catch their breath. When her heartbeat had calmed to a steady pace, Ana María sank onto the mattress next to her sister, searching through the heap of material to find one of her hands and grip it tightly.

"Did he hurt you?"

"Nothing more than a bruise," Isabel murmured.

"Even a bruise is too much, Isa." Ana María stroked her thumbs over her sister's knuckles.

"Yes, well, without your timely arrival, that bruise may have had companions." She shuddered. "I would not put it past the earl."

"Nor would I, which is why we need to leave."

Isabel sat up then, strands of hair falling out of her once-neat bun and cascading about her face. "But we can't. Not after what Tío Arturo said."

"I know." Pressing her lips together, Ana María looked down at their twined hands. "All I know is that Lord Tyrell is not done with us. Men like him will not allow themselves to be humiliated in front of a crowd without some form of retribution."

Breaking their hold, Isabel covered her face with her hands. "Lo siento. I wish I had not gone into that room."

Ana María nibbled on her lip as she pondered her sister. "Why were you in there, Isa? Is it true you were searching through his desk?"

Slowly dropping her hands, Isabel met her sister's eyes, her expression devoid of any discernible emotion. "I was lost."

"But that didn't really answer my question," Ana María pushed, arching a brow.

Isabel worked her jaw, fixing her gaze on the floor. "Don't you just wish we could go home? That we could find *something* to stop this—"

Isabel swallowed whatever other words she planned to say when the handle on the door jiggled. After exchanging a wary glance, Ana María padded to it and pressed her ear against the cool wood. A knock sounded a moment later.

"Ana, Isa, may we come in?"

Releasing a breath, Ana María quickly unlocked the door and swung it open to reveal Gabby, Lady Yardley standing close behind her. Without a word, Gabby dashed toward the bed and all but tackled Isabel in her rush to embrace her.

"I could kill that man for hurting you!" she snarled, tucking her face into Isabel's neck. "I may still do it."

Isabel blinked rapidly as her confused gaze met Ana María's, before she slowly wrapped her arms about their sister. "I pity any man who encounters you in a dark corridor."

"You're too generous, Isa. Any such man would be deserving of my ire."

"Well, ladies," the viscountess began, drawing their attention, "we must leave in the morning, for I will not spend another night in this cursed house."

"I wish we could leave now," Gabby grumbled.

"But where will we go?" Isabel asked, lines of worry appearing in the wings of her eyes. "Tío Arturo warned us to stay away from London for a time."

"I'm aware of your uncle's edict." Lady Yardley paced in front of the fireplace. "I will begin making inquiries. Perhaps Lady Hampstead will allow us refuge at their country estate."

"I would not anticipate such an offer." Gabby scowled. "Lady Mallory told me earlier this evening that her father, Lord Hampstead, is close friends with the earl."

"That explains so much," Ana María murmured under her breath, reflecting on her earlier conversation with the marchioness and the accusations she expressed.

"What was that, my dear?" Lady Yardley asked.

Ana María shook her head.

"I will send Consuelo up to help you all begin packing while I return downstairs." Lady Yardley patted her elegantly coiffured hair and sighed. "I just need a moment to settle my nerves. I'm so thankful the marchioness and I walked by the door when we did, because I'd hate to think of what that loathsome man was capable of."

"Well, rest assured, my lady, that no matter what the earl had tried, he would have met the sharp end of my hairpin in the process," Ana María declared.

Isabel directed a warm smile at her. "You should have seen her. Ana appeared in the doorway like the fearsome Cuerauá-peri. Her eyes were blazing and her lips were curled into a snarl. She was quite frightening, really."

Ana María dipped her head. "I don't like the thought of appearing frightening, but I will make an exception in this case, for I cannot adequately express how enraging it was to find Lord Tyrell with his hands on you."

"Thank you for being there, Ana," Isabel whispered, her dark eyes turning glassy before she looked away.

"I will always be there, Isa. For you and Gabby."

The sisters exchanged a sentimental look before Lady Yardley cleared her throat. "All right, ladies, let us resume this sweet moment another time, for now you must make haste to pack your trunks, for we leave in the morning, regardless of whether we have a destination."

Sleep was fitful that night, and Ana María tossed and turned among the moonbeams that shone through the cracks in the drapes. Sometime in the early-morning hours, sleep finally claimed her, for she jerked awake in a panic when someone shook her shoulder.

"It's just me, Ana," Gabby said, her pretty face filling her vision. "Lady Yardley asked me to awaken you so you can dress."

Ana María sat up and scrubbed her eyes. "Has she found somewhere for us to go?"

Gabby shook her head. "Not yet. At this time, she thinks we should return to London. She said we'd be safer at her home than wandering on the open road."

"That makes sense, I suppose." Ana María smoothed her hand over her plaited hair, imagining what awaited them when they departed from Tyrell Manor. "Our very first house party has been memorable, don't you think?"

"Most disastrous things are memorable, I'd wager." Gabby lifted the skirt of her nightdress and crossed her legs under her. "I wish I had been there last night to help you defend Isabel from the earl."

"Well, selfishly, I'm glad you weren't. Because then I would have had two sisters to worry about instead of one."

"I can take care of myself." Gabby's shoulders sank as she

picked at the hem of her nightdress. "I've often been left to my own devices, so I've had to learn to see to myself."

Ana María's heart suddenly lodged in her throat, and she opened and closed her mouth like a fish for an uncomfortable moment. It was no secret that Gabby, the third daughter, whom their father had longed to be a son, was often pushed off on las niñeras and later governesses. But their mother's affinity for Gabriela, who was made in her image, seemed to harden Elías Luna's heart toward her further. Ana María had always been so frustrated with her sister's exuberant antics, her lightning-quick temper . . . but spending this time with her in England had made it abundantly clear that Gabby had just wanted to be seen. To be valued. To be loved.

Carefully placing her arm about her youngest sister's shoulders, ignoring how they instantly stiffened at the contact, Ana María whispered, "I know you can take care of yourself, querida. But you shouldn't have to. Not all the time."

The starch gradually seeped from her frame, and eventually Gabby rested her head against Ana María's shoulder. The pair breathed in harmony for several minutes, the early-morning light enveloping them in a halo of peace and quiet.

"Is it wrong for me to be happy we're here?" Gabby asked, her voice barely a whisper.

"Of course not." Ana María leaned into her sister's side, causing her to sway. "But if I recall from our voyage, you were quite *vocal* about your unhappiness in having to leave Mexico."

"Oh, my mood fluctuates." Gabby snorted. "I'm sure that's not surprising to you."

"I don't know what you're talking about," she assured, although her frame shook with a suppressed laugh.

Gabby smacked her leg. "I miss home terribly. I miss Mother, and the staff. I miss waking up early, and stepping into the courtyard to be greeted by a warm sun and a balmy breeze. And yet . . ."

Ana María waited a moment, before she prodded. "And yet?"

"And yet, here, in this frigid, humorless place, I have been given liberties I never would have been granted at home." A breath expanded her lungs. "Instead of being known as Señor Luna's youngest daughter, the traviesa who causes trouble wherever she goes, I'm Miss Gabriela Luna, a proud Mexican and whatever else *I* decide to be."

Ana María smirked. "And what do you want to be?"

Lifting a shoulder, Gabby fidgeted with her hem again. "I don't know yet. But I'm determined not to be auctioned off to the highest bidder for use as a broodmare."

Gabby's jaw was locked tight, her hands clenched at her sides, as if she could contain all the rage and feeling of impotence that coursed through her body at such a thought. She speared Ana María with a piercing look.

"Father didn't even ask if you wanted to marry Señor Ramírez. He didn't even make the man court you before he proposed because Señor Ramírez had courted Father instead." She threw her hands into the air. "That makes no sense. You are the one who will have to live with him. Share a bed with him. Bear his children. And he wasn't even expected to get to know you aside from your name. Your *surname*."

Ana María tried to draw breath, but it abruptly felt like her chest had been cracked open, exposing everything to the light. Instinctively, she drew her knees up and hugged them close, as if she could hold herself together. Exhaling a ragged breath, she asked, "And what would you have me do?"

Coming to a halt, Gabby's face fell, her eyes sad and haunting. "What could you have done? What power do you have, Ana?"

Clenching her eyes closed, Ana María shook her head.

"That's what I want to change. We should have more authority over our own lives." A thudding sound caused Ana María to blink her eyes open, watching as her sister pounded her fist into her palm.

The door opened before Ana María could respond, and Isabel entered the room. She paused on the threshold, her eyes darting between the pair of them.

"Lady Yardley wants us dressed as soon as possible. She said she'll retrieve us as soon as the carriage is ready."

"Are we permitted to go downstairs to eat breakfast?" Gabby asked.

Isabel shook her head. "She asked us to remain here. She'd like to limit any possibility of us encountering Lord Tyrell."

Ana María and Gabby exchanged a glance, and then nodded.

"Well, I suppose I've lounged in this bed long enough." Throwing the covers aside, Ana María dropped her feet to the cold floor. "Will you help me dress so I don't have to bother Consuelo? I'm certain she's quite busy getting us prepared to depart."

Sometime later, Isabel and Gabby sat in the armchairs before the fireplace, with Ana María meandering about the room. Dark clouds hung low over the horizon, and fog clung to grass, casting a dreamlike quality over the landscape. How was it possible they had arrived just days prior? So much had happened in that time, from her first kiss to the horrid confrontation with Lord Tyrell. It was as if fate could not let her experience happiness for too long without raining down its displeasure upon her. She had reached for something forbidden, something her heart desired, and had been punished for it.

And then she recalled Gabby's passionate words, and she lifted her chin. She deserved good things. She deserved respect.

Gentle touches and soul-consuming kisses. Ana María deserved much more than polite regard; she deserved—she *demanded*—love.

A knock sounded at the door. Isabel snapped her copy of *Respuesta a sor Filotea* closed as she rose to her feet. "It's Lady Yardley. Are we ready?"

Gabby and Ana María nodded, shaking out their skirts, as Isabel opened the door . . . and all the air was abruptly sucked from the room.

Earl Tyrell crossed the threshold and swung the door closed before Isabel even had a chance to respond, the sharp crack of wood on wood echoing through the room and reverberating through Ana María's body. His blue gaze swept over them in icy regard.

"So it appears the whispers that you were preparing to leave were correct," he drawled.

The sisters remained mute as they cautiously watched the earl.

"Sit," he commanded, pointing down as if they were pet dogs he was bringing to heel.

Indignation fired through her blood, unfreezing her limbs and her tongue. "What is the meaning of this?"

Ana María purposely left off any honorifics, for the man deserved no such respect.

"I asked you to sit," he bit out, his eyes narrowed on her.

"And as I am not your pet, or your servant, or any other person beholden to you"—she narrowed her eyes—"I refuse."

A grin—unnerving and a tad taunting—split across his face, and Ana María unconsciously took a small step back. "Whatever made you think you were not beholden to me?"

"We'll be gone from Tyrell Manor within the hour, my lord," Isabel said, her tone firm.

The earl shook his head, his perfectly styled dark hair flitting across his brow. "I would think twice about doing that, for if you do, I will instruct my secretary to send off the telegram I have written to my *friends* in London."

"What do you mean?" Gabby demanded.

"I have many friends who have kept an interested eye on the three of you since you arrived." His lips twisted into a sneer. "My French friends."

The sisters gasped in unison, which drew a bark of laughter from the earl. "Aah, I see you recognize the delicate situation you find yourselves in."

He walked to the window, coming to stand an arm's length away from Ana María, his attention trained on the world outside the glass panes. "Didn't you think it odd you were invited here when we had not been properly introduced?"

They had. They *had* thought it odd. Lady Yardley had had every intention of declining the invitation until the rumors had begun to circulate . . .

"It was you who spread word that French intelligence was detaining Mexican nationals," she murmured on a harsh breath.

"My friends did that." He flicked a dismissive hand. "They knew getting you out of London was key, and my invitation would be a welcomed refuge."

"But why would they want us?" Gabby demanded, moving to link arms with her.

Time seemed to suspend for Ana María, for she knew what he would say. And she couldn't stop the awful truth from dripping from his lips.

"Because they know who you are. They know who your father is." Tyrell splayed a hand. "And they know how important he is to the rebel government."

"I don't—" Ana María swallowed and tried again. "I don't know what you're talking about."

The earl took a step forward, until his face hovered before her own. His eyes were slits of barely contained malice. "Of course you do. Because despite your lovely face, you are quite the clever girl."

Gabby dug her nails into Ana María's arm, vibrating with fury—or perhaps it was fear—and her sister's presence bolstered her nerve enough that she managed to hold Lord Tyrell's gaze without flinching.

With his face relaxing back into casual disregard, the earl spun away and prowled back to the door. Propping his shoulder against it, he looked almost bored. Ana María gritted her teeth when she realized he was blocking their escape.

"Your father is Elías Luna Cuate, the senior adviser to President Benito Juárez. My friends in French intelligence tell me that Mr. Luna is one of most influential men in the Liberal government. The same government that has been chased out of power." He crossed his arms over his chest. "But as that very same rebel government is continuing to cause trouble for Napoleon, I think they would be very happy to have the three Luna daughters delivered into their hands. Leverage and all that."

Sliding her gaze to Isabel, Ana María found her sister staring at Lord Tyrell with her mouth agape. Locking eyes with Ana María, Isabel seemed to say, *What do we do now?*

Stuttering a breath, Ana María finally said, "I suspect you want something for our continued freedom, then?"

"I knew you were a clever girl." He clapped his hands. "Now sit while I tell you my terms."

Locking her teeth together, Ana María dragged Gabby to the bed, where they sat, Isabel joining them. The trio linked hands, prepared to face his verdict together.

15

Stripping off his gloves, Gideon smacked them against his thigh as he climbed the stairs leading back to his chamber. His morning hack across the damp, foggy meadows had been meant to strip the memories of Ana María's taste, the feel of her willing, curvy body within his arms, from his mind, where they had been haunting him since the previous day. But even the crisp, fresh air could not exorcise her demons.

And as if those memories had not harassed him enough, he could add the glimpses he saw of her last night at the ball. Her stunning gold embroidered gown had seemed to capture all the light in the room and caused her to glow, making her the brightest object in his vision. Gideon had been helpless to look away, although he had tried his hardest by dancing with other women whose faces he could not even remember. But the real twist to the proverbial knife was that he had danced with each of her sisters, who were both charming and lovely, yet they were not her.

No one was, and Gideon knew, in the churning depths of his soul, that he would never meet another woman quite like her.

Dragging a hand across his brow, Gideon turned a corner

and came up short, quickly tucking himself, as best he could, into an alcove. Peering out, he spied Lord Tyrell exiting a door down the hall, a sort of self-satisfied smile on his lips that left Gideon's teeth on edge. He watched the man disappear in the other direction, whistling a merry tune. Whatever put the earl in such a good mood probably spelled misfortune for another poor person. He had heard about the confrontation the man had the previous night with a few of his guests, although he wasn't certain what it had stemmed from. Biting the inside of his cheek, he pondered whether the two were related.

Gideon glanced back at the door Lord Tyrell just exited. Did he know the guests staying there? The earl had left it ajar, and he battled an overwhelming urge to see if the occupants were in need of help.

Setting his jaw, Gideon stepped out of his hiding space and walked toward the door, intending to glance in as he passed. But as he did so, his gaze fell upon Miss Isabel, who had her face buried in her hands. All thoughts of walking by flew out of his mind, and Gideon pushed open the door, his eyes immediately traveling from Miss Isabel's bent head and landing on Miss Luna like a lodestar in a dark sky. Her face was ghostly pale, her eyes red-rimmed and swollen.

"What's happened?" he demanded, rushing to drop to his knee before her. "What did that fiend say to you?"

Ana María blinked down at him with large eyes, her mouth slack. "Wh-what are you doing here?"

"I just saw Lord Tyrell depart, and in much too jolly of a mood." Gideon reached forward to boldly grasp her hand. "Ana María, what happened?"

His use of her Christian name—a liberty he had never taken and she had never offered—seemed to snap her back into awareness, for she exhaled. "He threatened to deliver us to his French allies."

A stone settled in Gideon's gut. "His French allies?"

She nodded. "Apparently the earl has friends, as he called them, within French intelligence. You can surely understand why they might have a vested interest in—"

"The occupation of Mexico." Gideon rocked back on his soles but did not loosen his grip on her hand. "But why would they be concerned about you and your sisters? What would they gain by your imprisonment?"

Isabel lifted her head then, her eyes hollow. "They believe they'd gain our father's cooperation."

Gideon's eyes darted between them. "I don't understand."

"Our father is a top adviser to the Mexican president."

Oh. A roar filled his ears, and it took him a moment to realize it was the sound of his racing heart. *Christ, of course their parents were of some great importance, for why else had they been sent so far away?*

Gideon tried to swallow around his dry throat. "But why did you come here? Surely a man of your father's connections and power would have preferred to keep you closer."

Ana María's sigh rattled with a depth of exhaustion. "Our father wanted us to stay in Mexico, but our mother refused. She insisted we be sent here, entrusting our safety, as well as the fortune we carried, to her brother."

"Her brother?" Gideon frowned before his eyes went wide. "Do you mean Señor Valdés?"

She nodded, but it was Gabby who broke her silence. "Our full name is Luna Valdés, but we dropped the latter to keep our connection to our tío a secret. Which is also why we have made our home with Lady Yardley, rather than with him."

Gideon raked a hand along his scalp as he attempted to reconcile all the new details he'd just learned. So many puzzle pieces were abruptly sliding into place, like Ana María's quick grasp of international relations and her savvy political mind. She'd apparently been raised in the center of Mexican politics, with a presidential adviser as a father and an ambassador as an uncle.

Other memories slammed into him, and Gideon climbed to his feet, pressing his fingers to his temple as he sorted through them, vaguely aware that the ladies were watching him. Ana María had hinted that her life was not her own, which didn't stand out to him at the time, for most young women of wealthy families were often used as bargaining chips. It was an ugly reality. But knowing her connection to the Mexican government changed things so completely. Gideon glanced at her over his shoulder, his heart lurching at the lost look in her normally sparkling eyes.

Goddamn Lord Tyrell.

His chest expanded and condensed as he took a moment to focus, before turning to face them. "So Lord Tyrell has threatened to hand you over to his connections within the French government. What did he ask of you as an alternative?"

Gideon's skin began to tingle at the loaded look the sisters shared. When no one volunteered the information, he pushed. "He had to have asked for something. The earl is a schemer, and if he senses a way in which to benefit from others' misfortunes, he will not hesitate to exploit it."

He looked to Ana María, who held his gaze for a moment, before she wrenched her eyes closed. "The earl said that if I marry him, he will keep us safe from the French."

A punch to the gut was the only way Gideon could describe the painful sensation that ripped the air from his lungs in a labored whoosh. He staggered back a step and shook his head back and forth, the only word he could manage a simple "No."

"I don't have a choice, Señor Fox." Although she kept her eyes closed, she squared her shoulders. "Lord Tyrell knows about the fortune we brought from Mexico, and he wants it." Her laugh bordered on hysterical. "What better way to ensure our dependence upon him, while also securing a powerful incentive for the French to work with him."

"Ana, you can't marry that man." Gabby's voice broke, but her eyes sparked with intensity. "We did not escape war, travel across the ocean, and finally taste a bit of freedom for you to fall into the snare of such a vicious snake of a man."

Ana María hiccuped a breath and pressed her hand to her mouth for a long moment. "I'd be a countess, I suppose."

"As if you've ever cared about such a ridiculous thing as a title," Isabel declared. Biting her lip, she finally whispered, "I'm sorry, Ana. It's my fault you're in this situation. I'm the one who went in Lord Tyrell's study. I'm the reason you rushed in to save me and made a scene."

"Wait," Gideon cut in, holding up his hands, "what are you talking about?"

Isabel studied Ana María for a moment, and then sighed deeply, her shoulders curling in. "At the ball last night," she began, before launching into an explanation of the events that occurred the night prior.

When she was done, Gideon stared at the ground, struggling to keep his rage and disgust in check. In that moment, he wanted to track down the earl and throttle the man for even thinking he could treat two young women who were his guests so crassly. Such behavior could not be borne . . . though Lord Tyrell was attempting to punish Ana María still.

"Marry me instead."

His words dropped with all the weight of a bomb, and all three women reared back, their mouths falling open. And Gideon couldn't blame them. He had not even thought the words, so he was just as surprised to hear them echo about him.

But they rang with confidence.

Ana María slapped a hand over her mouth as she stared at him, unblinking.

Licking his lips, Gideon compelled the right words to come to him to make this better. To make her understand, for although he had no notion he would propose, and had certainly not weighed what a marriage to Ana María would mean, Gideon refused to take them back. Not when they tasted so good to say.

"If we marry, Miss Luna, I can protect you. I have connections and enough power to ensure that you, Isabel, and Gabby remain safe." He yanked on his waistcoat, alarmed to find himself out of breath. "But aside from protection, as your husband I can offer you a comfortable life filled with opportunities to do good works and push forth reforms that would make this world a better place to live for all people. I would respect you, even more than I do now."

Her gaze was unrelenting, her eyes staring into the heart of him. The secret part of him that was certain he would fall in love with her . . . and perhaps had already done so.

"And what do you gain?" Ana María dropped her hand and considered him, her face expressionless. "You offer me respect, safety, the chance to help you shape policy, but whatever do you gain from taking me as your wife?"

"Your share of the family fortune," Gabby interjected.

Gideon frowned at her for a moment, before looking back to Ana María. How could she possibly ask what he would gain? Wasn't that abundantly clear?

"What do I gain?" He furrowed his brow as he shook his head. "Miss Luna, I would gain *you*. The chance to welcome every sunrise by your side and say good night to every sunset. Just spending my life with you, orbiting around your smile and laugh, would make me the richest of men."

He didn't dare look away from her, tension leaking from his body at the soft hint of a smile that curved her pink lips. But it was immediately replaced by a harsh line.

"But a marriage to me could overshadow your work." Her chin trembled, but not her voice. "I don't want you to lose the support you've worked hard to gain for your global slave trade mandate."

"But I won't." Gideon advanced toward her, his gaze beseeching. That sense of rightness, of certainty had grown, rooting itself deep in his soul. "For so long my whole life has been working toward meeting that goal, trying to honor my grandmother's legacy. Her bravery and sacrifice. But also I . . ." He swallowed, and shook his head, determined not to admit more than was necessary. Ana María needed his strength in this moment, not his vulnerability. "Miss Luna, you are clever and brave and charming, and I know you will speak passionately and eloquently about these great evils I've been working against. We could form an admirable . . . partnership."

Pangs of alarm ricocheted through his head, shrieking at him to remember the powerful enemy he would earn in Lord Tyrell if he went through with such a plan. But Gideon knew—knew in the marrow of his bones—that he'd rather the earl be his enemy than for Miss Luna to be that monster's wife.

"And what of Señor Ramírez?" Isabel asked, her brows pulled low.

Gideon steeled himself, for he knew this portion of the conversation would require delicacy.

"What about him?" Ana María growled, propelling herself to her feet. She stalked to the door and spun about in a swish of crinoline and linen. "I told the earl of my engagement, and he did not care because Fernando is not here. My engagement to him will not shield us from Lord Tyrell's machinations. There is no way for him to help."

But Gideon could. Damn it, he was here and he could help. He could finally drop the pretenses that caused him to hold her at a distance—

"And Señor Ramírez was never her choice, Isa. You know that," Gabby pointed out.

"I do." Isabel rubbed her brow. "Yet once again Ana finds herself with few options."

Gabby made a rough sound in the back of her throat, but before she could reply, Gideon interjected. "I don't know what to say to make this better, ladies. You have been placed in a horrible situation in which a choice must be made, and for that I am sorry."

"Ana," Gabby exclaimed, throwing her arms wide as she stared at her sister, "there is *no* choice. Surely you know that."

"I know," she whispered in a quaking voice. Her eyes shot up to his, and she stared at him for a long moment. "I'd be happy to marry you, Señor Fox."

Elation streaked through his blood, hot and bright. Gideon took a minute to simply look at her, taking in the lines of her face, and while he wouldn't describe her expression as joyous, the soft curve of her lips and the shy twinkle in her eyes gave him hope.

She was to be his wife, and Gideon's heart lurched out of rhythm at the thought.

The sound of a throat clearing—he vaguely suspected it was

Gabriela's—snapped him from his daydream. "Right, well, first things first, we have to deliver you all safely from here."

"Lady Yardley left some time ago to make inquiries for where we can take refuge and to request the carriage be brought around," Isabel explained.

A knock sounded on the door, and they all froze. Gideon instinctively planted himself before Ana María, his mind praying that Earl Tyrell stood on the other side of the door so he had an opportunity to rip the man's throat out with his bare hands.

The door swung open a moment later, and the viscountess entered, a harried aura surrounding her.

"The carriage is still—" She drew up short, her blue eyes flying wide when she noticed Gideon. "Whatever are you doing in here, Mr. Fox?"

Before he could respond, Ana María stepped to his side and fit her arm through his. Her presence comforted him, although he knew he was the one who should be providing comfort.

"Much has happened since you left, Lady Yardley, including my rather sudden engagement to Señor Fox," she said, her tone calm, even as he detected a tremor in her frame.

The viscountess blinked at them for a long moment, before she allowed Gabriela to lead her to an armchair, which she sank onto like a stone in a bucket. "Someone please explain to me what is going on before I swoon."

Gideon remained by Ana María's side as she recounted the early-morning visit with Lord Tyrell, the man's frightful ultimatum, and Gideon's own arrival and subsequent offer. He was impressed by how well Lady Yardley took the news, nodding approvingly when Miss Luna explained that she had accepted his offer.

"Well, of course you should marry Mr. Fox. He would make a splendid match for you, and I've long thought that." Gideon took a step back when she flashed a glare at him. "Pity it took this situation with that vile Lord Tyrell for you to act."

"It does not trouble you that Miss Luna was engaged to another man?" Gideon asked with a shake of his head.

"Yes, but he's not here, now is he? And engagements can be broken." Lady Yardley scoffed. "I've been waiting for you to win her over."

Opening and closing his mouth as excuses and apologies tangled together, Gideon finally snapped it closed with an audible clack of teeth. Darting a glance across the room, he almost laughed at the disbelieving frowns on Isabel's and Gabby's faces. He chose to believe their expressions were because they doubted Lady Yardley's claim, not because they doubted him.

The viscountess shook her head at him one more time, before she smacked her hands on her thighs. "So I'm going to assume that the reasons the earl's grooms keep blocking my coachmen from bringing the carriage around is that they have been instructed not to by Tyrell? That villain."

"I'd wager you're correct, my lady." Gideon closed his eyes for a moment as he considered how he could best help the women leave Tyrell Manor. It would be a delicate thing . . . but then the earl wasn't aware that he was helping them. Subterfuge would be key.

Gideon swept his gaze across the women before looking down at Ana María. "I know where we can go. I just need to send a note as soon as possible so our host can expect our arrival. I also need to ask if he would be so kind as to acquire a special license for us."

"Remember, I'm not Anglican," she whispered, staring up at him.

"And neither am I." He flashed a quick, commiserating smile. "I'll do my best to secure the services of a priest."

Glancing back at the other ladies, he beckoned them to come closer. "Here is my idea to smuggle you lot out of here. We're going to need to act quietly but quickly. Are you ready?"

They nodded eagerly, and Gideon went about explaining his plan, a bit of confidence creeping into his tone with every word he spoke.

This would work, he told himself. By the end of the day, they would be on the road, racing to Dancourt Abbey and his new, unexpected future with Ana María Luna.

The carriage hit a rock and pitched Ana María into Isabel, who grumbled in her sleep. Flexing her stiff back as best she could in the cramped space, she pulled back the drapes on the carriage window and looked out on the darkening countryside that passed in a blur. Ana María had no notion of where they were, but she trusted Gideon.

Dios mío, soon she would be Señora Ana María Luna de Fox.

Allowing the drapes to fall back into place, Ana María rested her head on the seat back and closed her eyes as the day's events flashed behind her eyelids. How was it possible that the morning began with Lord Tyrell threatening to hand them over to the French unless she married him? Looking into his cold, menacing eyes now seemed like a lifetime ago, the terror and then resignation that followed a terrible memory. For then Gideon had appeared and made everything right.

He'd somehow found a groom willing to rush a message off to his friends, and then stealthily carried their trunks from their rooms, down the servants' staircase, to the wagon of a local farmer who had arrived at Tyrell Manor to make a delivery. After receiving a generous payment, the man had hidden the three sisters among the hay and boxes that littered the wagon, and then drove it to a nearby village to wait for Gideon and Lady Yardley.

Ana María was not sure how long they waited, curled up on the wagon floor, stifling sneezes and ignoring painful cramps, until Lady Yardley's carriage arrived. But after that indeterminate amount of time, they were hustled into the carriage, their trunks carefully but quickly stowed, and they were off, the team of horses thundering down the road and taking them to safety. She'd not had a moment to speak with Gideon, who traveled as an outrider next to the carriage, and Lady Yardley had made it clear when she finally settled in the cab that she was not in the mood to discuss what had transpired after they had been smuggled away. The viscountess had promptly fallen asleep, leaving the sisters anxious and on edge.

Glancing across the cab at the older woman, whose body bounced on the squab with every divot in the road, Ana María smiled. She imagined that Lady Yardley had not expected this amount of excitement or *chaos* when she agreed to serve as chaperone for her and her sisters, and Ana María was thankful for the older woman.

Several minutes later—or perhaps it was hours, for Ana María found it difficult to judge time in the dark cab—the horses began to slow and the carriage pitched to the right. A glance out the window showed her that they had turned down a drive of sorts. It appeared unmarked, but again, she could not be certain. Within a handful of minutes, the carriage jolted as it came to a stop.

"Have we arrived?" the viscountess asked, lifting her head and tapping under her eyes with her gloved fingers.

"I believe so." Ana María lightly shook Isabel's shoulder to rouse her.

The door to the carriage opened at that moment, and Gideon

filled the entry, a gas lantern held high in his hand. His gaze immediately went to hers.

"We've arrived, ladies. Are you ready to disembark and meet your host?"

"Indeed," Lady Yardley announced, clutching Dove in her arms as she squeezed her wide skirts through the doorway with Gideon's assistance.

Isabel and Gabby had finally stirred, and sleepily stepped from the carriage. When it was Ana María's turn, she took a moment to calm her sudden nerves, for she knew that when she stepped down from the conveyance, everything would change. If Gideon's friend had been successful in procuring a special license, they would be married within the week, if not sooner. She would soon be Mrs. Fox. He would be her *husband*.

She would likely never return to Mexico again.

The realization made her sway on her feet.

"Here, let me help you." Gideon grabbed her by the arm and carefully led her down the steps, taking the majority of her weight upon himself. When her feet finally hit the ground, he stared down at her for a moment, his brows crinkled in concern. "I know a good deal has transpired this day, and you have handled every obstacle admirably. You just have a short distance left to walk, and you can retire directly to your chambers. How does that sound?"

Exhaling deeply, Ana María nodded. "That sounds lovely, señor."

"Please call me Gideon." He reached up to tuck a strand of hair behind her ear, his hand lingering on her cheek. "I think you more than deserve to use that name."

"Well, then please call me Ana María." She leaned into his touch, closing her eyes. "Or Ana."

She sensed, rather than saw, his gentle but knowing smile.

"Come along, Fox, your future bride is no doubt famished."

Taking a step back, Gideon rolled his eyes. "I should apologize now for any outrageous behavior you may witness while you are here. If there was somewhere else we could have gone, I would have chosen it."

Peering around his shoulder, she spied the silhouettes of two gentlemen standing at the bottom of the entry stairs, a collection of servants waiting on the top landing to welcome them inside. "Who are they? Where are we?"

Gideon pivoted and, placing his hand on the small of her back, walked with her. "We are at Dancourt Abbey, the country estate of my friend Captain Dawson. I'm sure you recognize the Duke of Whitfield standing by his side."

Ana María could not smother her snort of amusement. "I'm certain my sisters were thrilled when they learned the identity of our hosts."

"I confess I heard Gabby exclaim something in Spanish that sounded suspiciously like a curse."

"Oh, I'm sure it was." She chuckled, reflecting for a moment that laughter was even possible after their tumultuous day.

"Miss Luna, I'm very happy to welcome you, Lady Yardley, and your sisters to my home," Captain Dawson said as they approached. His bow was crisply executed. "And I must confess that I am more than pleased to host your nuptials as well."

Dipping into a curtsy, Ana María smiled. "I still can't believe that I will be married."

"Nor I," Gideon added, scoffing when Dawson clapped him on the shoulder.

"Our best-laid plans never quite work out the way we expect," the duke intoned. Stepping forward, he reached for Ana María's hand and brought it to his lips, bussing her knuckles discreetly. "But so often they work out better than we could have imagined, don't you agree, Fox?"

Gideon huffed a breath at her side. "I need a dram of brandy before I'm prepared to hold a conversation with you, Whitfield." Stepping between the men, he grasped Ana María's hand with a small, private smile and pulled her after him. "My future bride needs to rest, for she has had a challenging day. Thank you for your hospitality, Dawson. I am in your debt."

"You are indeed, my friend," Dawson said with a smile. "But I shall endeavor to make repayment painless."

"Let us hope," Gideon replied, already leading her up the stairs.

Dancourt Abbey was what Ana María would call a well-appointed hunting lodge. It boasted no great works of art on the walls or lush Moroccan rugs. Instead, rich wood accents framed the towering casement windows that overlooked the darkened landscape, and polished oak paneling lined the walls. A fire roared in an imposing stone fireplace that took up the entirety of one wall, and the hearth was flanked by spacious leather armchairs and a cozy rug. What it lacked in stylish decor, it more than made up for in comfort, and tension seeped from Ana María's bones as she took in her surroundings.

Following the housekeeper up the narrow staircase, she peered about herself as they walked down the hall, noting the cleanliness of the home, which was always a good sign. At the end of the corridor, the housekeeper opened a door, revealing Isabel and Gabby already sorting through their trunks with Consuelo looking on.

"And here is where you and your sisters will be staying, Miss Luna." The older woman smiled. "The captain thought you may be more comfortable sharing a chamber together"—

she glanced at Gideon, who stood just behind her—"for now, at least."

A blush swept across Ana María's face and down her neck until she was certain her skin was on fire. Memories of the taste and shape of Gideon's lips flashed through her mind like a bolt of lightning, and soon she would be at liberty to indulge in all manner of carnal pleasures with the man who had fascinated her from the first.

As if sensing her thoughts, Gideon placed one of his hands on her waist—one of his very large hands—and squeezed.

Ana María was only just able to contain her shiver. "Thank you, Mrs. Ormsby. My sisters and I appreciate all your help, especially at this late hour."

"We are most pleased to welcome you. A maid will be coming up soon with dinner trays for you all."

The older woman bobbed a quick curtsy and bustled away, leaving her alone with Gideon. Ana María stood staring after her, not quite willing to enter the room yet. Her tongue felt frozen in her mouth, though, for she could not get out a word with Gideon standing so close to her.

But whatever words she managed, she was certain she did not want her sisters overhearing them. Ana María closed the door, steadfastly ignoring Isabel's and Gabriela's curious stares. Amusement . . . and something *darker* . . . sat on Gideon's expression when she looked up at him.

"I know this day has been quite a whirlwind," he began, stepping closer still.

"That is putting it mildly," she managed with a cracking voice.

He smirked as he looked down at her . . . and then his expression turned serious. "But now that you and your sisters are safe, I would understand if you've changed your mind about our *understanding*."

Ana María pulled her chin back. "Why would I change my mind?"

Gideon shook his head, his brow crinkled. "Ana, you've made it clear during the months of our acquaintance that much of your life has been dictated to you. You've been controlled by your father for his own ends." He dropped his hand from her waist. "Your time here in England was supposed to be your chance to spread your metaphorical wings, if you will, and it haunts me to think you would settle for me as your husband as a means to keep you and your sisters safe."

She missed his touch. But more so, Ana María appreciated that he seemed to understand how her time in England was supposed to be her chance to make her own decisions. Choose the life she wanted to live.

Summoning every ounce of courage she possessed, Ana María reached forward to grab his hand. Licking her lips, she forced herself to meet his curious eyes. "Just because the circumstances are inconvenient and not at all what I would have chosen for myself does not mean that this choice was hard. Had my attentions been free to give, I would have gladly paid them to you."

Her confession sparked a metamorphosis of his face, changing his expression from guarded acquiescence to fiery hope, the sight lifting a weight from her shoulders she'd not known she carried.

"I will be a good wife to you," she murmured, squeezing his fingers, delighting in the feel of his bare palm against her own.

"I know." Gideon brushed the back of his hand against her cheek. "Just as I know we will be happy together. I will make sure of it."

Ana María nodded, for she chose to believe he was right.

16

"My man of business arrived with the special license an hour ago."

Gideon pushed out his chair and stretched his back after several hours spent holed up in Dawson's small library. He'd been busy writing letters to Stansberry, as well as Lord Montrose, explaining what had occurred at Tyrell Manor two days prior. He knew the marquess would not be pleased, but truly, what was Gideon to have done? Even as he sat on the back of a horse he had borrowed from the kindly Lady Hampstead, the miles long and the road craggy, Gideon did not regret offering his help and protection to the Luna sisters. And he certainly did not regret his proposal of marriage to Miss Luna.

Ana María. Christ, how he loved the shape of her name on his tongue.

Rising to his feet, he reached out to grasp Dawson's hand. "Thank you for helping me procure it. I'm not certain I would have been as successful as you."

Dawson advanced to the sideboard, studying the selection before grabbing a decanter. "Care for a dram? To celebrate, of course."

Gideon offered his thanks as the door creaked open, Whitfield appearing like a wraith in the entry. He raised his brows in question. Or perhaps in greeting. One never knew with the duke.

"If we do not invite you in, does that mean you cannot cross the threshold?" Gideon drawled, accepting a tumbler from Dawson.

"You really are an arse, Fox." Whitfield kicked the door closed behind him. Sinking into a leather armchair, he propped his chin on his hand, a portrait of ennui. "And here I intended to congratulate you on winning the hand of the young woman who has transfixed you from the start."

Gideon propped his hip against the sideboard. "If I recall correctly, which I naturally do, it was you who first noticed Gabriela and brought the sisters to my attention."

The duke nodded his thanks to Dawson when the man offered him a glass, and spun it about, giving the alcohol some air. "And I have rued the day ever since. I should have known not to trust those pretty hazel eyes of hers."

"Is that who I heard you bickering with in the drawing room earlier?" Dawson asked, smiling over his tumbler.

"A duke does not bicker." Whitfield smirked when the two other men scoffed. Taking a long drink, he raised a shoulder. "But apparently my presence was enough to sour Gabriela's mood, and she felt compelled to tell me so."

Gideon and Dawson shared a chuckle. It was so diverting to see the normally caustic and unbothered Whitfield so perturbed.

"That's why you brought them here and interrupted my holiday, isn't it, Fox?" Whitfield pointed a finger at him. "Because you knew that she would be my own personal biblical plague."

"As much as I would like to say that such thoughts were on

my mind, in truth, I was simply intent on removing the women from that situation as quickly as possible," Gideon said, studying the alcohol in his glass.

The rush to depart Tyrell Manor had taken careful maneuvering and more than a few bribes paid, which Lady Yardley happily funded. The entire time they were on the road to Dancourt Abbey, Gideon had been on edge, looking over his shoulder to ensure the earl had not sent his men after them. Because he knew that leaving the manor would not be the end of the story.

As if he could read Gideon's thoughts, Dawson set his alcohol aside and leaned forward to brace his forearms on his knees. "I've stationed several of my men around the estate to monitor who comes on and off the premises. I also sent word to some old comrades of mine in London to see if they would be interested in providing security for the next several weeks as we determine what sort of a threat Lord Tyrell intends to be."

Gideon nodded, gratitude warming his skin.

"If it all works out as I have planned," Dawson continued, "they will be able to escort your secretary and Father Duncan here as well."

"That would be ideal." Gideon took a bracing sip. "When do you anticipate their arrival?"

"If your secretary telegraphs from the train station, we can expect them within six or so hours." Dawson's brows rose. "If that is the case, you can be married tomorrow. Or the next day, I suppose. Whichever you'd prefer."

Rubbing his forehead, Gideon sighed. "The sooner the better. I know Tyrell will cause trouble, and I want to cut him off at every pass."

"And we will do our best to help you," Dawson said, jerking his head at Whitfield.

"But what of your proposal, Fox?" Whitfield stared at him intently over his glass. "The whole reason you attended that infernal house party, and turned down the invitation to join us here, was that you and Montrose decided winning Tyrell's support was key. But now you've absconded with his quarry. That doesn't seem like a shrewd political move."

Gideon's cheeks expanded on an exhale. "Because it's not. Even so—"

"How could you not act?" Dawson finished with a shrug.

"You know you can count on me to assist you in any way needed to protect your bride and her termagant sisters." The duke tossed back the rest of his drink and extracted a handkerchief from his lapel, politely patting at his lips. "And as you also know, I have a deep-seated dislike for Tyrell. A greater fiend I have not met, and I can count many in my own cursed family. I would gladly put a bullet between that man's eyes if the deed is needed."

"Or perhaps stab a stake through his heart," Dawson asked with a teasing grin.

"Only if there are any stakes left after Gabriela Luna does her best to send me back to the underworld."

The day continued in a quiet manner, with the sisters keeping to either their room or the house, having been warned by Captain Dawson that for their own safety, it would be better to remain close to the estate. The housekeeper had offered each sister her own chamber, but none of them wished to be separated, drawing comfort from one another's presence.

While Isabel read, and Gabby stared out the window at the home woods surrounding Dancourt Abbey, Ana María sat at a small escritoire, fiddling with her pen as she wrote and rewrote a letter to her parents. What exactly could she say to them, having found she could no longer meet the expectations set for her?

She knew Fernando would not be heartbroken over their severed engagement, not when it was widely rumored how fond he was of his mistress, Señora Romero. Still, Ana María could not help but fret over what her father would say. She'd jumped to do his bidding her entire life, had strived to be a perfect daughter, and now she was to marry a man he'd never met.

Gideon was a rising star in Parliament, however, with power and influence within his grasp. And she would help ensure that those policies he championed would come to fruition. Ana María knew how to play the political game, having learned at her father's knee, and she would charm politicians all over England if it helped her ambitious husband achieve success. Surely that would count for something in her father's eyes.

Dropping her pen on the desktop, Ana María covered her face with her hands. With a strangled hiccup, she forced herself to admit that the real reason she was struggling with writing the letter was that she had to tell her mother that England would forever be her home now. Nevermore would she spend her mornings greeted by the Mexican sun or be wished good night by the Mexican moon.

Twin fires burned the backs of her eyes, and her throat closed around a sob as she dropped her head onto her arms.

"Ana, are you crying?"

She quickly shook her head, long used to denying her own emotions. But when a gentle hand landed on her shoulder, and another pushed hair off her brow, she lost her fight. Sobs tore free from her throat, from her soul, and she no longer cared about the tears that coursed down her cheeks.

"Querida, whatever is the matter?" Isabel crooned. Her hand rubbed soothing strokes on Ana María's back.

"Tell us, Ana." Gabby wrapped her hand around one of Ana María's own and squeezed her fingers tight. "How can we help?"

"There is nothing to help." Ana María barely recognized her ragged voice. "There's no turning back."

With a gentle pressure on her arm, her sisters managed to coax her to her feet and lead her to the edge of the bed, where she collapsed in a cloud of cotton skirts. Isabel tucked herself close on one side, with Gabby on the other, each linking their hands together in tight knots. With a rough sigh, Ana María rested her head on Isabel's shoulder.

"Ana," she began, her voice gentle and tentative, "are you crying because you don't want to marry Señor Fox?"

There was no judgment in her tone. No accusation. Although marriage to Gideon would offer them a protection they so desperately needed in that moment, Ana María knew that her sisters would not insist she go through with the ceremony if she decided the cost was too steep to pay.

"No." She cleared her throat. "No, that's . . . that's not it at all."

"Then what is it?" Gabby ran her thumb over Ana María's knuckles. "I've never seen you like this."

"You've never seen her like this because when has she ever been allowed to be vulnerable? When have any of us been at liberty to share, openly, how we feel about anything? What we think about anything?" Isabel pressed a kiss to the top of Ana María's head.

"Never," Gabby whispered.

Wetness fell on their joined hands, and Ana María glanced to the side to see tears pooling in Gabby's eyes and sliding down her cheeks.

The sisters communed in silence, giving comfort and receiving it in equal measure. Their contentious relationships of the past were but a shadow now; the long months in England, with only one another to turn to, had eased them into this new stage, where they could finally be sisters. As well as friends.

When the sobs no longer scorched the back of her throat and her eyes were dry, Ana María accepted a handkerchief from Isabel and blotted her cheeks. "My tears are not for my upcoming marriage. I admire Señor Fox greatly. In fact, I'm certain"—her mouth trembled—"it would be very easy to fall in love with him."

Isabel and Gabby tightened their hold on her.

"It just occurred to me while I was writing to Mother and Father that I may not see them again." Her voice broke, and she paused to collect herself. "I may never see Mexico again."

"Of course you will." Isabel bumped her shoulder. "After Presidente Juárez is returned to power, you and Señor Fox will visit and help strengthen relations between the two countries."

"Wouldn't that be glorious?" Ana María's laugh tapered off. "Do you think the war will ever end? Is it possible to reinstate Presidente Juárez?"

"It has to be," Isabel declared. "I won't consider the alternative."

After a moment's pause, Ana María asked, "If Gideon and I were to visit Mexico, do you suppose people would even welcome us? What sort of reputation will I earn for having broken my engagement to Fernando?"

"Ana," Gabby said sharply, seizing her gaze, "why are you worried about what the people back home think? Why are the opinions of Father's sect important? What they think of you, or by extension *us*, does not matter now. England will be your home, and this is where you will build your life. Those people are unimportant, as they always should have been."

Ana María nodded. Gabby was right. Of course she was. Hadn't their tío Arturo made it clear when they arrived that they no longer had to subjugate themselves to their father's rule? That his decree held no weight here? Yet Ana María still needed to be reminded of such. No longer was he owed her obedience. The only edicts she was now expected to honor were her own.

And, she supposed, those of her soon-to-be husband, although she suspected that her and Gideon's wants and desires would align themselves quite nicely.

"So much has changed, hasn't it?" Ana looked first to Isabel and then to Gabby. "I wanted to toss you off the ship countless times on the voyage across the Atlantic, and now the thought that you might make that trip back home without me is enough to reduce me to tears."

Gabby chuckled, smacking the back of her hand. "Why are you thinking of such things now? You are stuck with me for the foreseeable future, it would seem, for Napoleon and his men occupy Mexico still."

"Do you know, Ana," Isabel began, her jaw working on a pause, "that it's been hard living in your shadow? The perfect older daughter, who always knew the right thing to say and just how to say it. Father always propped you up as the example, and you never failed to rise to whatever measurement he set down for you. Dios mío, how I resented you."

"I'm sorry," she whispered, her eyes clouding with tears again.

"But you have nothing to be sorry for." Isabel turned about to face her fully, her dark eyes bright. "And it took us being here, *me* seeing *you* without Father to interpret the view, to realize that your supposed perfection came about at the price of your soul."

Ana María bit her lip and dropped her gaze, unable to meet her sister's eyes any longer.

"And I'm sure you had your opinions of us." Isabel's tone turned hard. "I suspect Father did that on purpose."

"Of course he did," Gabby readily agreed. "We were raised to be adversaries."

"No more." She nibbled on the inside of her cheek and then blurted out, "Will . . . would you both be willing to stand up with me during my wedding ceremony?"

Isabel rolled her eyes, and Gabby elbowed her playfully in the side. "We were going to do so whether you invited us or not."

Relief and affection detonated like firecrackers in her chest. "I don't even know if the British have bridal attendants."

"It doesn't matter anyway"—Isabel shrugged—"because you're Mexican and that's what Mexicans do."

A grin pulled her lips taut. "I appreciate the reminder."

17

Carriage wheels sounded over the gravel in front of Dancourt Abbey when Gideon was at the breakfast table the following morning with Ana María and her sisters. Whitfield had dined with them for a time, but when Gabby arrived, her frosty gaze falling on the duke the moment she stepped in the room, he had immediately risen from his seat and grumbled a goodbye.

But now they were to have more visitors.

Wiping his mouth with a napkin, Gideon tossed it on the table and looked to Ana María. "Would you like to greet Father Duncan with me?"

Her nod was immediate. "I would like that very much."

Taking his arm, Gideon escorted her to the front entry, where Captain Dawson already stood waiting. Isabel and Gabriela soon joined them, and the quintet stood along the top step, watching as the newest guests alighted. The older man was assisted from the carriage and looked up at them with a self-satisfied grin that made Gideon snort. Stansberry exited the carriage after him, a heavy satchel in his hands containing an assortment of paperwork that would keep Gideon busy for weeks.

All the weeks he planned to holiday with his new bride in the countryside.

Sliding his gaze to the right, he took in Ana María. She wore a plain blue day gown, which was devoid of embellishments aside from delicately embroidered butterflies on her bodice. Her hair was pulled back in a simple bun, making her appear younger than her four and twenty years. As if sensing his regard, she glanced up and met his eyes, the gentle smile that crossed her pink lips sending his stomach into somersaults.

"Now that Father Duncan has arrived, perhaps we should decide if an afternoon wedding would meet with your approval."

"Oh, of course." Her eyes went wide before they darted about. "Where will the ceremony take place? Is there a church nearby?"

Although she did not specifically say it, he knew she was questioning if the wedding would take place in a Catholic church. Her tense frame belied the importance of his answer, but then it was important to him as well.

"Not a church, but I have what I think may be a charming alternative."

"Is that so?" She peered up at him. "Are you going to tell me?"

Gideon looked down to where the old priest was climbing the stairs to join them. "I thought I could show you and Father Duncan together, and see if it will suit."

Ana María nodded before a smile slid over her face as she turned to welcome the older man. For some unknown reason, Gideon's throat felt abruptly tight watching his oldest and dearest friend greet his soon-to-be wife. The affection and respect both held for the other was palpable, and for the first time in a very long time, he considered what his life could be outside of politics. Even now, the hallowed halls of Westminster had lost a bit of their allure, knowing such a woman would be waiting for him at home.

"Gideon," Father Duncan murmured, turning to grasp his hands. "I'm honored beyond words that you wish for me to marry you to this lovely young woman."

Ana María blushed prettily by his side.

"Of course I wish for you to marry us." He leaned forward, as if to impart a great secret. "Your Mass is the only one that manages to keep me awake."

Ignoring how Ana María gasped in mock outrage, the older man chuckled. "The highest of praise, I'm sure."

"Truly, though, thank you." Gideon's tongue felt thick and unruly in his mouth. "It was short notice and a long way to travel, and I know you do not like to be away from the parish for too long."

"Do not worry, my boy." Father Duncan patted his hand with his own gnarled one. "I assure you that seeing you take a wife is an answer to my prayers. Your grandmother would be so very proud."

Gideon looked down at where their hands were clasped, blinking rapidly to keep his rioting emotions in check.

"Gideon was just telling me, Padre, that he wanted to show us where he thought we might hold the ceremony," Ana María said, touching his arm.

He sensed that she was aware he was struggling, and her question was meant to change the subject. Gideon was grateful.

"You have my interest. If my knowledge of Catholic parishes in this part of England is correct, there are none in the vicinity." Father Duncan looked to Ana María. "But at one time, there were churches, shrines, and abbeys dotting the countryside."

"That must have been lovely," Ana María breathed, a dreamy look on her face.

"And it still is." Gideon pulled out his watch and consulted it for a moment. "Perhaps we can meet back here in an hour's time and I can show it to you."

Father Duncan and Ana María exchanged an amused look, before nodding in unison.

Locked away in Dawson's study for the next three-quarters of an hour, Gideon and Stansberry argued over the wording for his marriage announcement to Ana María. His secretary had hoped that by getting ahead of their sudden departure from the Tyrell house party, they would be able to mitigate any scandal that resulted, and Gideon appreciated the man's forethought. However, they could not agree on the language, Gideon not wanting to reveal too much personal information for the sisters' safety, and Stansberry adamant that they create an impression that this was a love match. In the end, it was Whitfield who strolled into the study after overhearing them debating, and promptly took control of the endeavor, assuring Gideon that between him and Stansberry, their marriage proclamation would charm the ton.

Frustrated and eager to rejoin his bride, Gideon left the duke to it.

Now, Gideon led Ana María, her sisters, and the rest of their group on a short walk along a rambling path through the dense forest behind Dancourt Abbey. When they stopped at the edge of a clearing, Ana María stepped forward tentatively, her mouth agape.

"Here it is," Gideon announced with a swish of his hand.

The group was silent a beat, before Gabby said, "Señor Fox, are you mad?"

He snorted. "Allow me to explain what I'm thinking."

Stepping over a pile of crumbling masonry overgrown with

ivy and wildflowers, Gideon spun about in a circle with his arms wide. "This used to be the sanctuary at the original nunnery."

Ana María took a small step forward, her gaze turning critical. "It was?"

"The altar was there," he said, pointing at a spot across the way, "and here is where the altar boys would prepare the Holy Communion."

Father Duncan, Isabel, and Gabby followed his directions, and quietly stepped into the space.

"From what I have been able to determine, the original Dancourt Abbey was built in the early 1300s, and was the home for scores of nuns over the next three hundred or so years." Captain Dawson leaned against what had once been a narrow doorway leading into the sanctuary from a connecting interior room. "After Henry the Eighth stripped power from the papists, and founded the Church of England, the abbey slid into decline. The king did not strip it of its lands immediately, but over the next century, the abbey was forced to sell bits and pieces of its surrounding orchards, wheat fields, and grazing lands, until all that remained was the building itself."

Gideon watched Ana María as she held her skirts, stepping over bits of debris and picking up random items off the littered floor, when Isabel's voice dragged his eyes to her.

"How is it that you've come to know so much about this place, Captain?"

Dawson quirked his mouth. "Because it's the reason I bought the estate. The manor house is sufficient enough, and the home woods are expansive and offer plenty of game to hunt, but this"— he waved at the crumbling, ivy-covered ruins about them— "was the real incentive."

"But why?" Isabel pushed, advancing a step closer to the captain, peering at him as if he were some unknown creature she had only read about in a book.

"I've always been fascinated by history." Dawson swiped his glove across a windowsill that was now missing its windowpane, stirring up a small plume of dust. "The chance to own a piece of such a storied past was something I could not turn down. I'd like to restore it one day."

"Why?" Isabel asked, moving forward another step.

The captain stared at her for a moment. "Because I can, Miss Isabel."

Without waiting for her to reply, Dawson crossed to where Gideon stood with Father Duncan. "Will this suffice? I can have the servants clear away some of the larger debris and bring chairs for guests, as well as several tables to prepare Communion."

The priest's cloudy gray eyes swept over the sanctuary, before he looked up to stare at the royal-blue sky stretched above them through the crumbled remnants of the cathedral ceiling. A delighted smile spread across his wrinkled face. "It's perfect. This land has been sanctified, and God the Father can look down on Gideon and Miss Luna as they exchange their vows with each other."

With a knot in his throat, Gideon glanced at Ana María. Did she agree? Taking a step back, Gideon attempted to view the ruins through her eyes. The limestone bricks that had not fallen with the passage of time were covered in ivy and moss, with various wildflowers and brambles pushing forth between cracks in the old brick floor to bathe the debris in color. The open roof offered no protection from rain or snow, but provided an unhindered view of the heavens.

Gideon had heard of the grand cathedrals in Mexico City

and other parts of Latin America, and he was certain his bride had partaken of Sunday Mass surrounded by man's creative offerings to God. Ana María was already sacrificing so much to marry him, so perhaps he should find another space more worthy of her and her hand.

"I agree, Father," she exclaimed, spinning about in a cloud of skirts, her cheeks infused with pink. "If the servants would be kind enough to bring chairs here, and perhaps some padded stools for kneeling during the service, I think it will be perfect."

She reached out to grab Gideon's hand, her palm warm and her grip strong. "Can you imagine what this abbey looked like four hundred years ago? Its walls and furnishings may have been looted, but the spirit of the abbey lingers still. I would be very happy to be married here."

Gideon didn't bother to hide his smile as he looked down at her. "I would be, too."

The sound of Dawson's snort broke the moment as he pivoted toward the main house. "Let me tell Mrs. Ormsby what is in store for her and her staff this day."

"Thank you, my friend," Gideon called after him.

Dawson merely lifted a hand in acknowledgment.

"Is it true that white has become a popular color for wedding ensembles because Queen Victoria wore it when she married the Prince Consort?" Ana María asked.

"It is. White is lovely, but I still prefer a pop of color."

Lady Yardley lounged in a wingback chair near the window, a goblet of claret dangling from her fingers. The viscountess had spent a good deal of the day either in the drawing room scouring the newspapers for any hint of their quick departure from the Tyrell house party, or pacing along paths in the home woods, Dove by her side. When Tío Arturo had arrived later in the day, her spirits lifted and his report from London seemed to ease her mind, and the viscountess's customary vivacity returned.

Standing back to consider herself in the gilded mirror, Ana María ran her hands down the magenta folds of her dress. There had been no time to have a custom bridal ensemble made, so she'd had to choose from among the gowns she had brought with her. Consuelo had laid out several choices, but as soon as Ana María's gaze fell on the magenta gown with its gold stitching, she knew it was the one. Lady Yardley had tried to tell her it was too bold, too bright for a wedding, but she did not care. She'd been wearing the gown when she'd first set eyes on Gideon at the Montrose ball, and even then had known her life would never be the same. Now it seemed poetic that she would wear it while pledging her life to his.

Consuelo had styled her hair in a pinned updo with a strand of her mother's pearls interwoven among the curls. Ana María hoped she'd be able to return them to her one day.

A rap at the door preceded its opening to reveal Isabel and Gabby, each dressed in lovely jewel-toned gowns.

"Ana!" they squealed in unison, rushing forward to compliment her hair and gown.

"You act as if you've never seen me wear this gown before," she said with a snort.

"But we've never seen you wear it on your wedding day," Isabel declared, Gabby nodding in agreement.

Desperate to hide how her lip trembled, Ana María pressed a hand to her mouth.

"Do all brides cry?" Gabby asked, pressing a delicate lace handkerchief into Ana María's free hand.

"Only when you make them cry, Gabriela dear," Lady Yardley said from the corner, raising her glass of wine in salute.

Before Gabby could retort, there was another knock on the door. When Ana María bid them to enter, the door swung open to Tío Arturo, a subdued expression on his face.

"Mi hijitas, I am once again gratified to see you happy and hale," he declared as he shut the door behind him. "I had thought by sending you to the countryside, you would be safe. Instead, I sent you straight into the lion's den."

Ana María bussed her uncle's cheek. "But how could you have known what a villain Lord Tyrell was?"

"My dear, I pay well-connected men to provide me with such intelligence. I made decisions about your safety—the beloved daughters of my beloved sister—based on that information." Tío Arturo dragged a hand down his face, weariness clinging to him. "I should have known of the man's connection to the French, and I am sorry I didn't. You wouldn't be in this position now if I had not failed you."

It seemed that a good deal of people had been fooled by the earl, and Ana María refused to punish them for it. "You did not fail me, Tío. Isa, Gabby, and I know you have done your best. You entrusted us to Lady Yardley, after all."

The viscountess chuckled. "That's why you're my favorite, Ana María."

"Liar," Gabby shot back.

Rolling her eyes at her sister, Ana María stepped forward and wrapped her arms around her uncle's waist. "Even if I hadn't been forced to choose, Señor Fox would have been my choice."

Tío Arturo pulled back, his arms tight on her shoulders, his probing gaze sweeping over her face. "Are you in earnest?"

She nodded, hoping her eyes reflected the truth of her words.

"Well, then." He swallowed, his gaze holding hers. He'd once said he saw her mother in her eyes, and Ana María wondered what he saw now. "I'm so very happy for you, querida. Felicidades."

"¡Felicidades!" her sisters added, their spirited sincerity making her heart sing.

"Let's make our way to the abbey." He winged out an arm to her. "We don't want to keep your groom waiting."

Grinning at her sisters, Ana María hoisted her skirts with one hand and wrapped the other around her tío's arm. "I'm ready."

A quarter of an hour later, Ana María stood with her uncle and sisters just outside of the dilapidated doorway that led into the former interior of the sanctuary. Gabby had peered around the frame and excitedly exclaimed that the staff had swept up most of the debris and laid a long, green runner from the door to the makeshift altar. Vases and baskets filled with a vibrant array of blooms had been plucked from the surrounding meadows to breathe color and life into the space.

"And these are for you," Isabel said, suddenly thrusting a small bouquet of wildflowers into her hand.

Ana María glanced down at the delicate blooms in surprise. "Where did these come from?"

Isabel lifted a shoulder. "Gabby and I picked them for you."

The blossoms grew blurry as her eyes filled with tears. Sucking in a breath, desperate to contain all the happy emotions bubbling up inside of her, she turned to Tío Arturo.

"Gracias con todo for offering to walk me down the aisle in my father's place." She brought the small bouquet to her nose and inhaled. "But I'd very much like to have Isabel and Gabby give me away instead."

Startled gasps sounded around her, but Ana María kept her gaze trained on her uncle, willing him to understand how important this was for her.

"That's not quite how things are done," he began, before he chuckled. "But then most couples aren't married in the crumbling ruins of old abbeys."

"Perhaps that's something they should reconsider," she offered.

"Por supuesto." Tío Arturo smiled down at her. "Of course your sisters should give you away. You have been through much together, and I'm certain the idea would make your mother very happy."

Bending down, he bussed her cheek. "I wish you all the happiness, mi hijita."

Ana María watched him disappear through the doorway, leaving her alone with her sisters . . . and the birds, crickets, and butterflies that made their homes in the ruins of the old abbey.

A slender hand grasped one of her elbows, and another latched on to its twin. Ana María dropped her gaze to where they were linked, her heart swelling over how much had changed.

"Are you ready?" she asked, lifting her chin.

"Of course we're ready," Gabby declared before she sobered. "Are you ready to become Señora Fox?"

Ana María didn't hesitate. "I am."

With that, the women moved in tandem to walk Ana María to her waiting groom.

The ceremony and Mass went by in a blur. She knew she kneeled and stood when she was supposed to, spoke the correct words when required, and otherwise behaved as a willing bride should. Nevertheless, the whole affair was like a dream bathed in the golden light of sunset, and the only discernible thing she could focus on was Gideon's handsome face. His soft smile as he spoke his vows to her. The burning embers in his eyes when she repeated hers back to him. And when Father Duncan announced them man and wife, Ana María committed the look of triumph, of complete happiness that blazed across his mien as he leaned down to press a kiss to her lips, to her memory. The kiss was gentle, even chaste, but it sealed their union, and there was no turning back. It terrified her as much as it filled her with elation.

Perhaps Gideon understood that. Mayhap the gravity of their new reality was assaulting his nerves as much as her own, for he pulled her close, his strong arms wrapping snugly around her waist.

"I'll endeavor to make you happy," he whispered against her cheek.

"Igualmente," she replied.

He released her then, and Ana María immediately missed his warmth. Her heart stuttered when he weaved his fingers with hers. "Let's celebrate, then, Mrs. Fox, with our friends and family."

She nodded, eager to face all that was to come.

18

He was a married man.

It felt almost incomprehensible to him, although one look at Ana María solidified the *rightness* that had rooted in his marrow from the moment he proposed.

When she had appeared at the end of the aisle in the abbey, Gideon had not been able to take his eyes from her. She wore the magenta gown. The gown she'd worn the first time he'd seen her, imprinting her likeness on the backs of his eyelids like a meteor streaking across a midnight sky. She'd been but a beautiful mirage then, always on the horizon and never quite corporeal enough to be real, the promise of her tempting him despite knowing better.

But now she was his.

Gideon reminded himself of this as they chatted with their family and friends at dinner that night, partaking of the scrumptious feast that Dawson's staff had prepared. Anytime Ana María laughed, anytime she smiled, anytime she looked at him with an intriguing mix of bashfulness and beguiling charm in her velvet eyes, he was reminded that she had become his oasis in truth, and Gideon could not comprehend how he had gotten so lucky.

How was it possible that the woman he'd wanted from the first, the clever beauty who continued to intrigue him despite his valiant efforts to push her away, was now his wife? Gideon hardly knew what to think, so for once, he simply decided to feel. And his stomach flipped and his chest went tight—as did his trousers—every time Ana María directed a smile at him. For today, Gideon decided that would be enough.

He watched her out of the corner of his eye now as she chatted with Whitfield, who sat on her opposite side. His friend had been an amiable companion who hadn't monopolized her time or engaged in overt flirting. Gideon had been friends with the duke long enough to know Whitfield was adept at making a woman feel as if she were the center of the universe, and he wasn't certain what he would do if Ana María fell prey to his charms. But his concerns were for naught, for Whitfield was friendly but respectful, and Ana María kept a hand over her husband's, as if she needed proof Gideon still sat at her side. He was more than happy to remind her, as many times as she needed.

Yet he couldn't help but wonder what would happen after the festivities had concluded. They may have shared a passionate kiss—*no*, a soul-consuming, blood-burning kiss—but that did not mean his new bride wanted to consummate their marriage. The thought of knowing Ana María was his and not being able to touch her, to taste her, left his jaw throbbing.

Gideon walked with Ana María up the stairs now, her body close to his side, her jasmine scent wrapping seductively around him. His thoughts tumbled about one another; should he bid her goodbye at the door? Should he enter after her and offer to play lady's maid? Should he leave her to undress on her own, and come to her chamber later in the night?

The walk to her room was short, and before Gideon knew which way was up, they stood facing each other. Her cheeks were dusted in scarlet, her chest rising and falling with nervous breaths. Dark eyes studied his face, and he glimpsed a question there . . . one Gideon breathlessly hoped she'd ask.

Ana María dropped her gaze as her pulse thudded visibly at the base of her throat. "W-would you like to come in?"

Of course he would. The night's promise of passion had tempted him throughout the day, like a simmering reverie he clung to even while reality swirled about him. But as time passed, it had occurred to him that they had never had a conversation about their expectations for their wedding night. Ana María may have turned willing and pliant under his touch once before, but that didn't mean she was interested in immediately consummating their union. Perhaps she needed to be courted. Wooed. Ana María deserved for there to be trust between them, and maybe he could earn her trust—*and* give her pleasure—tonight.

"Ana," he rasped, "I'd like nothing more."

Her throat bobbed on a swallow, and she opened the door, stepping inside and watching owlishly as he entered after her. Gideon turned to look at her as the door clicked shut, and watched as she wrung her hands, her dark eyes wild as they darted over his face.

"I don't know what to do," Ana María blurted out into the silence, her palms flying up to cover her mouth, her countenance draining of color.

His darling wife was nervous, and that would not do. With a silent plea for the right words, Gideon took a step toward her.

Ana María held her ground, and he was relieved to see her gaze soften a tad.

"You know we don't have to do anything you're not ready for, right?" he whispered.

Ana María nodded.

Gideon came to a stop before her, his gaze holding hers. "We could just talk, if you'd like."

Her lips tipped up. "I do enjoy our conversations."

"As do I." He allowed his smirk to turn sly. "But I enjoy kissing you, too."

When she chuckled in response, Gideon moved to enfold her in his arms, burying his face in her hair.

After a pause, her arms wrapped around his waist, and Ana María turned her face to bury it in his chest. Her body heaved with the force of her breath. Having her this close was so satisfying. Knowing there was no faraway fiancé to keep them apart, no critical eyes, no wagging tongues. Ana María was his wife, and he clenched his eyes closed as he considered all that meant.

Scrambling for a smidge of his renowned self-control, Gideon pulled back to meet her gaze. "Ana dear, do you know what to expect tonight? Aside from interesting conversation?" he added with a squeeze of his arms.

She froze. "I think so. I found the anatomy books in mi abuelo's library, so I think I understand the mechanics."

Mechanics? Right. Gideon worked his jaw as he debated how to continue.

"It's just . . ." Her brows knit together. "It's just so frustrating."

Her distress caused Gideon to slide his palms along her jaw to cup her face. His thumbs smoothed across her cheekbones, humming in the back of his throat. "What's upset you?"

Closing her eyes, Ana María leaned into his touch. "I hate

not knowing what's expected of me. I despise being ignorant, especially of something so intimate."

"I'll show you," he said, his voice dropping an octave.

"I know." She blinked her eyes open, staring up at him solemnly. "I know you'll be gentle, because you're a good man, Gideon."

He pressed his cheek to hers, overcome by her faith in him.

Eventually pulling back, he met her eyes. "Will you help me undress?"

"Oh." Her mouth fell open, her pink tongue flicking out to wet her lips. Gideon locked his jaw to bite back a groan. "Of—of course."

Her hands trembled as she reached for his tie, deftly freeing the knot and sliding it from around his neck. Gideon studied her face as she peeled his dress coat from his shoulders, noting the pulse racing at the base of her throat and the flush spreading across her cheeks and disappearing beneath her dress. Christ, but he couldn't wait to map her skin and discover all the places he could turn it crimson.

When Ana María plucked the last button free, she paused, her pupils blown wide as she stared at his chest. Gooseflesh danced across his skin under the heat of her gaze, and Gideon held himself still, determined his lovely new bride would have the chance to look her fill. She was trusting him with so much, and he was determined to put her at ease. Eventually, he set about removing his cuff links, before he reached for the hem of his shirt and ripped it over his head, tossing it aside with no care for where it landed.

If her gaze had been a gentle caress before, it was a scorching weight now, and Gideon all but preened at the dazed expression on Ana María's face. But when she sank her teeth into her plump bottom lip, his thoughts shifted.

"Would you like to touch me?" he grated, already anticipating the decadent feel of her hands on his skin.

Her throat worked on a swallow. "Sí."

With a tentative step forward, Ana María extended her hand toward his chest and paused when a loud crinkling sound filled the air. They glanced down in unison. A piece of paper lay crushed under her foot, and his lungs stuttered as she bent down to retrieve it. With his heart beating a staccato in his throat, Gideon watched as she held it up, her brows dipping low as she studied it. Comprehension dawned like a blazing sun across her face.

"You . . . you kept it?"

Pulling it apart with her fingers, Ana María revealed the Darwin lecture program she had folded into a makeshift fan all those weeks ago, the crisp creases doing nothing to mar the print.

"I just . . ." He shook his head.

Ana María pressed her palm flat against his chest, right over his thundering heart. "You just what, Gideon?"

He met her gaze after a painful pause. "I just needed to keep a part of you close. No matter how small."

She clamped her eyes closed, and he bit his tongue rather than demand she open them and reveal her thoughts to him. It had been a silly impulse to grab her discarded program that day at the lecture, but he'd carried the crumpled fan in the interior pocket of his coat—right over his heart—ever since. It had been a comfort to him when he thought she could never be his, and now it was a bittersweet token of how long he had pined for her.

Sable eyes opened slowly, their depths soft and tender. Without a word, Ana María wrapped her arms around his neck and rose up on her toes to snare his lips with her own.

His existence narrowed to the exquisite feel of her, the lush taste of her, and the tempting promise of all that was to come. Gideon ran his nose along her jaw, nipping at her flesh, as he unwrapped her arms and dragged a hand lower down his body.

"Will you help me with the buttons *here*, little wife?" he rasped.

Her chest heaved with her rapid breaths, but Ana María's nimble fingers had the buttons lining his placket undone within the space of three heartbeats. She lingered, though, her knuckles grazing over where he was hard and aching for her.

With a growl, Gideon pushed the trousers from his hips and down his legs, kicking them away as if they had offended him. Now he stood before her in nothing but his drawers, which left little to the imagination in his aroused state.

When Ana María's face blanched, he realized he may have frightened her. Running his hands up her back, he dragged his fingers across her shoulders, kneading them into her tense muscles. Eventually, he tenderly cradled her neck with his palm.

"Have I shocked you?"

"I was just a bit overwhelmed." She tilted her chin up to meet his eyes. "You're just so . . . so . . . much."

"Oh, darling, I've only given you a glimpse of how overwhelming I can be." Gideon twined his fingers in her hair and gave it a small tug, his tongue tracing across his teeth as his gaze devoured her. "You've overwhelmed me from the first and every day since, and I intend to exact my revenge."

To her credit, Ana María did not cower at his words. Instead her eyes grew heavy lidded as she whispered, "A true gentleman would not seek revenge on a young woman."

"Perhaps not." Giving in to temptation, he ran his thumb over her bottom lip. "But whatever gave you the idea that I'd be a gentleman in the bedroom?"

And with that, his mouth crashed down on hers.

As Gideon molded her to him, he realized she tasted richer, more decadent, and when he stroked his tongue along the seam of her mouth, he thought he knew why. Because this kiss was not a stolen moment. The guilt, the uncertainty, that had flavored their last kiss was no more. Ana María was *his* now, and he was hers, and Gideon intended to savor this moment, and every moment to come.

Ana María broke their kiss but did not step back, her brisk breaths coasting across his lips.

Gideon nipped at her earlobe. "Do I have leave to make you more comfortable?"

Her pupils dilated, and she nodded.

"Thank God," he exclaimed, spinning her about to work free the buttons that ran up her back.

Endless minutes ticked off the clock until Gideon was successful in freeing Ana María of her cumbersome gown and multiple undergarments, groaning in the back of his throat as his fingers skimmed over her bare shoulders, dragging the sleeves of her chemise down her arms. Gideon was granted a brief view of her lusciously full breasts, with their pebbled, toasted brown nipples, when Ana María enfolded him in her arms, pressing her curves to his chest and snaring his lips in a fiery kiss.

Somehow Gideon managed to walk them to the bed. The backs of her knees caught on the mattress, and she fell back with a gasp, sprawled before him in all her golden-skinned glory. Her legs were shapely and toned, flaring out into a pair of supple thighs that Gideon could not wait to bury his face between. His gaze traced over the swell of her hips, traveled up her navel, until it reached her breasts, and Gideon choked on a breath.

Ana María brought her arm up to shield her body, and Gideon shook his head. "No, darling, don't. Let me look at you. I've been *starved* to look at you."

With her lip caught between her teeth, Ana María slowly lowered her arm, and Gideon delighted in the roses that bloomed across her skin. Just the sight had him rubbing a hand along his straining length . . . but he paused when he caught Ana María staring at his movements.

"Do you like it when I touch myself?" he asked, snaking his hand inside his drawers to grasp his cock and give it a tug.

She nodded, her pink tongue flicking at her bottom lip.

"Do you touch yourself, too? When you're all alone, and no one is there to see you?" Gideon angled his head to meet her gaze.

Her eyes widened, but then she looked away, her cheeks stained red.

"Aah, you do." He sank to his knees before her and clasped her ankle. "Will you show me how you touch yourself, little wife?"

Ana María whipped her head about to meet his gaze, her eyes feverish.

"Don't be frightened," he purred, dragging his hand from her ankle to her knee. "I just want you to feel good."

She continued to stare at him, her inhalations uneven. When she uncurled her fist, and trailed her hand down her navel, Gideon bit back a moan.

With her forehead puckered in concentration, her fingertips carefully combed through the coarse dark hair that covered her womanhood. A great gust of air escaped his lungs when Ana María finally ran the pads of her fingers along her slit.

This was not the first time she had touched herself. Her confident, sure strokes told him as much as he watched open-mouthed as his beautiful, innocent bride brought herself pleasure. Gideon's hungry gaze followed the slight tremors that traveled in waves under her skin, noting how her pretty nipples hardened into greedy little points. But when her hand began to move faster, desperate sounds falling from her kiss-swollen lips, Gideon didn't hesitate to offer his assistance.

Gently spreading her knees wide, he settled his shoulders between them as his hands kneaded comfort into her thighs. "Let me help you, darling."

And pushing her hand away, he leaned forward and wrapped his lips directly around the aching nub at the top of her sex.

Ana María's back arched off the bed, a loud, low keen filling his ears as she tangled her fingers in his short curls, anchoring him to her as she undulated her hips. Gone was the polite young woman who had charmed all of London, and in her place was this lush siren intent on finding her release, and Gideon was a mere servant to her pleasure.

"Don't stop," she cried, her head thrashing about on the bed.

Gideon had no intention of stopping. Not until she was twitching and boneless beneath his hands.

Releasing her nub with a wet pop, he teased it with his fingers before he dragged them down her wet seam and paused at her entrance. "You're so lovely here, Ana."

She clenched her eyes closed as she angled her pelvis into his touch. "Please, Gideon."

"Please what, darling?" He cocked a brow. "You have to say it."

Shaking her head back and forth, Ana María finally opened her eyes, her irises pinpoints. "Por favor! Husband, I'm so close."

Ana María claiming him as her *husband* ripped a growl from his chest, and without preamble, Gideon leaned forward to flick the tip of his tongue across her nub while he slowly in-serted a finger into her wet heat.

"Yes," she shouted, her hands scrambling at his shoulders, and her nails scouring his flesh.

Gideon knew she was close when her words morphed into sounds, desperate and feral. And when he took a particularly long suck on her pretty nub at the same time he crooked his finger within her heat, her back bowed as a high shriek escaped her lips. Gideon continued his ministrations until her legs had stopped shaking and her gasps of pleasure had turned into whimpers.

Sitting back on his haunches, Gideon surveyed his handi-work. With her black hair twisted about the bedsheets, a thin sheen of sweat coating her sun-kissed skin, and her lips red and raw from his kisses, Ana María—*his wife*—looked like a woman who had been well loved.

And now Gideon hoped for some of her love in return.

Quickly stripping off his drawers, he climbed onto the bed and prowled over her. Smoothing hair back from her face, he leaned down to press a kiss to her lips. Ana María moaned into his mouth, her arms eagerly wrapping around his neck.

"I need you," he whispered, stroking his tongue against hers. Ana María snagged his bottom lip between her teeth and sucked it. "I know. Show me what to do."

With a groan, Gideon dropped his head to the valley be-tween her neck and shoulders, inhaling deeply of her scent while he used his knee to spread her legs. When he'd settled comfortably within the cradle of her hips, he grasped his cock and ran it up and then down her warm flesh.

They moaned in unison, hers hitched and breathy, his bro-ken and fevered.

When his member slotted into place, Gideon pulled back to meet her eyes. "I'll be gentle, but this may hurt."

"I trust you," she whispered, a small, brave smile twisting her lips.

And because Ana María trusted him, he found the strength to go slow, stopping to allow her time to adjust to his size. His dear wife did not utter a word, although her nails bit into his shoulders as her chest moved with her strained breaths.

When Gideon was finally seated in her tight heat, he whistled between his teeth, every inch of his skin on fire and his body begging to move. "My God, Ana—I've never felt anything so amazing."

She released her grip on his shoulders, stroking a hand down his spine to his backside, where she squeezed his bottom as she arched her hips. "Ándale, Gideon."

With a choked laugh, he readily obeyed. Pulling his hips back slowly, the exquisite drag, the sheen of her wetness coating his cock, made his eyes roll back, and he slumped forward, resting his head on her breast. Christ, she was perfect. Everything about her seemed specifically crafted for him, from her tight wet heat, to the soft sounds she made as he pumped into her, to the fierce way she held him close. After a time, Ana María began to roll her hips with his thrusts, not content to lie back and let him have his way with her. Oh no, not his Ana. She was just as determined to grasp her pleasure as he was.

When the pull of her became too much, and his movements began to falter, Gideon dipped his mouth to the shell of her ear and whispered, "Wife, it's time to come for me."

And he leaned down to lick a stripe across her nipple, sucking it into his mouth with a growl.

Ana María seized around him, her body tensing as her lips opened on a silent scream. Gideon was helpless to resist the way she clenched about him, her body squeezing and coaxing his to follow her into sweet, mind-shattering oblivion.

In the heated, sticky aftermath, Gideon slipped free from her embrace to clean them both of their exertions before he rejoined her on the bed. As he enfolded her in his arms, his breath escaped him in a long sigh, jostling her head from where it lay on his chest. She offered no protest, though, so Gideon held her a bit tighter.

"Was I too rough with you?" he eventually asked.

Ana María shook her head. "Of course not."

Relief swept over him, and he pressed a kiss to the top of her head. "I confess that you made me a bit crazed."

"That's a very flattering sentiment," she said, running her nails over his chest.

"But it's true. I've desired you for so long, yet even my fantasies could not possibly compare to *this*."

"I was worried."

Gideon grasped her shoulder until she met his gaze. "Why?"

Pressing her lips together for a long moment, Ana María finally expelled a breath. "You've sacrificed your career, your proposal with Lord Montrose, to save me and my sisters, and I would have been distraught if you had been disappointed in this as well."

Horror, mixed with a smidge of chagrin, churned in his gut. He didn't know what to say to alleviate her concerns, so Gideon opted for honesty. "Ana, love, I am ashamed it took the awful ordeal at the house party to spur me to action. But please know that even when I tried to keep my distance, I was fighting a losing battle."

His chest suddenly felt tight, and with his throat stinging, Gideon swallowed convulsively. Whatever was the matter with him?

"Are you all right?"

Looking down into her dark eyes, he nodded. For his chest still felt tight and his throat still ached, but suddenly the idea of not kissing her was more than he could bear. So Gideon crashed his mouth onto hers, uncaring that their teeth clanked together and instead reveling in the way her hands automatically combed through his hair, hitching him closer as her tongue eagerly moved alongside his.

Pushing all other thoughts away, Gideon sank into her embrace, into her kiss, and let his new wife captivate him for a spell.

19

The next fortnight passed in a fever dream. If Ana María closed her eyes, her thoughts were composed of writhing limbs, whispered words, heated kisses, and the hungry sounds of ecstasy. She walked about with a smug smile on her face, even though her body bore testament to her husband's love bites, kisses, and overeager finger marks. Ana María had been an enthusiastic participant in their lovemaking from the start, so the physical imprints of Gideon's eagerness for her had never been a concern.

Until he rubbed his thumb over one such bruise as they lounged in bed and cursed.

"I'm so sorry, Ana," he murmured, studying an offending spot.

With her brows knitted, she shook her head. "For what?"

"I shouldn't have been so rough with you." His cheeks were pink.

"You were hardly rough with me." Ana María pressed a kiss to his jaw. "And I quite like these signs of your passion."

Gideon buried his face in her hair, and his fingers stroked along her skin for a time. Ana María allowed his heartbeat, nestled under her ear, to lull her into boneless relaxation. It was quiet moments like these that she had begun to treasure, collecting them like gems to hoard and save for the future. A future she knew would bring challenges. She closed her eyes as a bit of reality intruded upon the idyllic world they'd created for themselves.

"Do you know if my uncle has received word from my parents?"

He dragged his knuckles over her shoulder. "If he has, he's not told me. Do you expect to hear from them?"

"The last letter I sent was announcing our impending wedding." She released a long exhale. "I'm certain my father will have something to say about it."

Gideon went still under her ear, and even his thrumming heart seemed to suspend on invisible tenterhooks. But then he ran his fingertips along her scalp and down through the strands of her hair, his touch soothing anxieties she'd not realized she carried.

"Would you tell me about him?" he whispered. "Your father?"

It was Ana María's turn to go still. After working her jaw for a moment, she asked, "Why do you want to know about him?"

"Because he's your father. And according to you, he is a powerful figure within the Mexican government." Gideon cleared his throat. "Yet he sent you and your sisters away, to the other side of the world, with no protection."

"And a large portion of the family's fortune. Don't forget that detail."

Bitterness filled her mouth, and she burrowed her head into Gideon's side so she did not have to meet his gaze.

Once again, his hand stroked over her skin, and gradually the tension seeped from her limbs. "Yes, your uncle explained the finances when we discussed the marriage settlements." Gideon paused and then added, "You once said that I was like him. Your father. Why would you make the comparison, love?"

The term of endearment had tears burning the backs of her eyes, and Ana María held her breath to stifle them. What could she tell him? She racked her brain for the effusive praise that used to fall so effortlessly from her lips, like sheet music she could play on the piano with her eyes closed.

But the words would not come. Without the constant barrage of instruction and recrimination, the seeds of her obedience had scattered in the breeze.

"He was born in a small village in Michoacán." Ana María pushed herself up into a sitting position, drawing her knees into her chest as she wrapped her arms about them. "Mi abuelo— my grandfather—was a farmer, and my father was determined not to be one as well."

Fixing her eyes on the counterpane, she continued. "Mi abuela was Purépecha. They were a fierce people who were never defeated or subjugated by the Triple Alliance, and Abuela Sesasi was so proud of this. And it was that pride that made her determined that her sons would elevate themselves to positions among the criollos and penisulares who ruled the country."

"And those are the members of the upper class?"

She nodded. "Yes. The Spanish natives who came to Mexico to exploit its people and natural wealth, or their Mexican-born children. They remain at the top of the social hierarchy even now, some forty years after Mexico won its independence from Spain."

"Europeans love their caste system," he droned, bumping his shoulder into hers.

"Most people seem to favor a social order," she said, her voice sad to her own ears. "People are quite content as long as there is someone else below them on the ladder or they believe climbing higher is a possibility."

"I suppose your father's Pur . . . ?"

"Purépecha."

"Pur-é-pecha," he enunciated slowly, "ancestry did not command the sort of respect or prestige needed to elevate his status?"

"Indeed not." Ana María pressed her lips into a firm line. "Their prestige was obliterated as soon as the conquistadores defeated Moctezuma."

Ana María's acrimony pulsed like a telltale heart. Swallowing her rancor, she unclenched her jaw enough to continue. "My father met Señor Juárez in Mexico City. The men, both from humble origins and with visions of what Mexico could be if it embraced social and economic reforms, became fast friends. Their ambitions, their charisma, granted them entry into circles wary of anyone who did not boast Spanish antecedents. It's how my father met my mother."

Gideon slowly wrapped an arm about her shoulders, pulling her once more into his side. "You haven't spoken much of your mother."

"Probably because I fear I'm too much like her."

The truth charred her tongue and ushered unwelcome tears to her eyes.

Her husband said not a word, his presence by her side a comfort.

"She was the daughter of Spanish nobility. Three times removed from the royal line of succession. María Elena Cordova Valdés could have married anyone, but she fell in love with the son of a Michoacán farmer."

"So it was a love match?"

"Perhaps on her side." Ana María snorted. "But I suspect my father was enamored of her connections and sizable dowry. Both have aided his political career."

Gideon's breaths played with the delicate hairs along her crown. "And that's why you compared me to him."

It wasn't a question, so Ana María did not try to persuade him otherwise. "You're both men from modest beginnings, clever and successful despite the obstacles placed in your way." She reached for his hand, lacing their fingers together. "But where my father has always been self-serving, Gideon, you have been gracious. Selfless, even. I once believed you and he to be similar, but I know now I was wrong."

He pressed a kiss to her temple, holding his lips against her skin. "How do you know that?"

"Because marrying me could bring you headaches and complications." Ana María cupped his cheek. "Even so, you married me anyway."

"Ana," he murmured, reaching to pull her into his lap. With her legs resting on either side of his hips and his arms wrapped around her waist, Ana María felt safe. Precious. Wanted. "I may wish that happier circumstances had brought us together—"

"Well, you are quite stubborn," she whispered, leaning forward to peck his lips.

"But I am quite content with how events have . . . transpired." His mien turned contemplative as his thumbs rubbed patterns into her thighs. "We've been circling each other for months, so our marriage seems apt."

Gideon arched his pelvis then, rubbing his cock along her heat, split open over him. Clenching her eyes closed, Ana María bit back a moan.

"We've been in our own sphere since we said our vows. I've

barely seen my sisters, and we've eaten more of our meals in this suite than we have anywhere else."

"And do you regret that?" He punctuated his question by flicking his tongue against her nipple.

She whimpered. "N-no. It's been lovely. B-but . . ."

"But what, little wife?" Gideon wrapped his lips around her nipple, giving it a firm suck, before he released it with a loud pop.

Ana María choked on a gasp.

"What was that?" he asked, as his hips flexed under her, his cock nudging against the ball of nerves at the apex of her sex.

She gnashed her teeth together. "What w-will happen when we . . ." She wet her lips. "When we return to London and our marriage overshadows your bill? When my lapses become fodder for your e-enemies?"

Gideon stilled, his eyes locking with hers. "We will face the talk together. You are the daughter of a premier politician, and I have no doubt that you'll have thoughtful and shrewd ideas that will help make my work in Parliament that much more effective. And one day in the near future, the feats of your clever mind will eclipse any presumed notions the public has about you, and my friends and enemies alike will know I married far above my station."

With those emphatic words, he kissed her, a meeting of lips that incinerated her doubts and sparked a hot, intense emotion in her heart.

An emotion she had no time to contemplate because Gideon lifted her hips and grasped his cock to slot it against her opening. "That's it, sweetheart," he purred, "look at how well you take me."

Ana María slid down his length and tossed her head back on a low moan as her thighs settled against his. Planting her hands on his chest, she dug her fingers into his firm muscles as she undulated her hips, and the only emotion pumping through her veins was white-hot desire.

The wicked words that tumbled from Gideon's lips spurred her to move faster, pushing her closer and closer to the precipice.

Just like that, darling. Yes, be as greedy as you want.

So good, Ana. You're so, so good.

And when she finally tumbled over the peak, her legs locking about him, and her thighs quaking as tremors of bliss radiated across her skin, Ana María cried out his name, certain he would be there to catch her.

Isabel had marked out the path over the course of the past week. While Ana María was occupied with her new husband, and Gabby was busy avoiding the duke . . . or *antagonizing* him, Isabel had been paying close attention to her surroundings. Being offered refuge at Dancourt Abbey had been a boon, for while she considered Captain Dawson a cad, he was also a cad well-connected within the British military. If anyone had the information she was searching for, it would be him, she reasoned.

So after she had retired to her shared chambers for the night, she had read and pretended to sleep until Gabby's breaths grew deep and the house became still around them. Only then did Isabel rise, don a modest dressing gown, and tiptoe from the room.

She dared not light a lamp or candle, not wanting to call any undue attention to herself, so her progress was slow as she navigated down empty halls, the only sound the whisper of cotton about her legs. As she drew closer to Captain Dawson's study, her heart began to race. Surely the man possessed useful information she could send home . . .

Stepping into the room, Isabel shut the door and leaned back on the wood, her eyes sweeping across the dim space. A gas lamp burned on a side table between two armchairs flanked by several tall bookshelves crammed with all manner of books. Her mouth grew dry at the thought of exploring Captain Dawson's collection, although she did not have high hopes for its contents, considering what she knew of the man.

Pushing aside thoughts of his striking blue eyes, Isabel turned to consider the opposite end of the room, stress lifting from her frame when she spied a large desk tucked under a grand beveled window. Her steps were quick as she crossed the room, her palm just settling on the cool desktop when the sound of a throat being cleared met her ears.

With a gasp, she stumbled backward, her frightened gaze landing on a tall figure sitting behind the desk, in the darkest corner of the room. As she watched, the figure rose to his feet and stepped closer, the faint light illuminating the handsome face of the man she had been so careful to avoid.

"Miss Luna, I was wondering how long it would take you to give in to the temptation."

She shook her head back and forth, strands of hair feathering against her cheeks. "I don't know what you mean, Captain."

The man raised a brow. "After what Fox told me about what transpired with Lord Tyrell, I would have thought you'd learned your lesson about sneaking around a man's study."

"I thought this was the library." Isabel fancied her voice sounded confident. "I couldn't sleep and thought a book might assist me."

"Indeed. But the books are quite obviously located on the other side of the room."

Isabel smothered a cringe. "Oh, are they? I had not noticed."

The corners of his eyes narrowed ever so slightly, and he

stepped out from around the desk. "Would you like some assistance in selecting a book?"

No, I would not, Isabel thought, biting down hard on her tongue to keep her irritation in check. It was rotten luck to encounter the captain, but it was a streak of bad luck she was determined to break.

"What do you suggest, sir?" She canted her head. Despite herself, she was genuinely curious about which book he'd recommend. Probably something scandalous.

"Hmm," he murmured, making his way toward the closest shelves. Glancing back at her over his shoulder, Captain Dawson ran a long finger down a book spine, and for some inexplicable reason, Isabel fought back a shiver. "There are several etiquette books here, with instructions for young ladies on how to behave at balls and house parties."

Despite how fire swept up her throat and over her cheeks, Isabel schooled her expression, determined not to reveal how much he had embarrassed her. She wasn't acting for her own interests, but to assist her country . . .

She flicked her fingers as if she'd found something offensive on them. "Oh, I've read my share of those books, and find them terribly dull. Just more lectures about the kind of behavior expected of women while my male counterparts behave as boorishly uncivilized as they choose, with no one in society batting an eye."

Isabel capped her sentence by flashing him a pointed look.

To her surprise, Captain Dawson chuckled, the flash of his smile brightening the space and throwing her off balance. Blast the man. "Well, then tell me, Miss Luna, what kind of books would you be interested in?"

Lifting her chin, she shrugged. "Well, I've been reading several books about swordplay, as well as a book about jujitsu. It seems prudent for a young woman to learn how to defend herself should she ever be accosted by a rogue in a dark room."

The smile fell from Captain Dawson's lips, but his eyes continued to glint as he studied her. "In that case, try this one. It's about the dangers of double identities."

The captain slid a slender book from a nearby shelf and handed it to her. Isabel accepted it with a wary nod, glancing down to read the title. *East Lynne.*

"I suspect you'll find it quite interesting," he said as he paced to the sideboard and reached for a decanter, pouring himself a glass. "But it's quite scandalous, so don't let Lady Yardley see it in your possession."

"Oh," she whispered, staring down at the book cover. "Gracias."

"Now, I would offer to escort you back to your room, but knowing you can see to your own safety, I wish you good night."

Isabel bobbed a quick curtsy and escaped the room. As she raced back up the stairs, Isabel held the book tight to her chest, intrigued by it . . . and possibly by the man who gave it to her.

20

A soft knock on the door pulled Gideon from sleep. Rubbing the heels of his hands into his eyes, he blinked them open, noting that a faint glow of waning afternoon sunlight filtered through the curtains. He and Ana María had spent the majority of the day in bed, wrapped up in each other. Turning his head, Gideon soaked in the sight of her. Positioned on her side, with the sheet pooled about her waist, Ana María had tucked a small fist under her cheek. Her black hair lay draped across her face, loose strands fluttering with her breaths. A tinge of smugness settled in his bones, for his wife looked exhausted but satiated, and Gideon dragged his palm along her arm to pull her close—

A knock sounded on the door again.

Biting back a curse, Gideon carefully extracted himself from the bed, doing his best not to wake his bride. Slipping on a robe, he padded to the door and cracked it open. Consuelo, the sisters' maid, greeted him with a shy smile before carefully averting her eyes to the side. A dinner tray ladened with food was in her hands. Gideon's stomach rumbled at the delicious scents, and he took the tray from her with a quiet word of thanks. He pivoted to shut the door, but paused.

"Please ask Mrs. Ormsby to have hot water brought up. I'm sure my wife would appreciate a bath."

Consuelo bobbed a curtsy and departed.

Over the next half hour, Gideon partook of the roasted chicken, pudding, and boiled potatoes that had been delivered, while admiring his slumbering bride. In an effort to be productive, he tried to read through several committee reports Stansberry had organized for him, but his attention was a waning thing, for he found it difficult to contemplate business when his lovely wife slept several feet away. Gideon had been circumspect for so long in regard to Ana María. He relished the fact that he could now admire her whenever he wanted for as long as he desired.

Eventually, Consuelo returned with a small contingent of footmen, each carrying a large bucket of steaming water. After positioning a screen before the bed to maintain Ana María's modesty, Gideon allowed the men to enter and fill the large bathtub in the adjoining chamber. When they had first arrived at Dancourt Abbey, Dawson had apologized profusely for the lack of modern bathing facilities, explaining that such renovations would begin the following year. Gideon did not mind the arrangement, however, and after the servants had departed, he discovered he was eager to bathe his new wife.

Sinking onto the mattress next to her, Gideon gently brushed the hair back from Ana María's face, his fingers stroking along the sharp line of her jaw.

"Darling, I've had a bath drawn for you," he said in a low-pitched voice. "Come, let me tend to you before the water cools."

Long black lashes blinked open, and it took Ana María several seconds to focus on him. "A bath?"

He nodded. "I thought you might enjoy it."

"A bath sounds divine," she mumbled, stretching her arms

overhead, and then she giggled and shielded herself with the bedding when she noticed how Gideon stared at her with hooded eyes.

"You are insatiable," she chided, rising to her feet with the sheet firmly in her grasp. Ana María turned toward the connecting bathroom and smiled at him over her shoulder as she walked away.

Gideon quickly followed, wrapping his arms around her waist and pressing a kiss to the tender spot below her ear. "I'll never get enough."

Ana María smiled up at him. "Well, try to control yourself long enough for me to tend to my ablutions."

"I'll help you."

She cocked a brow. "Will you?"

A smirk crept over his mouth as he grasped her hand and led her to the steaming copper bathtub. "Someone needs to wash your back." Curling an ebony strand of hair around his finger, Gideon felt his blood heat. "And your hair."

Without waiting for her reply, Gideon grasped her shoulders and spun her about. "Now get in before it turns cold."

Allowing the sheet to pool at her feet, Ana María gingerly stepped into the water, sinking below the surface with a long moan. Gideon clamped his teeth together at how his body responded to her pleasure. After adjusting himself, Gideon pulled up a stool and sat at the side of the tub, his gaze eagerly taking in her wet and pink-tinged skin.

"This feels glorious," Ana María drawled, smoothing loose curls from her face before she relaxed her head against the rim of the basin. "Thank you for thinking of it, Gideon."

Grasping the soap and a strip of cloth, Gideon worked it into a lather before grabbing her arm and massaging the soap into her skin. "I wanted to take care of you."

Her dark eyes turned to molten sugar as she looked him. "You did?"

Reaching for her leg, Gideon rubbed his thumbs into the arches of her feet, before massaging the delicate hollows of her ankles. Snaring her gaze, he trailed his soapy fingertips over the backs of her calves, along the sensitive skin behind her knees, to the supple flesh on the insides of her thighs. "You're always so intent on taking care of others, ensuring they're well, but who takes care of your needs?"

A breath hissed from her lips when he teased the sweet folds between her thighs. "*I'm* going to take care of your needs, darling. Do you want that?"

Ana María bit her lip. "Yes. Por favor."

Gideon chuckled as sin curled about them in the damp air, and he slipped a finger inside her. "Please what, my love?"

Wrapping her hands around the rim of the tub, she angled her hips into his touch. "Make me feel good."

Leaning forward, he stole a kiss from her breathless lips. "I so love it when you ask."

An hour later, Ana María walked by his side through the dark woods behind the manor house. After he'd brought her to release, Gideon had washed her hair, delighting in how her midnight locks curled about her face and glinted almost blue in the gas lamps. He'd helped her dress in a plain cotton frock and then served her dinner. She ate heartily, not once complaining that the food was no longer hot. When Ana María was full and sated, Gideon had tucked a blanket under his arm, grabbed a lantern, and invited her to walk with him.

"Where are we going?" she asked now, holding his hand tightly as they made their way around a bend.

"You'll see," Gideon said. "Our destination is just up ahead."

Within fifty feet or so, he brought them to a halt, the shadowed outline of the convent ruins rising from the trees directly ahead.

"Why did you want to come here?" Ana María looked up at him. "And at this time of night?"

"Let me show you."

Tugging her hand, Gideon led her carefully through the crumbled interior of the priory before they found themselves standing in the sanctuary, a twinkling swath of the heavens unfolded before them through the missing ceiling. Spreading the blanket across a mossy patch of earth, Gideon pulled Ana María down to sit next to him, his arm wrapping about her shoulders and bringing her close to his side. They tipped their heads back in unison to look at the patchwork of constellations glittering in the dusky Devonshire sky.

"Que hermosa noche," Ana María whispered, her voice full of wonder.

"Indeed," he agreed, his eyes intent on her face rather than the spectacle above.

They were silent for several minutes, the peaceful ambiance cocooning them in its embrace. But when Ana María sighed, long and loud, Gideon immediately darted his gaze to her.

"I dread when the time comes for us to return to London."

"I do, too," Gideon admitted. "It will be like waking from a dream. The very best of dreams."

Ana María turned until her cheek rested on his shoulder. "Things will be so different. I'm not ready for reality to change this happy accord we've found."

"Then let's do our best to keep it."

She went still. "What do you mean?"

Gideon kissed the top of her head. "What I mean is that there's no reason we can't carry on as we have since the wedding."

"As loath as I am to admit it, I don't think it would be prudent of us to lock ourselves away and engage in carnal exploits all day long," Ana María pointed out, her cheeks scarlet.

"Probably not." Gideon's chest shook with a suppressed laugh. "Although I would like that above all things."

Ana María fiddled with a sash on her dress. "Gideon, what do you expect of me? As your wife?" Something in his expression must have reflected his confusion, for she heaved a breath. "My mother served as my father's hostess. Is that what you'd want of me?"

Tracing his fingers down her forearm, Gideon linked their hands together. "If that's something you would feel comfortable doing, it would be very helpful. I'm confident I would have the most charming hostess in London."

Her lips twitched, but she did not smile. "What else?"

Gideon's brows stitched together. "I suppose I will leave that to your discretion. There may be times I'd like for you to accompany me as I meet with constituents and electors, or to attend dinners and parties with other politicians and their wives."

"Would it be possible . . ." Ana María hesitated, pressing her tongue to the top of her mouth. "For me to help you draft your proposals?"

"Christ, I had hoped that you would."

Her dark eyes widened. "Truly?"

"Of course." Gideon slid his hand along her cheek to cup the base of her head. Leaning down, he kissed her, slowly and gently. "You are the most discerning woman I know, and have seen places and experienced things I can only imagine. I would be very grateful if you shared your opinion and insight about the work I do."

"Gideon," she breathed against his lips, "we're going to do so many great things together."

"I hope so, love," he declared, before he surrendered to her kiss and all the promises it held.

"I've almost forgotten what you looked like."

Ana María rolled her eyes. "I missed you, too, querida."

"You look well." Gabby's expression turned to teasing. "You glow . . . in a very satisfied way."

She looked at her sister askance. Although she knew what Gabby was referring to, the traviesa, she refused to encourage her nonsense. "I find I am quite happy with my marriage."

"It would seem so, considering how you and Señor Fox have hidden away like ardillas pequeñas." Isabel pulled her eyes from the trail ahead of them to smile at her. "We've missed your calm presence, but I suppose it's something we should get used to."

And the bubble she and Gideon had blissfully occupied rudely popped. Once they returned to London, her life would revolve around her husband and their new marriage. No more would she awaken to Gabby curled into a ball, fast asleep by her side. Isabel would no longer tell Consuelo to retire early, declaring the sisters would play lady's maid for each other. Just as they had forged a bond with one another, they were destined to sever it.

Fire singed up her throat, and Ana María blinked back tears as she affixed her eyes on the back of her mare's head as they ambled down the path.

Captain Dawson had sent word with the couple's breakfast tray that he was taking Isabel and Gabby out for a hack about the estate, and issued an invitation to join them. Gideon had not wanted to leave the warmth of their chamber, but Ana María missed her sisters and thought an afternoon ride was just the thing. She was able to persuade her mulish husband with shrewd negotiation tactics she'd learned in their marriage bed, and Gideon had eventually been convinced.

He rode in front of her now, next to Captain Dawson and Mr. Monroe, the gamekeeper, the former occasionally pointing out certain sights and features along the way. Ana María had eventually fallen behind to ride between her sisters, enjoying the crisp breeze and the rolling meadows dotted with sheep and cattle.

"We've received a letter from Father," Isabel announced into the silence.

Ana María gasped, swinging her head about to look at her. "We did?"

She nodded, not taking her eyes from the path. "Tío Arturo had the letter forwarded here. Apparently, all the missives we've penned him and Mother since we arrived did not warrant a response, but word you had married an Englishman prompted him to finally put pen to paper."

The bitterness was palpable, and rather than excuse their parents' behavior, as she would have been tempted to do in the past, Ana María held her tongue. Isabel had every right to her anger over their parents' lack of regard.

"What did it say?" Ana María finally asked.

"Read it for yourself," Isabel said, extracting a folded piece of parchment from a pocket in her habit and extending it to her.

Squaring her shoulders, Ana María took it, noting her father's handwriting. Her stomach flipped, and she was abruptly nauseated.

"Maybe read it when you are alone." Gabby waved a hand about. "There's no use ruining such a beautiful day by reading the words of a man a whole ocean away."

"And no matter what he wrote, it won't change the fact that

Gideon and I are now married." Ana María stared at the letter until her father's writing blurred before her eyes. Sucking in a halting breath, she tucked it into the inner pocket of her jacket. "Did Señor Ramírez send a letter as well?"

Isabel shook her head. "Tío Arturo said he sent him word before he departed London for the wedding, but has not yet received a reply."

It was a relief. Despite the brokered nature of their engagement, Ana María did not dislike Fernando and hoped he could find happiness as she had.

Flexing her hands around the reins, she asked, "Was there any news of the war?"

"Some. I imagine Father was worried about the letter being intercepted," Gabby said.

"What did he say?" she pushed.

Isabel's chest rose and fell on a breath. "The French and monarchists have agreed to invite Ferdinand Maximilian, an Austrian archduke, a *Hapsburg*, to serve as emperor of Mexico."

"¿Qué?" A buzzing sound filled Ana María's head. "Mexico is to be a monarchy again? And a European is to rule us?"

"We were New Spain, and apparently now New France." Gabby's gaze drifted to the surrounding hills. "We are no closer to returning home than when we left."

And Ana María would not be returning home. In England she would remain. Cold, dreary England with its bland food and judgmental harpies, and—

Ahead on the trail, Gideon looked over his shoulder, his gaze immediately finding hers. He stared at her for a heartbeat, until his brow ticked up in question. Affection swelled in her chest that he knew her well enough by now to sense her distress, and Ana María flashed him a wobbly smile. Gideon's eyes softened after a moment, and he faced forward again.

"He's completely smitten."

"He's not looked at us once. Have you noticed?" Gabby snorted. "He only has eyes for Ana."

Heat bloomed in Ana María's cheeks, and she ducked her head while Isabel and Gabby continued to tease her as their horses carried them down the trail, weaving between trees, sunlight glinting through the canopy and painting the world in amber.

Ana María's thoughts wandered back to her father's letter, and then to the ongoing conflict at home. Maybe Gideon could help. Perhaps once he'd succeeded in passing his abolition bill through Commons, he would be open to discussing how Parliament could aid her countrymen in ejecting the French. One of the first things she'd learned about Gideon was that he had a cunning political mind, and Ana María was certain that if he turned his attention toward the subject, he could help Tío Arturo find the support necessary for the British to align with the deposed Juárez cabinet.

The men had come to a stop on the trail ahead, the gamekeeper pointing to a cluster of sheep on the ridge across the sprawling meadow. Ana María brought her mount to a stop at Gideon's side, and she strained her eyes to see what about the flock had captured their attention.

"The bank along that stream there was unstable, and we had ordered the flocks to be kept away from this pasture until we could assess the danger." The gamekeeper pulled his hat from his head and wiped at his brow. "Apparently someone was not aware of the order."

"Do you think some of the lambs or ewes may have fallen in?" Captain Dawson asked, peering at the flock through a spyglass.

"Quite possibly."

"Then let's make haste to rescue those we can." The captain turned to Gideon. "Would you mind escorting the ladies back to the manor?"

"I'm going to help you." Gideon swept his gaze over the three of them. "The more hands to help, the better. I hope you don't mind, Ana."

"Of course not. Do what you can." She made a shooing motion with her hands. "I will see you later this evening."

Isabel and Gabby assured the men that they had walked the path before and were confident they could make it back to the estate with no escort. Nevertheless, Captain Dawson sent a groom along with them, ensuring the man was armed with a pistol, as a precaution.

Ana María wrinkled her nose at the detail, but held her silence. Although they had seen and heard nothing from Lord Tyrell since they'd arrived, Captain Dawson had continued to be vigilant.

After a tip of his hat, Gideon rode off across the pasture after the captain and gamekeeper. She watched him go, her chest a tad tight to be separated from him for the first time since they had been married.

"Don't cry, Ana. You and Señor Fox will be back in each other's pockets in no time," Gabby teased, winking at her as she urged her horse into a trot.

"Be kind, Gabby," Isabel admonished before she smirked. "Ana is allowed to be overwhelmed after being let off her leading strings."

Ana María glared at them, but she couldn't hold the expression for long. Truly, she enjoyed their teasing, and was happy she had an afternoon to spend in their company without being distracted by her husband and—

The groom riding in front of their group abruptly jerked

back on the reins, causing his gelding to rear up on its hind legs with an agitated whinny. Her lungs seized when her gaze landed on the reason for his reaction.

Lord Tyrell sat atop a white horse on the path before them, two men flanking him on horseback. Before Ana María had a chance to catch her bearings, the groom had extracted the pistol at his hip and pointed it at the men.

The earl did not react to this show of force, his mien blank and almost bored. So when the sharp crack of gunfire came from the left, Ana María clutched at her ears as a mounted man appeared from the shadowed forest, a smoking pistol in his hand. A thudding sound pulled her head about, her eyes widening in horror to find the groom lying in a puddle on the ground. A ringing sound filled her ears, and Ana María reeled as she stared at the groom's unmoving body—

"Ana, run!"

Blinking and disoriented, Ana María looked about, but it was as if she were viewing the unfolding action from under water. In a haze, she realized her sisters were galloping away in opposite directions as if the hounds of hell were on their heels.

She needed to allow her sisters time to make their escape, for suddenly all she cared about was keeping them far from the earl's clutches. Her father had taken away all her opportunities to be Isabel and Gabby's elder sister, and she was determined to do all she could for them now.

So pushing down the fear surging like acid up her throat, Ana María raised her chin, carefully averted her gaze from the fallen groom, and met the earl's cold eyes straight on.

Tilting his head to the side, Lord Tyrell considered her as if she were an exotic bug trapped within his net. "Have you already grown so bored with your new husband that you won't even attempt to escape?"

She willed herself not to respond in any way, for his remark was crass and not deserving of her attention.

The thundering of distant horse hooves and raised voices met her ears, and she turned toward it. Gideon was coming. Ana María sensed his rapid approach in her bones.

And abruptly she was wrenched from her saddle and thrown unceremoniously over the thighs of one of Lord Tyrell's men, the saddle pommel slamming into her gut and robbing her of breath.

"Let's make haste to the train station. I wanted the three, but this one should make things much more satisfying."

Ana María clutched fruitlessly at the saddle strap, frantically trying to unclasp it as the horses bolted into the surrounding forest, weaving around trees and cutting through underbrush. She knew that she could be seriously injured, or worse, if the saddle slipped free and she crashed to the earth, but it was a risk she was willing to take to ensure she was not stolen away. From Gideon. From her sisters.

She glimpsed her captor raising his hand in her periphery a moment before a searing pain radiated from the back of her head, causing stars to dance before her eyes. In the next moment Ana María's world went black.

21

The distant pop of a pistol sent icy spears shooting through his blood.

Gideon jerked the reins of his mount until the beast turned about, and he rotated his head as he tried to determine which direction the sound had come from. He'd said goodbye to Ana María not a quarter of an hour earlier; surely that was not enough time for danger to find her.

And then a figure on horseback burst through the tree line. Curved low over the saddle, it was hard to determine whether the rider was Ana María or one of her sisters . . . until he noted the green habit. Isabel had been wearing green.

Wrapping the reins tightly about his hands, Gideon closed his eyes, willing himself to breathe through his rising panic. Whatever happened he needed to be calm. Despite the emotions churning like an angry tempest inside him, he was determined to think logically.

While Gideon had been calming himself, Dawson had raced out across the pasture to meet Isabel, vaulting from his mount as soon as he was near and plucking her from her saddle with swift moves.

"What's happened?" he demanded as Gideon approached, his hands tight on her shoulders.

He'd never seen Isabel so pale, her breaths ragged and her bottom lip trembling as she stared up at his friend. "It was Lord Tyrell."

"What did he do?" Dawson's tone was far more gentle than Gideon had ever heard it.

Isabel's throat bobbed for a second, and she finally clamped her eyes closed. "He appeared from the forest with three men. They shot Ned."

Dawson turned to stone, his jaw working. Gideon abruptly remembered that Ned had served with Dawson in the Crimean War, and guilt lanced his chest.

"And what of Ana María?" Her name stuck to the roof of his mouth. Belatedly, he asked, "And Gabby?"

"Gabby fled in the opposite direction, and Ana . . ." She shook her head, her black eyes shining with unshed tears. "I don't know."

That was all Gideon needed to know. Without a word, he swung up on his mount and galloped away in the direction Isabel had come from. Ana María *had* to be safe. Surely she had made her escape after Isabel, and that was why her sister was unaware of her whereabouts.

Because the alternative was more than Gideon could bear.

His horse thudded down the path, the landscape rushing by in a blur that mirrored his thoughts. Gideon rode to the main road and pulled up, spinning about, his eyes frantically scanning the landscape. Where was she? She couldn't be—

"Fox. Fox!"

As he turned his horse about, his shoulders sank as his eyes locked with Dawson's. Panic crept along the edges of his vision, and his lungs labored to catch a breath as fear squeezed them tight.

"Isabel and Monroe have returned to the estate. Apparently Gabriela had already arrived. Whitfield and my men will meet us at the train station"—his breath stuttered—"while others t-tend to Ned."

Gideon felt for Dawson and the loss of his friend, but his terror for Ana María made everything else pale in comparison. Knowing how crass this made him, he simply nodded, unable to trust his own voice.

There was so much he hadn't told her. Just that morning he had awoken to find her curled into his side, her flawless face relaxed in sleep and devoid of the constant energy that seemed to radiate from her every move. He'd stared at her for countless minutes, memorizing every dip and curve, every wisp of eyelash and subtle change to her expression, for every single detail was precious to him. And Ana María continued to believe he'd married her out of convenience.

Shame eventually overrode his discretion. "Why the train station?"

"Because I'd wager all of the abbey that the earl will head for the coast. He threatened to turn them over to the French, right?" When Gideon nodded, he raised a palm. "So I doubt Tyrell has changed his mind. And if he is going to deliver her to his allies, it will be in a place where they can make a fast escape."

Of course Dawson was correct. Tyrell had told the sisters he wanted to deliver them to the French for favors, and the most efficient way to do so was to travel to the nearest port, which meant Torquay.

He steeled his spine. Ana María needed him, and thus *he* needed to keep his wits about him.

"Let's not dawdle, then. It doesn't appear as if Tyrell has much of a head start, so if we're lucky, we may be able to intercept them at the train station." Dawson suddenly ripped a glove off and ran his hand roughly along his jaw. "I am sorry, Fox. I promised you and your lady wife that you would be safe here, but despite that . . ." The words died as the captain dropped his head to his chest.

"You have nothing to apologize for." Gideon clapped a hand on the man's shoulder. "You opened your home to us with short notice, hosted a beautiful wedding, and allowed me to take over your study so I could see to my parliamentary duties—"

"And don't forget that I provided you with a whole separate wing of the estate to utilize for your honeymoon."

Gideon snorted, a welcome moment of levity soothing the tension simmering under his skin. "And that." He sobered. "You have been a generous host, and I will forever be grateful to you, my friend."

Dawson put on his glove and gathered up his reins. "Well, don't thank me yet. Save it for when we recover your wife."

Sucking a breath deep into his lungs and exhaling it noisily, Gideon nodded. "Knowing Ana, she's probably already set about rescuing herself."

Not waiting for a reply, Gideon nudged his mount in the flanks and urged it into a gallop, his lead directed toward the train station. Closing his eyes, he sent a quick prayer on the breeze that they would arrive in time.

Awareness returned in shades of light and sound.

First it was a rumble that broke through the fog that consumed her, a steady beat that encouraged her heart to follow suit. Next it was a sharp light piercing through her eyelids, making her whole body wince in discomfort.

But it was the stench of bay rum cologne that ripped her cruelly awake.

Ana María stared up at a paneled ceiling draped in red brocade, and it took her several blinks to realize it swayed back and forth. Frowning, she rotated her head and bit back a groan when pain lanced across her scalp.

"I was wondering when you would come to. Darren assured me he hadn't hit you hard, but then the man is a brute."

The voice conjured a cascade of memories, each visceral and disarming. The hack through the abbey's home woods with her sisters. Lord Tyrell appearing on the trail. Captain Dawson's man crumbling like a broken doll to the ground.

Pushing herself upright, Ana María swallowed a surge of bile as her gaze swept over the cramped carriage interior. Aside from the earl sitting on the squab across from her, they were alone. But a quick glance out the window revealed a horde of outriders surrounding the carriage. Dios mío, she had no notion of how she would even attempt an escape.

"Where are you taking me?"

The earl didn't look up from the piece of parchment in his hand. "Torquay."

The name rang in her head like a cannon blast. If Lord Tyrell was successful in transporting her to Torquay, would Gideon know? Would he be able to reach them before the earl's allies smuggled her out of the country?

"I don't understand why you think the French would be at all interested in me." A breath shuddered past her lips. "My current knowledge of the war is gleaned from the British papers, which are glaringly lacking in coverage. And I've yet to receive a letter from my parents because sending written communication is a challenge when a foreign army has invaded your country."

She held her breath, hoping Lord Tyrell hadn't checked her person and found the unread letter from her father.

Snorting, the earl dragged his serpentlike gaze to meet hers. "My contacts do not care if you're married, ignorant, or penniless. Your value lies in your connection to Elías Luna Cuate. If he wants you safely returned to him, he will surrender the whereabouts of Benito Juárez or find some way to pay your ransom." His forehead furrowed. "I suppose the French could ransom you back to Fox or your uncle, but I find I do not care."

Unease slithered along her spine. "You know my husband will demand justice."

Lord Tyrell returned his attention to the paper in his hand.

"I can see the headlines now." Ana María raised her hands as if she were reading a broadsheet headline. " 'Lord of the Realm Abducts Wife of Star PM.' "

"How trite." Tyrell rolled his eyes. "Why would I be concerned about an upstart nobody whose time in power is a fleeting thing? Come now, Miss Luna, I thought you were clever."

"It's Señora Fox, my lord, and you'd do well to remember that."

Her head pounded the devil's tune, fear and helplessness coalescing like tar in the back of her throat, but Ana María would not let the earl intimidate her. She'd lived her entire life at the knee of the formidable Señor Luna Cuate; had married the smartest, most ambitious man of her acquaintance; grasped the tenuous bonds of sisterhood and reinforced them with love and loyalty; and had found the person she desired to be on the foggy shores of a far-off country. Ana María was not the same young woman she had been when she stepped from that ship months before; gone were the submissiveness and restraint.

She refused to ever be a pawn in her own life again.

"Miss Luna, Mrs. Fox, I really don't give a damn." Lord Tyrell carefully folded the paper in his hands and set it on the seat next to him, his mien bored. "My man has already sent word to the Home Office that I've detained a Mexican national who has used her connection to a member of Parliament to send top secret information to the French government. Of course you will be far from British shores by the time officials arrive, but the impending investigation and publicity will spell the end of Fox's career." His lip curled. "It's exactly what the upstart deserves."

Ana María opened her mouth to lance him with a scathing retort, when the carriage jerked to a stop, sending her careening forward to slam into the seat next to the earl and knocking all breath from her lungs.

Leaning over her as she gasped like a freshly caught fish, Lord Tyrell pushed the curtains aside and peered out.

"It appears we're here." He extracted a gold watch from his pocket and flipped it open. "And we made excellent time."

Rising to his feet with feline grace, the earl swiped his top hat from a hook by the door and pointed at her with it. "Stay here. I'll return to collect you shortly."

The cabin was bathed in sunlight as he swung the door open, and Ana María shielded her eyes from the glare. Still, she watched as Lord Tyrell paused in the doorway, the brightness behind him hiding his expression.

"My men are patrolling these docks, so an escape attempt would be foolish. I cannot vouch for how you would be treated if you were to fall into the wrong hands."

With that ominous threat, he stepped down the stairs, the door slamming shut behind him.

Ana María scrambled to the window, sweeping the curtains aside with an impatient hand. A gangplank seemed to stretch from her window to the belly of a large, three-mast ship, sailors scurrying about its deck like busy bees in their hive. Dread curdled in her stomach as her gaze landed on Lord Tyrell speaking with a group of men standing nearby, one gentleman in particular occasionally stepping aside to field questions from sailors. The other men appeared to listen intently as the earl spoke before breaking out into chatter, gesticulating their hands about. And then while she watched, they turned in unison to look at the carriage, causing Ana María to squeak and drop the curtain back into place.

Sinking onto the seat, Ana María gripped her head in her hands. What was she to do? Her brief peek outside had revealed the earl had not been exaggerating when he said his men were crawling all over the docks, loading and unloading ships. She couldn't imagine her presence would go unnoticed.

Maybe there was a weapon Lord Tyrell left behind. Ana María dropped her hands and peered about the small cabin. Surely it contained something she could use to defend herself. When her gaze landed on the earl's satchel tucked under the seat, she scrambled to her knees to pop it open.

It was filled with neatly organized documents, and she impatiently pushed them aside as she searched for a pistol or knife, *anything* of use. But a weapon was not to be found.

Sitting back on her heels, Ana María growled. There had to be something to help her here. She slammed her hand down, her palm cracking against the wooden floor and wafting a wave of air that disturbed the papers Lord Tyrell had been reading earlier. Her scalp tingled, and with her lip caught between her teeth, Ana María settled on the seat and reached for a stray sheet. It took her a moment to understand what she was reading, but when the carefully penned script revealed its importance, a gasp caught in her throat. Ana María stared at the parchment, unblinking, as various ideas tumbled about through her mind, until she folded it and tucked it under the boning of her corset.

Her attention immediately snapped back to Lord Tyrell's satchel. What had been a disappointment just moments ago was now brimming with potential.

With a quick look out the window to confirm the earl was still occupied, Ana María dragged the satchel onto her lap and studied its contents. In this moment, escape may not be a possibility, but she had every intention of ensuring Earl Tyrell paid for his treachery.

The door to the carriage swung open several minutes later.

"Come now," Lord Tyrell said, beckoning with his hand as if she were a timid dog. "My friends desire to meet you."

Ana María arched a brow. "And if I would rather not meet them?"

"You assume you have a choice in the matter." The earl propped his leg on the first carriage step, his expression darkening. "Now do cooperate or else I will be forced to insist, and my insistence may come at the expense of your dignity."

Setting her jaw, Ana María marched forward to extend her hand to the man.

Oh yes, she would have her say. Whether in this life or the next, Ana María was determined to exact her retribution.

22

"What if we're wrong? What if they took her to London, and not Torquay after all?"

Dawson cast his eyes heavenward, and then turned to peer out the window as pasturelands gave way to town sprawl. "The train attendant said they boarded the Torquay train."

"But what if he lied?" Gideon halted his pacing, his body swaying with the motion of the train. "What if Tyrell paid him off and he told us Torquay to throw us off their trail?"

When he and Dawson had galloped into the train station, Gideon had all but thrown himself from the saddle, dashing about the platform, calling for his wife. He'd been about to demand a search behind the ticket counter when Dawson had grabbed his arm and explained Tyrell and his men had been spotted boarding the Torquay-bound train . . . which had departed some fifteen minutes prior.

An unholy sound crashed against the back of Gideon's teeth, and he'd pressed a fist to his mouth to keep from lashing out.

"For the love of God, sit down, Fox." Whitfield peered at him from over the newspaper he was reading, as if their train ride were for a jaunt at the seaside. "Dawson has men searching every stop along this line, and I sent a wire to London alerting the ambassador of what had transpired. I also sent one along to Dawson's contact at the Home Office."

Gideon whipped his head about. "You did?"

The duke pushed his spectacles up the bridge of his nose. "Of course I did."

"I've heard *whispers* in the Home Office that Tyrell was being watched." Dawson narrowed his eyes. "I never learned why, but *now* I have very strong theories."

Raking a trembling hand through his hair, Gideon perched on the edge of a seat, his leg bouncing up and down like a metronome. The adrenaline coursing through his blood was the only thing keeping his panic at bay. If the earl was successful in delivering Ana María to the French, after she had fled a war and crossed an ocean to escape them, Gideon would bloody well march on Paris himself.

"I've never seen you like this, Fox." Whitfield folded his newspaper and set it aside. "If it wasn't for this wretched situation, I'd be delighted to see you so passionately consumed with the welfare of another person."

"She's my wife!" Launching to his feet, Gideon stared unseeing out the window. Pressing his forehead to the cool glass, he whispered, "I've never felt more helpless in my life."

His friends were quiet for a pregnant moment, until Whitfield spoke again. "And you feel helpless because you care. A great deal, it would seem."

Gideon glared at him over his shoulder. "Of course I care. Like I said, Ana María is *my wife*."

"Yes, I'm aware. I was at the wedding." Whitfield crossed his arms over his chest as he stared at him. "But what I find . . .

amusing . . . is that this was supposed to be a marriage of convenience. You help the former Miss Luna with her unfortunate situation with Tyrell, and in return you gain a beautiful and wealthy bride to host your dinners and warm your bed. A fortuitous bargain, indeed."

"Will you get to your fucking point, Whitfield?" Gideon snarled.

The duke, insufferable as the day was long, chuckled. "My point is that you seem to have fallen in love with your convenient bride."

He opened his mouth to laugh—or deliver a scathing retort—but such a response died a quick death on his tongue. Rather, he gaped at his friend as the truth washed over him. For all his talk about focusing on his proposal with Montrose, Gideon had forgotten it when he'd learned Ana María was in danger. The decision had been effortless, and he'd not questioned it since.

"That was quite rude of you, Whitfield, to call attention to such a thing when Fox hadn't even realized it himself."

"You knew?" Gideon demanded.

"Of course I did. You've left your chamber only a handful of times since your wedding night. Stansberry said your correspondence to London has been reduced to a trickle." Dawson huffed an exaggerated chuckle. "I've never swived a woman who made me want to forgo good company and ignore my responsibilities."

Gideon didn't know what to say.

"Ana María is"—he coughed into his fist—"quite *special* to me, and I am grateful to you both for helping me to bring her home."

"That wretch thought he could traverse onto Dancourt Abbey

land, take the life of an honorable man, and steal away another man's wife." Dawson pounded his fist against the windowpane. "I would have pursued the man with or without your help, Fox."

Locking his teeth together, Gideon nodded.

"And I'm here because Mrs. Fox"—the duke held up a hand—"I beg your pardon, Señora Fox, made you smile before I could. And for that, I owe her my loyalty."

At a loss for words, his throat choked with affection for his churlish friends. Gideon turned away.

"The seaside station approaches." Dawson turned steely eyes from the window to Gideon. "The docks are not far."

"And what is the plan? I admit that my emotions are a bit fraught—"

"Just a tad." Whitfield held up two fingers.

"But even I know it would be best not to proceed directly to the docks without a plan in place," Gideon continued, ignoring the duke completely.

Dawson rubbed a hand across his stubbled jaw. "I suspect Tyrell will have men at the station, ready to report our arrival or stop our progress."

"So what do we do?" Gideon's cheeks puffed on an exhale. "Is it possible to sneak off the train in some manner?"

"That's what I was thinking. Let me have a word with the attendant," Dawson said, rising to his feet.

Whitfield extended a hand filled with several sovereign coins. "This should make the discussion more fruitful."

The captain snorted. "Indeed."

A half hour later, Gideon, Dawson, Whitfield, and a handful of the captain's men slunk down a narrow alley adjacent to the docks. They had managed to slip from the train through a small door used to load trolley services, separating and blending into the crowd until they met again at a local telegraph station. Dawson disappeared inside and exited a scant moment later, a strip of paper in his hands.

"The Home Office indicated several men will be joining us," he'd said.

The coordination of government assistance filled Gideon's lungs with relief. Lord Tyrell was a powerful man, but Gideon appreciated the reminder from his friends that he was not without his own connections.

Now Dawson craned his head around the corner of the building. "Here comes Walter." He looked back at Gideon. "He should be able to tell us what's happening further down the boardwalk."

A dark-haired man with an equally dark beard stepped around the corner of the alley, the bill of his brown hat tipped low over his eyes. His gaze immediately fell on the captain, huddling to confer with him in whispered words. After a short exchange, he stepped back with a nod and disappeared in the direction they had come.

"Walter's located Lord Tyrell's contingent," Dawson said. Catching sight of Gideon's questioning expression, he added, "I sent him a dispatch before we left Dancourt Abbey, and he's been monitoring the docks."

"Thank God you had the wherewithal to think of such a thing," Gideon responded, puffing his lips on an exhale.

Amusement touched Dawson's mouth for a passing moment. "The earl and his men are several blocks further up the docks. Walter's going to meet the Home Office gents at the telegraph office and bring them to meet us."

"And Ana?" Gideon forced down a swallow. "Did Walter see her?"

Dawson shook his head. "He didn't, but there's a carriage parked along the boardwalk."

Gideon pressed his fingers into his temple. Ana María had to be in that carriage. She had to—

"So here's what we're going to do"—Dawson motioned for Gideon, Whitfield, and the other men to come closer—"and we need to act fast."

The captain explained his plan, and Gideon did his best not to interrupt, biting his tongue, for Dawson was the experienced military man. However, when he assigned Gideon to stand on the other side of the street and alert them to the approach of additional carriages or men, he put his foot down.

"I refuse to act as a lookout while you lot rush in to rescue my wife."

Whitfield groaned. "Don't be difficult, Fox. We have to be fast, and can't afford for you to lose control of your emotions—"

"Lose control of my emotions? I just want my wife to be safe—"

"So do we." Whitfield snatched his spectacles from his face and massaged the bridge of his nose. "So do we, my friend."

All the fight fled from Gideon's limbs on a long exhale. He ran a weary palm across his brow. "I'm sorry. I know you're all trying to help. Just . . . all the unknowns are difficult to contemplate."

They were. Endless scenarios twisted and morphed in his mind: Ana María in the belly of a barge headed to Paris, at the mercy of men who conquered her country, terrified and alone and far out of reach.

The duke's heavy hand fell on his shoulder. "One day in the future I'm going to remind you of how undone you were in this moment, but I assure you that at least for now, I understand."

Gideon flashed Whitfield a rude gesture, but chuckled. "I do not look forward to it."

After some additional discussion, the men crept from the alley, each heading in various directions per Dawson's plan. With his hat pulled low over his ears and his chin tucked into his collar, Gideon shoved his hands into his coat pockets and ambled down the street, perching himself on the corner of the building directly across from the black carriage parked next to the gangplank. His fingernails bit into his palms from how tightly he held himself, his limbs quivering with his desire to rip the carriage door open to see if it contained his bride.

But he would not foil their plans. Dawson had his men surveil the area, and they strategically planned their maneuvers around what they'd learned. Plus, the Home Office would join them. When he had been consumed with terror for Ana María, his friends had taken the reins of the rescue effort, and its success would be in thanks to their level heads.

Ignoring the rivulets of perspiration that trailed down his neck and spine, Gideon sucked greedy breaths into his lungs in an attempt to remain calm. Alert. Focused.

All of his good intentions scattered like chaff in the wind when Earl Tyrell appeared in his line of sight. Gideon watched with his blood roaring in his ears as the older man walked around the carriage and gestured for a footman to open it for him. Squinting his eyes, Gideon tried to make out figures or shapes within the dim interior, with no luck. But abruptly the earl extended his hand into the carriage, and several heartbeats later, a familiar glove appeared from the shadows and clasped it.

His surroundings disappeared, the noise and smells of the docks melding into the void as Gideon's entire focus settled on Ana María as she descended from the carriage steps. Her jaunty hat was askew, inky locks tumbling about her shoulders, and her habit bore smudges of dirt and debris. Regardless, she was hale. So beautiful and dear that Gideon struggled to breathe around the sob tearing up his throat.

And then one of Tyrell's men grabbed her roughly by the arm and pushed her in the direction of the gangplank, causing Ana María to stumble. Gideon was stalking across the road before he had a moment to consider his actions, extracting the cane he had tucked into the folds of his coat, and flipping it open with the flick of his wrist. There was a blade tucked inside the cylinder, and Gideon was more than prepared to use it.

As he rounded the edge of the carriage, he paused, a bit of cognizance taking hold. Gideon swung his head about, looking for any sign of Dawson or his men, eventually expelling a breath when he spied the captain perched on a tall stack of crates and barrels, a rifle trained on the men below.

As he peered around the corner of the carriage again, a feral sound ripped from his throat when he spied his wife thrashing against the hold of two men who dragged her toward the waiting ship. His mind went blank, all thoughts bleached white by the searing fire of his anger. Rushing out from around the carriage, he cried, "Ana!"

Ana María whipped her head about, her dark eyes latching on to him from across the distance between them. And rather than seeing fear in her gaze, he glimpsed a blazing anger. An anger to match—likely even surpass—his own.

Gideon sprinted down the plank after her, skirting groups of men yelling for him to stop, and smacking others aside with his cane.

Everything seemed to explode about him. Gunshots crackled through the air in between exclamations, groans, and curses. Stumbling to a halt, he tugged on his earlobe as he scanned the chaos surrounding him. In that moment, a hulk of a man came rushing at him, a cudgel in his beefy hands, and Gideon readied his cane to strike him . . . but a loud pop echoed, and the man lurched to the side, collapsing in a heap several yards away. Not bothering to confirm whether the man was dead, Gideon raced after his wife, catching glimpses of the back of her head through the stampede of sailors and workers fleeing the gunfire. A gap in the crowd provided him a view of Ana María scuffling with one of her captors, the other nowhere in sight, and Gideon weaved through bodies to reach her. The crack of pistols and the whoosh of bullets streaking through the air made dread tingle like ice across his skin, but his fear for his wife raged like an inferno through his blood.

Pushing past a trio of men running in the opposite direction, he saw that Ana María was suddenly yards away, still grappling with her guard. Before the man knew what she was about, Ana María managed to wrest her hand free from his grip, grasp the pin from her now-mangled hat, and jab it deep into the fleshy part of the man's forearm. He let her go with a pained wail, and she hoisted up the long skirts of her habit and ran straight for Gideon.

He met her halfway, enfolding her into his embrace, pressing his cheek to hers as he soaked in her nearness.

Except Ana María planted her palms on his chest and shoved him back. "Estoy bien. Vamos!"

Grasping his hand tight, she led him back through the melee.

But within a few steps, Ana María gasped as she stumbled to a halt, and without thought, Gideon stepped in front of her, terror gurgling up his throat.

"Put the gun down, Tyrell," he ordered, his tone crisp but calm.

The earl shook his head, his outstretched arm quaking as he

aimed a pistol right at the center of Gideon's chest. "Step aside, Fox."

"No." With a nudge, he maneuvered Ana María farther behind him. "Are you mad? How do you possibly think you'll get away with this? Home Office men are here, for God's sake."

"Home Office officials?" He snorted. "Do you not think I have my own connections at the Home Office? Connections who would be all too happy to corroborate my story that your wife was attempting to steal British secrets—"

A loud whack rent the air, and Lord Tyrell cried out in anguish as his pistol clattered to the boardwalk. Clutching his hand gingerly, he whimpered as Gideon jumped back in surprise.

"I see you're still an insufferable windbag, Tyrell." Whitfield tapped the cane he used to crack the earl across the wrist on the wood planks below their feet. "Don't you ever get tired of hearing your own voice?"

"You're a disgrace to your family name, Sebastian," Tyrell growled, cradling his injured arm to his chest. "Your father always said you were a hopeless disappointment, and now I know why."

Whitfield cocked his head to the side. "And I always assumed you were his friend because you were also a wretched shit stain of a man. It's quite gratifying to see I'm right."

The earl's face turned a florid shade, but after a pause, he lifted his chin. "If you help me leave from here now, I will reward you handsomely."

"I don't need anything from you," Whitfield bit out.

"That's not what I heard."

"Well, you heard wrong." The duke leaned forward on his cane. "I can't say I'm surprised you're mistaken because—"

The earl rushed Whitfield before he or Gideon had a moment to draw breath. In one instance the older man looked weak and pathetic, and the next he had collided into the duke with the force of a locomotive. Gideon leapt forward to help his friend, when a loud crack rattled his eardrums. Lord Tyrell fell to the boardwalk with a satisfying thud.

Gideon, Ana María, and Whitfield stared down at the earl's broken body, stumbling back as a halo of red puddled around him. Whipping his head about, Gideon met Dawson's eye as he lowered his rifle.

"There's a carriage waiting just there"—Dawson gestured with his chin to a conveyance blocking the road—"to take you back to the train station. Whitfield and I will speak with the Home Office officials. Considering a lord of the realm lies dead on the dock, they're going to want to know everything that transpired."

Gideon wrapped an arm around Ana María's shoulder and tucked her close to his side. "Tell me more at Dancourt Abbey."

Dawson's gaze bounced between them for a moment. "I'm relieved you're safe, Mrs. Fox. Now have a safe train ride back to the abbey. I'll have a few men accompany you."

"Thank you, Dawson." Gideon turned to the duke, who continued to stare at the earl's body. "Whitfield, I can't begin to thank—"

"Then don't." The duke looked up, his blue eyes shuttered and a sad smile on his lips. "Take your bride from here. We'll talk soon."

With a swallow, he nodded dumbly, before sweeping Ana María away.

Gideon lost track of time in the rush to the train station and then as they boarded the train headed west toward the abbey. His movements were mechanical, his mind detached from his body. The only thing he knew for certain was that Ana María was with him. Her hand was in his. Her scent was in his nose. His eyes would never get their fill of her lovely face.

Only when they were seated in a private train car, tucked closely together as their bodies swayed as one to the rocking motion, did they finally exchange words. It was Ana María who broke the silence.

"I'm sorry," she whispered, her face buried in his chest. "I'm sorry that meeting me, *marrying* me, has caused you so much trouble."

"Ana," he began, but she spoke again before he could continue.

"The earl had horrible plans to use my abduction to discredit you, and I wasn't sure if you or the authorities would arrive in time"—she plucked at the buttons on his waistcoat—"or if I would find myself a captive of the French. But I was determined to cause as much trouble as I could along the way."

Sliding from this lap, Ana María slipped a hand into her bodice. Gideon watched her movements with a frown, the expression deepening when she pulled free several folded pieces of parchment. Unfolding one, she handed it to him.

"I found this among Lord Tyrell's paperwork. I think you'll agree that the Home Office will be quite interested in it."

Gideon looked down at her offering, the recesses of his mind registering that the paper was a shipping manifest of some sort. But he found he had no interest in it. No interest in the earl or anything else.

Accepting the paper from her, he flung it to the side, uncaring where it landed.

"Ay, Gideon," she exclaimed, "what are you doing? You have to read it. This could be exactly what you need to pass your proposal."

"It doesn't matter. Tyrell's dead."

"But he could still be a threat to you, mi amor." She ran her knuckles along his cheek. "We don't yet know the lies the earl circulated about you. Or me. He very well may have poisoned society against us, and we'll *need* this information."

She grasped at the other slips of paper she had stolen away in her bodice, unfolding them with urgent hands. "There could be damaging details in here as well. I didn't have much time to look through all of the earl's belongings, but I grabbed whatever looked important. Surely something in here can help with you—"

"Ana," Gideon said wearily, grasping her hands. With the adrenaline now dissipating, fatigue was settling in his bones. "Let's not discuss that now."

"But I found ammunition that will help you secure the votes you need for your proposal with Lord Montrose." Her voice dropped to a whisper. "Gideon, I thought this was important to you. A way to honor your grandmother's legacy."

"It is important. It will always be the work of my heart. But, darling, may I please have a moment to just be grateful you are unharmed? That you are in my arms, once again, where you belong?" With a gentle tug, Ana María sank onto his lap. Gideon brought his hands up to cradle her face, his eyes finding hers. "In every second since I heard that gunshot echo across the home woods at Dancourt Abbey, my thoughts have been focused on *you*. Your safety. Your happiness. I've been crippled by helplessness that I could not ensure either. I've always prided myself as a man who accomplished difficult things, but with you gone, I fell apart. Without the help of my friends, Tyrell would have succeeded and—"

She silenced him with a kiss. "But he didn't, mi amor. I'm safe here with you."

"And I am so grateful." A tear slipped from the corner of

Ana María's eyes and trailed down her cheek. He brushed it away with his thumb. "Because I love you. I love your clever mind and your kind heart. Your droll wit and your stunning beauty. I love your passion and your zeal, and I am the luckiest of men that you call *me* husband. For now, bringing you home is all I care about.

"The time will come, much sooner than I'd like, when we will have to tend to the mess that villain Tyrell has left us with. And there is no doubt that despite our claims, some will use what happened on this day as proof that I am unworthy of the power I've earned. Not long ago, the fight to prove otherwise would have left me frustrated and demoralized. But that was before you, Ana." Gideon pressed a kiss to her trembling lips. "You think that our marriage has caused me trouble, but you've only brought me joy. Strength. I have gained a partner I know will be by my side as I will be by hers. We can do the difficult things together. It's why I'm so certain my proposal will meet with success, because we will fight for it together."

"You wonderful man. ¡Me encantas!" She chuckled against his lips. "I love you, too, so allow me to tell you how we can turn this dreadful situation to our advantage."

He frowned but Ana María continued before he could reply.

"I was raised by a politician, Gideon, so trust me when I say that we need to strategize as quickly as possible." Ana María nipped at his chin. "If you want us to fight together and accomplish great things, for Britain and Mexico, the work starts now."

His heart felt as if it had swelled to twice its normal size. Gathering her close, Gideon buried his face in her hair, riotous emotions—pride; awe; wild, blistering love—churning inside of him. Meeting his wife's tenacious gaze, Gideon smiled. "Tell me what you're thinking, darling."

EPILOGUE

"Ana, are these really all of the invitations you and Gideon have received?"

Peering over her shoulder at Gabby, who stood rifling through the basket Stansberry used to sort the post, she nodded. "Those are the ones Stansberry deems worthy of our attention."

"So there are others?" Isabel asked, a dubious note to her voice.

"Apparently so."

She crossed the drawing room to sit next to Isabel in front of the large arched window that welcomed in the warm afternoon light. She and Gideon had moved to the elegant townhome on Upper Belgrave Street about a month after they returned to London, and Ana María had immediately set about to furnish the space. With her sisters' help, she had filled the rooms with comfortable chairs and settees, colorful rugs, stylish draperies, and tasteful pieces of art, some of which were done by Mexican artists Tío Arturo helped her procure. Although Isabel and Gabby continued to reside with Lady Yardley, under the pretense of allowing the newlyweds their privacy, they visited almost daily, the rooms and halls rarely devoid of their laughter and antics. Ana María was thankful Gideon did not seem to mind, often joining in their banter and teasing. Several times she watched him excitedly discuss a new scientific advancement with Isabel or patiently teach Gabby how to play chess, and she marveled that the somber, serious man she met all those months ago was just a facade that masked his warm and engaging nature.

"It seems that *Times* article Miss Assan wrote did wonders for your reputation," Isabel said over the top of her book.

Ana María raised a shoulder before turning to thank a maid as she set a refreshment tray on the gilded table between them. Pouring a cup of café, she set a cake on a saucer before handing it to her sister. "Miss Assan merely wrote a detailed account of Lord Tyrell's dealings with the French."

"Dealings?" Gabby plopped onto the sofa next to her with a huff. "I'd hardly call passing British military endeavors to the French simple *dealings*."

"I still cannot believe the earl thought he would get away with such a thing," Ana María said, handing her youngest sister a cup.

"Power and privilege are apparently potent intoxicants." Isabel punctuated her words by slamming her book shut.

"Gracias a Dios you had the wherewithal to steal the earl's papers." Gabby's hazel eyes were wide as they met hers. "He went to great lengths to slander you and Gideon."

Stansberry had tried to warn Gideon through the post that stories were beginning to circulate in the papers that something untoward had occurred at the house party. The speculation fluctuated widely, from reports that Ana María and Gideon had been caught in flagrante delicto, or that Gideon had assaulted the earl after arguing about his proposal, to Isabel and Ana María stealing valuables from Tyrell Manor. However, the

Home Office officials who later interviewed Ana María had asked them not to discuss what had occurred in Torquay until after they concluded their investigation, leaving them in an uncomfortable position when they returned to London. While Gideon did not have the luxury to delay his work in Parliament any longer, Ana María kept a low profile, only leaving the house to attend Mass. But when word of Earl Tyrell's death and the Home Office's posthumous investigation into his ties to the French hit the papers, Gideon decided it was time to tell *their* story.

It helped that the manifest Ana María had taken from Lord Tyrell had been for a ship the earl owned that detailed trips from a known slave trader's port in Angola to one in Brazil. Ana María would never forget the tortured look on Gideon's face when he'd finally read the document. He had immediately shared it with Miss Assan, the reporter at the *Times*.

The subsequent article about Gideon's work with Lord Montrose, the earl's deplorable threat to turn Ana María and her sisters over to the French, and then her ultimate abduction had hit with all the weight of a lead bomb. They had fielded interview requests, an invitation for a private meeting with the Queen and Prince Albert, the prime minister had praised Gideon in front of both houses of Parliament, and the invitations had come in droves. Ana María still struggled to forgive and forget the treatment she had been subjected to before the *Times* article had proclaimed the truth, and thankfully Gideon and her sisters had understood this, not pressuring her to accept any invitations she was not ready to, no matter how Stansberry fretted.

For that was not the only reckoning to be had.

"Señora, a letter has been delivered for you," a maid announced as she entered the room. She held out a weathered envelope to Ana María. "Mr. Stansberry wanted you to receive this immediately. It's from Mexico."

Ana María accepted it slowly, gingerly, her eyes quickly scanning over the script on the front. It was in her mother's writing.

After the maid had departed, Ana María made no move to open the letter. The last correspondence she had received from her parents had been after her wedding. That letter had survived her abduction, and she'd finally read it with Gideon in their bed at Dancourt Abbey. Predictably, her father had been irate that she had broken her engagement to Fernando Ramírez, lamenting the circumstances that led to it. Although he seemed slightly pleased that his new son by marriage was a member of Parliament, he also accused Gideon of being a fortune hunter, no doubt intent on claiming the Luna fortune they had smuggled from Mexico. Gideon had laughed at that assertion, for he'd instructed Stansberry to open a safe box at the nearest bank for the sisters' fortune, ensuring Ana María, Isabel, and Gabby had ready access to it.

Gideon was not present to read this new letter with her, and Ana María almost tucked it away for his return, until she met Isabel's soft gaze. Swallowing, she turned to Gabby, who looked at her with an equally gentle expression. Expelling a breath, she plucked the seal free.

It was written in their mother's graceful, flowing script. The opening salutation made it clear she was the true author of the letter, and not merely their father's stenographer.

Mi hija,

I hope this letter eventually finds its way into your hands. I include you y tu nuevo esposo in my prayers and hope you both are muy contentos.

Your father has been quite busy in the fight with the French, and recently he's met with victory thanks to the information you shared with Arturo. The Liberal leadership was not aware such weapons shipments were being received and dispersed in Tampico, but because of your quick thinking during a frightening situation, our soldiers were able to intercept the parcels and distribute the contents among our supporters or sell them for additional supplies.

"Ana," Gabby whispered, drawing her eyes up. "Look at how you've helped Mexico."

"Th-that's not what I was trying to do. I was just sc—"

"¡Claro que no!" Isabel affirmed, a fond look on her face. "But despite your fear, you did so anyway."

With a nod, she dropped her gaze to the letter in her hand, the words now blurry.

After Ana María had arrived at Dancourt Abbey and rested for a day or so, she and Gideon had finally read through the items she had taken from the earl and carefully hidden away in her bodice. Most were financial documents, but stuck to the back of an invoice was another manifest detailing shipments into Tampico, Mexico, that had made Ana María tuck her face into Gideon's neck and weep.

Because of you, mi amor, the Liberal forces have the supplies they need to fight another day. I'm so proud of you, and I know your father is as well.

Please tell Isabel and Gabriela I pray the Rosary for them every day and miss them dearly, as I do you. Give my love to your Señor Fox, with the hope we will meet one day.

"We're proud of you, too, Ana," Gabby interjected as she dashed at her cheeks. "Seeing how happy and confident you are now, compared to how sad you were when we left Mexico, is . . . inspiring."

Pressing her trembling lips together, she glanced at Isabel, who offered a tremulous smile in agreement.

The drawing room door opened then, and Gideon stepped into the room, his tender charcoal eyes finding hers. He'd been working longer hours at Westminster, taking more meetings, and agreeing to accept more social invitations, which allowed him and Ana María to engage with the elite members of society that just weeks ago had shunned them. With Lord Tyrell's misdeeds splashed across the broadsheets, his allies had quickly tried to distance themselves from the late earl and throw their support behind Gideon instead, and he was gracious enough to allow them to do so if only to see his objectives succeed.

"Good evening, wife. Sisters," he said, skirting around the back of the sofa to buss Ana María on the temple. He snatched a biscuit from the tray before sinking into an adjacent armchair.

"Try again, Gideon." Gabby tsked as she shook a finger at him. "You should know the proper greeting by now. How are you to greet our family when you one day visit Mexico if you do not learn Spanish?"

Her husband rolled his eyes, but wiped his mouth with a napkin, cleared his throat, and obediently said, "Buenos tardes, mi esposa bonita."

Ana María and Isabel snorted in unison, but Gabby nodded approvingly and then gestured with her hands for him to continue.

With a long-suffering sigh, he slowly enunciated, "¿Cómo estuvo su día?"

"Estuvo bien, cariño," she whispered, her voice cracking as

love and affection ballooned in her breast. He always tried so hard for her. For her sisters. Because that was the kind of man he was.

Gideon hesitated, his brow dipping low as he considered her. "Is everything all right, darling?"

She could only manage a nod, a knot of tears in her throat. But she hoped her happiness, her love, shone in her eyes. "Now that you're home, everything is perfect."

AUTHOR'S NOTE

It all started with a random search of immigration records.

While brainstorming a character for another project, I thought to research immigration records to better understand who was emigrating to Latin America post-1850. I stumbled across data about the number of Mexicans emigrating to England, and wondered aloud about the reasons that would necessitate such a move. Like a bolt of lightning, I remembered the Second French Intervention, and within a half hour, I had the beginnings of the Luna Sisters series all mapped out and a fire in my belly to write their stories.

Before the start of *Ana María and The Fox*, the three sisters are sent from Mexico by their parents when the French defeat the Mexican army at the Second Battle of Puebla in 1863. The Battle of Puebla may sound familiar to you because in the year prior, the vastly outnumbered Mexican army managed to defeat Napoleon III's forces at Puebla on May 5, 1862, in what is now commemorated in the United States as Cinco de Mayo. It was one battle in a six-year war, and is *not* the battle that won Mexico its independence (that was won from the Spanish in September 1821). Their victory at the Second Battle of Puebla paved the way for the French to march on Mexico City, and set up the action of our story.

I find it impossible to discuss the Second French Intervention of Mexico without discussing the United States, Mexico's closest ally. At the time French forces were landing on Mexican shores, the Civil War had begun, so the US government could not afford to enforce the Monroe Doctrine, which was a US foreign policy first enunciated in 1823 that opposed European colonialism in the Western Hemisphere. Thus, Napoleon III was able to assert his advantage, although the United States continued to officially recognize the Benito Juárez government. In fact, after the Civil War had ended, the US lent its support to the Liberal government to oust the French from Mexico in 1865. Such an ending is exactly what the Luna sisters were hoping for!

Since the American Civil War was occurring at the same time that Ana María and her sisters fled Mexico, I felt it was important to incorporate the continued struggle to abolish slavery. Although the British Empire had abolished the international slave trade in 1807 and the United States in 1808, enslavers continued to do business in other parts of the world. By the time *Ana María and The Fox* begins in the summer of 1863, the Atlantic slave trade had been dealt a crippling blow thanks to the Lyons-Seward Treaty. Signed by the United States and Great Britain, the treaty aimed to suppress the slave trade in American and British ports, and was championed by the Lincoln administration, which was keen to keep the British from supporting the Confederate states in the interest of reopening the cotton trade. Gideon briefly touched on this in his discussion with Lord Tyrell during the house party. The treaty outlined measures that forcefully targeted vessels that were suspected of transporting enslaved Africans. The treaty was incredibly effective, but the horrific practice continued in countries such as Brazil and Cuba. And this is what Gideon's fictitious measure with Lord Montrose was attempting to eradicate.

As for Mexico, slavery was fully abolished in 1837, although strides had begun after the country declared its independence from Spain in 1821. In fact, Mexico was seen as a haven for freedom-seeking enslaved people. Author Alice Baumgartner estimates in her book, *South to Freedom: Runaway Slaves to Mexico and the Road to the Civil War*, that some three thousand to five thousand enslaved people fled south over the Rio Grande to Mexico in search of freedom, and many Mexicans were sympathetic to the cause, something that infuriated bounty hunters. In a February 2021 article by NPR's John Burnett titled "A Chapter in U.S. History Often Ignored: The Flight of Runaway Slaves to Mexico," scholar María Hammack states that "under Texas law, Mexicans and enslaved persons were not allowed to be found together or to collaborate or even speak to each other." In earlier versions of *Ana María and The Fox*, Ana María and her sisters discuss their country's history of abolition with Gideon, as well as the complexities of Mexican society and the position of their Afro-Mexican neighbors within it.

An important aspect mentioned within the story but not elaborated upon was that many members of the European elite viewed the French occupation of Mexico favorably. There were reportedly celebrations held throughout France when Mexico City fell to Napoleon's armies. The quote Arturo shared with the sisters about how Napoleon was praised for defeating "one of the most degenerate and despised races of either hemisphere" was taken from an actual newspaper at the time (per *Maximilian and Juárez* by Jasper Ridley). The nuance surrounding the French Intervention as it related to Mexican, French, British, and United States politics and culture is impossible to

sum up in a book focused on the romance between two characters, but I will continue to share snippets of this time in history
in future Luna Sisters books.

This is a big-picture summary of the historical events and
figures that shaped the story behind Ana María and Gideon's
book. As a MexiRican (Mexican American–Puerto Rican) woman
who has spent the majority of her life living an hour north of
the US-Mexico border, I was thrilled I could blend my cultural
history with my love of the Victorian era. I look forward to
sharing more of Mexico's heritage and history with readers in
book two of the Luna Sisters, *Isabel and The Rogue*!

ACKNOWLEDGMENTS

Ana María and The Fox is the book of my heart. For the first time, I've had the opportunity to write about characters who share my rich, proud history and look like me. I poured a hefty bit of myself into Ana María, but also into Isabel and Gabby. Writing their stories was, and is, a dream, and seeing this book released into the world has me thinking of all the people who made this dream a reality.

My amazing editor, Sarah Blumenstock, grasped from the beginning what I wanted to do with not only Ana María and Gideon's story, but the entire Luna Sisters series, and patiently and expertly helped me shape this book into one I can be proud of. To the entire Berkley team, who have been so supportive of me and *Ana María and The Fox*: Liz Sellers, Cindy Hwang; Katie Anderson and the art department, who graced this book with the most STUNNING cover; Alaina Christensen, the production editor, who took my words and turned them into a beautiful, real-life book; Angelina Krahn, the copyeditor, for her stellar but gentle eye; and to my marketing and publicity team, Yazmine Hassan, Jessica Plummer, and Hillary Tacuri, for working so hard to get Ana María and Gideon's story to readers!

To Jessica Brock and Kristin Dwyer of Leo PR, for holding my hand through the rollout of my print debut!

Publishing is hard, but it's easier to manage when you have dear friends who celebrate your successes, boost you through your rejections, and brainstorm with you when you've written yourself into a corner. Elizabeth Bright and Lisa Lin are those friends to me, and I'm so grateful for their friendship.

To the talented, kind, and incredibly supportive authors of my LatinxRom group, who welcomed me and championed my books from the beginning: Natalie Caña, Zoraida Córdova, Adriana Herrera, Alexis Daria, Angelina M. Lopez, Ofelia Martinez, Priscilla Oliveras, Mia Sosa, Sabrina Sol, Nadine Gonzalez, Sera Taíno, and Aleera Anaya Ceres. *Ana María and The Fox* has them to thank for its title! Special thanks to Ofelia for always being available to help ensure my use of Spanish was correct!

To the members of the 321 Write group, especially Elle Pond, Elsie Day, Tristen Crone, Mish, and Sacreblue. I wrote *Ana María and The Fox,* as well as book two, with them during writing sprints, and their passion for storytelling and fandom is such an inspiration.

To my fellow Berkletes, especially Elizabeth Everett, Alicia Thompson, Jenna Levine, and the Latinas de Berkley group of Alana Quintana Albertson, Isabel Cañas, and Jo Segura: thank you for giving me a space to share my publishing highs and lows. I'm so thankful for you!

My career as an author would not be possible without the continued support of my real-life romance hero, my parents, my siblings, my in-laws, and my extended family, who are the first to offer praise and preorder my books . . . but are quick to keep me grounded as only family can.

And last but certainly not least, to my agent, Rebecca Strauss. It was Rebecca who first recognized the magic in my Luna Sisters idea and encouraged me to write it. And through every step of the process, be that crushing rejections or euphoric success, she was a steadfast voice of motivation and praise. I will forever be grateful for her faith in me and my storytelling abilities.

Ana María AND The Fox

A LUNA SISTERS NOVEL

Liana De la Rosa

READERS GUIDE

DISCUSSION QUESTIONS

1. Ana María and her sisters are members of the criollo class (the Mexico-born children of Spanish parents), a status that rewarded them with a certain amount of social clout in Mexico. In what ways did their privilege and social status change when they arrived in London, and how did it stay the same?

2. Ana María told Gideon that he was cut from the same cloth as her father. Why do you think she made that comparison? Do you think it was an accurate assessment?

3. Ana María's, Isabel's, and Gabriela's personalities reflect their birth orders in many ways: the pressure Ana María feels to be perfect; Isabel's drive to be useful; Gabby's need to be seen. How do you think your birth order—or your experience as an only child—has affected you?

4. The Luna sisters grew up in an environment that fostered competition rather than interpersonal relationships, but their time in London helped Ana María, Isabel, and Gabby form sisterly bonds for the first time. How do you think this deeper level of sisterhood helps them?

5. Male friendship is important in the world of the Luna sisters, especially for Gideon, who grew up in very different circumstances than the people he now works and socializes with. His close friendships with Sebastian, the Duke of Whitfield, and Captain Sirius Dawson prove invaluable when Ana María is abducted. Do you enjoy reading about male friendships? Why or why not?

6. Gideon and Ana María encounter microaggressions throughout the book; Gideon because he's a Black man in a position of power and Ana María as a foreign woman of color in a predominantly white space. How do you think these microaggressions shaped how they moved through society?

7. While attending the house party at Tyrell Manor, Gideon muses on how much of the wealth accrued by the ton over the generations was derived from the exploitation of peoples throughout the British Empire. When reading historical narratives, do you like seeing behind the curtain of gentility and wealth, or do you prefer the history to be romanticized?

8. The effects and evils of colonization are touched upon throughout the book. Which of the observations that Ana María and Gideon make are still accurate now?

9. How do you think the ton and fellow members of Parliament reacted to Gideon and Ana María's marriage?

10. At one point, Gideon feels as if he has to choose between his work and the spark he feels with Ana María. When reading a historical romance, do you prefer the leads to instantly give into their attraction, or do you enjoy a slower burn?

11. Pressure from society is a huge aspect in this book and the historical romance genre overall. How do you feel when you read about the way people once cared so deeply about societal etiquette and norms . . . and do you think that concern has really changed?

Photo courtesy of the author

Liana De la Rosa is a historical romance author who writes diverse characters in the Regency and Victorian periods. Liana has an English degree from the University of Arizona, and in her past life she owned a mystery shopping company and sold pecans for a large farm. When she's not writing, Liana is listening to true crime podcasts and pretending she's a domestic goddess while she wrangles her spirited brood of children with her patient husband in Arizona.

CONNECT ONLINE

LianainBloom.com

f **𝕏** **⊙** LianainBloom

Ready to find
your next great read?

Let us help.

Visit prh.com/nextread

Penguin
Random
House